all that MATTERS

FELICE STEVENS

Published by Good Man Press

ISBN: (eBook) 979-8-88949-043-2
ISBN: (Paperback) 979-8-88949-044-9

First Edition, May 2024
Printed in the United States of America

Cover Art by Reese Dante
Photographer: Miguelanxofoto
Model: Emilio Alcaraz

Edited by Keren Reed
Copy Editing and Proofreading by Flat Earth Editing
Additional Proofreading by Lyrical Lines

Dedication

To everyone, everywhere, searching for their dreams.
And to my family for giving me mine.

Acknowledgments

Thanks to my editor Keren Reed for everything you do. To Hope and Jess from Flat Earth Editing, thank you for always going the extra mile, plus. Thank you to Dianne from Lyrical Lines for the super eagle eyes. And thank you to Reese for not only the most gorgeous covers but also for always being there.

And always, thank you to the readers for reading the stories I love to write. Your support means everything.

Chapter ONE

"Good morning, folks, step inside and find a seat; then we'll be on our way."

Nico Andretti put on the hearty Welcome-to-New-York bullshit voice he'd perfected after years as a sightseeing guide for the iconic double-decker tour buses that tourists flocked to in Times Square. While he wasn't using his college degree in business, one day he'd go for that master's. Life had a way of sidetracking him, but he had his eye on the prize.

The truth was, Nico enjoyed his job. He got to meet interesting people from all over the world while riding around the city, made some nice tips, and occasionally he got a hot guy's number.

Not a bad gig.

He grinned, thinking of the last guy he'd met—a

divorced father of twins, who'd promised his kids the ride of their lives to see the city before they went home the next day to England. Later that night, as the kids had slept in their room down the hall in the Marriott Marquis, Nico had given Daddy the ride of his life.

Yeah, life was pretty damn good at the moment.

The bus filled up quickly, and Nico was about to tell the driver to close the door and take off when he spotted a harried man pushing through the crowd, waving his hand.

"Wait, please."

The tour buses ran every half hour from the pickup spot in Times Square, and normally Nico would tell the driver to leave, but this guy seemed so desperate to make this particular bus, he waited.

"Hold up, Dave. We got one more coming."

Windblown and breathing heavily, the man almost tripped over himself coming to a stop. Thick golden-brown hair fell over eyes the rich amber color of Nico's favorite whisky. The man adjusted the leather computer case hanging from his shoulder, and Nico took note of the discreet but stupid-expensive designer logo. His brows rose. They didn't usually get people on a sightseeing bus who'd drop thousands on accessories, but hey, he was all for it.

"Thank you so much."

"You know we run these all day long."

Perfect white teeth flashed in the man's handsome face. "Yeah, but I have a meeting at two, and I leave tomorrow morning. I've never been to the city, and I wanted to make sure I got the earliest bus possible to see it all. So thanks again."

"No problem. There are seats in the back or on top if you'd like."

"Great. Appreciate it." The man dipped his head and handed him a ticket, and Nico couldn't help but notice the thin gold band on his finger. Of course he was married.

All the beautiful men were. Mentally, he slapped himself. Married to a woman, most likely, with a perfect life at home—house, kids, golden retriever.

That didn't stop Nico from giving him the eye as he made his way to the rear of the bus. And speaking of rears… *damn*. That was one beautiful ass. He blinked.

Mind out of the gutter, you perv.

With a flourish, Nico picked up his microphone. "All right, everyone, take your seats, and let's start. Welcome to New York. As the song goes, it's been waiting for you." People chuckled. "We're here in Times Square, known as the Crossroads of the World. But did you know that in the early 1800s it was called Long Acre after London's carriage district? William Vanderbilt had his horse exchange located here, when obviously there were no skyscrapers and cars, just wide-open spaces with some tenement-style buildings. The name was changed to Times Square in 1904, when the *New York Times* moved its offices here."

People murmured in surprise. Nico liked to give this introduction as a way for people to get a sense of what the city, now crowded with people and cars, must've looked like over one hundred and fifty years earlier. It kept their minds off the snarl of traffic they were inevitably stuck in. Nico took the time to grab a sip of water as people craned their necks, oohing and aahing as they traveled down Broadway. When the bus finally broke free, Nico continued.

"Now we're passing the Empire State Building, no longer the city's tallest spire, but still a world-famous structure. Many native New Yorkers will tell you they've never been to the top."

"I've seen it in so many movies." A woman who sat with her daughter sighed. "So romantic."

They made stops along the way, passing the Flatiron Building and the designer shops in SoHo. People got off and on, most of the time barely noticing him. Occasionally someone tipped him, which was nice. He only made about twenty dollars an hour as a tour guide, and in a city like New York, that didn't go far, but it gave him the freedom to make his own schedule, allowing him to keep working at the family restaurant. By the end of the night, his feet might hurt, but there was never a doubt that he'd help out. They all did—family helped family. He also saved every penny by living at home, in the basement apartment of his mother's house, so he could eventually pursue his dreams.

Amid all the comings and goings, Nico noticed Mr. Gorgeous Ass staying put and staring out the window, taking pictures as they drove by Chelsea Piers and Hudson Yards. He grinned, enjoying the sight of a first-time visitor to the city. Surprisingly, the man had stayed on even when they passed through SoHo—considering the labels he wore, Nico would've sworn he'd want to get off and hit up the stores.

Most of the people exited the bus at the stop for the Statue of Liberty and picture-taking. Mr. Gorgeous Ass passed by him and hesitated. "Am I allowed to stay on for the ride back to Times Square?"

"Of course. You won't be late for your meeting later."

"Thanks. I just want to grab some pictures."

"We won't leave without you, I promise."

His face brightened, and laugh lines fanned out from those smoky, golden eyes. Nico put his age around forty, a good twelve years older than him, but his body was in peak physical condition. A thin black sweater stretched across a broad chest, and well-cut gray slacks hugged his powerful thighs. When he exited, Nico forced himself not to gawk at that fabulous ass.

Dave took a pull from his bottle of Diet Coke. "Gonna run out and take a quick leak."

"Go ahead." Nico sat in a vacant seat in the front row. "They'll be a few minutes, and I'll collect the tickets from any newbies coming on."

With a salute, Dave hustled to the diner on the corner, where he always stopped to pick up a muffin and a coffee. Nico scrolled through his phone, checking social media. His cousin, Joey, had posted pictures of his trip to Florida with his longtime girlfriend, Teresa. It pissed Nico off that Joey had scheduled his vacation without asking him, but as he was the one without a significant other, he let it slide.

Footsteps and loud voices heralded the return of the passengers, so he stuck the phone into his pocket and pasted a smile on his face. Company policy was clear—no phones were to be used during the trips—but Nico figured since they'd stopped and he was alone, no harm, no foul.

He collected the tickets from the new passengers and noted that his gorgeous out-of-towner hadn't yet returned. Dave was at the corner, and Nico knew they couldn't sit and wait for someone to daydream at the famous sights, no matter how good-looking they were. Spying the man's golden-brown hair above the fray, he called out, "Bus is leaving."

Mr. Gorgeous Ass snapped to attention and hurried to the curb. "Sorry. I got lost in my head."

"Not a bad place to be."

The man shot him an unreadable look and found his seat, where, Nico noticed with surprise, he'd left his computer bag.

Oh, buddy, you are such an easy mark.

Feeling like he had to say something to clue them in, Nico first gave his new passengers the spiel with the route information uptown, then said, "I want to give everyone a friendly word of advice. New Yorkers have a reputation as being tough and unfriendly, but that's usually because we're busy rushing somewhere. Truth is, we'll always help you out in your hour of need. But you gotta be smart. Watch your personal belongings. Don't go leavin' your stuff on the seat if you get off the bus, or puttin' it next to you on the subway if you take the train. Ladies, don't hang your bag behind you on your chair. You don't wanna ruin your vacation 'cause some sticky-fingered bozo made you as an easy mark." He grinned. "That public service announcement is brought to you by your friendly neighborhood travel guide, Nico. Now, let's talk about Chinatown."

As he gave a brief overview of immigration and the historic Five Points area, Nico noticed his bus crush glance at the computer case by his side. A red flush rose over his cheeks. Nico had tried to be subtle and not make the tourist feel bad, wanting to warn people to be savvy and smart in the nicest way possible. Hopefully the guy understood Nico meant well.

The downtown loop normally took approximately ninety minutes start to finish, but there was a protest and a broken-down truck, so it was closer to two full hours before they returned to the final stop in front of the M&M's store. People filed out of the bus, thanking him, some pressing tips into his hand and tipping Dave the driver as well.

"Thank you. Thanks, everyone. Enjoy your day, don't play three-card monte on the street—because you'll never win—and if you want some great, homemade Italian food in Brooklyn, stop by my family's place—La Dolce Vita—in Bay Ridge, Brooklyn."

Last off the bus was the gorgeous tourist, who handed him a twenty-dollar bill. Nico's eyes widened—in all the years he'd been doing this job, he'd rarely seen more than a five.

"Oh, uh, thanks. I really appreciate it."

"No, thank *you*, Nico. I enjoyed your stories about the city. You made the trip much more enjoyable with your extensive knowledge."

"I'm glad you found it helpful. Now you can eat lunch and make your meeting. Have a safe trip home."

"Thanks. I will. Next time I'll try to stay longer. I definitely need more than two days here."

Nico would've loved to keep talking, but a line was growing for the next group. "You do. Hope to see you again on your next trip."

A sigh of regret escaped Nico as he watched the man stride away and get lost in the crowd. He faced the group of people waiting curbside.

"Give me a few minutes to clean the bus, and you can come right on." Carrying a ten-gallon trash bag, he walked through the center aisle, peering at each seat, picking up discarded cups, fast-food wrappers, and newspapers people had left behind. At the rear of the bus, he spotted a leather wallet on the floor.

"Shit," he muttered, picking it up. When he opened it, the face of his gorgeous stranger stared up at him from the driver's license. "Ford St. Claire, Fort Lauderdale, Florida." Why did that name seem like a perfect fit?

"Nico, you done?" Dave called out.

He shoved the wallet into the back pocket of his pants. He had another five hours until his shift ended, so he couldn't do anything about it at the moment. "Yeah, Dave, coming right away."

He finished clearing the trash, disposed of it, then began taking the tickets and introducing himself to the crowd.

On his next break, he pulled out the wallet, and though he felt a little creepy doing it, searched through it to see if he could tell where St. Claire was staying. Some of the receipts in the billfold pointed to the bar inside the Knickerbocker Hotel and the Charlie Palmer at the Knick restaurant. St. Claire had ordered a gem lettuce salad, the New York Strip, and a martini.

"Not surprised. Classy place for a classy guy." Not that Nico had ever been. It was way out of his league. For now. But one day…because Nico had plans. Big plans and faith. One day he'd be able to walk in there and order anything he wanted off the menu.

By five thirty he'd finished, counted his tips—ninety dollars—and pocketed the cash. "See you in a few, Dave," he said over his shoulder as he descended the bus steps.

"Yep. Good crowd today."

Nico nodded and set off to file his timesheets then continued on toward the Knickerbocker Hotel.

The clerk greeted him with a pleasant expression. "May I help you?"

"Yes. I'm here to see Ford St. Claire."

The clerk typed something into his computer. "I'll ring his room." The phone rang and rang with no answer. "I'm sorry, but there's no answer."

An unexpected complication. Nico had figured St. Claire would have returned to the hotel by now. "I can wait." He took a seat, attention focused on the door. At five forty-five, St. Claire walked in, and striding quickly, made his way to the elevators. Nico jumped up.

"Mr. St. Claire. Wait."

His steps slowed and he turned around, puzzlement written on his handsome face. Their eyes met, and Nico guessed the moment St. Claire recognized him, because his brows shot up.

"Hello. You're from the bus, correct?"

"Yes." Nico smiled. "I imagine you were frantic when you discovered your wallet missing? I'm here to return it." He extended his hand, and with a face filled with pure relief, St. Claire took the billfold.

"Oh my God, thank you so much. I called your company, but they said no one had turned anything in. I thought it was lost forever and I'd be stuck."

"Not a problem. Glad I could help." Nico turned to go.

"Wait. Please let me give you something for your trouble."

Normally, Nico wouldn't have minded taking a tip from a customer, especially one he'd gone out of his way for, but something stopped him.

"No, it's fine. Enjoy your night and have a safe trip home tomorrow."

As he walked out, his phone buzzed.

"Hey, Ma."

"Hey, yourself. How was work?"

"Good. Anything wrong?" Nico had the night off and was looking forward to hanging out in the city with his buddies.

"Nah. Just wanted to tell you that me and Aunt Justine are going to the movies, so I might not be home later."

"That's nice. You girls have fun. I'm calling up Anthony and Jack to see if they wanna hang out."

"Good. Maybe you'll meet someone nice and settle down. Like Anthony."

Nico gazed up at the sky as if the clouds could help him. "Ma. I'm not looking for a boyfriend."

"Why not?"

"I dunno. I'm just not."

"That's not an answer."

Nico had learned that the easiest way to deal with his mother's nagging about his personal life was to cut her off before she got rolling. "Well, it's all I got. Now give Aunt Justine a kiss for me, and I'll talk to you tomorrow. Bye."

"But—"

He ended the call mid-squawk and texted his buddies in their group chat.

Anyone up for pizza at John's, then Stonewall?

Anthony was the first to answer.

Sounds good. I'll see if Sergio can join us.

Nico rolled his eyes. Sergio was Anthony's newest boyfriend, and though Nico had zero desire to spend the night watching them make out in front of his face, he didn't want to go home and watch television. He checked the time.

Great. See you around 7 at John's. Pepperoni and mushroom?

Jack chimed in: *No can do. Got me a date with a hot mechanic.*

Jack worked as a contractor and filled in at his parents' plumbing supply store in the neighborhood. Nico snickered to himself.

Have fun plugging his leak.

Jack sent him a middle-finger emoji.

Nico checked the time. Six o'clock. He made his way to 42nd Street and hopped on the subway. As always on a warm summer day, the Village was crowded, and Nico slid down his shades, giving himself a chance to surreptitiously admire the butts and broad shoulders. He sniffed the air when a few gym bros passed by, getting faintly turned-on by the scent of their sweat and musk. Man, he was horny.

There was a small crowd at John's, but he ordered their pizzas and waters and found a table. He spied Anthony walking in, hand in hand with Sergio, and waved.

"Yo. Over here."

They slid into the booth opposite him, and their pizza and drinks arrived a minute later.

"Oh God, I'm starving. We had fourteen cases." Anthony groaned. "I swear I've never seen so many assholes in one day. Literally." Anthony was a lab tech at a gastroenterology center in the city, and he was responsible for prepping the patients coming in for colonoscopies and other procedures.

Sergio grabbed a slice and sank his teeth into it. "*Mmm.* So good. We're running our end-of-season sale, and it's the same. How many pairs of leggings and sports bras do these people need? And in black, too? Girl, just buy Gap, I swear." He stuffed more pizza into his mouth. Anthony gazed at him, eyes soft with indulgence.

"You're obviously doing something right, baby, because the customers love you. Sergio made top sales associate for the second month in a row." He kissed Sergio's cheek and nuzzled his neck.

"You're so supportive, baby." Sergio snuggled into Anthony's chest.

Sergio worked at lululemon and was wearing their latest, head to toe. He and Anthony had met when Sergio sold him a new outfit for the gym. They'd been dating for about three months, and at twenty-one, Sergio was the youngest man Anthony had ever dated.

Finished with chewing, he and Anthony began to kiss. Exactly what Nico had feared. He downed his water.

"Are we finished? Can we get over to Stonewall now? I really need a drink. Unless you two would rather get a room?"

Sergio disengaged his lips from Anthony's, sporting a cat-that-drank-the-cream smile.

"Sorry," Anthony muttered, looking anything but. "Yeah, sure. First round's on me."

"Baby, you're so generous." Sergio swooped in and pecked him on his lips. "I can't wait to get you home and thank you properly."

"*Marone a mia*. For fuck's sake," Nico cursed.

The walk to Stonewall took them about fifteen minutes, and it was already crowded when they arrived. Anthony brought him his whisky, and Nico leaned against a post, people-watching while Anthony and Sergio picked up their drinks at the bar. Anthony's hand wandered to Sergio's ass and squeezed it. Sergio shifted closer, and they kissed. Anthony had confided to Nico that he'd never had a lover like Sergio and couldn't keep his hands off him whenever they were together, a fact he was proving each time Nico met them.

Sergio rubbed up on Anthony while Anthony's hand kept busy on his ass. A little annoyed, somewhat amused, and strangely turned-on, Nico forced his gaze from his friend and, holding his glass to his lips, he scanned the room checking out the scenery, and froze. His heart did a double beat.

There, at the door, stood Ford St. Claire.

Chapter
TWO

Ford stood for a moment, his eyes taking a few seconds to adjust to the dim interior of the bar. Dammit, he knew he should've had something to eat besides the salad he'd chewed without tasting, but he had to make sure he got to the Stonewall Inn. It was the landmark he'd most wanted to see on his short visit, but when his wallet turned up missing, he'd been afraid that would never happen. He'd berated himself for being that stupid tourist who got pickpocketed.

When the tour guide, Nico, had shown up at his hotel with it, Ford could've kissed him. Truthfully, it was something he'd wished he'd had the nerve to do, lost wallet or not, because Nico was the most beautiful man he'd ever seen.

He blinked, staring into the crowded room. It was as gritty as he'd seen in pictures or imagined, with a pool table in the corner and long tables filled with a mixture of cool, exciting people and gawking tourists like him. He'd hoped to grab a seat and people-watch, but that looked out of the question, so he decided on one drink, and then he'd leave to get something to eat.

He blinked and rubbed his eyes. It couldn't be…but it was. Ford didn't know whether to turn and walk out, or to put one foot in front of the other and fulfill a fantasy. No time to think because here he came, a disbelieving expression on his handsome face.

"Mr. St. Claire?"

Nervous now, he wet his lips. "Hi, Nico. Fancy meeting you here."

"Funny, that was going to be my line." A quick glance to his hand, and Ford realized Nico had seen his ring. *Dammit.* Why the hell was he still wearing it?

Because Lenny had given it to him on their tenth anniversary, and after so many years, it had become part of him.

Self-conscious, he twisted the ring around and around. "I, uh, I'm not married. When we met in med school, it wasn't legal, and after we moved in together, we talked about it occasionally but never followed through." Something always came up—mainly Lenny's dick inside someone else's ass, he'd learned. "Plus, Florida made it hard as hell for gay people. About a year ago, Lenny decided he didn't want to be with me anymore, but we still co-own our practice." Not the actual story, but it was neither the time nor place to get into details.

"That must be awkward."

"We come in on different days, so it's not too bad."

The taut lines of Nico's face softened, and a smile curved those luscious lips. "All I gotta say is, it's his loss. My gain."

Ford's dick twitched. For a year, his libido had lain dormant, frozen in a body made impotent by the death of his relationship. And now, it seemed, it was waking up. Not that he planned to act on it, because that wouldn't be him.

Well, the old Ford. Maybe it was time to try something new and be himself rather than the person others wanted him to be.

"I was going to get a drink and sit, but…" He glanced around the crowded space. "It doesn't look like there's room."

The hand on his elbow startled him. "How about we try one out of two? Let's get you that drink." Ford allowed Nico to lead him to the bar, squeezing past people talking and laughing. And kissing. He gawked at the two men swallowing each other's tongues. "What do you want?" Nico asked.

"Extra-dry martini." He spoke without taking his eyes off the couple going at it, hot and heavy.

"Don't mind them. They can't keep their hands off each other whenever they're together."

"Or their mouths."

Nico cackled. "That's a good one. Lemme get you that drink."

Nico ordered for him and raised his glass of whisky. "*Salute.*"

"Cheers." They locked gazes as they sipped.

"I never expected to see you again after I returned your wallet. Especially here."

Heat rushed to Ford's face. "I, uh, I—"

"Let me guess," Nico murmured, shifting closer. "You've never been to a gay bar."

"No, I have. I mean…" He gulped his drink. God, he was so out of his element.

"Is this your first time since your split?" Eyes the color of the Caribbean Sea glinted, and Ford spied the pink tip of his tongue. "Are you looking to meet someone for some fun on your last night here?"

Did Nico think he was coming on to him? Did he want

to have sex with Nico? For a brief moment, the world tilted as Ford imagined what all that hot, naked skin might feel like, but he didn't want the man to think he was a tease. He couldn't change overnight. "I'm not here to do that. It would be foolish."

"Foolish, how?" Nico's dark brows drew together.

Face flaming, Ford glanced at the crowd and whispered, "I'm leaving tomorrow, and I'm not going to...*be* with someone I just met. That's not me. But Stonewall is iconic. I wanted to see what it was like."

"So, you weren't married, but you were together for how long?"

"Twenty years."

Whistling, Nico nodded. "Long time. And you never...?"

"I-I'd rather not talk about it," Ford rushed in.

The lies, tears, and betrayal. None of that belonged here, in this space where smiles met smiles and laughter reigned. Ford wondered if he'd ever be happy again.

Drink finished, Ford looked for somewhere to place the empty glass, and finding none, he stood squeezing it, hoping it wouldn't break in his hand.

"Let me get you another."

Before he could say no and that one drink was his limit, especially on an empty stomach, Nico plucked the glass from his hand and left him to go to the bar. Ford used that time to ogle the younger man's body without fear of getting caught. His admiring gaze swept over those broad shoulders tapering to a narrow waist, where slim-cut pants cupped a perfect ass. *God.* His breath grew short. What would it feel like to touch him? Nico spoke to someone next to him and laughed, his face so alive and bright, Ford couldn't imagine such unfettered happiness.

Nico returned with his drink. "Here you go."

Ford vowed not to drink it and simply hold it for show. He didn't want to get drunk. He might do something foolish.

Like act on his desire to kiss Nico.

"Thanks."

"So you're from Florida? You like it there?"

Ford shrugged. "It's okay. I could do without the hurricanes and humidity, but my apartment faces the water, so it's nice to sit outside on the terrace."

After their breakup, Ford bought a high-rise apartment on the Intracoastal, and at night he'd sit and watch the boats sail past, wishing they could carry him away to a new life. One where people he'd once believed were his friends didn't whisper as he passed by, nor gave him fake sympathetic smiles.

"Sounds nice," Nico mused. "They have places like that in the city—overlooking the river, you know? They're out of my reach right now. But one day…" He took a sip of his drink.

"One day? Is being a tour guide your full-time job?"

"For now. And I help out at my family's restaurant in Bay Ridge. That's in Brooklyn." He grinned, and Ford couldn't help smiling in return. There was something so joyful about Nico. "Maybe one day you'll get to visit the city again, and you'll come eat there. I'll make sure you get good service." He winked, and a hot flush rose through Ford. They'd only just met, but he enjoyed this teasing and back-and-forth. It reminded him that life existed even though he often felt dead inside.

"Maybe. There are always seminars and events going on. This was a quick trip for me to give a deposition—expert testimony in a legal case. Normally they would come to me, but I wanted to see New York City. When I volunteered to come over, they were happy not to have to make the trip."

"Sounds complicated." Nico's brows rose. "Whaddya do for a living, anyway?"

"I'm a dermatologist."

"One of those doctors who give Botox treatments?" Nico

shuddered. "I can't imagine sticking a needle in my face."

"You don't need any work. Your skin is still supple and firm."

"Yeah?" Nico's gaze turned heated. "I'm definitely firm."

"Uh, yeah, okay." Red-faced, Ford ducked his head. "Botox and fillers are a significant part of the practice, but we do much more than that. We treat skin diseases and do aesthetic treatments and cancer detection. My specialty is surgery to remove growths—malignant and benign. It's more than getting rid of wrinkles."

Impressed, Nico nodded. "I shoulda known, considering how good your skin looks." Nico's fingertips brushed his cheek, and Ford froze. "Soft and smooth," he murmured.

"I, uh, moisturize and always use SPF." His throat closed, and forgetting his earlier promise, Ford gulped half his drink. "Occasionally use laser treatments and light therapy. And of course, stay out of the sun."

"I love the sun. When I have the time, I lie out in my backyard where it's nice and private." A wicked grin kicked up his lips, and his eyes sparkled like sunbeams on the surface of the water. "No bathing suit means no tan lines."

"Oh, uh, you should still use sunscreen. Even if you don't burn, you can still damage your skin. People your age are coming in with problems because they don't take care of themselves properly."

Here he was, with the most gorgeous man he'd ever seen, and what was he doing? Talking about wrinkles and skin disease.

Smooth, Ford.

He drank the rest of his martini.

"You okay? You seem kinda nervous." Nico cocked his head.

"N-nervous? N-no. I'm okay. Just taking in all the sights." His smile was weak at best.

"*Mmhmm.* Me too. And I like what I see."

Flustered and forgetting his glass was empty, Ford put it to his lips.

"Thirsty? Have some of mine." Nico handed him his whisky.

"I-I shouldn't."

"Go on. We all do things we shouldn't, but that's the fun of being alive."

The thought of putting his mouth where Nico's had been sent a shocking thrill through him, and before he knew it, he'd swallowed the harsh liquor.

"Oh God, that's awful," he gasped. It went down like fire but settled warm and comforting in his belly.

"It just takes a while to get used to. Have another," Nico urged. "The first time's always the hardest." Nico offered his glass again.

"Maybe just one more," he mumbled and took another drink. "You're right. It didn't taste half as bad." He licked his lips.

"It's like sex. The more you have, the better it gets." Nico winked.

Ford wasn't so sure. Lenny had loved sex, and when they first got together, they were young and they'd had sex as often as they could. But for him, the stress of residency and then setting up the practice had put his sex drive second. They'd gone from sex every morning and evening to twice a week. Lenny had complained at first, and they'd talked about it. Ford, constantly worrying about failure and not doing the right thing, had argued that their responsibility to the practice took precedence and there was nothing wrong with cutting back on the sex. Lenny had agreed without complaint.

Ford should've known Lenny had given in too quickly.

The *buzz* in the room had risen to a dull roar, and his head pounded. Hazy from a healthy dose of lust and alcohol, Ford swayed, and Nico caught him. "Whoa. You okay?"

"I think I need to leave. I have to get up at five to get to the airport."

"Okay, let's get you back to your hotel."

"I can do it. I'm at the Kickerblocker…I mean, Lickerboner." *Dammit.* He knew what to say but couldn't get his mouth to form the words.

Shaking with laughter, Nico slid an arm around his waist. "I know where you are. I'll make sure you get there."

He leaned on Nico as they walked out into the street. Nico took out his phone, and Ford was pushed into the back seat of the waiting car. To his surprise, Nico sat beside him.

"You're coming too?"

"I have to make sure you get home okay."

Ford clasped his hands tight and concentrated on not getting sick as the stop-and-go traffic played havoc with his head. A few times his stomach lurched, and he feared he'd embarrass himself, but Nico must've read his mind and opened the window, letting the cool night air in.

"Thank you. I can't believe I did this. It's not me."

Nico didn't seem concerned. "Don't beat yourself up over it."

They reached the hotel, and again, Nico took control, supporting his waist as they entered the lobby. Ford's tongue was thick and his head still spun, while his stomach did slow somersaults. "I'd better get upstairs 'cause I might make a fool of myself in the lobby." He swallowed.

"What's your room number?"

"1602."

Nico led him to the elevators, and he thought for moment he was in trouble when the elevator took off, but he managed to keep it together until they reached his room. Nico put a hand inside his back pocket.

"I'm not grabbing a feel, just getting your wallet out for the hotel key."

"S'okay." They were of similar height, and his head

lolled onto Nico's shoulder.

"Come." Nico tugged on his arm, and he sprawled onto the bed while Nico kneeled in front of him and took off his shoes. "Go to sleep."

"You're being so nice to me, and I don't deserve it." He tried to smile, but his lips trembled, and to his horror, a river of tears rolled down his cheeks.

Mercifully, Nico ignored his drunk-ass rambling and swung his legs onto the bed. "I'll set your alarm for tomorrow to make sure you don't oversleep. Bye, Doc."

The last thing Ford heard before he passed out was the *click* of the door as Nico left.

The blaring of the alarm woke Ford, and he lay for a minute with his eyes closed, feeling like death. Vaguely recalling Nico bringing him to the room, Ford flung an arm over his eyes and groaned.

"I can't believe I started crying. What a pathetic jerk."

He ordered room service, then took a long, hot shower. A snail mucin face mask and caffeine pads over his eyes to reduce the puffiness helped somewhat. By the time he left for the airport, he was feeling halfway human.

Ford sat at the gate, sipping an extra-large latte, and popped two Motrin. He should be chugging water to rehydrate, but at the moment, caffeine to get his brain working was paramount.

As a first trip to the city, Ford understood the appeal. There was something to be said for its anonymity. When all hell broke loose at home, he'd retreated, only leaving his apartment for the office, but he couldn't escape the people who stopped, stared, and whispered.

Isn't that the guy whose partner was caught sleeping with the senator's son in the limo?

Don't forget the parties on their yacht.

I heard he was sleeping with their pool boy too.

That poor man. Imagine having your sex life plastered all over the news.

Humiliation burned deep like a brand seared to his skin. The past year had been a blur of misery and pain. The perfect life he'd tried so hard to build had upended, and in shambles, Ford gave Lenny their beautiful house on the Intracoastal and the yacht, no longer able to live in a place where visions of Lenny fucking random people stalked his every waking minute, as well as his nightmares, not the least of which were if Lenny had been careful with all his random partners. For peace of mind, he made sure to get tested every six months.

In his seat on the plane, Ford sipped the pre-takeoff water offered by the flight attendant and closed his eyes, thankful that the NSAIDs had begun to do their work. The plane taxied, and as they flew up and over Manhattan, he glanced down, imagining he could see Times Square, wondering if Nico was giving another tour.

Wondering why he cared.

Chapter THREE

"You shoulda seen your boy here last week. He was making all the right moves on this older dude and left with the guy." Anthony's brows waggled. "Had a good night there, Nico? Eh? Eh?" he sniggered.

Nico threw daggers at him. "Shut up. And how would you know? You and your boy toy were going at it like you were making a porno flick. I thought you'd whip it out right in front of everyone."

Anthony's face grew red. "Don't call Sergio that. And I can't help it if he can't keep his hands off me." He flexed, and Nico and Jack both rolled their eyes and groaned. Anthony loved wearing tight T-shirts that showed off his muscles and tats, although lately Nico had noticed he'd leveled up his wardrobe from Hanes to Alo and lululemon. Definitely the new boyfriend's influence. Anthony had never cared what the hell he'd worn before he'd started dating Sergio.

"*Marone a mia*, are you fucking serious with this bullshit?" Was it possible Anthony was so taken in by this twinky kid? He'd always gone for the gym-bro type with tats and bulging biceps. A mirror image of himself.

"Yeah, I am. Matter of fact, Sergio's moving in with me next month." Anthony's words hung in the air like a challenge to Nico, daring him to say something negative.

"No shit. Good luck." Perhaps sensing the tension, Jack raised his beer, while Nico sat with his jaw hanging open. An elbow to his side from Jack forced him to speak.

"Yeah, good luck."

"Gee, thanks," Anthony responded, sarcasm dripping from his words. "I've given enemas to people more enthusiastic. What? You don't approve? Not that I need it, but let's get it out in the open. Why don't you like Sergio?"

Nico drank some whisky and popped a stuffed mushroom from the plate of appetizers into his mouth, using the chewing time to gather his thoughts. "I don't *not* like Sergio. He's a cute kid. But you got real serious, real fast. And he's unlike any of the other guys you've been with—the total opposite, in fact."

"Yeah, exactly. Maybe I was looking for the wrong thing all along." Anthony didn't get passionate about much besides the Mets, food, and the gym, so to see his brown eyes blaze and his finger pointing in Nico's face was surprising. "Once I met him, I didn't need no one else, 'cause he makes me feel good about myself. Like I can do anything. He treats me like a king, and I treat him like he's the best thing that's ever happened to me 'cause you know what? He is." Anthony played with the rim of his glass. "Sometimes when you know, you know."

Dumbfounded, Nico had to ask. "Are you in love with him?"

Underneath his scruff, Anthony flushed pink, and he

shrugged. "I mean, I've told him, yeah."

"I think it's sweet." Jack nudged him again. "Don't you, Nico?"

No, I think he's being led by a pair of blowjob lips.

But he couldn't say that if he wanted to keep his head attached to his body. "Yeah, sure. Definitely."

The server came with their food, but none of them began to eat. Tension radiated in the booth of the diner where they often congregated after work. Anthony, determined bastard that he was, refused to let it go. "You don't get it because you've never been with nobody who's put you number one. Someone who thinks of you first."

"That's 'cause I'm not looking for a boyfriend. I'm fine as is."

Anthony snorted. "Bullshit you are. This is all because of Prickface Payson."

A knot twisted in his stomach. "I don't wanna talk about it."

"He hurt you," Anthony said softly. "Don't think I forgot."

"Well, I have," Nico lashed out. "So fucking drop it and let's eat. I had a full day of tours, and I'm starving." He picked up his burger and took a big bite. Jack, ever the peacemaker, began to ramble about his latest job putting in tile in a house in Howard Beach and how the woman propositioned him, hoping she could get a reduction in the price.

"I had to tell her—very nicely, of course—that I don't play for her team."

Nico managed a faint smile, but Anthony's words remained stuck in his head like a fucking earworm of a song. Why had he brought up Payson? He'd managed to stuff away the fucker's cruel words into a black place he hadn't visited in years.

"Anyways, tell us about the mysterious older man,

Nico." Anthony kicked him under the table. "Lemme tell you, the dude made a beeline for our boy here, and the two of them were into each other the whole night." He took a bite of his burger, chewed, and swallowed. "Guy looked like he had serious bucks—Sergio made his shoes as Gucci. You get in?"

"Oh, yeah?" Jack set his turkey sandwich on the plate, big blue eyes wide with interest. "Tell us. No secrets between us Brooklyn boys, ammirite?" He and Anthony raised their glasses.

"Nah," Nico protested. "It wasn't like that. He was on a tour that morning and lost his wallet on the bus. I found it and returned it to him at his hotel. It was dumb luck that he showed up at Stonewall that night."

"But you left with him. Nico Andretti don't strike out."

"Yeah, well, maybe if I'd made a move, but the guy had a little too much to drink. It wouldn't have been nice."

"Who are you?" Anthony gawked. "What happened to love-'em-and-leave-'em Nico?"

Nico lifted a shoulder. "This was different."

"How?" Anthony persisted, eyes narrowed.

"It just was. Can we stop with the twenty questions?" He continued eating, alternating between frustration and annoyance as Jack and Anthony discussed him as if he weren't present.

"Maybe he likes the guy," Jack was saying. "It could happen."

"Oh, trust me," Anthony the know-it-all declared. "Our boy was into him. They were staring deep into each other's eyes."

"Yeah?" Jack darted a glance to him. "Did they kiss? Nico don't usually go for that in public."

"Almost. I'm telling you—"

"Are you fucking kidding me?" Nico smacked his hand on the tabletop. "*Dacci un taglio!* You two clowns are really gonna sit and talk about me like I'm not here?"

"Ooh, someone's pissed. You always start speaking Italian when you get mad."

"Then listen to me, for fuck's sake."

Unimpressed by his outburst, Anthony finished his burger. "You ain't sayin' nothin', so I'm drawing my own conclusions."

"Well, pick up a crayon and draw this. Nothing happened. Period. Not everything is always about sex. *Marone a mia*, can't a guy talk to another guy without their dicks being involved?"

"A guy, yes. You? Not so much. I've known you since we were two. You can't pull that shit with me. Why is it so hard to admit you like the guy?" Anthony's brows shot high, and a crafty smile quirked his lips. "Ohhh, wait a sec. I know."

Tense with anticipation, Nico attempted nonchalance as he popped the last few fries into his mouth. "Yeah? What do you know?"

"You wanted it, but he turned you down. Damn. I don't think that's ever happened before."

"You're so stupid." Nico was ready to be done with the conversation. "And you don't know what the hell you're talking about." Thoroughly disgusted, he pulled out his wallet and threw some bills on the table. "I'm outta here."

"No, come on, dude. Stay." Jack grabbed his arm, but he pulled away and left the booth.

"Nope. Have fun talking shit about me." Without looking back, he stalked out of the restaurant and into the night.

Walking home, he ignored the happy couples he passed. He and his friends had made plans for the evening, but that was obviously a wash. Over the years, they'd had their little spats, but Nico sensed a shift in their friends group—Anthony wrapped up in Sergio, and Jack dating a bunch of different guys, looking for something, but for what, Nico didn't know.

Nico liked the thrill of the chase and a hot new kiss every time. Each man was a present to be opened and played with, but after, he easily became bored. He'd tried to see if the dating life was for him, but when the guy became clingy because they'd spent the night together, that was his cue to step away and say good-bye. Nicely, of course, with a kiss of regret and an it's-not-you-it's-me speech. His mother raised him to be a gentleman and never be cruel, though life had treated her like shit.

He reached his mother's house and sat on the steps to the porch. The Marzettis next door were having a fight, their shrieking voices reaching him from their upstairs bedroom window. Nico had no idea why they stayed married. From what his mother told him, Joe was a serial cheater, and Christine always eventually found out. Each time Joe would apologize, buy her a piece of jewelry, and nine months later another kid would be born. They were up to five now.

The yelling stopped, and Nico looked up. Their shadows merged and clothes were tossed into the air.

"Looks like number six is on the way," he muttered. "Crazy idiots."

He couldn't understand it. Why stay married if you were only going to cheat? Then again, his mother had gotten the rawest deal. After dating for five years, with a huge wedding planned, his sperm donor—because Nico refused to think of that bum as his father—bailed on her. He'd been cheating on her for months with the assistant at his dental practice.

A month later his mother discovered she was pregnant, and his father had wanted nothing to do with her or the baby.

Naturally, his *nonno* was enraged and threatened to go after him. With a baseball bat. Nonna intervened, saying his mother was better off without a man who would treat a woman so shamefully. The entire family rallied around her, helping his mother through her pregnancy, and Nico was raised with his cousin who lived down the block from them. Aunt Justine was like a second mother to him, and Uncle Louie stood in as a surrogate father, cheering him on at his ball games and helping him with what college to go to.

Until Uncle Louie decided he was bored and left Aunt Justine after twenty-five years of marriage to "find himself." Where he found himself was with Brenda Rozetti, a very young, big-breasted waitress at the restaurant Nico's grandparents had owned and given to their daughters when they retired. Aunt Justine refused to give him a divorce, and they hadn't spoken in almost ten years.

All of which left Nico with a sour taste in his mouth for relationships, marriage, and fidelity in general. In the end, everyone screwed the one they said they loved.

His ass hurt from sitting on the hard cement, so he opened the gate and unlocked the door to his apartment. With both Nonno and Nonna gone, his mother wanted him to take over the two stories of the house, and she would live in the little apartment downstairs, but he refused. No way would his mother live in a basement.

Inside, he stripped to his boxers, poured a Scotch, and turned on the ball game. Wouldn't kill him to stay in for a night. His feet were tired anyway, and he wasn't in the mood to talk to some rando.

As he sipped his drink, an ad came up on the television for some fancy Manhattan dermatologist specializing in laser surgery. Immediately, Dr. Ford St. Claire came to mind. Not that he'd been far from it in the past week. St. Claire would always be the one he let get away, but he stood by his decision not to take advantage of the man. Drunk sex wasn't his style, even if the man was insanely good-looking and Nico had desperately wanted to know what his kisses tasted like.

Nico opened his laptop, typed in St. Claire's name, and up popped the website of St. Claire's office—Fresh Faces. He clicked on the About Us tab, and there he was. A sweep of golden-brown hair, those lion-like amber eyes, and the most kissable lips Nico had almost come into contact with.

As one half of the founding partners of Fresh Faces of Fort Lauderdale, Dr. St. Claire is dedicated to helping patients achieve healthy, clear skin. He specializes in the diagnosis and treatment of various skin diseases, including skin cancer, and is one of South Florida's top Mohs surgeons. Dr. St. Claire is happy to offer patients lifestyle coaching, both in person and virtual, to assist in their goal of looking young and staying healthy.

A native of Florida, Dr. St. Claire attended the University of Miami for college and medical school. He did his residency at Broward Health Medical Center, and along with Dr. Leonard Nova, opened Fresh Faces of Fort Lauderdale.

Recalling that St. Claire's partner was his ex, Nico clicked on the About tab for Dr. Nova and was met with a photo of a dark-haired, dark-eyed man with a wide, fake smile. Instant dislike rose in his gut. He never trusted a man with fake-as-hell, too-white teeth. He'd bet the man cheated. He had that scummy appearance of someone who couldn't keep his dick in his pants. Why would anyone want someone else when they had a man like Ford St. Claire at home?

"Lifestyle coaching, huh?" Nico rubbed his chin. "Maybe I should think about it. He did tell me to watch my sun exposure. And the consult is free."

Long after he'd filled out the form, Nico was still grinning.

Chapter FOUR

"All done, Mr. Rosenstein, and I'll send that mole that popped up last month for a biopsy."

Ford helped the elderly man off the examination table as his assistant handed Mr. Rosenstein his shirt. His hands were shaky, yet he put the clothing on without help.

"Thank you, Doctor, for making the time for me. I feel so much better now that you've seen me." He held Ford's wrist tightly as Ford walked him to the waiting room. Normally he'd have his assistant do it, but Mr. Rosenstein was his first patient when he'd been a medical student and had stayed with him all these years, so Ford felt a little protective of the man, especially since he had no family. He and his wife had started out as snowbirds from New York City, and he'd moved to Florida permanently after she passed away. They had no children, and he now lived with his aide in a modest apartment in Sunrise. He came every three or four months for a skin-cancer checkup, though Ford had said once a year would be fine. Ford suspected it was more out of loneliness and a need to get out and talk to someone than a desire to be physically checked.

"Always, Mr. Rosenstein."

"How are you doing? That one not giving you any trouble, is he?"

Ford's lips twitched. Mr. Rosenstein had never liked Lenny—the one time Ford had been ill and Lenny'd taken over his patients, Mr. Rosenstein had confided that he thought Lenny was a schmuck.

"You can do much better. I know it's not nice to say that, but I'm old. I've reached a point that I can say what I want."

"No, we worked it all out, and I'm fine."

Mr. Rosenstein gripped his arm tighter. "You're young and good-looking and a doctor. Most of all, you're a good person. A *mensch*. What more could anyone want? There's someone for you. Like my Lillian used to say—a cover for every pot."

"I'm fine. Really. Don't worry about me. You take care of yourself. That's most important to me." He spotted the man's aide waiting in the reception room. "Jim? Here he is. All good to go."

Jim helped Mr. Rosenstein to the desk to check out, and Ford returned to his office to review the next patient's chart. From his early morning review of the schedule, Ford anticipated a busy day—predominantly Botox and fillers, but those could be done in no time. He also had a Mohs surgery, rashes and a few nasty burns to treat, laser treatments, and chemical peels.

He preferred to keep busy. It kept his worries at bay— that he couldn't do this, that he wasn't good enough. He knew it wasn't true, that he didn't need Lenny to keep his end of the practice going. Their system of not being in the office at the same time worked well for now. Ford anticipated that eventually they would have a discussion concerning the dissolution of the practice, but the thought of more lawyers and endless meetings made his head spin. All he wanted to do was work.

His phone buzzed.

"Dr. St. Claire, Ms. Montrose is here."

"Send her in."

The first of his six purely cosmetic procedures of the day. He went to work.

Five hours later, he sank into his office chair with a groan. The door opened, and his assistant, Marisol, stuck her head in. "That's it for the day, Dr. St. Claire. All you have left is a virtual appointment. It came in last night, and Susan forgot to put it on your list." She rolled her eyes. "That one needs to start thinking less about her boyfriend and more about the job."

Ford rolled his shoulders and managed a smile, which morphed into a yawn. "Mention it to Adriana. She's the office manager."

"I will. Anyway, the appointment isn't for another twenty minutes." She adjusted the cap she wore over her curls. "I have it on your portal."

"Thanks, you're the best."

"I know." She grinned and waved. "I'll see you on Wednesday."

"Have a good one."

He and Lenny split the practice by days—Ford came in Monday, Wednesday, and in the afternoon on Fridays. Lenny was Tuesday, Thursday, and Friday mornings. Each had their own assistant, and when the scandal hit, the first thing Ford had done was gather Marisol and the rest of the staff to reassure them that even though their work hours had changed, their salaries would remain the same. It wasn't their fault that the doctors' personal lives had imploded.

Lenny was too busy doing damage control, giving interviews to the local news reporters. Being the face of the practice, he had a wonderful working relationship with the media, and somehow the spin was sympathetic to him.

Ford rubbed his eyes and scanned the virtual appointment as he sipped his coffee. "What the…" It couldn't be.

Nico Andretti? Was that his last name? Ford frantically replayed their conversation but didn't recall Nico mentioning his last name. The age seemed right—twenty-eight—and Ford winced. He was fourteen years older than Nico, and he'd never felt his age more than that night at Stonewall together. Nico was so at home with the crowd and didn't appear to mind the public kissing and touching.

The computer dinged, signaling someone had entered the waiting room for the virtual meeting. Glancing at the time, Ford saw he still had two minutes to spare. He jumped up from his chair to gaze in the mirror and straightened his tie. A quick comb-through of his hair, a spritz of hydration to his face, and he was as ready as he could be.

Maybe it won't be him. And why does it matter? He's 1100 miles away.

Still, his heart thumped like a drum when he clicked the link. The computer blurred, then cleared. And there he was on the split screen, as gorgeous and sexy as Ford remembered.

"Hey, Doc." Nico grinned and waved. "How's it goin'?"

"So it is you. I saw the name, but I wasn't sure."

"It's me. In the flesh." He winked. "So to speak."

"How have you been?" Ford drank in Nico's face, his beautiful aqua-blue eyes and soft lips. "You're looking well."

"Aside from it bein' hot as hell, I'm fine."

"Trust me, you don't know hot in the summer until you've been to South Florida."

"Is that an invitation? I can check my vacation time. I haven't been to the beach yet." Nico flexed his biceps, and Ford had to pinch himself to keep from drooling at the muscles bunching under all that tanned skin. This appointment was getting out of hand, and Ford took a deep, steadying breath and got them back on track.

"Do you have a question about a skin problem?" He scanned the intake sheet Nico had filled out. "There's not much information here."

"Well," Nico demurred, tapping his perfect cheekbones, "you say you give lifestyle coaching, right? That skin is the body's biggest organ and needs to be kept in tip-top shape. So I was interested in that."

"You want me to be your lifestyle coach?"

God, that might be the death of me.

"Yeah, what do you say?" Nico's eyes sparkled, reminding Ford of the waters off the shores of Turks and Caicos. "You can give me tips on looking young."

"You are young." Ford sighed, not without regret. "But the first thing is what I already mentioned. Stay out of the sun. You look tanner than the last time."

"*Mmm*, yeah. I spent the weekend in the backyard. But I think I got a sunburn. Can I show you?"

Ford's eyes narrowed. "I don't see anything on your face. Your nose isn't red or peeling."

Nico rose to his feet, and Ford almost swallowed his tongue. All Nico wore was a pair of boxers that did nothing to hide the outline of his thick cock. And, dear God, he pulled down the waistband to reveal the neatly trimmed edge of his pubic hair. Saliva pooled in Ford's mouth, and his breaths came short.

"No, but see? Right there?" His fingers trailed along

the edge of the wiry hair before resting on the jut of his hip bone, where it was, in fact, red and angry-looking. "I think I missed a spot with the sunscreen."

Ford's hungry gaze devoured Nico's half-naked body. Washboard abs with a sprinkling of dark hair. Powerful, muscular thighs. A rapidly stiffening dick that bulged through the thin boxers. Ford couldn't tear his eyes away. Christ, he was hard in his office. He had to stop this. Now. This was the kind of desire he'd heard of and never imagined he'd experience, yet here he sat in his office, barely able to breathe, feeling as though struck by lightning.

"You can sit. I've seen enough," he barked out, and Nico raised his brows at the sharp tone. "Sorry," he apologized.

"S'okay. Long day?"

Relieved that Nico had listened and was once again hidden, Ford redirected the conversation to the reason they were talking in the first place.

"They're all long. As for that burn, have you put anything on it?"

Nico's brows drew together. "Nah, I just got it today. I had a half day of tours and some time until I had to go help at the restaurant, so I laid out in the backyard."

"What SPF do you use?"

"I dunno, fifteen, maybe?"

Ford grimaced. "That's nothing. You should use at least forty-five. Now, for that burn, put some aloe-vera gel on it. That'll hydrate it, but unfortunately, the damage is done. When it gets less red, use some vitamin E oil and massage it in every day. That will help minimize scarring. It's why I stress good care from the beginning."

Nico nodded. "Okay. Guess I shoulda covered up the jewels better. I've been using a washcloth."

"That's not large enough. You need to use at least a hand towel."

Nico's lips kicked up in a wicked grin. "Thanks for noticing, Doc."

Ford could feel his face heat. "Uh, well, anyway. What else would you like to discuss? About your skin and keeping healthy, that is," he added hastily.

Nico scrunched up his face in thought. Damn, he was adorable.

"Well…I know water is important. How much should I be drinking?"

"You do know that you can get all this information online. Do you really want to pay for a coach?"

Nico propped his chin in his hand. "You got me, Doc. Fact is, I was watchin' the game the other night and saw a commercial for those fillers and shit, and it reminded me of you."

A thrill ran through him, and despite himself, he had to ask. "You thought of me?"

All trace of humor faded from Nico's face. His gaze turned dark and sensual, and he ran the tip of his tongue over his lips. "Yeah. You were kinda out of it when I left you, and I hoped you made your flight okay."

Ford flinched and cast his eyes downward. "Oh, yeah, that wasn't my finest hour. I guess you figured out I'm not much of a drinker."

"That's for sure," Nico teased.

Nico wasn't being mean. That was simply part of his brash, in-your-face type of humor, something Ford had rarely experienced, except with patients who'd relocated from up north.

"Well, I should thank you again for being so nice. I was pretty embarrassed."

"Why?" Nico sounded genuinely surprised. "Happens to the best of us. Everyone needs to let go sometimes."

Let go? If Ford let go, he'd crash to the ground, ending up in a million pieces of heartache.

He shrugged. "I was a stranger. You didn't have to be nice."

"I'm a nice guy, didn't you know?" Nico returned to that flirty teasing that made him so damn enticing, Ford could talk to him for hours. But he had to stop.

"So to finish up, you need to make sure you drink enough water—what's your body weight?"

"Two hundred, give or take." He ran a hand over his flat stomach, and Ford followed his movement. "I don't like to bulk up, but wanna make sure I stay in shape. I think it's working, don't you, Doc?"

Ford blinked. "Yes," he replied faintly. "It's definitely working." He licked his lips. "Uh, so at two hundred pounds, you should be drinking about one hundred ounces of water."

Nico's big eyes grew comically wide. "A hundred? That's nuts. If I did that, I'd be running off the bus to pee all day."

"You can do it in the morning when you wake up and then at night."

But Nico didn't look convinced. "I dunno. I'll have to see."

Ford's office line buzzed. "Hold on a second." He pushed the intercom button. "Yes, Adriana?"

"Dr. St. Claire, Dr. Nova is here. He'd like to speak to you."

His stomach tightened. "Here? In the office?"

"Yes, Doctor."

What the hell was Lenny doing at the office? It wasn't his day. "Tell him I'm on a virtual appointment. I can speak to him later."

"I told him. He said he'll wait."

Ford clenched his teeth so hard, his jaw ached. "I'll be there shortly." He ended the call and returned to Nico, who'd obviously heard everything. "Sorry. I shouldn't have taken the call in the middle of your appointment. I was just afraid it could be an emergency."

"That your ex?" Nico asked, ignoring his apology and clearly more interested in his conversation.

"What? How…how did you know?" Had Nico read the papers? He'd mentioned a Google search. The Internet was forever, and Ford knew he could run but not hide from Lenny's dirty escapades, which would follow him to his grave.

"You mentioned you work together."

"Oh. Yes, it was him. Well, it was nice talking to you, Nico. Please make sure to put aloe on that burn and use a higher sun protection factor the next time you're outside. Just because you have more melanin in your skin doesn't mean it can't suffer lasting damage."

"I will, Doc. Thanks. I'll talk to ya."

Ford doubted it. As nice as it had been to escape for the past hour, there was little reason for Nico to call him again.

"Bye."

He turned off the computer and took a few deep breaths, practicing the calm his yoga instructor had taught him. He'd need every arrow in his measly quiver to go up against Lenny.

Upon exiting his office, he heard Lenny's voice, and tension immediately swirled in his gut.

I will not let him get the best of me.

"Adriana, when is he—never mind, there he is. Ford, come with me," Lenny ordered, but Ford stayed put.

"No. You came to see me. We can go to my office." He turned on his heel and marched back behind his desk. "Sit."

Lenny, of course, remained standing and crossed his arms. "I wanted to talk to you about the office."

"What about it?"

Was he going to walk away, leaving him with full ownership? Ford had neither the capital nor the desire to run the practice on his own.

"I want to bring in someone to handle the cosmetic stuff. We're getting too busy with the Botox and fillers for two doctors, and the practice can't handle all the patients."

While Lenny's reasoning was sound, something didn't seem right, but Ford couldn't put his finger on what it might be.

"I don't want another partner."

"Not a partner. This would be an employee." Lenny met his gaze without any guile, but still, Ford found it hard to trust him.

"And you have someone in mind."

"As a matter of fact, I do. Dr. Jose Diamond. He's excellent at what he does."

Derision curled his lips. "I'll bet. Did you check his medical qualifications, or was the blowjob he gave you enough to pass the interview?"

Lenny didn't even seem embarrassed. "Your jealousy is showing, babe."

"Jealous? Of who, you?" he sputtered. "That's a joke."

"Of course you are. I'm out every night, having fun, and you're home alone in your prison in the sky."

"If sex with people you'll never see again and having people talk behind your back means success, then yeah, you're winning," Ford sneered. "I loved you, and none of it mattered. Twenty years, and you can dismiss it like it was a blip. Like it was nothing."

How did this happen to them? There was a time when Lenny had been his world, his everything. He'd given Lenny his love, his heart, only to have it tossed aside like day-old news.

"I'm not interested in hearing how much you miss me. Jose is top in the field. He'll get a percentage of what he works on, and we take the rest. Win-win."

Damn him. Even at his strongest, Ford was no match for Lenny's confidence and arrogance. From the beginning it had been like that—Lenny, the rich guy from Coral Gables, and Ford, the scholarship student from the "bad" part of town. Lenny would laugh and tease him, calling Ford his "walk on the wild side."

Ford had been completely dazzled by the life Lenny introduced him to, falling under the spell of the beautiful people, elegant parties, and expensive clothes. Lenny swept him away to a life he'd only watched on television.

Until it all ended abruptly mid-series, his life canceled without warning.

Ford gritted his teeth. "I don't miss you. Trust me. What percentage were you thinking?"

"Forty percent for him. We take sixty."

It wasn't a bad business decision. The cosmetic treatments were nothing more than busy work, taking up more and more of the practice's time. The extra income notwithstanding, Ford much preferred to work on people who had true problems with their skin.

"Fine. Get the contract to my lawyer."

A big smile broke out over Lenny's face. "Perfect." He checked his Rolex. "Oops. Gotta run. I've got a dinner date in Miami, and the traffic on 95 is a killer."

And like a whirlwind, he was gone.

Ford slumped in his chair. How was it possible that Lenny was the wrongdoer and yet he wound up on top? Even a sex scandal rolled off his back. The man truly was Teflon.

He stared dispassionately at the computer screen, reading the notifications that had popped up during his virtual appointment with Nico and his talk with Lenny.

Send follow-up to Nico Andretti, re: appointment

With regret, Ford deleted it. Much as he enjoyed talking to Nico, there was little reason to continue with him.

Haircut appointment at 10 a.m. Manicure 11:30 a.m. Facial at 3:00 p.m.

Ford confirmed all three.

The American Academy of Dermatology's annual meeting is next month, and there's still time to register. Join us for three fabulous days in New York City!

It used to be that Lenny went to all the conferences, and now Ford understood why. The parties and networking, and then Lenny would come home, insatiable for sex, demanding new positions, using toys he'd picked up that would leave Ford blushing.

"Let's try it this way, baby," he'd whisper, and Ford had taken it as a sign of how much Lenny had missed him. Only now he realized Lenny was merely continuing what he'd started while away.

"Maybe it's time for me to see what's out there."

Ford clicked the link for the conference information and began to read.

Chapter FIVE

Anthony found Nico in the kitchen of La Dolce Vita and cornered him behind the register. "Whassamatta with you?"

"Nothin'." Nico smiled at Marie Vitale, with whom he went to high school. "Here you go. I got your chicken parm, eggplant rollatini, a kiddie meatballs and spaghetti, a side of sautéed broccolini, and tiramisu." He handed a bag to the little girl next to Marie. "And a coupla sprinkle cookies for you, Missy, on the house. Tell your daddy I can't wait to see him come in himself for dinner."

Marie brushed back a tear. "Aw, thanks, Nico. You're a doll. How much do I owe ya?"

"Nothin'. You just tell Jimmy to get better and that we're all rooting for him. Anything you need, we're here for you. We're honored to help out New York's finest."

Marie's husband had been shot while busting up a

fentanyl ring, and the bullet just missed his spine. It had been touch-and-go for a while, but he was walking again after months of therapy.

Anthony nudged him. "That was nice of you. Marie's been through hell."

"I know. We take care of our own."

"So you gonna answer my question? What's wrong? You're all mopey and shit."

"Don't be stupid. I'm fine. Just tired. It's hot as fuck outside, and I'm doing tours every day and working here."

"Sounds like all work and no play makes Nico a dull boy." Anthony glanced at the clock on the wall. "It's ten o'clock, and you're closing in a little while. Let's go out tonight. I'll be your wingman. You need to get laid. That'll make you feel better."

"Shh." He smacked Anthony on the shoulder. "Don't talk about sex in my mother's restaurant. That's disgusting—like a sacrilege."

"She ain't here no more. What's the big deal?"

It had emptied out, so it was only the two of them and the cooks in the kitchen. Bobby, Anthony's cousin and their busboy, had left for home. Nico started counting the cash in the till.

"It just is, okay? And where's your boyfriend? Why isn't he here with you?"

Like a proud papa, Anthony puffed out his chest. "He got chosen to go on some work retreat. They go away for a coupla days and get all Zen and shit."

"Oh brother," Nico mumbled.

"Anyways, I don't wanna go home yet. Let's get a drink at Maxie's."

"You're not gonna stop naggin' until I say yes, right?"

"Nope." Anthony drummed on the counter. "So let's get a move on."

"All right, all right. Cool your jets. Lemme close up."

Maxie's was the neighborhood bar they'd been going to from the time they'd hit twenty-one. It was within walking distance of the restaurant. Anthony's uncle, Frank, was behind the bar and waved to them as they entered.

"Hey, boys. Good to see you. C'mon, siddown. I got your whisky, Nico." He poured him a hefty splash of Macallan and set the tumbler in front of him. "Anthony, here's your beer. How's your mother, Nico? She good? Feeling okay still?"

"Thanks, Frank. Yeah, she is, thanks." Nico clinked his glass to Anthony's.

"Beautiful woman. Always so sweet whenever I come by the restaurant. Tell her I say hi, okay?"

"I will," Nico promised, and not for the first time, wondered if Frank had a little crush on his mother. Frank's wife had died about seven years ago from breast cancer, and ever since, he'd seemed a little lost. Nico glanced around. "Busy night."

"Yeah, it's hopping. Got the Mets on, if you wanna order some wings and stuff."

"Nah, but thanks. I just came from the restaurant and had baked ziti for dinner."

"Set me up with some of them wings, Uncle Frank." Anthony tapped the bar top. "I didn't have dinner."

"Why not? The boyfriend didn't cook tonight?" Frank punched the order into the computer screen.

"He's not home."

As Frank teased Anthony about Sergio, Nico checked out the rest of the bar. The pool table sat empty, but there was a group of guys sitting at a table, watching the game, an empty pitcher of beer on the table between them. One of them had thick blond hair and beefy arms. He booed when the Dodgers pulled ahead of the Mets with a three-run homer, and met Nico's eyes across the bar. A slow grin spread over the guy's face, and the familiar tingle of arousal rolled through Nico.

He sipped his Scotch, and when Blondie stood and crossed the bar, coming toward him, he turned away, smiling into his glass.

Anthony whispered, "Smooth move. Not even here five minutes, and you pulled one." He shifted over, making room for the man, who slid in between them.

"Yo," the guy called out, his voice rough. "Hey, over here. Lemme get another pitcher of Bud."

Nico frowned. He didn't like the bossy tone the guy used to speak to Frank. Not even a please? Who the fuck did he think he was? Only two bartenders were working, and they were both busy.

"Mets suck ass this year," Blondie said to him as he waited. He had pale-blue eyes, a nose that had obviously been broken several times, and full lips.

"Yeah."

"I'll bet you do too." Blondie's lips hit his ear. "Meet me in the bathroom in five." He banged the pitcher against the shining wood railing. "If these fuckers ever move their asses. Jesus Christ, they need to hire people with IQs higher than their age. Come on. I need beer here."

Annoyed now, Nico moved away from him. "Hey, chill out. They're doin' the best they can."

"Yeah? Well, this is a business, and they need to take care of their customers." He eyed Nico. "Tell you what. I'll wait on the beer, and you come with me. I can't wait to get you on your knees."

On the other side of the man, Anthony coughed, and Nico drained his glass, then set it on the bar top with a *thump*. "I don't think so." Ignoring Blondie, whose shocked face led Nico to believe people rarely told him no, he looked over at Anthony. "You ready?"

"Yeah," Anthony said. "Let's roll."

Nico turned to Blondie. "I don't get on my knees for anyone, and sure as hell not for an obnoxious piece of shit who doesn't know how to talk to people right." He took out a twenty and handed it to Frank, who was working the tap in front of him, filling the asshole's pitcher. Anthony did the same. "Frank, love you. See you soon."

"Okay, guys. Take care."

The stores and many restaurants on Fourth Avenue were closed this time of night, but the bars and coffeehouses remained open. "Guy turned into a douchebag, huh?"

"You heard the way he talked to Frank. That doesn't fly with me."

"You wanna go somewhere else and hang out? Get a cup of coffee?"

They reached the corner. "Yeah, sure."

They opted to sit outside and ordered cappuccinos. The night had turned balmy, and sidewalk cafés were filled, enabling Nico to enjoy his favorite sport—people-watching.

"So what's wrong?" Anthony sipped and licked the foam from his lips.

"Nothin'. Like I said, I'm tired."

"Eh, that's bullshit. You've been in a funk for a while now. Even Sergio mentioned it."

Nico snorted. "Yeah? He knows me like that?"

But Anthony remained serious. "Laugh, but it's the God's honest truth. You think 'cause he's a young guy he don't know nothin', but he's…whaddya call it, *perceptive*. Before he left, he says to me, 'Make sure you see Nico and find out why he looks so unhappy.' "

"Oh, uh, well, that's nice of him." Nico felt bad for thinking so negatively of the kid. He should lighten up.

"So? What's the deal?"

Nico curved his hand around the cup. "No deal. Haven't been feeling it lately. Happens sometimes, you know?"

"Not to you. Last few times we all went out, you left early."

Nico didn't answer right away. He watched the people

walk past, couples arm in arm, some laughing and holding hands, others silent, side by side. "I'm just…I dunno, in a funk. Wondering if I'm wasting my time with the tour work, thinkin' I should maybe go back to school."

"Huh. You ain't talked about that in a while."

"Yeah, well, I don't like to in case my mother overhears. She gets all upset still, since I shelved it to take care of her." He sighed and drank some more of the milky, cinnamon-laced coffee. "Maybe it's all a pipe dream."

"Don't say that. You can always go back to school. And maybe you gotta, like, adjust and shit. Instead of owning your own company, work yourself up into management. Then you can make suggestions."

Nico hadn't thought of that. He'd always been focused on owning a business. "Yeah? You think?"

"I mean, you got a college degree in business, and you know your shit. You ain't a slouch."

One thing he could always count on was Anthony's support. The brother he never had.

"Thanks, bro. Maybe you're right."

"I know I am. You love doing it, and the people love you. Every time I go on one of your tours, I see how the people eat up your spiel. I bet you're their most popular guide."

"Yeah, I mean, Carlos, the supervising dispatcher, says that a lot of repeat customers ask for me by name when he reads the information on the ticket bookings that come in."

"See what I'm sayin'?" Anthony pressed on. "That's good. Maybe one day you could casually, like, drop a hint that you're looking at moving up in the company. See what they say. That's how I got to be the supervising tech." He finished his cappuccino. "I'm thinking of goin' back to school and becoming a physician's assistant. I can make a lot more money."

"You should. You'd be great."

"Thanks, bro." He slanted a glance at Nico under his

thick lashes. "It would be good, especially if Sergio and I get married."

Shock zinged through him. "Married? Are you kiddin' me? Damn. It hasn't been that long. Only a few months."

Anthony's cheeks pinked. "Yeah, but I ain't never felt like this before. I was talking to my mother, and she said it was like that with her and my pops. When you know, you know." He shrugged, and Nico wondered if this was the beginning of the end for their group. Joey and Teresa would be getting married soon, and now Anthony and Sergio? Suddenly chilled, he rubbed his arms. Would he be the one left behind? No real job to speak of, and no one to love and love him in return.

They paid the bill and walked toward home. Anthony lived about five blocks from him, and they parted ways on the corner of Third Avenue and 78th Street.

"Talk to you." They hugged, and then Nico stood there for a moment, watching Anthony cross the street and disappear into the night.

Once home, he sat in bed with his laptop and looked to see if any management jobs were open with the tour company. His jaw dropped when he saw the salaries were more than three times what he made as a tour guide.

"Whoa. Maybe Anthony was right."

He started taking notes.

Summertime was prime tourist season in New York City, second only to the month between Thanksgiving and Christmastime. Today he only had a half day of tours scheduled—for the past month he'd been going nonstop, and he was fucking tired. This was his last tour of the day, and he planned on picking up lunch and heading over to the park to catch some rays. He grinned, thinking how the sexy Dr. St. Claire would be proud that he'd upped his sunscreen game to SPF 45.

"Everyone have your tickets ready, please." He stood outside the doors of the bus and took each one from the passengers as they passed by him. "We're almost set to go." He took a swig from his coffee cup, and the lid fell on the sidewalk. "Dammit," he muttered as he bent to pick it up. He turned to gulp as much of the coffee as possible before tossing it into the garbage can. He couldn't carry an open cup on the bus.

"Would a bottle of water suffice?" a deep, husky voice asked, and Nico's jaw dropped as he spun around.

"What the hell?"

Ford St. Claire stood in front of him, in all his gorgeous flesh.

"Hello, Nico. Remember me?"

Remember you? I jerked off to you every night for weeks. Hmm. Maybe he should keep that private and act casual.

"Yeah, of course. How ya doin', Doc?"

"I'm well." He handed him his ticket. "Here for the tour."

Nico stuck the ticket in his folder. "Why're you taking the same downtown loop when you could do the uptown one? You've already seen these sights."

"I know. But when I called and asked which bus route you were on, they told me this one. I came to see you again, Nico, not the Statue of Liberty."

Rarely if ever tongue-tied, Ford's honesty left Nico at a loss for words. "Oh, uh, yeah. That's nice. Uh, you'd better take your seat." Regaining his composure, he tried to make light, even though St. Claire's words shocked him to the core. "And hold on to your wallet this time."

"I plan to," Ford assured him. "I'll need it to take you to dinner tonight. If you're free, of course."

His stomach jumped, then did a free fall even as his heart slammed and explosive thrills burst through him.

"Oh, uh, sure. I think I am."

Ford's gorgeous face lit up, and his eyes glowed. "Great. I'd better take my seat." The man had beautiful style, and that morning he wore a pair of almost-white jeans with a dark-green polo that set off the golden sparks in his eyes. A dark swirl of chest hair peeked out of the shirt.

St. Claire mounted the steps, his fabulous ass only inches away from Nico, who sighed at its perfection. As he did the first time, Nico tracked St. Claire's progress as he made his way to his seat. This time he wouldn't be saying good-bye when the tour was over, and his mind went haywire at the possibilities.

Had St. Claire—*Ford*—really come to New York to see him?

Several times during the tour, he caught Ford's eye as he spoke and was proud that he'd managed not to stumble over his words. He'd never looked forward to the end of the day so much.

Close to two hours later, Dave turned off the bus and discharged the passengers on Broadway. Waiting by the door, Nico offered restaurant and other city advice, and stuffed into his pocket the tips people handed him. Ford had hung back, waiting for the bus to empty out, and approached him after everyone had left.

"So…you're done for the day?"

"I am." Nico shifted his crossbody bag to the front. "Just have to drop my paper work in the office, and I'm free."

"I'm at the Knickerbocker again. Can you meet me for lunch?"

Nico thought fast. He was supposed to have a shift tonight at the restaurant, but no fucking way was he going to miss this opportunity. His cousin would have to change with him.

"Yeah, sure. Where should I meet you?"

"What do you feel like eating?"

He couldn't keep a smile from overtaking his face. "Anything you want."

Ford blushed. "Uh, well, you know the city, so it's your choice."

"Definitely not in Times Square. Wanna wait inside the Hershey's store for me? It's air-conditioned, and I'll meet you there in a few."

"Sure."

Stomach swirling with anticipation, Nico hurried to the building where the Hop to It bus company office was located, put in his time sheets, and gave the dispatcher the tickets.

"Have a good one, Nico. See you on Saturday."

"Yeah. You too, Carlos."

He had a day off before returning to the job, and hopefully it would be spent with Dr. Gorgeous Ass.

On the way to the Hershey's store, Nico thought about where to go for lunch and what a man like Ford St. Claire would like. No Papaya King or Shake Shack, for sure. Nico imagined him in classy restaurants with tablecloths, fresh flowers, and tuxedoed waiters. Places where a glass of wine cost as much as a bottle at the spots Nico frequented. Much as Nico would've loved to experience one of New York's best restaurants, he didn't want to seem greedy by suggesting somewhere expensive.

"I know." Decision made, he hurried over to the store, where he found Ford, looking like a damn *GQ* model, browsing the candies.

"See anything you like?" he whispered in Ford's ear, and he jumped slightly. He turned around and gave a shy yet utterly sensuous smile.

"Yeah. I do."

Nico itched to kiss those soft lips but refrained. "Hungry? Do you like Mexican?"

"Yeah, sure."

"I have a great place, not far."

Dos Caminos was located in the W Hotel and was midpriced. When he and Anthony graduated from college, they went there and got tipsy on margaritas, ate platters of nachos, steak tacos, and finished off with churros in *dulce de leche* ice cream. They topped off the night with a ride home to Brooklyn in an Uber.

Seated inside, Nico ordered a margarita, while Ford ordered his martini. "You're not going to have a margarita?"

Ford shook his head. "Tequila and I don't mix. It's not a pretty sight."

They ordered guacamole for the table, and Ford chose the chicken fajitas while Nico opted for nachos. Their drinks came, and Nico raised his glass.

"To unexpected lunches." They sipped, and Nico crunched a chip from the basket. "So…what're you doin' back in the city?"

"The national meeting of dermatologists is being held here. Normally my ex goes, but this time I decided to come." There went that cute little smile again. "For obvious reasons."

His fingers tightened around the glass in his hand. "Yeah? Meaning?"

"I think you know."

He did, but Ford St. Claire wasn't some random he picked up at a club. He was class, and given his own past, Nico wasn't sure he should trust his gut, which told him this man wouldn't bash his heart to pieces. He shoveled some chips and guac into his mouth to give his brain a chance to catch up to his body.

"I-I'm really glad to see you. How long is your conference?" Acting casual, Nico was already planning how he'd sweet-talk his cousin, Joey, to cover for him. He wanted to spend as much time as possible with Dr. Ford St. Claire.

"Three days." Ford's gaze locked on his. "Does that work for you?"

He couldn't help the grin breaking across his face. "It sure does."

Chapter SIX

Was he ready for this? And what exactly was he thinking "this" would be?

Ford piled chicken, beans, and *pico de gallo* on the tortilla, rolled it up, and took a bite. This trip was important for networking and keeping up-to-date on cutting-edge procedures, but who was he kidding? He would skip any and all meetings to be with Nico.

Supposedly, there was no fool like an old fool, but sitting in that lively, vibrant restaurant with Nico woke him up from the frozen landscape he'd painted himself into. He hadn't been out with another man since he and Lenny split. His blood ran hot, and he rolled up his last tortilla and held it out to Nico.

"Want some?"

Slow heat rose in Nico's beautiful eyes, and his fingers curled around Ford's wrist as he leaned forward to take a bite. "*Mmm*, delicious," he hummed, and Ford shivered but decided to stop flirting. He couldn't play games with someone as sexually sophisticated as Nico. He wasn't in the same league.

Maybe not even the same universe.

"Are you busy for the rest of the afternoon? Maybe you can show me the sights I never got to see last time."

"I'd love to." Nico's eyes twinkled. "I can take you places you've never been."

Ford had little doubt of that and gulped his water. What was happening? This wasn't Ford St. Claire, the mild-mannered dermatologist with the steady hand. The man who'd been satisfied with sex a few times a week, if that. The calm and peaceful waters he'd spent years carefully cultivating now churned in waves, threatening to drag him under, where wildness waited.

They finished their meal and walked outside to the heat and hot sun hitting them in the face like a wet blanket.

"This feels like Florida," he remarked. "I'm spoiled by living in air-conditioning."

"I was going to suggest Central Park, but it's so hot… How about a boat ride? We can do a Circle Line tour—it takes you from the Hudson River to the East River, and it'll be cooler on the water. We can sit inside where it's air-conditioned."

"That sounds nice."

And it was. Of course Nico was the perfect tour guide, peppering the guide's facts with funny stories of his own that left Ford laughing. They walked off the boat, and he couldn't stop staring up at the towering skyscrapers as they walked toward Twelfth Avenue.

"It's really beautiful. I can't even imagine what it must be like in one of those apartments at night with the lights twinkling."

"Me neither. But one day, maybe I will," Nico said with a determined expression, and Ford admired his tenacity.

"I'm thinking you can accomplish anything you want."

"Yeah?" Nico's smile turned wistful, but he said nothing further, and Ford pulled out his phone to call for a car.

"What would you like to do for dinner?" he asked once they were in the Uber. Nico's thigh pressed hard against his, and he wished he was the type who could throw caution to the wind, bring him upstairs to his room, and have wild, crazy sex.

"I chose lunch. You get to pick now."

"That's not fair. I only know my hotel and the places my ex used to talk about."

"He's from the city? What places did he mention?"

"No. Lenny and I are both from Florida." Ford thought for a moment. "He'd talk about the Palm, Mr. Chow, Buddakan…we ate at all the ones in Miami."

"I've never been to any of them." That beautiful mouth drooped, and Nico gazed at the floor of the cab.

Ford sensed his withdrawal and didn't like what he suspected, but again, he couldn't say what he truly felt. That Nico deserved to be taken to the finest places and shouldn't be self-conscious.

"Didn't you say your family owns a restaurant? Why don't we go there? I bet the food is better than at any of the big, hyped-up places. I never get to eat homemade." When he was young and had to fend for himself for dinner, it was mostly boxed mac-and-cheese or whatever microwaved or canned stuff was on sale at the supermarket. His mother spent most of the money she earned from dancing at the strip club on cigarettes, booze, and bad decisions.

"It sure is." Nico slanted him a look from under his lashes. "But it's nothing fancy, like you're used to. Just lettin' you know."

A pang hit his heart. If Nico only knew they were far more alike than they were different…Ford had grown up in one of the poorest trailer parks in Miami, and spent his childhood listening not to the waves of the ocean pounding the shores, but the sound of his mother's boyfriends pounding her face in.

He squeezed his eyes shut for a second. "I'm not a snob. Trust me."

Nico lifted a shoulder. "If you wanna."

"My conference starts tomorrow, so I don't have any commitments tonight. I'd like you to show me the New York tourists don't usually see. I can change, and maybe we can have a drink at the hotel, then go to eat?"

"Sounds like a plan, Doc."

They reached the hotel, and he brought Nico up to his room. He'd been upgraded to a mini suite, and Nico lounged on the sofa, while he took out a pair of jeans and a T-shirt.

"I'll be right out."

Nico shrugged. "Mind if I turn on the television? The Mets have an afternoon game."

"Go ahead. Of course."

Ford shut the door behind him and stripped off his clothes. He was probably reading too much into Nico's mood shift. After all, they barely knew each other. Wasn't that the point of spending time with him? Although Ford had no idea why he was stressing about this. His life was in Florida, and Nico's was here.

He checked his reflection in the mirror and decided to spray on a little cologne. Lenny had introduced him to something other than drugstore brands, and though the prices were shocking, he indulged. He left the bedroom and found Nico immersed in the game, sprawled on the sofa. Muscular thighs filled out his pants, and the white polo shirt he wore showcased his smooth, tanned skin.

Imagine coming home to a man like Nico every night…

When Lenny's infidelities had come to light, Ford's desire had died along with their relationship, which made his reaction to Nico confusing. As much as he'd struggled to remember how much he'd once loved Lenny, now all Ford could think about was the man in front of him.

"Ready?" He put a smile on his face, attempting to act casual.

"Yeah, sure." Nico swung his legs to the floor and rose to his feet. "You smell good."

His face grew hot. "I, uh, put some cologne on since I didn't have time for a shower."

Nico's stare grew heavy-lidded, and he moved closer. "It's nice."

Ford inhaled the scent of Nico. Sunshine, saltwater, and sweat. It was a mind-altering combination assailing his senses, and he ached to kiss him but forced himself to walk away. He couldn't be so forward. "Let's go have that drink."

"You okay?" Nico's dark brows drew together. "You seem kinda jumpy."

Ford blinked. "Uh, no. I'm not. Why would I be?"

"I dunno. You tell me. Are you hungry?"

Nico licked his lips, that raspy voice going straight to his dick.

Yeah, I'm hungry, all right. I want to taste your tongue in my mouth.

"I could use a drink and then some food."

"I thought you weren't a big drinker."

His equilibrium restored, Ford opened the door and let Nico pass before exiting.

"I'm not. I had one at lunch, and I'll have one now. That's no big deal."

They found a seat, and their server appeared immediately. "What can I get for you gentlemen?"

"An extra-dry martini for me. Nico?"

"Macallan neat."

"Anything to eat?"

"No, thank you." They had a small bowl of mixed nuts between them, and he popped a few into his mouth. "So how has your summer been going?"

"Good. Been working hard." Nico chewed his lip. "I've been thinking of applying for a new job."

"Really? I thought you loved being a tour guide. And didn't you say you wanted to own your own business, or was that my imagination?"

"Yeah, I did, but me and my friend were talkin', and I realized it wouldn't be possible—not a tour-bus company like where I work. So I've been lookin' into management positions with them instead."

Ford wanted to hear more about Nico's future plans. "And you think you'd like that? You're so good with the public, wouldn't you miss the tours?"

Nico propped his chin in his hand. "Yeah, maybe. But it doesn't pay enough. I could make over a hundred grand if I switched, which is a hell of a lot more than I make now. And a management job would let me save up for an apartment."

"Where do you live now?"

A faint flush stained Nico's cheeks. "In the basement of my mom's house. I help her around the house and stuff since she's alone."

"That's being a good son." He paused, unsure whether to ask but feeling he had to say something. "Your father—"

"I have no clue about the bastard," Nico cut him off and gulped his whisky. "He left my mother right before the wedding. She found out she was pregnant a month later, and he didn't give a damn."

Their younger years were eerily similar, although his father—whomever he was—never had any intention of marrying his mother. Ford doubted he even knew his mother's name when they had sex in the back of his car.

"I'm assuming she had family support. It's not easy to

raise a child alone."

"Yeah, we're all close. We lived in my grandparents' house, still do—my mom inherited it after they passed, God rest their souls. My aunt lives down the block, and me and my cousin help out at the restaurant."

"It must be nice to have a tight-knit family."

"They can be a pain in the ass sometimes, always up in my business, but yeah. They're all right."

Despite his words, Ford could tell there was tremendous love for the people in his life.

"Will they be at the restaurant tonight?"

"Yeah, there's always one or two of us there. Tonight it's my cousin Joey. I had to switch shifts with him to go out with you."

"I hope it wasn't too much trouble."

Nico winked. "I gave him no choice."

Ford's heart gave a happy jump. He'd never had the opportunity to flirt or have dates in high school—even if there were gay kids, no one wanted to associate with the "trailer trash" as he'd heard them whisper behind his back in the halls. After school, he spent all his free time reading in the library, which had helped him get a scholarship to college. He'd met Lenny during his first year of med school, and Ford had been eager to shed his less-than-stellar background, embracing Lenny's attention, happy to be molded into the person Lenny wanted him to be.

"I'm glad."

They locked gazes, and again, he had a crazy thought to say, *Fuck dinner, let's go upstairs*. He wanted Nico inside him. He'd been cold and empty for so long, his heart hollow and dry from all the tears he'd shed over a failed relationship that had stolen half his life.

The server stopped by their table. "Another round, gentlemen?"

"No, we have dinner plans, thank you," Ford replied.

"I'll charge it to my room, if you could give me the check."

"Of course, sir." He presented the bill, which Ford signed. He found Nico watching him.

"Are you sure you want to do this?" Nico asked.

"What, eat dinner? Yes, I'm starving, and you promised me a home-cooked meal." He reached into his jeans pocket for his phone. "Should we call a car?"

Nico regarded him thoughtfully. "Yeah, I guess so. The train would take forever."

"I've never been on the subway," he remarked.

"No need to start now," Nico snickered. "Seriously, if we were stayin' in the city, I'd say go for it, but to get out to where we're going, the R train'll take forever. No way I'm wasting so much time."

"I understand. But isn't Brooklyn part of New York City?" Ford was confused. "Anyway, give me the address, and I'll call the car."

"Nah, I'll do it. It'll be faster." He grinned. "Trust me." He swiped a few times. "Done. They'll be here in five, so we should hustle out. And to answer your question," he said as they walked side by side to the street, where Ford's eyes grew wide at the hordes of people crowding the sidewalk, "real New Yorkers call Manhattan 'the city.' All the other boroughs are known by their names."

"Ahh, gotcha."

The car arrived, and Ford watched the city pass by him as they drove over the Brooklyn Bridge and onto the highway. "This is Brooklyn? Where you live?"

"Not right here. It's a little ways away, in an area called Bay Ridge. Lots of Italians lived there, but now it's a big mix of Muslims, Asians, Greek, and Irish."

"It really is a melting pot," he mused. They continued on the highway, alongside the river.

"Here's the exit."

The car exited and drove through quieter streets than

Manhattan—the city—Ford corrected himself. Private homes mixed with apartment buildings, but there wasn't that frenetic hustle. He liked it as much as those high-rises by the river.

They stopped in front of an unassuming storefront with the name *La Dolce Vita* written in gold on the window. Half of the ten tables in the restaurant were full. The delicious smell of tomato sauce and garlic in the air had his stomach growling.

Nico nudged him. "Don't think I didn't hear that. C'mon. Let's siddown."

"Nico, whassup?" A tall, dark-haired, brown-eyed man a little older than Nico yelled from the door leading to the kitchen. They had similar features—the jaw shape, the high cheekbones—so Ford surmised this was Nico's cousin. "I thought you weren't gonna be here?" The two men hugged.

"Yeah, but my friend here wanted a good, homemade meal, so where else was I gonna take him? Doc, c'mere." Nico motioned him over. "This is my cousin, Joey. Joey, this is Dr. Ford St. Claire."

Joey's brows shot up. "Not gonna lie, that's a mouthful."

"You're right, so please just call me Ford."

"You got it. Have a seat, and Teresa will bring you the menu."

"Tre's here?" Nico didn't see Joey's girlfriend.

"Yeah, well, when I took your shift, she decided not to go out with the girls and instead she's here helping out." He winked and lowered his voice. "It's good for the future, ya know? When we get married?"

"Congratulations. When's the wedding?" Ford asked.

"Shh. It ain't official yet. I wanna be able to get her the ring she's been droppin' hints about. I almost have enough to pay for the whole thing. I don't wanna have to pay it off."

Nico leaned in close. "Joey and Teresa have been dating for about five years. She's a great girl."

A young woman approached them, her jet-black hair pulled back in a simple ponytail, big brown eyes sparkling beneath a thick fringe of lashes. "Nico, you bum, what're you doing here after you ruined my night?" She laughed and hugged him. "I'm just kiddin'. Who's this?" She eyed him up and down. "Well, now I see why, and I ain't mad about it. Hi, I'm Teresa." She held out her hand, and laughing, Ford shook it. He liked these brash people who loved hard and spoke their minds.

"I'm Ford, and it's nice to meet you too."

Joey put an arm over Teresa's shoulders. "Ford's a *doctor*," he said with emphasis. "He and Nico are gonna have dinner."

"Yeah? I'm a NICU nurse at Maimonides. What hospital do you work at? And follow me."

Ford's head spun at her rapid talk, but Nico took it in stride, and soon they were seated at a corner table. A busboy came by with a heaping basket of crusty bread and olive oil and filled their glasses.

"Thanks, Bobby."

"No problem, Nico."

Joey sauntered over. "So you gonna have red or white?"

Ford cocked his head and looked to Nico. "Up to you."

"You planning on pasta, or you want chicken or seafood?"

"I don't know. I haven't seen the menu."

Joey snorted. "And you ain't gonna. Whateva you want, we can make. It's family."

A little stunned, Ford didn't know what to say. "Oh, I…I honestly don't know."

Turquoise eyes smoldering, Nico leaned in close. "How about I order for both of us. You trust me?"

Ford's heart beat double time, and he nodded. "Yeah, I do."

Chapter SEVEN

What the hell was he doing bringing Dr. Ford St. Claire here to meet his family? He'd had the opportunity to go anywhere he wanted in the city and have the meal of a lifetime—Ford had said to take his pick—and yet he'd chosen his family's little place where he'd grown up and spent practically five nights a week. Not to mention, his cousin and Teresa would be dissecting their every move.

"Hello? Earth to Nico." Joey waved a hand in front of his face. "Whaddya wanna order?"

He had nothing to be ashamed of. If Ford wanted to know how the real people in the city lived, he was gonna get a taste of it.

"Okay, bring us some baked clams, burrata, and calamari to start. Then we'll do mussels in white wine with linguine, baked ziti, and throw some eggplant in there too, and chicken parm with a side of sautéed spinach." He checked in with Ford, who sat watching him with his jaw hanging open. "What?"

"That's a lot of food."

"Nah. You'll see. We'll finish it all, no problem."

Nodding, Joey wrote on his pad. "He's right. Once you start eatin' it, you can't stop. I know you're havin' chicken and mussels, but I'm gonna bring you a nice red. It'll go good with everything."

He disappeared, leaving them alone. Soft opera music played in the background, reminding him of dinner with his *nonno* and *nonna*.

"If the food tastes like it smells, I'll be in heaven."

"Don't worry, you'll be hearin' the angels singing." Nico took a hunk of bread and dipped it in olive oil. "Have some."

"I don't usually eat bread."

Now it was Nico's turn to stare. "What? Who doesn't eat bread, especially good bread like this? Wait a sec. You aren't one of those carb counters, are you?"

Ford turned red. "Uh, I mean, I try not to have too many carbs, and I eat mostly protein and veggies."

"*Marone a mia,*" he muttered. "Listen, Doc. Food is like sex. You can never have too much if it's good. A little bread isn't gonna hurt you. Go ahead," he urged. "And make sure you dip it in the oil."

Cheeks adorably pink, Ford did as told.

"It's delicious. I guess now that I'm not working full-time in the practice, I can work out more. I do yoga, but maybe it's time to try other things."

Nico thought Ford was pretty damn perfect as is and forced his dirty mind away from thinking of him in skimpy, tight pants. "I'm sure there's a gym in your building, and a pool. Or you can bike, do all kinds of shit like that. You live in Florida."

Teresa plunked on the table two platters filled with their

appetizers. "Florida? Who lives there? You, Ford?"

"Yes. Fort Lauderdale."

She eyed Nico, then Ford. "What kinda doctor are you again?"

"A dermatologist."

"Yeah?" She studied Ford. "You do Botox? 'Cause your face is smooth like a baby."

Ford smothered a laugh, and Nico huffed. "Jesus, Tre."

Luckily, Ford took it in good humor. "No. I don't. But I have plenty of patients who want it, and fillers. People are obsessed with looking young. I prefer to take care of myself and age gracefully. You're young and have beautiful skin. You obviously take care of it."

She flipped her hair. "Yeah. I drink lotsa water, no tanning like these dummies do, and tons of moisturizer. But anyways, how'd you two meet?"

"Smooth, Tre." Nico dipped a crunchy calamari in the spicy red sauce. "I mean, nothing like the third degree while our food's getting cold."

She glared at him. "You gonna bring a guy here and think we don't have questions? You stupid or somethin'?"

Ford laughed out loud. "I took one of Nico's tours a month or so ago and left my wallet on the bus. He returned it, and we happened to run into each other later that evening. We talked, and when I came back for a conference this week, I surprised him by taking another tour."

"Yeah? Happened to run into each other? In New York City?" Her pretty brown eyes narrowed. "That's a good one."

Nico could see she had her doubts. "It's the truth."

"One of them funny coincidences, huh? Okay, I'll buy it. Well, eat up. Here comes Joey with the wine."

"Jesus, it's like having dinner onstage," Nico grumbled. He should've known this would happen. He'd never get a chance to talk to Ford one on one.

"Hey, Nico?" Ford took a baked clam. "Don't stress.

We have all night."

They shared a smile, and he relaxed. What was he so nervous about? This was his life, take it or leave it.

Joey set two wineglasses in front of them and poured Ford the wine to taste. "Whaddya think? Pretty good, huh?"

Knowing Ford would never say anything bad, Nico expected a quick "yeah, of course," but again Ford surprised him.

"It's a Pinot Noir, right? I taste the cherry. It's very good—my favorite red. Thank you, Joey."

"You got it. I could tell you got good taste." Puffed up, Joey poured more into Ford's glass and then his. "He's a good guy, Nico. Don't be stupid."

"Shut up," he growled, and Joey walked away. "Don't pay attention to him." He picked up his glass. "*Salute*."

They clinked and drank. Ford was right. It was delicious.

They ate their appetizers, and Nico could see Ford wasn't faking his enjoyment simply to make him happy. When he tasted the burrata, his eyes rolled to the back of his head.

"Oh God, this is amazing."

Pride swelled in Nico's chest. "It's good, ain't it? We get it fresh every day from this old guy who makes his cheese by hand."

Ford licked his lips, and a powerful surge of lust rocketed through Nico. It had been over a month since he'd gotten laid, something unheard of for him, but the desire to hook up wasn't there. Between the two jobs, he was running on fumes and had little time to think about anything else. He crunched more calamari. Lately his head had been wrapped up in figuring out what to do with his life professionally. His personal life could wait.

Watching Ford from beneath half-lowered lids, Nico knew he'd give his left nut to spend the night with him. Fuck, he was dying to kiss him, almost from the first second he saw him. And Nico Andretti wasn't the type to wait. But not this time. Ford had said that night at Stonewall that he didn't have sex with men he barely knew. It wasn't a tease on his part—Ford might be older, but there was an innocence about him that brought out a protective instinct Nico hadn't been aware he possessed. Nico sensed deep hurt from his ex and something else he hadn't yet figured out. Maybe he'd get more answers tonight.

They finished off the starters as the main courses arrived. Ford groaned. "I am in so much trouble."

Nico suppressed a grin.

You are if I have anything to say about it.

Teresa set plates in front of them. "Enjoy, guys."

"Have some more wine." Nico refilled their glasses. "Looks good, yeah?"

"It does. Very good."

Nico felt Ford's gaze on him and held it. *Well, damn.* A throb of lust hit him low in his belly. The night was looking better and better. He scooped out some baked ziti and put it on Ford's plate, then took some.

"So, how'd you get the name Ford? Is it like one of them old, Waspy family names? Were you named after your rich grandpa or something?" He placed a chicken cutlet on top of the ziti to make room for the mussels.

In the process of cutting his chicken, Ford hesitated. "No. I was named Ford because my mother got pregnant in the back of a Thunderbird and she thought Ford sounded classy." He chewed his food as Nico sat stunned by the revelation. "At least that's her claim, but of course, she could've been lying. She was a master at it."

Well, damn. That was not the story he'd imagined when thinking of the classy Dr. St. Claire. The fact that Ford continued to eat as if nothing he'd said was mind-blowing only proved Nico's theory. Ford held a whole lot of hurt inside him, and Nico was caught up in fervently wanting to know more.

"Hey." Nico surprised himself by putting his hand over Ford's slightly shaky one and giving it a squeeze. "We all got shit we have to deal with."

Ford jerked his head in a nod and drank his wine. Nico decided to table the discussion for the moment and concentrate on the two of them.

"Feel like going out after we finish?"

"Where to?" Ford mopped up the sauce on his plate with the last of the bread, and that made Nico stupid happy.

"We could go to Stonewall again." He wasn't ready to take him to Maxie's. One set of family members was enough for the night.

"Or someplace new. I always heard stories about those rooftop bars overlooking the city."

Nico's heart sank. He didn't have the money to spend like that, and he wasn't dressed for it. "I don't think I could get us in there," he said quietly.

Ford met his eyes. "Then we don't go. Stonewall it is."

They finished their meal, and without asking, Teresa brought them over a tiramisu to share and Joey followed with cappuccinos.

"God, I don't think I can take another bite." Ford groaned, the sound going straight to Nico's dick. He wanted to hear what Ford sounded like naked and under him, begging for his cock.

"Sure you can. Here." He cut a small piece off and held it out to Ford, who instinctively licked his lips and leaned forward. "Come on, Doc. Let loose. Just for one night."

Something hot flared in Ford's honey-colored eyes, and he allowed Nico to slide the fork between his lips.

"*Mmm*," Ford hummed, and Nico felt the vibration all the way to his fucking toes. "So good."

"Yeah. So good."

Eyes locked, he took a piece and licked the fork, watching the unmistakable lust rise in Ford's eyes. They finished the dessert, and Ford gulped down his ice water.

"I-I need to use the restroom. Where is it, please?"

Nico pointed to the corner, and Ford left. Joey and Teresa hurried over.

"Dude, what the hell was that? I felt like I was watchin' a porno flick."

"Ew, Joey, you're disgusting." Teresa gave him a shove, but her eyes sparkled. "But he is so into you. And he's hot, even if he is older."

"What the hell does that mean, even if?" Nico demanded.

"Jeez, chill out. I'm just sayin', usually you go for guys your age. This one's different. And he's got class."

"He does," Nico agreed. And not just because he had money. Ford might've dropped a bombshell about his less-than-perfect childhood, but he'd sure as hell made something of himself.

Teresa nudged Joey. "Sam wants to pay. He's at the register." Joey took off. "You like him."

Nico shrugged. "I mean, yeah. What's not to like?"

"Don't play cute with me." Her voice dropped. "I know you. You've never brought nobody here for dinner. He's special."

"He lives in Florida, Tre."

"So? That's why God invented planes. And FaceTime. Lemme tell you something. That guy hasn't had enough of you yet. You must've weaved that sexy Nico spell around him, because he is into you, like the cream in a cannoli shell. Take him home and have some fun."

Of course Teresa assumed they were having sex—Nico doubted she'd believe him if he told her they hadn't even kissed. From the corner of his eye, he spotted Ford approaching. The way his shirt clung to his broad chest and his jeans molded to his body left Nico breathless.

"It's complicated."

"Why? 'Cause he makes more money than you? Or

that he's way older? You ain't still lost in your head from that no-good asshole, are you?" When he didn't answer, she leaned in closer. "Those things are bullshit. You're no slouch. Don't go thinkin' you ain't good enough just 'cause he's a doctor and has money." A customer called her over, and she hurried away.

"Ready to go?"

Ford returned to the table. "Yeah, I'm ready." He had his phone in hand. "I'll get us a car. How much do I owe—"

"You're kiddin', right?" Nico waved a hand in the air. "Family don't pay, and you're with me."

But Ford didn't move. "I have to give something to Teresa and Joey for serving us." He fished out his wallet and took out two fifty-dollar bills. "Give me a second."

Nico watched, his heart filled with some unidentifiable emotion. Maybe there really were good-hearted people left in the world. Teresa hugged Ford, and Joey slapped him on the back.

Nico spied the car pull up outside. "Our ride's here," he called out. Ford gave one last wave, and Nico kissed Teresa and hugged Joey. "Catch ya later."

"Be good," Teresa said, and he snickered.

"I always am."

Ford had already entered the car, and Nico slid in next to him.

"Thank you for that amazing meal."

"Well, I didn't cook it, but I'm glad you enjoyed it."

"Can you? Cook, I mean," Ford asked.

"Yeah, of course. I started helping with the sauce when I was two years old. My *nonna* would sit me on the kitchen counter next to the stove with a spoon and show me how to stir. I can make everything we serve in the restaurant. What about you?"

Ford made a face. "My mother knew how to make coffee. That and cigarettes were her main diet. We didn't even have an oven in our trailer. Just a stovetop and a microwave. If it came from a box or a freezer, I'd make it for dinner because I was home alone. She'd get her boyfriends at the strip club to buy her dinner, but there was never anything left over for me."

Trailer? Strip club? Home alone? Horrified by the bits and pieces Ford had begun to share of his story, Nico kept silent, but he reached out and took Ford's hand in his and squeezed tight. He felt an answering pressure, and they sat that way as the car traveled into the city.

Nico noticed they were heading up the West Side Highway and thought it odd, but maybe there was traffic. When they passed the usual exits for the Village, he leaned over to Ford.

"I don't think this guy knows where he's going. We're getting close to midtown."

Ford held his hand tight. "I know. I told him to take us back to my hotel. I hope you don't mind."

Nico smiled, picked up their entwined hands, and kissed Ford's knuckles. "I don't mind at all."

Chapter EIGHT

Dear God, why the hell was he so nervous?

Nico couldn't be considered a stranger, not now after they'd spent the day together. He'd met his family and suspected from their comments and joking innuendos that they assumed the two of them were already sleeping together. His body throbbed, empty and yearning.

Did he want that?

He'd only ever had one lover—on their second date, Lenny had brought him to his parents' beach house on Star Island, and on silken sheets, fueled by endless glasses of champagne and promises of forever, Ford gave him his virginity. Lenny had assured him that the more sex they had, the less it would hurt, and while he learned to enjoy the physical part, he much preferred the cuddling and kissing afterward. At the five-year mark, Lenny tried to convince him to spice up their sex life, suggesting toys, threesomes—which Ford had no interest in—or sex in public places. He once followed Ford into the fitting rooms when they were shopping, in an attempt to have sex—*"Don't you think it's hot, knowing people are right outside?"*—but Ford had refused. Lenny sulked and withdrew. Later he'd apologized, saying he wasn't going to pressure Ford anymore. Ford supposed that was the beginning of Lenny's infidelities.

He glanced at Nico's profile, instinctively knowing this was a man who didn't need games. His lush mouth promised kisses that made Ford blush and his heart pound.

The car stopped.

"We're here," Nico said. "Ready?"

Ford nodded. He was. So ready.

Hand in hand, they walked up to his suite, and after he unlocked the door, Nico took the card key from Ford's shaky fingers and set it on the table. A light from the bedroom shone a golden glow into the living area.

"We'll take it as slow as you want. Okay?" Nico's long fingers mapped the lines of his face. "But I've been dying to kiss you since the first time I saw you."

Unconsciously, he licked his lips, and Nico's lustful gaze burned hotter. "Me too."

A smile lit Nico's face, and twin dimples popped. "Let's make it happen, 'kay?" Nico's hand slid to his nape.

He expected a kiss like Lenny's—harsh and demanding, with tongue and teeth. Instead, Nico rested his lips on Ford's, briefly at first, light as a butterfly, brushing gently, over and over, leaving Ford shaking.

"You taste perfect," Nico breathed, then nipped his bottom lip, sucking it. He tangled his fingers in his hair, anchoring him. "So damn sweet," he whispered before settling his mouth over Ford's.

Ford moaned at the touch of Nico's tongue seeking entrance, and he sucked it greedily, feasting on it like a starving man. Hot, slick, and soft, it rubbed and danced with his as his heart pounded, roaring in his ears.

"Oh God, oh God." He wanted to tear his clothes off and roll naked on the bed with Nico, feeling all that flesh pressed to his. No one had ever made him feel so uninhibited and free.

"You like this?" Nico dipped his head and took Ford's face between the palms of his hands, capturing his mouth. Their kisses intensified, growing more frantic and heated, messy, wet, and wild.

"I do, please, please." He was begging and pleading—for what, he wasn't certain, but knew only Nico could give it to him. Blood burning, he waited on the precipice of something endless, ready to burst into a thousand pieces.

"Tell me what you want," Nico murmured, nuzzling into his neck, nipping him, then kissing the sting away.

"I-I don't know." He hung his head. "I'm sorry."

Nico tipped up his chin and brushed their lips together. "Don't be. I have no problem taking it slow. But you drive me crazy, and I couldn't help myself." He rested their foreheads together, noses touching, their breaths mingling.

"You've thrown my life into chaos," Ford admitted. "I don't…I've never done this with anyone else, but I wanted to be alone with you so badly."

"I like being alone with you too." Nico rubbed their cheeks together, the raspy late-night stubble delicious against his fevered skin. Ford melted into him, and Nico took his lips, leaving behind a trail of fire wherever they touched.

"I'm not ready to sleep with you." He waited for Nico to walk away. Hoping he wouldn't.

"I know. You're not that kind of man. I respect that."

"I enjoyed myself tonight." Ford allowed himself the luxury of touching Nico, running his hands over his chest and shoulders, feeling the dips and curves of pure hard muscle.

"Told you the food would be amazing." Nico kissed

the tip of his nose.

"It was, but that's not why."

"Yeah?" Nico quirked a brow. "What, then?" And Ford knew he wasn't fishing for a compliment.

"I loved the hominess. It felt like I was in someone's kitchen. Your cousin and his girlfriend were so welcoming and friendly. And they care about you." He wasn't looking forward to his lonely existence once he left New York.

"We're in each other's business all the time, but yeah, they've got my back and I've got theirs. Thick and thin, we're there for each other."

It was a concept Ford was a stranger to, yet he yearned for all the same. "You're lucky."

Nico kissed him, ran his nose down his cheek. "You got no family? What happened to your mother?"

Not the conversation he wanted to have with a gorgeous, sexy man in his hotel room.

"I'd rather not talk about it."

Nico fixed him with a stare and nodded. "Okay. Whatever you want."

Ford glanced at the clock and saw it was nearly eleven. Early for Nico, he suspected, but he had a breakfast at eight, followed by a full day of lectures to attend. "Another kiss?" Regret laced his words. "And I'm afraid we'll have to call it a night. I have an early start tomorrow, and it goes all day."

"What about after?" Nico began placing those gentle yet searing kisses on his lips, leaving him craving more, and Ford clung to those broad, strong shoulders. "Can I see you?"

"You want to see me again?"

Nico stopped, his lips hovering. "Yeah. Unless you don't?" He took a step away but Ford clutched his shirt.

"No," he blurted out, and at Nico's wicked grin, heat rushed through him. "I-I'd love to see you again." He hesitated but decided to hell with it. They always said to speak from your heart. "I'm here for three nights, counting this one. I'd like to spend them all with you."

Nico crushed their lips together, tongue thrusting to meet his. Head fuzzy with desire, Ford gave in to Nico's power and sucked until Nico growled and broke free.

"If I don't stop, you're gonna be naked." Blue eyes glittered with a dangerous light, that full, swollen mouth gleamed wet, and a flush rested high on his cheekbones. Ford bit back a whimper of despair.

"Maybe I was wrong."

Nico chuckled and wiped his hand over his mouth. "Nah. You weren't." He leaned in for a swift kiss. " 'Cause when— not if, but *when*—it happens, it's gonna take the whole night for me to do what I want to you."

That weird, fluttery feeling tumbled through him at the thought of Nico and him naked. Together. Teetering on the edge, Ford found his voice and sanity in time to ask, "How will I reach you? I don't have your number."

Nico took out his phone. "Gimme yours, and I'll text you."

Ford recited it, and a moment later felt a buzz in his jeans pocket. "I got it."

"So text me when you're ready tomorrow. Let me know what you wanna do."

"Whatever you want. I'm in your hands."

A slow smile crept across Nico's face. "Yeah? I like the sound of that. I'll figure somethin' fun."

And then he was gone, leaving Ford not only alone but lonely. With his exit, Nico had taken all the energy from the room. Lenny used to be the one to carry the conversation at a party, while Ford stood by his side, never knowing if he'd say the right thing. Lenny would tease him, calling him arm candy, which would annoy Ford, but as usual, he remained mute, afraid to make waves.

He'd kept silent about many things, but that had led to a life of discontent. The best thing to come out of their split, aside from leaving a cheating lover behind, was that Ford had found his voice for what he did and did not want.

And he wanted Nico.

He changed for bed, set his alarm, and closed his eyes. For the first time in a year, he was excited to see what the next day brought.

"Is this seat taken?" an older man asked, silver hair shining under the overhead lights.

Ford, finishing his first cup of coffee, pulled out the chair next to him. "It isn't."

"Good, good. I got stuck in uptown traffic and was afraid I'd miss the coffee." A server appeared, poured him a cup, and presented the dish of eggs, bacon, and potatoes, at which the man made a face. "A travesty," he grumbled. "You'd think it being a dermatology convention, they'd choose food high in antioxidants."

Ford chuckled at his outrage. "I agree. I take my greens powder with me everywhere. But as long as I have my coffee, I'll be fine."

The man's eyes twinkled behind black-framed glasses. "You youngsters are smart." He took a sip of coffee. "Bruce Sandler."

"Ford St. Claire."

"Where's your practice, Ford?" Sandler made small talk as he picked through the pastry basket, deciding on a lemon scone.

"Florida. Fort Lauderdale."

"Get a lot of basal cell and melanoma down there?"

He grimaced. "Unfortunately, yes."

"We're seeing it on the rise here as well. I'm in SoHo.

All the people who thought they were invincible in their twenties, slathering themselves with baby oil or nothing at all, are now in their fifties and sixties, suffering from that failure to use sunscreen and take care of their skin."

"I agree."

Sandler peered at him. "Fort Lauderdale, *hmm*?" Seeing the wheels turning in Sandler's mind, Ford tensed, anticipating what was coming next. "That doctor…"

"Is my partner, yes." He didn't feel the need to elaborate.

"Ah." Sandler's expression was thoughtful. "Has it affected your practice at all?"

"Surprisingly, no."

Sandler broke off a corner of his scone. "I guess a juicy sex scandal brings in the curious. From what I remember, his troubles had nothing to do with the practice."

"No one has ever complained about Lenny's work. And we're busier than ever. In fact, we're in the process of hiring another doctor to do the cosmetic work. Anyway, I'm looking forward to the lectures, especially the micro needling and new innovations in hair growth. There's so much coming on the horizon."

"A shame he couldn't keep it in his pants," Sandler mused, returning to the subject of the scandal, and Ford, still shocked at the brash outspokenness of New Yorkers, choked on his English muffin. Sandler chuckled. "Oh, come on. It was all over the news, even up here. And you certainly have nothing to be ashamed of—I recall it all now. At least the way it played out on television, you were merely the long-suffering partner. Are you staying in the practice or thinking of relocating up here?"

"Moving here? N-no, I hadn't thought of it." Although now that Sandler mentioned it, living in New York and seeing Nico all the time was an enticing fantasy he could dream about. But right now, that was what it was. Fantasy. His life was in Florida, and Nico's was here, and…why the *hell* was he thinking about this again? "I had to fly up last month for some expert testimony, but this is my first extended trip to New York."

"I hope you enjoy it. I'll be winding down my practice in the next five years, when my lease is up. My wife and I are going to split our time between here and California, where our grandchildren are."

"Sounds like a plan."

"Not one you have to think about. You're a youngster."

A woman in a sleeveless pink sheath stepped to the microphone at the front of the ballroom. "Welcome, Doctors."

"I guess we're off to the races," Sandler remarked.

It was a full, exhausting day of lectures, demonstrations, and meeting reps, who gave him bags filled with samples of every kind of cream, serum, pill, and powder imaginable. By five thirty, he collapsed in his room and lay on the bed. He switched on his phone, which he'd turned off during the day. Several notifications popped up from Nico.

Hey. Wondering if you'd have time to meet for lunch. Got a break.

Half an hour later: *Guess not. See you tonight.*

At four thirty: *So what's the plan for tonight?*

Twenty minutes later: *You there? Lemme know what's up.*

Crap. He hoped it wasn't too late and called Nico instead of texting.

"Hello?"

"Nico? It's Ford. Sorry, I was tied up in the conference. So many lectures and demonstrations." He hesitated. "Did you go home, or are you still here?"

"I'm hangin' out in the lobby downstairs."

A ridiculously happy grin spread over his face. "Great. I just have to shower and change. Did you think of where you want to go for dinner?"

"Yeah. And it's casual, so don't worry about your

clothes." His chuckle was warm and low, sending tingles through Ford. "Matter of fact, the less the better."

"Huh?" Nervous excitement built up through him. "Where are you taking me?"

"See you soon."

The call ended, and Ford scrambled to get ready. He figured Nico was teasing him, and after showering and checking the weather to see that it was brutally hot, picked a short-sleeved white linen shirt and tan shorts. He slipped his feet into a pair of comfortable sandals, grabbed his wallet and phone, and left the room.

Plenty of people milled around the lobby, but Ford immediately saw Nico. The tumbling black waves and tanned skin were a perfect foil for the bright-blue shirt he wore. Thin cotton pants caressed his legs, and Ford sighed. Nico was so damn beautiful.

And Ford was in over his head.

Nico lifted his head from scrolling on his phone and met his eyes. A blinding white smile flashed across his face, and he hopped out of his chair.

"Hey, Doc," he greeted him. "You're looking hot as fuck," he murmured only for his ears.

His face burning, Ford blinked rapidly. "You just stole my line."

Nico knocked his shoulder. "Ready to go?"

"Are you going to tell me where?"

"Nope." Nico took his hand and squeezed it. "You gotta trust me again."

"I do."

"The beach?" Ford stared at the swarms of people strolling on the famous Coney Island boardwalk.

They stood on the sidewalk, and Nico pointed. "And that's where we're gonna eat."

"Nathan's?"

"Don't be a food snob. Fried clams, french fries, and hot dogs. Food of the gods. C'mon."

The line snaked outside of the restaurant, but they finally ordered, and while he waited for the food, Nico went to find a place to sit.

"It's a zoo out there," Ford protested. "You'll never find a place."

"Oh, ye of little faith." Nico kissed him and patted his cheek. "That's why I'm doin' it, not you. It's like ridin' the subway. You gotta know where to stand and pick up on the cues."

And sure enough, he walked outside, laden with the tray, and found Nico in the corner at a table for two.

"You were right."

Nico smirked and popped a fried clam into his mouth. "I usually am. Let's eat."

Everything smelled delicious, and Ford dug in, knowing when he returned home, he'd be eating strictly protein and vegetables. But for now, with the sea breeze in his hair and Nico across the table, he happily threw his strict diet out the window. A few pounds gained was worth it to be alive.

They demolished their food, and he groaned, flopping back in his chair. "Oh my God, that was so decadent. I still don't understand how you can eat like this"—he waved his hand over the remains of their meal, then toward Nico—"and look like that."

Nico's grin was wicked. "It's a talent. I work out. In many different ways."

Ford's heart sank, figuring Nico's euphemism for working out was sex, and lots of it. "However you do it, I don't have the metabolism at forty-two that I used to at twenty-eight."

"I dunno, Doc. You look pretty damn good to me. Now come on. Let's take a walk."

They dumped their tray and headed to the boardwalk. They walked with the crowd, stopping at a frozen-custard stand, where a cute blond guy with the nametag Alexi swirled him a cone.

"Aren't you going to get one?" Ford asked Nico.

"Nah, I'll just take a lick of yours." Nico leaned over.

"No way." Ford laughed, holding it aloft. "Get your own."

Alexi took his money. "He's like my husband. Always trying to steal my custard." He had a Russian accent and a charming smile. "Right, Cam?"

"That's 'cause yours tastes sweeter, baby." A good-looking man with a deep velvety voice slipped his arms around Alexi's waist.

"Thanks." He pocketed the change.

"Let's go on the beach," Nico suggested and kicked off his sneakers. "Feel the sand on our toes." Ford slipped off his sandals, and they walked on the sand to the water's edge. He finished his cone and licked his sticky fingers.

"I hardly ever go to the beach."

Nico stared at him. "Get the fuck out. You live in Florida."

How to explain without sounding stupid? "Lenny didn't like to go. He hated the sand."

"What about what you like? So far all I hear is what you did for him. What'd he ever do for you?"

Feeling uncomfortable, Ford dug his toes in the sand and let the water rush up to his ankles. "I'm here now, aren't I? At the beach?"

The harsh lines of Nico's face softened. "Yeah. Sorry, I didn't mean to get up in your face, but shit like that pisses me off."

"I just don't want to waste time with you, talking

about him." The waves rolled in again, rinsing their feet. He wondered what Nico would look like dripping wet in the shower.

God, I'm in so much trouble, but I can't help it.

"Maybe we should go back to the hotel?"

Apparently, that was the right thing to say, because Nico smiled and kissed him. Soft and sweet, his lips moved over Ford's.

"I like the way you think."

Chapter NINE

Nico held tight to Ford's hand in the car on the ride to the hotel, as if afraid he might bolt. It wasn't a silly thought—Ford was as skittish as a virgin, which, if Nico hadn't known better, he would've suspected. But the man sure as hell didn't kiss like one. His lips tingled, recalling the hot press of Ford's mouth from the previous evening and the slick, delicious taste of his tongue. It was better than any ice cream he'd ever tasted.

Ford was like a bottle of champagne you were unaware had been shaken—you assumed it was going to have some fizz, but when you opened it, the contents exploded in your face.

Ford was a man filled with bubbling contradictions, and Nico was ready to pop his cork, but only if Ford was willing. He didn't mind giving it a twist or two, but Ford had to want it.

By the time they arrived, it was close to nine p.m., and Ford slowed his steps as they entered the lobby. "You want a nightcap?"

He waved at the restaurant, and Nico, much as he longed to go inside, gave a rueful glance at his casual pants that were wrinkled from wearing them all day. For the first time, he was uncertain. "I-I dunno. Are you sure? I don't want people to stare at me because I'm not dressed good enough."

Ford's expression softened. "I'm positive. And trust me, they're going to stare because I'm going to be with the best-looking man in the place."

Still filled with misgivings, Nico couldn't resist. "All right. But I think you got that wrong. That's my line."

They were seated quickly and ordered drinks, and Ford decided on a cheese platter. Nico gazed around the café. "I guess you were right. There's a buncha people like me here."

Ford tipped his glass in Nico's direction. "I don't think there's anyone here like you."

Nico sipped his whisky, but the liquor wasn't what warmed him, deep in his belly and his heart. Going on dates wasn't how he rolled—he'd learned years earlier that revealing his true self to someone else was a risk he wasn't willing to take. But none of that mattered now. The past was irrelevant. He was here, sitting with Ford, whose eyes held the promise of good things to come.

Besides, he'd be gone in a few days. If his mother's illness had taught him anything, it was to enjoy every second of life.

"Not hungry?"

"Huh? Oh, yeah. Looks good." He roused himself and scanned the platter, picking up a couple of cheese cubes and popping them into his mouth. "Tastes good too."

Ford's brows drew together. "What's wrong?"

"Nothin'."

"Are you feeling okay? You got so quiet."

He put a smile on his face. No use in ruining their time together. "Nah. I'm good. Just tired from working. I promised to take Joey's next shift 'cause he's been taking mine."

"Oh, damn, I forgot about that." Ford sounded disappointed.

"Why? What's it got to do with you?"

"Well…tomorrow night—my last night—they have a cocktail party and dinner dance. It's at The Pierre. I thought maybe…maybe you'd like to come as my guest."

Damn. The Pierre was high class. After walking past it for years, he would've loved to get to see what it looked like on the inside. As a guest.

"I dunno," he demurred, and watched the consternation rise in Ford's eyes. "I promised Joey, and I've been slackin' off because—"

"Because of me, right? I'm sorry, Nico. I didn't mean to cause trouble."

"No way. You didn't. But I don't feel right about askin' him again."

"I understand. It was just an idea." Ford blew out a frustrated breath, and Nico thought fast.

"I mean, I'll probably miss most of it, but we close at ten thirty. If I dress at the restaurant, I could probably be there by eleven thirty." He chewed his lip. "But that's probably too late, huh?"

"For the dinner, yes," Ford said, and Nico couldn't understand why his chest hurt. "But," he continued, "not for me. No matter when you get here, I'll be waiting. Because then I'll get to see you one more time."

Nico held out his hand, and Ford took it.

"Enough already, Tre. I'm not askin' him."

"I'm tellin' you, Joey won't mind."

It was eight in the morning, and he and Teresa stood on the corner of 77th Street and Fourth Avenue, waiting for Joey to come out with their coffees from the bodega. They met every morning to take the R train into the city for work—Teresa would change at Jay Street for the F train, while Joey stayed on with him until he got off at 34th for his job at H&M.

"Joey won't mind what?"

His cousin held out the tray, and they took their coffees. Nico glared at Teresa. "Nothin'."

She rolled her eyes and made a face at him.

Unaware, Joey pulled out his phone to pay for the fare. "How's the doctor? He still here?" They descended the steps to the station, and Nico saw the train was delayed—of course—and wasn't coming for fifteen minutes. *Fucking city.*

"Yeah. He leaves tomorrow. I took him to Coney Island yesterday."

"Giving him that New York experience, huh?" Leaning against a post, Joey drank his coffee. "You give him the Nico experience yet?" He smirked, and Nico grew hot.

"Shut up. It ain't like that. He's not the type you just bang and walk away from." But why, Nico couldn't say, as that had been how he'd handled his sex life for years. No strings, no promises. It had been what he'd wanted ever since his heart got stepped on.

So why was doubt creeping in? Despite all the joking he did over Anthony and Sergio's over-the-top PDA, a tiny part of Nico wanted that. Wanted someone so into him, they couldn't stop looking at him as if he were the sun and they orbited him. He wouldn't mind a man who couldn't keep his hands off him in public, unafraid to show how happy he was to be with Nico.

He wanted someone to care.

"I liked him," Teresa declared. "He's classy, unlike those bums you usually fool around with. He's got an education, and it's good that he's older. You need someone who respects you and treats you good. I can tell he likes you. A lot."

Joey tossed his cup into a trash bin. "I'm just fuckin' with you. He's a good guy, and like Tre said, into you."

"Yeah," Teresa, interjected. "Which is why—"

"Nothing. Stop it," Nico growled and peered down the tunnel. "Where the fuck is this train? I'm gonna be late."

"Why what? Tell me already," Joey insisted.

Nico kept silent, but Teresa couldn't control herself.

"Ford invited Nico tonight to a fancy dinner party with a bunch of other doctors. *At The Pierre.* I told him we wouldn't mind takin' over his shift so he could go."

"And I said no. You've taken over my shifts the past two nights. It ain't right."

The train screeched into the station, and Nico walked inside with Joey and Teresa right behind him.

Joey was truly upset. "Babe. You know I'd do it, but I got us tickets tonight for the Mets. On the field, right behind first base. They cost me a ton."

Disappointed, Nico put on a smile. "It's okay. I told Ford I'll go over after I finish at the restaurant. No big deal."

Teresa frowned but stopped arguing with him.

Nico made it to work on time, and when he picked up his paper work, was pumped to find out from Carlos that they were starting an executive training class soon.

"Fill this out by Monday, and you'll be notified if you're chosen."

"Thanks."

"Bus is waiting." Carlos was a man of few words, and

Nico saluted him and ran out. On his way, his phone rang. Seeing it was his mother, he groaned but knew he had to answer it.

"Ma, I'm at work. I can't talk right now."

"Yeah? Good. Then you can listen. I just got off the phone with Teresa. Are you crazy? You're gonna give up a date with a doctor, who wants to take you to *The Pierre*, so you can work in the restaurant?"

"What am I supposed to do? Joey can't make it, and there's no one else who can replace me."

"Yes, there is. Me 'n Justine'll do it."

"Wha—no way. You're not supposed to overexert yourself, even if your scans are clear. That's what the doctor said. I ain't gonna let you—"

"Look at you. Not gonna let me. It's my restaurant. Mine and Justine's."

"Yeah, I know, Ma. But when you stopped 'cause it was too hard to be on your feet every day, me 'n Joey told you we'd do it. Same for Aunt Justine." His mom had been diagnosed with cancer and was just recovering from that battle, while his aunt was dealing with COPD. "You both worked there for years to put us through school and give us whatever we needed. Now it's our turn."

"I know. And every night I thank God I had you. Both you boys are angels from heaven. And so is Teresa. She's like the daughter I never had." He heard her sniffle, and his heart squeezed. There wasn't anything he wouldn't do for his mother. And that included missing out on a night with Ford so she wouldn't have to push herself to make him happy.

"She's the best, and so are you. Now I gotta go."

"I'm not finished talkin'."

"Yeah, but I am. I'm workin'." Nico approached the bus and scanned the line. It already looked like the bus would be crowded. "I'll talk to you later."

"You sure will," she warned.

It was, as he'd predicted, an extremely busy day but typical for a summer Saturday. He didn't mind—it made the hours pass quickly. Ford had texted him, and at lunchtime he took a few minutes to read and reply, in between sandwich bites.

I'm at my second lecture of the day, this time about oxygen therapy for the skin. I spent my breakfast listening to talks about chemical peels and laser treatments. After lunch, I'll be learning about new innovations in hair growth. I'd rather be sitting on a bus tour with you. Will miss being with you at dinner.

It all sounded important and heavy.

I wish I could be there. But Joey has field seats for the Mets game. I couldn't ask.

I understand. But you'll be here later?

Yeah, definitely.

If by any chance you get off early, meet me at The Pierre. Cocktails start at 7 in the Cotillion Ballroom, and the dinner is at 8 in the Regency Ballroom.

Nico sighed, imagining the glittering lights and well-dressed people. Payson had gone to high-profile parties and events in hotels like The Pierre, but he'd never invited Nico.

"It's not for a plus-one."

"You don't want to be with a bunch of boring suits."

"We'll have our own party together."

Nico should've known it was all lies and deceit. The ugly truth was, Payson hadn't wanted him there. The only place good enough for Nico had been in Payson's penthouse apartment.

Sirens blaring, a police car raced by, and cabs honked all around him. Sidewalk vendors hawked their cheap knock-offs. Who was he kidding? These streets were his reality, not fancy dinners in ballrooms with people who made millions of dollars.

I doubt it, he texted back, *but thanks.*

He couldn't stay miserable, though. After his last tour was finished, he turned in his sheets and tickets and counted his tips. Over two hundred dollars. He was banking some serious cash this summer—he'd already made a thousand dollars. The best year ever, yet his mind wasn't on the bills in his hand, but on the man from Florida and the invitation he'd had to turn down.

His phone buzzed, and seeing it was Anthony, he ignored it. It stopped but then immediately started up again, so he answered.

"What's wrong? You break up with the boyfriend?"

"No, you idiot. Come outside."

"What?"

"Stop talkin' and get out here. I can't stand here all day."

Totally confused, he left the office and found Anthony pacing the sidewalk outside the building, two Macy's shopping bags in his hand.

"What's goin' on?"

"Here." He thrust the bags at Nico. "Joey called me and explained the sitch with you and the hot doctor. So me 'n Sergio are gonna go to the restaurant and help out. Your mom and Justine will be there to supervise, and we'll make sure they don't overwork themselves."

"What the hell are you talkin' about? You and Sergio? You ain't never waited tables. And I told my mother—"

Anthony snickered. "Since when does your mother take orders from you? Anyways—"

But Nico wasn't finished. "How are you and Sergio gonna manage?"

"Sergio waited tables at Applebee's before he got this job." An evil grin lit his eyes. "You think we're gonna let you miss this chance? A date with a rich doctor? No way."

Nico grunted. "What the fuck is this, *The Bachelor*? And I'm not seeing him 'cause he's got money. Don't be a fuckin' idiot. It's not like that."

"I know that, dummy. Now, look. I went to Macy's, and some sales guy helped me pick this out. You and him wear the same size, so he told me it would fit okay. There's also a shirt and a tie. I got them on sale; you can pay me back later. Plus, I FaceTimed Sergio from the store because he knows all about this shit, and he gave me the thumbs-up. If you hurry, you can get dressed quickly and make the dinner."

His head spun. "Wait, what? You and Joey did all that just for me to be able to go to this dinner?"

"Yeah. I mean, we know you like the guy. You can admit it. There ain't nothin' wrong with sayin' so. It's us."

A swell of love for his friends and family rose inside him. These were the people he could always count on, no matter what. He didn't even need to ask—they knew what he needed and came through in the clutch.

A sudden thought hit him. "I don't have shoes. I can't go in these sneakers."

Panic struck Anthony's dark eyes. "Shit. I didn't even think about that." He chewed his lip. "I got it. Here, take mine."

"What? Your shoes? Bro, that's—"

"Just do it. I can't stay. Sergio's waiting for me, and we gotta go get ready for later."

There he and Anthony stood, trading shoes in the middle of Times Square, and not a single person stopped to look or paid them any attention. Nothing shocked anyone in New York City, and this proved it. Not that he should be surprised—Times Square had The Naked Cowboy, drag queens, a man with a giant python on his shoulders, and assorted people dressed up—or not dressed, in some cases. Two men exchanging footwear was low on any tourist's list of "Bizarre Things We Saw Last Night at the Crossroads of the World."

Nico slipped his feet into Anthony's loafers. "These are nice. I should get me a pair."

"Yeah, you should. Class up your act."

"Thanks, man. I-I don't know what to say. Appreciate it. And make sure you tell Sergio thanks." Again, he was surprised and touched by the support from Sergio, considering his less than enthusiastic response to him and Anthony dating. Showed how wrong first impressions could be.

"I will. Call me tomorrow. I wanna hear all about it."

"I promise."

They hugged, and Anthony ran to the train, while Nico returned to the office, hoping Carlos hadn't left yet. He banged on the door.

"Carlos? You there?"

At the shuffle of footsteps, he heaved a sigh of relief. The door opened. "Didn't you leave?"

"Listen. I don't have time. I gotta change." He rushed past Carlos to the bathroom.

"What's up? You got a hot date or something?"

He stripped and took out the shirt, ripping off the tags. Plain white, no problem. Buttoned it up, found the tie. Blue flowers, not his style, no big deal. He put it on quickly and pulled out the suit. Dark gray, and Anthony was right. It fit like a dream.

"Anthony, you done good," he muttered as he stuck his feet into the loafers. He stuffed his pants and shirt into the bags and ran out to where Carlos stood. "I gotta leave this here till my next shift."

"I can't guarantee nothin'."

"Whatever." Nico wrote his name on a sticky note, stuck it on the bag, and shoved the whole thing into the bottom drawer of the desk. "Thanks, man."

"Lookit you!" Carlos whistled, and Nico's cheeks grew hot.

"I gotta get across town. Thanks for waiting."

"Have a good one."

Nico raced to the street and had no problem finding a cab. Traffic was a horrendous snarl, and it cost him a small fortune in taxi fare, but he made it to The Pierre with five minutes to spare before the cocktail thing was about to start. He took a second outside to catch his breath and settle his nerves.

Steady as he'd ever be, Nico walked inside and stood in the lobby, drinking in the space. It was as elegant as he'd imagined—all hushed and clean, with crystal chandeliers and marble floors. Intimidated, he discreetly wiped his sweaty hands on his jacket.

"This ain't no Holiday Inn, that's for sure," he murmured. He walked up to a desk marked *Concierge*. A man in a suit that probably cost more than he made in a week glanced up.

"May I help you?"

"Uh, yeah. I'm lookin' for the, uh, doctors' dinner? There's a cocktail party first?" He didn't remember the name of the ballroom and pulled out his phone. "The Cotillion room?"

He had no idea what a fucking cotillion was.

The man's perfectly groomed brows rose, and Nico braced for a confrontation, but he answered pleasantly. "Yes. Take the elevators on the left to the second floor."

"Okay, thanks."

With that accomplished, he stood outside a large ballroom, staring at a sea of men in suits and women in cocktail dresses. How the hell would he find Ford?

"*Marone a mia*, you're a dumbass." Nico could've slapped himself on the head. "Text him and tell him you're here." He found Ford's number and sent him a message.

A man in a tuxedo approached him with a sour face. "I'm sorry, but this is a private event."

Nico smiled. "Yeah, I know. I'm meeting someone here."

"Oh? Who?"

Bristling at the man's obnoxious tone, Nico remembered

he was at The Pierre hotel, not Canarsie Pier, and couldn't tell the guy off. Even though the douche could use a punch to his pinched-in face.

"Dr. Ford St. Claire." He spied Ford making his way through the crowd. "Who's right there." He waved, and Ford rushed over to him.

"You made it. What happened? I thought you had to work tonight?"

"Dr. St. Claire, you invited this person?" the walking dickhead asked.

"Yes, why? Is there a problem? The invitation said 'and guest.' *This person* is Mr. Nico Andretti, and he is my guest." One hand resting on Nico's shoulder, Ford waited for a response.

At Ford's haughty tone—which Nico had to admit was a big fucking turn-on—the dickhead wilted. "No, not a problem at all. We just have to make sure no one is trying to come in who doesn't belong. Enjoy your evening." He slunk away.

"Asshole," Nico muttered. "Probably going to look for someone else's night to ruin."

"Never mind him." Ford met his eyes, and Nico forgot about the rude jerk and everything else except the heat in Ford's gaze. "I'm really glad you're here, Nico. This night just got a whole lot better."

"Yeah. For me too."

Chapter TEN

Ford couldn't believe Nico was here. And looking like he'd stepped out of the pages of a fashion magazine. But when he stopped thinking with his dick, his heart lurched painfully as he watched Nico. He could read his body language. Nico felt he didn't belong, especially after the way he was spoken to by the event manager, and Ford vowed to make sure he was where he was supposed to be. At his side.

"Want to get a drink?"

"Sure."

Ford took Nico's hand. "Follow me."

At his touch, Nico met his eyes, and Ford smiled at him, giving his fingers a squeeze. They made their way through the crowd, and though several people caught his eye, signaling they'd like to talk to him, he continued on. Over the past two days, he'd come to realize that while he didn't know these people, they knew Lenny. And, he discovered, there were two camps: one was comprised of people wanting to get the scoop about their lives and how they could still practice together, and the second group were those who were only too happy to tell him of their sexploits with Lenny and how Ford was better off without him.

He had little to no desire to speak with those people at all, and thought he'd have to suffer through the night and wait until after to meet up with Nico. Now, with Nico's appearance, the entire tenor of the evening shifted, the weight of the scandal lifted, and he felt light and free.

"This is something else," Nico mused, craning his neck. "I've never been in this kind of hotel. Me 'n my friends would walk by, but I never went inside. I promised to tell everybody all about it."

"So what happened? How come you don't have to work tonight?" They reached the bar, and Ford ordered. "One Macallan neat and one extra-dry martini, please."

"You remembered my drink?" Nico said with surprise, and Ford wondered why. Had he never been treated like the special person he was?

"Yes. I remembered."

I remember everything about you. The way you kissed me. The heat of your skin. Your breath echoing in my ear. How you felt when I held you. I haven't forgotten one damn thing.

Ford took a quick gulp of his drink to get a grip while listening to Nico.

"Anyway, my best friend and his boyfriend are gonna take my shift. My mom and my aunt will be there to watch. They're not supposed to be on their feet too much."

"Why? Aren't they well?" Ford hated the thought of Nico struggling to care for a sick parent.

"My mom's in remission, but the cancer left her weak. And my aunt's got COPD. They come in to check on the kitchen and sometimes take over the register, but that's why me 'n Joey took over the restaurant for the most part. We think they should just close it down and retire. Their houses are paid off, and my grandparents had big life-insurance policies that went to them when they passed. Me 'n Joey 'n Teresa—when she's not workin' late—are there in the evenings. They don't need the headache."

"Has your family always owned it?"

"My *nonno*—my grandfather—he started the restaurant, and he loved it. He and my *nonna* were there every day. Now it's become more of a burden for my mom and aunt. But they feel obligated, even though my grandparents are both gone." Nico shrugged.

"That must be a difficult choice for them to make. They're lucky you and your cousin have agreed to help."

Nico gazed at him. "It's family. We stick together."

Nothing he would know about, so he kept quiet and sipped his drink.

Nico scanned the room. "So, all these people are doctors?"

"Dermatologists, to be exact. And yes. Along with their plus ones." He smiled into Nico's eyes. "And by the way, since I didn't have a chance to say it, you look very nice tonight."

Nico's face turned red. "Thanks. I didn't know I was coming, so Anthony went and bought me this stuff. I don't even have a suit that fits anymore. It's been years since I've worn one."

"I have to wear one every day." He grimaced. "And that was a very nice thing your friend did. You have such a great group of people around you."

Ford wondered, if he ever had a crisis, who would he call? There was no one, as Lenny seemed to have inherited all the people in their lives. *Guess juicy sex scandals make for better dinner companions and friendships than quiet evenings at home.*

"Dr. St. Claire, good to see you again."

He turned to see his breakfast companion, Bruce Sandler, smiling at him. "You as well. Have you been enjoying the lectures?"

"Not as much as this Scotch." He held up his glass, and Nico chuckled.

"Are you here with your wife?" Ford asked.

"No. She gave up on these events years ago. Said the women were all trying to look forty years younger than they were, and she couldn't be bothered. She's at home with our two dogs, watching her murder shows on television."

Nico snickered. "Sounds like my mom. I get nightmares from them, but she says they relax her."

Sandler directed his attention to Nico. "We haven't met. I'm Bruce." He held out his hand.

Ford watched as Nico hesitated a split second. "Nico."

"I detect a Brooklyn accent. Is your practice in Brooklyn?"

"I'm not a doctor," Nico stated, his jaw set hard. "I give tours on the hop on, hop off buses in Times Square."

Ford could see Nico square his shoulders, as if bracing for a negative comment. He hoped Sandler was as kind as he'd appeared to be and held his breath.

"My grandkids always want to take those buses when they come in from California," Sandler mused. "Must be interesting to meet so many people from all over the world. Plus, you have to love the city and know its history."

Nico blinked, and for a moment seemed at a loss for words. "Uh, yeah. I mean, I've lived here all my life and always loved visiting the landmarks, but also the hidden places that tourists never get to see."

"The real New York," Sandler agreed. "Is that how you two met? You were giving a tour that Ford took?"

Nico looked to him, and Ford answered. "Yes. The first time I came to New York was earlier this summer, to give expert testimony on a case. So when I decided to attend this conference, I made sure to find Nico."

"Always good to have a friend who's a native take you around." Sandler finished his drink. "Make sure you show Ford a good time, Nico. He's going home tomorrow, back to the grind."

Nico glanced at him, lips quirked in a smile. "I think that could be arranged."

A punch of lust hit him in the belly, and he struggled to catch his breath. Ford wished they could go to his hotel room now and skip the dinner. But hearing how Nico's family and friends had banded together to help him prepare for the date, Ford vowed to show him how much he appreciated the trouble they'd all gone through to make this happen.

"Nico's already taken me to his family's amazing Italian restaurant, and to Coney Island and Nathan's." Ford hummed with pleasure, remembering. "It was so good. I haven't eaten like that in forever."

"Lucky you." Sandler groaned, clearly envious. "My doctor gave me a warning—absolutely no fried foods. Did you have the clams? You had to have had the clams."

"Clams, hot dogs, and fries. I couldn't pick which one was better."

"Because they're all good. I wish my doctor wasn't such a stickler. They never let you have any fun once you hit sixty-five. And I'm seventy-two now, so he's watching me like a hawk." He made a face. "God, I love Italian food. *Cacio e pepe*, chicken *parmigiana*..." Sandler sighed. "All gone, forever."

"You could eat light," Nico suggested. "We prepare fish or shrimp in white wine."

"You might want to leave the city and go to Brooklyn. It's worth the trip," Ford heard himself bragging and decided to shut up.

Sandler, however, was canny and peered at him over his glasses, then eyed Nico. "You're young—what, twenty-five, twenty-six?"

Ford hoped there wouldn't be any snarky comments about Nico's age.

Luckily, Nico took it in stride. "Twenty-eight."

Sandler waved him off. "Still young. A kid. And you look like you take care of yourself."

"I try," Nico said, and Ford was proud Nico wasn't uncomfortable with all the talk about age. "I'm going to get another drink. Anyone want a refill?"

Ford shook his head.

"I'll take another, thank you." Sandler set his glass on the tray of a passing waiter. "We'll need it to make it through the dinner." He waited for Nico to move out of earshot. "Ford, may I be frank with you?"

"I hope so." Ford focused on Nico. Damn, he was a lucky man.

"It's about Nico."

Ford, busy daydreaming about what would happen later when he and Nico returned to his hotel room, blinked back to awareness. "What? I'm sorry. Did you say Nico? What about him?"

"Of course, you can tell me to shut up and mind my own business, but you seem like a very decent man."

"Thanks, but you said you wanted to talk about Nico, not me." Again, he cursed Lenny for putting him in this position where he'd either have to listen to people telling him they felt sorry for him or expect details of his personal life they had no right to.

"Bringing that young man here was brilliant. He turned plenty of heads when you walked in here with him. I'm sure someone will inform your ex you came with a date. You know what they say—living well is the best revenge, and from the way Nico looks at you, he'll treat you very well."

There was a crowd by the bar, and for once Ford was glad to have a moment. "We, uh, barely know each other."

"Look, I'm an old man, and you don't have to listen to me, but I've been around the block a few times. What Nova did to you was lousy. And the fact that you're still practicing with him tells me you're a nice guy—probably too nice, but that's another story for a different day. I think you probably let him run the show in both your personal and professional lives, which is fine, I get it. My wife is the boss, and I wouldn't have it any other way. Thing is, we respect each other."

Ford's face flamed hot. "And Lenny didn't respect me, is what you're saying."

Sandler's eyes were kind. "A good person wouldn't have done what he did. We both know that. Lucky for you, you're young and have your whole life ahead of you. There's nothing wrong with letting loose while you're at a conference—after all, you're not together anymore. Have that fling with a kid like Nico."

Drinks in hand, Nico approached them, and Ford allowed himself to appreciate the sight. While model-gorgeous in casual clothes, Nico was simply stunning in a suit that clung to his well-muscled thighs. Ford already knew what lay beneath that worsted wool—he'd felt the bulge of a thick cock.

But while Sandler assumed it was all physical between them, Ford enjoyed being with Nico, listening to him talk about his friends and family and watching them all interact. There was a realness about Nico that was missing from the people he'd spent time with. Nico wasn't about to hide or change who he was to fit in.

Nico handed Sandler his drink, but his gaze rested on Ford. "Everything okay? You look kinda funny."

Ford's lips ticked up for a brief moment. "No. It's all good."

They went in to dinner, which was typical for a conference—discussions about the lectures and samples received from the sales reps, plays seen and museums visited. The food was nothing special, but Nico seemed to be having a good time. A woman who had introduced herself as Dr. Dylan from Arkansas took a *petit four* from the plate of desserts on the round table and fixed her pale eyes on Nico.

"You're a tour guide? How very interesting," she drawled, in a tone that left Ford feeling she believed it was anything but. It set Ford's teeth on edge. Nico remained unbothered and popped a *macaron* into his mouth.

"It can be. Some people are nice and treat me and the bus driver well—they ask questions and say please and thank you…common courtesy, you know? But you get some who think they're above it all. Too good to talk to us." A lazy smile raised the corner of his lips, and he quirked a brow. "You know the type."

Her face flamed, and Sandler, who sat next to Ford, smothered a laugh. "I knew the kid could take care of himself," he murmured.

Ford leaned in close to whisper in Nico's ear. "Do you want to leave or stay?" He sensed Dylan's eyes on him and could almost feel the disgust rolling off her in waves.

"I want to be alone with you." Nico's husky voice went straight to Ford's dick. His blood burned, and his heart pounded.

"Let's say good-bye."

Nico's grin was full of the devil.

"Good to meet you all." He rose and shook Sandler's hand.

"The same," Sandler said. "Ford, if you ever find yourself in the city, stop by my office. Here's my personal cell number." He extricated a card from his wallet and took out a pen. And though Ford understood it was unlikely they'd ever see each other again, he did the same, and tucked Sandler's card into his wallet.

"Thank you. And come visit in Florida if you make it

down there."

"I will. Nico, good to meet you."

"You as well."

Ford took Nico's hand, and they left. "I'll get a car back to the hotel. You can stay, right?"

"If you want me to."

Their car came, and Ford, feeling braver and freer than ever, kissed him on the sidewalk with hundreds of people walking past.

"I want you, Nico."

This time he took the initiative, and when they entered his room, he pressed Nico up against the door and took his mouth. Nico groaned and sucked his tongue while grinding his pelvis into Ford's.

"You drove me crazy all night." Ford licked into Nico's mouth, tasting the combination of Scotch and sugar from the desserts. It was heady, and he deepened the kiss, his hands framing Nico's face.

"Let me make you feel good." The scruff of Nico's face rasped his cheek, sending a jolt of lightning to his balls, and he fought for control.

"You do," Ford gasped as he pushed Nico's jacket off. "You make me feel. Period."

Nico's hands touched his belt, and their gazes clashed. Ford nodded, and Nico crushed their lips together, his tongue stroking Ford's as he undid the belt and opened his slacks. Ford moaned as Nico's fingers played with the bulge of his throbbing cock through his briefs.

"Please, Nico. Please."

"Shh. I'm gonna take care of you."

No one had ever taken care of him—not his mother, nor Lenny. He'd been on his own. Until now.

Nico sank to his knees, taking Ford's pants and briefs with him, and they fell around his ankles. Ford's cock rose, painfully engorged and leaking from the tip. "I thought you were perfect before," Nico said, "but this is a work of art." Nico gripped him, licked the crown of his cock of all the sticky precome, and tickled the slit. "Fuck, you taste good."

"Nico, oh God." Ford reached out and buried his fingers in Nico's silky, dark hair. Nico hummed as his lips sucked down the length of his shaft, flickering and tonguing the pulsing vein. Ford flung his head back as his hips pistoned. "Oh God, oh fuck. Please, please."

"*Mmm…*" Nico was humming around his dick, the vibrations of his mouth like spikes of electric shocks to his nerves.

He was flying…soaring…drowning in hot pleasure and greedy desire. All that wet heat surrounding his dick sent his eyes rolling. Lust grabbed him by the throat, and he was gone.

"Nico," he sighed and came, jerking endlessly in Nico's mouth. Ford had no idea how he remained standing, and with hazy eyes, watched Nico sit on his heels. "That was…I have no words." He held out a hand and pulled Nico to his feet, then reached for Nico's zipper.

"You don't have—"

He silenced Nico with a hard, claiming kiss. "Aside from the fact that you gave me the most intense orgasm of my life, did you think I'd leave here without knowing what you taste like? Let's go to the bedroom." He kicked off his shoes and stripped off his pants and briefs.

"If you're sure." Nico licked his swollen lips, and Ford's dick stirred. He hadn't had sex twice in a night in years, but Nico made him feel twenty-five again.

"Trust me. I am." Never taking his eyes from Nico's, he

took his hand, and they entered the bedroom. Twenty years of hiding. Of hurting. Of knowing that no matter how he'd tried to fit in or change, it never made a difference. He'd never been wanted.

Nico had awakened the sleeping giant of desire, and Ford wanted it all.

Like Nico had done for him, Ford unzipped his pants, and along with his briefs, tugged them over Nico's hips.

"You're gorgeous. Even more than I imagined."

Nico's abs were ridged and muscled, his thighs like tree trunks, and his dick…Ford couldn't stop staring at its length and girth. He shivered, imagining it filling him, splitting him in two. Nico grasped himself, and the sight of that reddened tip in his fist, the slick sound of his hand, sticky with precome, had Ford panting.

"Jesus, the way you're looking at me." Nico's aqua-blue eyes had turned almost black with undisguised hunger, his silky hair hanging in his eyes, meeting the thick, dark lashes.

"I need…please." Ford kneeled and kissed along the length of Nico's dick before sliding it into his mouth.

"Ahhh, God, that's so good." Nico hissed, his fingers touching Ford's face as he bobbed his head, tongue curling around the tip and slit. He plunged down, sucking hard. "Mother of God." He flexed his hips, sending his dick to the back of Ford's throat.

He gagged for a second, unused to the size, but quickly found his rhythm. "So good," he gasped when he licked and sucked the fat, leaking crown. He grasped Nico's balls and squeezed them as he rose and fell on Nico's thick shaft. Nico's hips moved faster, punching in swift, strong jabs, fucking his face, and Ford loved it. Wanted it harder.

Hearing Nico's harsh cries, feeling his body tense and the sweat pouring off him, Ford grasped the thick root of Nico's cock and sucked.

"Ahh, fuck me, fuck." Nico held his head and came,

filling his mouth and throat. Ford milked his balls, drinking all the hot, sweet cream Nico gave him. After it was over, he nuzzled into the crease of his thigh.

"That was amazing." Ford sighed, the headiness of the sex still buzzing through his body.

Nico joined him on the floor, and they kissed, tasting each other on their tongues. It was as if they shared pieces of themselves, and he wanted more of Nico. All of him. Everything.

"You're staying, right?" He rubbed his cheek to Nico's, feeling his smile.

"I'd like that. What time is your flight?"

Ford groaned. "Fuck. I picked an eight a.m. flight. There are still a couple of lectures tomorrow morning, but I wanted to make sure I'd get home in time to get ready for Monday morning." He hung his head. "We could've spent the morning together. I'm sorry."

Nico kissed him softly. Slowly. Their lips learning the shape and taste of each other to hold on to when the miles separated them. "It's okay. I think we'd better set the alarm because I'm not ready to let you go to sleep just yet." Ford watched Nico reach over and pull out his phone. "Done. Now get on the bed, Doc."

Hearing Nico order him to bed was a fucking turn-on, and he stiffened. They lay side by side, and when their shafts aligned, Nico took them in hand and began a rough, hard stroke. Ford gasped, burning from his toes to his head, and hissed at the movement on his still-sensitive flesh.

"You like that, don't you?" Nico nuzzled into his neck, sucking and biting, and Ford rutted against him, breathless and caught up in a pleasure so bone deep, when he came again, it was like shattering into a thousand shining points of light. Nico's come spread warm and sticky over his stomach, and they lay together, hearts pounding, kissing and inhaling each other's breaths.

"I'm going to miss you, Nico." Loath to move, he held Nico tight.

"I'm gonna miss you too, Doc."

After that, there was nothing more to say. Ford closed his eyes.

Chapter
ELEVEN

The next morning, Nico walked out of the hotel with Ford. They held hands and kissed.

"You should've stayed sleeping. Checkout is at eleven."

"Without you, it's nothing," Nico said, his forehead resting on Ford's. "I didn't want to be there alone." He didn't give a goddamn how corny he sounded. Something had changed. Being with Ford at that dinner, being seen for the first time, Nico wanted to be a couple. Wasted nights of aimless hookups didn't compare to holding Ford's hand as they walked together or hearing him cry out his name as he climaxed.

The car stopped, and Ford wheeled his suitcase to the rear. Nico waited by the passenger door. Ford cupped his face. "I'll call you. I'm not letting you go."

"Sure. I'll talk to you." Nico forced a smile, knowing

Ford would go home to his million-dollar world and friends, but what could he do?

"I mean it, Nico. We'll figure this out." Ford kissed him. "I had the best night of my life with you."

The little he knew of this man was that he didn't lie. Nico clung to him, and for a hot second, he allowed the dream to be his reality. "I did too. I won't forget about you."

"You better not."

And then he was gone. Even at five a.m., Times Square had people strolling through, but without the frantic intensity. Nico walked to the train, paid his fare, and wasn't surprised that there were hardly any seats. The city was alive twenty-four hours a day, seven days a week, and these were the night-shift workers coming home. He found a seat in the corner two-seater and settled in for the long ride home.

The entire evening with Ford had made him realize how empty his life was. Joey had Teresa, and Anthony had Sergio. He could hang out with Jack and keep meeting guys at bars or the beach and get laid every night if he wanted. A few months ago, that was his life, and he'd been content.

Until Ford showed him the difference with a single kiss, shooting his life to hell.

"Fuck," he muttered, and the woman next to him shifted away. She probably thought he was one of those subway nuts who talked to themselves.

He wasn't stupid enough to think he was in love with Ford, but he sure as hell liked every single damn thing about him. It had been less than an hour since they'd separated, and fucking hell, he missed him already. It had never been like this, and Nico wasn't quite sure how to deal with it. Usually a hookup was fine, and they parted with a pat on the ass and a hurried good-bye, the guy's presence swept away like cobwebs with a broom.

Not Ford. The man was unforgettable. The way his eyes crinkled shut with laughter, or turned hot and hazy with lust when he looked at Nico naked. There wasn't a doubt in Nico's mind that Ford wanted him. But Nico didn't want it to only be about sex, though that had been fucking amazing.

Nico wanted Ford out of bed as much as in between the sheets. He just wasn't sure Ford wanted that as well.

He got home near six thirty, changed into shorts and a T-shirt, and hung up the suit. Aside from the incredible sex—the best he'd ever had, and he could still feel the heat of Ford's mouth on his dick—it had been an interesting evening. He'd enjoyed talking to the older doctor, Sandler, and most of the other people Ford had introduced him to, but the snotty bitch at their dinner table? Yeah, that was what he'd expected more of.

He turned on the coffee machine, then lay on his couch, waiting for it to brew.

He poured a cup and his doorbell rang. He peeked through the curtain, sighed, and opened the door.

"Hey, Ma. Come on in." He checked his watch. "I been home ten minutes. What took you so long?"

"Don't be fresh." Only five feet tall, Joanne Andretti's large personality made up for what she lacked in height. "You look tired. How was the party? Tell me about it. The Pierre is fancy stuff."

"Sit down. You want a cup of coffee?"

"Yeah, sure."

He brought her a mug and put out some biscotti. "Here ya go."

"Okay, so tell me. About the party and this man. 'Cause Joey and Teresa both haven't stopped talkin' about him."

"Yeah? What'd they say?" He knew they liked Ford but wanted to hear it from his mother.

"That he's the only guy they've ever seen you interested in. And he talks to you nice. Not stuck up because he's from money."

"He's not, actually. He didn't grow up with money, but

he's a doctor, and I'm guessing he makes a lot. He's also older than me." Not that it made a difference. His body was gorgeous, and Nico couldn't stop thinking of how good he'd tasted.

"Yeah, they said." She sipped her coffee and nibbled a biscotti. "How old, exactly?"

"He's forty-two." It occurred to him that Ford was as close to his mother's age as he was to Nico's, but he didn't want to think about that at the moment. "I mean, he's a doctor, rich and successful, and I'm just a tour-bus guide."

"Don't you put yourself down." She set her mug to the side and wagged her finger in his face. "You got lots of things going for you—a successful business in the restaurant, and you own a house, and you're gonna go for a management position."

"Ma, come on. It's your house that you put in my name along with yours. Same with the restaurant—it's yours and Aunt Justine's. And I gotta apply for the position. Which reminds me, I need to do that today. Deadline's tomorrow."

"You'll get it. You're a smart man."

He sighed. "I dunno. I'm feeling like everyone knows what they're doing in life. Joey's a manager at H&M, Anthony's going back to school to be a physician's assistant, Teresa's a nurse, and Jack's got the contracting business. Why am I so unsure?"

His mother gazed into his face. "Maybe I shouldn't have kept you from your father. Maybe he could've been positive for you, even though he was a big negative for me."

"No," he snapped. "I don't want to know anything about him. A guy who can walk out on his fiancée right before their wedding is no good. And did the son of a bitch ever ask to see me? No."

His mother paled and twisted her hands in her lap. "Look, Nico. There's something you need to know."

Cold sweat popped up on his skin, and his stomach

dropped. "Is…are you sick again? Tell me. Please."

"No. I'm fine. My last scan was clear."

The room, which had gone gray, brightened and came into focus. He took several deep breaths. "Thank God." He crossed himself. "So, what is it? Nothing else matters."

"It's about your father."

"I told you I don't wanna hear about that bastard. He doesn't exist as far as I'm concerned."

"But he does," his mother whispered. "God forgive me for what I did to you."

Nico started to shake. "Ma, what're you saying? Just tell me."

"I…lied to you. I've been lying all these years." She stared at the floor. "He…he never knew about you. I didn't tell him—couldn't. My father forbade it."

"What? No. Ma, what're you sayin'?" His teeth began to chatter.

"I'm sorry. *Per favore, perdonami*, Nico. I'm so sorry." She crossed herself.

He was cold, yet sweat poured from him. His heart pounded, and his chest hurt. He struggled to take in air as the enormity of her words slammed into him. Like he'd been hurled headfirst into a brick wall.

"You said he didn't give a damn. That he didn't want me." His stomach cramped, and Nico thought he might throw up. "You…Nonna and Nonno…you all said he wasn't interested in having a baby." The words caught in his throat. "You said he never cared."

Teary-eyed, his mother played with the ends of her hair. "We thought it would be the best for you. Your father…he never contacted me after he walked out before the wedding. Why would he care?"

Nico's head spun. "But maybe he woulda. If he'd known." He sputtered, "I can't…I don't understand. All these years you let me think he didn't give a damn about me."

"I'm sorry. It was me he didn't give a damn about. I have no idea if he would've wanted to know I was pregnant, but I was so hurt and angry. It was almost thirty years ago. Things were different then. I couldn't go against my parents. They said if I told him, they wouldn't help me. My father would kick me out of the house. You can't imagine…where would I have gone?"

She began to cry, and he sat on the arm of the chair next to her. "Ma, it's okay. Don't get all worked up about it. It's okay."

"It's not." She wiped her eyes. "I'm sorry. I shoulda said something to you years ago, but they died, and I got sick, and…I was such a coward. I was afraid you'd hate me for what I did."

"I could never hate you," Nico reassured her, and it was true. He loved his mother and couldn't imagine being in her shoes—in her twenties, reeling from being dumped, finding out she was pregnant, unmarried. He'd always looked up to his grandparents for taking care of his mother when she decided to keep him and raise him on her own. He'd heard the stories—how some old-school families forced their children into marriages to save face. Or made them give up the baby if marriage wasn't an option. That could've been him, and he shuddered, thinking how close he'd come to never knowing his mother. Now he saw the price she paid.

Still…he didn't know how to feel about this revelation. To discover after twenty-eight years that his father didn't know he existed left him bewildered and broken. All along he'd been told what a bastard he was. Nico wasn't sure whether he should laugh or cry. Or throw something at the wall.

And now for the hardest part of all. It was a delicate question, but it needed to be asked. "Do you, uh…do you know where he is?"

She lifted a shoulder. "Yeah. He lives on Long Island,

where he always wanted to. I think Merrick or somewhere on the South Shore."

"Oh." A thought struck him. "Did…is he married? Does he have kids?" The possibility that he had half siblings freaked him out slightly. There might be a whole other group of people he shared DNA with.

His mother still couldn't face him and kept her gaze fixed firmly on the floor. "I saw somewhere online he was married, but I don't know about anything else. I didn't want to think about it."

Unable to sit still, Nico paced the room. "I-I can't believe this. After all these years…"

"Are you…do you think you're gonna try and find him?"

Nico's laugh was bitter. "How? I don't even know his name. You've never told me, and everyone always called him 'that bastard.' "

"Do you wanna know?"

Nico rubbed his face. He'd had such a good weekend—a *great* weekend—and he'd come home on a high. Now he felt as empty as a deflated balloon, lying in the gutter.

"I'm not sure. I can't wrap my head around it. I-I need to be alone."

Head hung low, his mother nodded. "I understand. I'm sorry, Nico. I know it's not enough and you're angry with me." Without another word, she left his apartment, and he heard her slow footsteps on the stairs to the house.

It was a struggle not to run after her and tell her it was going to be okay. All his life, it had been the two of them, and she'd always been his cheerleader, so proud of him to became the first in their family to graduate from college.

"My son, the college man."

After her diagnosis, he gave up on business school, stayed and helped take care of her so the burden wouldn't rest solely on his aunt Justine, who wasn't well herself. It was a bad time for them all, but Nico never cared. She'd always been there for him, made every baseball and soccer game, and she was the first person he came out to, secure that she'd love him no matter what. She needed him, so he was there, no questions asked.

"How could she do this to me? I had a right to know…" Shaking and nauseated, his vision blurry, he sank to the floor. "It's not fair." He wiped at his face. "I gotta get out of here." He stuck his feet in sneakers, grabbed his wallet, phone, and keys, and left.

At just after seven on a Sunday morning, he passed people going to church, along with desperate coffee seekers hitting up Dunkin' and Starbucks and the corner bodegas. Unfortunately, there were also dog walkers, and he spotted Joey and Teresa walking Lulu, their pit-bull rescue.

"*Marone a mia,*" he cursed to himself as they waved to him from the end of the block. They'd want to know all about his night with Ford, and he was not in the right headspace for it.

"There he is. How'd it go, dude? Was it awesome?" Joey smacked him on the back as he bent to scratch Lulu behind the ears.

"It was really nice. I had a good time."

Teresa's eyes narrowed. "What's wrong?"

Dammit, she knew him too well. "Nothin'. It's seven in the damn morning. What the fuck could be wrong?" he snapped.

"Chill out, dude. Don't talk to Tre like that," Joey grunted.

Instantly contrite, Nico rushed to make it right. "Sorry, Tre. I'm just in a mood, ya know? I din'mean it."

"I know, don't worry. You 'n Ford still cool?" She put a hand on his arm. "You didn't have a fight or nothin', right?"

"No, we had a great time." He checked his watch. "Matter of fact, he's taking off in an hour."

"Oh, so that's it." She winked. "You miss him already.

You gotta have some vacation comin'. Why not go to Florida to visit him? After all, me an' Joey took off for that weekend and you had to cover for us on short notice."

"Yeah. That would be a good idea," Joey agreed like a fucking bobblehead.

"I'm not pushing myself on him."

Joey frowned. "You ain't thinkin' he's like that asshole Prickface, are you?"

"Payson," he muttered, hating that someone from so long ago still took up space in his head. "No."

But he must've sounded unconvincing, because Joey ignored him and kept on babbling. "Yes, you are. I know you. And I know what's goin' through that pretty head of yours."

"Yeah, what?" He cursed for engaging when he should've walked away.

"Because Prickface was a rich dude who led you on, letting you think he was more than a summer thing, you're thinking Ford is gonna be like that too 'cause he's a doctor and has money. Am I right?"

"I dunno." He shrugged. "Maybe." Not really. After their night together and how Ford stood by his side at the dinner, he doubted Ford would treat him like a boy toy. Good for sex but nothing else. But better to think about that than his mother's devastating news. That was something he absolutely didn't want to talk about yet.

"I don't get that vibe."

Despite himself, Nico laughed, and Lulu barked and wagged her tail. He petted her. "How would you know?"

"I dunno. Maybe 'cause he took you to that fancy-ass party. Prickface would never. He was only interested in bumping uglies in the dark."

Nico's face burned. "Shut up. Don't talk like that in front of Tre."

On her phone, Teresa put up a hand. "Don't mind me. I don't hear nothin'."

Joey pulled him aside. "Look. I know Prickface hurt you bad and put all this shit in your head that you're not good enough 'cause you don't have a big job and didn't go to a prep school. But he was a bitch and a dick. You're damn good enough—the best."

"Yeah? I dunno."

"Well, I do," Joey said staunchly. "And I bet Ford knows it too."

Even though his shitty mood had nothing to do with his one failed love affair, Nico huffed out an exasperated sigh. "Ford didn't say nothin' about seeing me again. He didn't ask me to come visit. And I ain't gonna invite myself, so don't talk to me about headin' down to Florida." He rubbed his eyes. "Listen, I'm not in the best mood right now. I'm just gonna walk it off."

"Fine, we'll walk with you." Joey tugged on Lulu's leash. "Let's go."

"Alone, please." He stood his ground, unblinking.

"Okay, dude. But if you wanna talk, I'll be home. Alone." Joey petted Lulu. "Just me and my girl."

"Yeah, I gotta go in for a shift at noon for twelve hours." Teresa hugged him. "Whatever it is, it's gonna be okay."

"Yeah." He hunched his shoulders and took off. He was glad they thought so because Nico wasn't so sure it would ever be all right again.

An hour later he returned home and lay on the couch. It pained him to know his mother was upstairs, as wounded and upset as he was, but he couldn't make himself go talk to her. His phone buzzed, and he tensed, thinking it was her.

He'd never ignored her texts before and he wouldn't

now, but what he saw made him forget his crappy mood.

Hi. I have Wi-Fi, so I thought I'd text. I had a great time last night. Hope maybe you'd think about visiting me the next time you have vacation.

Nico walked around the room with a big, goofy smile on his face. The pain of his mother's lies slipped from his mind. All he wanted was to return to that hotel room and have Ford hold him and tell him how wonderful he was.

Hi. I had a great time too. I'd love to visit. I can check my schedule.

Ford responded immediately.

Let me know. Any time is good.

The world looked a little brighter when he set the phone aside. He hadn't even had a chance to truly appreciate the evening with Ford. Seeing how wild and uninhibited Ford became under his lips and tongue led Nico to believe there was untapped sexuality within the quiet man. What a damn fool his ex had been. His body hummed, thinking of the opportunity to spend time together.

His phone buzzed, and he sighed, seeing it was Joey.

Doing okay? I can call up Anthony and Jack and order some pizzas.

He hesitated, but maybe talking it out with the guys was what he needed.

Yeah, sure. See you at 12. I gotta do some things first.

He got a thumbs-up and thrust everything out of his mind except filling out the job application. He ignored the footsteps outside his window and pulled up his old résumé, concentrating on getting the dates right. He took a few breaks to microwave a breakfast sandwich and gulp some more coffee.

"Okay, that does it." He double-checked everything, hit Send, and went to take a shower.

At noon, he knocked on Joey's door and listened to Lulu's barking. Shushing her, Joey opened the door, and

Nico was surprised to see everyone already there, with the pizzas on the table.

"Beer's in the fridge," Joey offered after giving him a hug.

All eyes were on him when he took a plate and two slices, then opened a beer.

"What?" It was like being a bug under a microscope.

"How was the date?" Anthony asked. "The suit looked good, right?"

"Yeah, it was perfect. Thanks." He met Sergio's eyes. "Especially you, Sergio. I'm sure you were the one with the most input." He tipped his head toward Anthony. "That guy's taste is up his ass."

"Hey," Anthony barked. "Except in boyfriends." He wrapped an arm around Sergio.

"Yeah. Except that."

Sergio smiled at him. "Thanks, Nico. I'm glad it went well."

"It did. But now he's on his way home."

"When you goin' to Florida to see him?" Jack chewed on his slice.

In the past, after his hookups, he didn't mind joking about them with his friends. But not now. What he shared with Ford was special and between the two of them only, and he intended to keep it that way.

"I dunno. I got other things on my mind."

"I knew it," Joey hollered. "Me 'n Tre said that, but if it ain't about Ford, then what?"

Nico needed a long swig of beer before answering. He set the bottle on the kitchen island. "My father. It seems my mother and Nonno and Nonna lied to me."

"What?" Joey's jaw dropped, and the others stared at him in shock. "Lied about what?"

His hands trembled. "He never knew she was pregnant. She never told him, even though I was told she did. Nonno told her if she let him know she was pregnant, they'd turn her out and wouldn't help her. So she didn't. She told me this morning, and I have no idea what to fucking think or do about it."

"Did my mother know?" Joey questioned.

Nico shrugged. "I dunno."

"Damn," Jack and Anthony spoke in unison. Sergio frowned.

"What are you gonna do? Are you gonna see him? Do you even know where he is?"

"Yeah. My mother said he lives on the Island. She said he's married, but I dunno if he ever had kids…I might have brothers or sisters. How fuckin' crazy is that?"

"I think you should see him," Sergio stated unequivocally.

"How come?" Nico was curious to hear his explanation.

" 'Cause both of you were done wrong. And he should know he's got a son, and you should have a chance to have a father. If you don't, you'll always wonder *what if?*"

Anthony dropped a kiss on Sergio's head. "I think Sergio's right. You don't gotta run and do it today, but you should. Eventually."

"My dad died when I was seven." Sergio's eyes filled with tears. "I only got a hazy memory of him, but it's better than none at all. I can't imagine any parent wouldn't want to know his own kid."

"Maybe," he hedged, hating that now his personal business was out there for gossip. It made his skin crawl. "How about we watch the pregame show? And I wanna eat my pizza."

Joey turned on the set, and they resumed eating pizza, drinking beer, and yelling at the sportscaster's odds for who was going to win the World Series. Nico sat with Lulu's head in his lap, thinking about his mother, his father, Ford, and what the hell he was going to do next.

Chapter TWELVE

"How was the conference, Dr. St. Claire?" Marisol asked. "It's been such a crazy week, I never had a chance to ask. Did you get to fit in any sightseeing while you were in New York?" She sighed. "I've always wanted to go. My boyfriend's from there, and he says he wants to take me to visit his family. They all live in the Bronx."

It was late afternoon on Friday, and with their appointments for the day finished, they were in his office, reviewing the charts, but he was happy to take a break and chat. "It was very eye-opening and educational. And yes, I got to see some really interesting parts of the city, thanks to a native who took me around. And of course, I ate great food."

"I bet it was eye-opening, Ford. I saw the pictures."

Arms crossed, Lenny stood at the doorway, a sneer curling his lips. Ford's stomach sank. "Marisol, will you excuse us?" All week, he'd been avoiding Lenny's snide emails about his "conference companion."

She gathered up her files and phone and fled the room. Ford didn't blame her. He was extremely lucky she and the rest of the staff had, for the most part, stayed after the scandal broke. It had been uncomfortable, to put it mildly, to work in an office with reporters parked outside and he and Lenny not speaking.

"What are you doing, Lenny? You're not supposed to be here right now. You're breaking our contract."

Ignoring him, Lenny strode inside, hands in his pockets, oozing that irritating combination of confidence and arrogance only being born into extreme wealth brought. Thick dark hair lay perfectly cut, his face was tan but unlined thanks to monthly treatments, and his wardrobe attempted to appear casual, but Ford knew it cost more than most people made in a month. Lenny was battling aging with all the tools in his arsenal, using himself as a human test model for any new product they received in the office.

"Where'd you find the boy toy, *hmm*?" Lenny raised a brow and eased into the chair Marisol had vacated.

Ford's throat turned dry, but he tried to affect nonchalance. "What're you talking about?" Why did he always, *always* feel second best with Lenny? Maybe because for twenty years, he'd listened to Lenny's subtle put-downs. How he'd lifted him from his trailer-park life to the luxury they'd lived in. How lucky he was Lenny loved him.

Lenny sneered. "Oh, come on, baby. You think I don't know about your little fling?" He examined his nails. "I got a bunch of texts and pictures from people I know who were at the conference."

"You had people spying on me?" His voice shook with fury.

Snorting, Lenny rolled his eyes. "Don't flatter yourself. *They* contacted *me*. Said you were smiling and flirting with some young guy in a cheap suit." Lenny's shrewd gaze was assessing. "What did you do, hire an escort?"

It was a struggle to hold his anger in check. "Don't be stupid," he snapped. "It's none of your business what I did. Or do."

Lenny's pale-blue gaze sharpened. "Or *who* you did? Are you actually having sex with someone you picked up at a conference?" He laughed. "How clichéd. For your sake, I hope you used a condom. Don't want a nasty surprise popping up. Those fuckboys aren't discriminating. They'll bang anyone with a bankroll."

"And you would know, wouldn't you?" Ford shot back.

"I don't need to hire someone to have sex with me. But that's sort of your world, isn't it? Or your mother's. I guess you can take the boy out of the trailer park…" He rose to his feet, grinning. "Gotta run. Don't want to be late for my date."

Cold dread washed over him as Lenny sauntered out. He'd told Lenny he'd lived in a trailer park and was on scholarship only after they'd exchanged I-love-yous. Knowing Lenny loved him gave him that level of intimacy and caring he'd craved, and Ford had opened up—to an extent. He'd never mentioned his mother or lack of a father. Obviously, Lenny's family had done some digging, discovered what he'd hidden, and Lenny had waited for the right time to use it against him.

He hung his head in his hands, waiting for the shaking to stop. His phone buzzed, and when he glanced at it and saw Nico's name, his heart gave a funny bounce. They'd texted all week, and Ford missed his exuberance for life, his humor, and the way simply being with Nico made him feel seen. Although something felt off, and Ford had meant to ask him what was wrong.

He picked up his phone and accepted the FaceTime. Nico appeared on the screen and Ford didn't realize how much he'd missed him until that second. The sparkle in eyes was missing, as was his teasing smile.

"Hey, Doc. How's it goin'?" Nico was behind a counter at the restaurant.

"I'm well. What's with you?"

"Nothin'. Here at the restaurant, workin'. Same old, same old, you know how it goes."

Ford wasn't buying it and decided to push back. "Yeah, I know how it goes. But you look upset. Is something wrong?" It occurred to him that Nico had applied for that management program and maybe hadn't been accepted. "Any news on the program you applied to?" He tried to word it as delicately as possible.

"Nah, it's too early, according to my dispatcher." Nico chewed his lip. "Uh, listen. I was wonderin' if you'd be home later. Like around eleven."

"Yes, why?"

"I need to talk to you about somethin', and I can't do it here."

Ford's heartbeat picked up speed. "Are you okay?"

"Not really." Ford heard voices out of the camera's eye. "I gotta go," Nico said. "Talk to ya later."

The screen went dark, and Ford was left hanging, wondering what the hell Nico was talking about. He shut down his computer and put the files in order. The office was empty except for the staff. Behind the front desk, Adriana and Marisol were speaking quietly but stopped at his approach.

"Ready for the weekend?" he asked. "Any plans?"

"Too hot," Marisol complained. "My boyfriend and I are gonna stay home and watch movies."

"Yeah. I'm not leaving my air-conditioned house. My husband and I sent our kids to my parents." Adriana laughed. "First time in months we'll be alone. How about you, Dr. St. Claire?"

"Same. Home and staying cool. Have a great weekend,

and I'll see you on Monday." He was halfway to the door when it occurred to him to ask, "How's the new doctor working out? What do you think of him?"

Marisol and Adriana shared a look, and Marisol shrugged. "I guess he's okay. Dr. Diamond, he doesn't talk to us, really."

Adriana added, "Dr. Nova had a software system set up specifically so all the cosmetic procedures go directly to Dr. Diamond. We schedule the appointments, and then Eva, his assistant, handles it all."

Ford wondered what that was all about, but his mind was too preoccupied with Nico and his problem. Let Lenny deal with it.

"Makes sense. After all, he was hired to take the load off us, so I guess it's working. Keep cool, and I'll see you on Monday. Thanks for another great week." He turned to leave.

"Dr. St. Claire?" Marisol called out.

"Yes?"

Marisol glanced at Adriana, who nodded. "Me and Adriana just wanna say we're glad you worked everything out and didn't leave the practice. We love working with you."

Emotional from her words, Ford needed a moment to recover. "Thank you. That means so much to me. I love working with you all too. And I'm not going anywhere. Be careful driving home."

He reached his condo off Las Olas Boulevard and couldn't wait to shower and change. All the while, nervous anticipation trickled through him. What was Nico planning on telling him? From his odd behavior, he couldn't tell if it was bad news relating to the two of them or something else.

He gazed at the clock. Three more hours. He sighed and entered the large en suite bath. The shower, like everything else in the apartment, was brand-new and high-tech, with two showerheads and big enough to fit "at least three or four people," the grinning realtor had told him, which he'd ignored.

He dressed, made a martini, and took it out on the terrace, where he sipped and watched the boats sail past. Did Nico want to end it? Whatever *it* was between them. Maybe he'd come to his senses and realized Ford was too naïve to be his lover, that he wanted someone with more experience. For him, the sex they'd had was explosive and exhilarating. With Lenny, he'd been submissive and reactive, never taking the lead. Lenny had been in control, concentrating mostly on bringing Ford to as many orgasms as possible. He'd always said he loved to watch Ford come apart, but now Ford wondered if it was simply Lenny needing to control their sex life, as well as everything else.

Being with Nico, even only for that one night, felt like a partnership, each of them concerned with the other's satisfaction.

"Does this feel good? How about this?" Nico asked, his lips leaving a trail of fire where they touched, and Ford nodded, drowning in desire. Every time Nico touched him, everywhere his lips and fingers landed, Ford came alive.

"Let me do the same for you," Ford whispered, kissing him, licking him, and Nico stroked his face, blue eyes brilliant as he gasped in pleasure.

It had been the single most sensuous evening of his life. Ford pinched his eyes shut, cutting off the memory. He left the terrace, ordered a salad, and when it came, ate it without much of an appetite, still lost in that hotel room where he'd found himself.

By eleven, Ford was convinced that Nico wanted to be nice and end it as friends. And Ford had rehearsed his response: it was too difficult to keep up a long-distance relationship; he agreed they were too far apart in age; but sure, let's be friends—both knowing the texts would soon dwindle to nothing.

His computer beeped with a FaceTime, and chest

hurting, he blew out a hard breath and put on a smile before answering.

"Hi, Nico."

"Hey, how's it goin'?" Dark shadows rested beneath Nico's heavy-lidded eyes.

"That's my question. You look tired."

Nico yawned. "Yeah. Well, I haven't been getting much sleep this week."

"Is that connected to what you wanted to talk about?"

"Uh-huh." Nico grunted and shifted the laptop on his stomach. "I need your opinion on something."

Ford's brows pulled together. "Okay, sure. Whatever you need."

"I got some news, and I'm not sure what to do about it. I…wanted your advice." He chewed his lip, and Ford waited, stymied now that the conversation wasn't going as he'd anticipated, his heart banging.

Was Nico's mother sick again? Was Nico sick?

His stomach cramped. "I'm happy to help you, anyway I can. Is it something medical?"

At Nico's shake of his head, relief poured through Ford.

"My mother told me my father never knew she was pregnant. She and the whole family lied to me."

As Nico related the shocking story, Ford had a wild idea to pack a bag and fly to New York to comfort him. The thought of Nico sitting alone and dealing with life-altering news hurt his heart. The suffering on Nico's face was so intense, so heartbreaking, he reached out to touch the screen, as if he were sitting in front of him.

"Jesus. I don't know what to say to that. I'm so sorry. What're you going to do?"

"I don't know. I've been thinking about it all week. I can't sleep. And I usually see my mother every day, just to check up on her, but I haven't since she told me. I feel like shit about it, but I'm also so mad that they all lied to me."

"I understand how you feel. It's a huge betrayal."

"So why do I feel so bad for my mom? I've never not talked to her for this long. But every time I think of going upstairs, I get nauseous. I can't go into that house, where my whole life was a lie."

Ford itched to hold him, but there was nothing he could do except offer solace and advice, as well as be the sounding board Nico needed.

"I don't think you should look at your life as a lie. Your mother loves you, and thirty years ago things were different. Your grandparents were traditional and pretty strict, I'm assuming?"

"Yeah. Especially my *nonno*. He was the head of the family, and his word was law. I don't think I ever saw anyone say no to him."

"So did she have a choice? She lived in their house and worked for them. With no other means of support, she was tied to them, a hundred percent. What a terrible, horrible decision she was forced to make, but really, there was nothing else she could do." Ford sighed, the pain he felt for Nico overwhelming. "Have you thought of contacting him?"

Shiny-eyed, Nico shrugged. "I didn't even ask his name."

"But your mother knows it."

"Yeah." Nico hung his head. "I don't know what to do." He lifted his gaze. "What would you do? You said you didn't know your father. What if you could meet him now? Would you?"

"Maybe. My situation is different." Ford grimaced. "I barely knew my mother. And she had no clue who my father might've been. She wasn't very discriminating in whom she showed attention to."

Except him. She never had time for a hug or kiss. After child services once paid a visit, she'd made the minimum effort to get him to his doctor's appointments for his school vaccines and have food in the house for him to eat. The old lady in the next trailer would watch him, but she died when he was ten. He'd cried like a baby; she was more of a mother to him than his own. She'd rock him to sleep and read to him. After that, he'd basically taken care of himself.

"That sucks. I'm sorry. I didn't mean to bring up bad memories."

Ford rushed to reassure him. "You didn't. I barely think of those days anymore."

"You did real good for yourself. I don't blame you." Nico rubbed his face, and Ford could see the battle in his eyes. "I haven't."

Nico's self-defeat hit Ford hard. "Is that the problem? You think your father won't be proud of you?"

"He's a dentist. I'm nothin' special."

"Don't ever say that," Ford lashed out. "You are special. Everyone has something special about them." He read the doubt in Nico's eyes. "You went to college, and you have ambition to move up. Not everyone who's a success has to wear a suit and tie and work in an office. More importantly, you're a good person. You know how I know that?"

Looking unimpressed, Nico lifted a shoulder. "I dunno."

"Because you have friends and family who would go above and beyond for you. They went out of their way to make sure you could go to that dinner with me."

"We do that for each other. It's how it is. You know."

Ford met his eyes. "No, I don't. I don't have people I can count on. Not one single person."

Nico leaned in, the blue of his eyes as clear and sparkling as the ocean a few miles away.

"Yeah, Doc. You do. You got me."

Chapter
THIRTEEN

Nico woke up early Saturday morning, knowing it was time. Speaking to Ford and seeing him had put his head in the right place, made the hurt easier to bear. Funny how that happened.

After showering and getting dressed, he sent a quick text to Ford.

Taking your advice. Talking to my mom.

Ford responded immediately.

Good. You'll feel better. Let me know how it goes.

He left his apartment and mounted the steps to the house. Using his key, he let himself in and called out, so as not to scare his mother, "Ma? It's me."

She appeared at the end of the hallway that led into the kitchen. "Nico. Is everything okay?"

"Yeah. I mean, no, it's not okay. That's why I'm here.

Can we talk?"

Solemnly, she nodded. "I just made some coffee. Come into the kitchen."

He followed her, and on the round kitchen table he spotted a box of Entenmann's doughnuts and a mug of coffee. He picked up a chocolate-covered one and took a bite.

"Put a plate under it. You'll get the table fulla crumbs," his mother scolded.

"Sorry." With a sheepish grin, he put two plates on the table and sat.

His mother faced him. "What did you wanna talk about?" Hopeful brown eyes met his.

"I did a lotta thinking this week. I know…I mean, I can't imagine what it musta been like for you when you found out you were going to have a baby. But Nonno? He was like that?" Nico had so many memories—good ones. "It's so hard to believe because he was so nice to me."

Her lips trembled. "Of course he was good to you. He loved you best of all. You were a boy. To me, he was an ogre. My father never forgave my mother for having only girls. He was so old-school—a woman belongs in the home, cooking, cleaning, and having children."

That Nico could believe. At home, his grandfather would sit like a king, never lifting a finger, while Nico's grandmother and mother waited on him. Nonna did all the cooking in the restaurant and took care of him, her children, and the house. Nico's mother and aunt had worked in the restaurant since they were teenagers, and Nico remembered his grandfather supervising from his table of cronies.

"I'm surprised he wanted you to keep the baby."

His mother's eyes widened. "He would've never made me get rid of it. That would've been a sin to him. But once you were born and he was told you were a boy? He was afraid if I told Ray—your father—he would take the baby from me and insist on giving you his last name." His mother's voice broke. "My father would never let that happen." Her voice dropped. "He became enraged when I argued with him."

"Argued about what?"

Her hands covered her face. "When I got sick, I told myself it was God's payback for hiding the truth from you. That he was punishing me."

"Ma, no," he protested, hating the harsh tone of her voice. "Stop it. Don't say that."

She took a sip of coffee. "I always wanted to tell Ray, not because I thought he'd come back to me, but because it was the right thing to do."

"But Nonno wouldn't let you."

"Oh, no." Her lips trembled. "When I told him what I was planning, he got so angry. Pounding the table, yelling. He called me terrible names." Tears fell down her cheeks. "He told me he'd lock me in my room if I tried to go anywhere."

Something about all this was bugging him. "Ma. What did Nonna do when all this was happening? Why didn't she try and help you?"

"You don't understand. Your grandfather, he wasn't a very nice man. God forgive me." She crossed herself. "But you?" Her smile was tremulous. "You were the boy he always wanted. He loved you unconditionally and gave you everything. There was nothing he wouldn't do for you. He loved Joey just as much, but Louie was his father. You had no one but him."

A chill ran through him. Much as he wanted to deny his mother's words, Nico knew they were true. His grandfather had doted on him—taken him to ball games, the zoo and toy store, where all Nico had to do was point, and he'd get whatever he wanted. Nico could do no wrong in his *nonno's* eyes. He'd spent hours in the restaurant after school, helping and learning, but also listening to Nonno and his friends. From those conversations, Nico had learned it was in his best interest to keep his sexuality a secret from his grandparents. As much as they'd loved him, Nico had known better to have expectations that they'd understand and accept him.

"I think if they knew I was gay, that unconditional love might not have stood up."

His mother nodded. "You're probably right. He wasn't enlightened. Like I said. Stuck in the old ways."

Nico reached out a hand to her, and she hesitated only a second before taking it. "I'm lucky I had you. And still do. I'm sorry, Ma. It was a shock to hear—something I never expected. I didn't know what to say, but I love you."

Her lashes fluttered, and Nico spotted tears. "I know. And I'm sorry to have sprung it on you out of the blue. It was wrong of me, but carrying a secret like that all these years…it was killin' me." She paused. "Do you think you'll wanna meet him?"

"Maybe," he hedged. "I'm not ready just yet. I need to be in the right headspace."

"I understand. His name is Ray Gargano. In case you wanna look him up."

Nico thought about how strange it was now to have the name of his father. "Can I ask you a question, Ma? You don't have to answer. I'm just curious."

"Yeah, sure."

Nico bit his lip. "Do you…do you think my father walked out on you because he didn't like Nonno and the way he was? Because Nonno was so controlling?"

His mother played with her hands, the bright-pink nails flashing when the morning sunlight hit them. "Probably. He didn't like my father and the way he'd talk down to women. Ray used to say, 'When we get married, he better not think he can tell you what to do anymore.' "

Nico frowned. "Sounds like he had a bit of a temper too. You never told me how you two met." They'd never talked about his father at all.

"Me 'n Justine were at the movies. He was on line behind me for popcorn and started talkin' to me." A tiny smile flickered on her lips as she gazed at him. "He was so handsome—you're the spitting image of him. Tall, with wavy dark hair, and the most beautiful blue-green eyes, like the ocean." She sighed. "I think I fell in love with him right away. He asked for my number and was so respectful when he showed up. Brought me and my mother flowers. I thought he was perfect."

"Nobody's perfect. He shoulda never gotten engaged if he had a problem with Nonno."

"We dated for five years. He was in dental school when we met and wanted to wait until his practice was doin' okay. Nonno didn't like it and thought he was stringin' me along, so we set a date."

"You shouldn't have let Nonno push you like that."

Sorrowful brown eyes met his. "I was caught between them, wanting to please both. Ray had plans. He wanted to move to Long Island—he hated the city." She sniffled. "My father didn't want that. He was so set in the tradition, how he was brought up, in Italy. *Family stays together.* That's what he'd say, and Ray would disagree. About eight or nine months before the wedding, we were having Sunday dinner here, and Ray told us he'd been talking to real estate people and wanted me to look at some houses with him. My father became so angry, and they had a huge fight. I said we should wait until we were married, and Ray got so mad at me. Said I was takin' my father's side over him, and that I was gonna be his wife, so I should be on his side."

Nico listened, angry for the situation his mother was put in—pulled apart by two domineering men. "Ma, it's not your fault. And that's no excuse for Ray cheating on you."

Her eyes filled again. "He said I wasn't giving him everything he needed. I was too much of a daddy's girl and needed to grow up. I shoulda been stronger. Told my father

I loved Ray and it was our decision, not his."

"It's still wrong, what he did," Nico said stubbornly, defending her. "You don't cheat. You break it off. He wasn't a good man either; I don't care what you say. You don't mess around on someone you love." He left his seat to hug her. "I'm sorry you had it so rough. But you know, you're still young. You could meet someone."

She laughed. "I haven't been on a date in over thirty years. I wouldn't know what to do."

Nico thought of Frank and decided he wasn't above playing matchmaker. "You know Anthony's Uncle Frank?"

"Yeah, sure." She selected a cinnamon doughnut from the box and put it on her plate. "Nice man. So awful about Valerie. She was such a nice girl. We all grew up together, like you, Joey, Anthony, and Jack. Shame she could never have children."

"Well, I think Frank likes you."

A cute pink blush stained his mother's cheeks. Despite her illness, his mother looked close to a decade younger than her fifty plus years. She'd lost her thick, dark hair from the chemo, and when it grew back silver, she'd decided to keep it. It only enhanced her rich brown eyes and high cheekbones.

"Don't be silly. We've been friends for years."

"He told me specifically to say hello and called you beautiful. Said you were always sweet to him at the restaurant. Every time I see him, he asks how you are."

A self-conscious smile tipped her lips. "He's very nice, but that doesn't mean anything. He's bein' polite, is all."

Nico knew better but decided not to push it. He'd talk to Anthony first and see if he agreed.

"I'm glad we talked, Ma. I don't wanna have secrets between us no more, okay?"

"I agree. No more."

He picked up his doughnut and took a big bite.

"Have you heard from that doctor?"

"Yeah, we talked last night."

"That's an unusual name. Ford."

He grinned. "No, Ma, he's not Italian. But I think you'd like him."

"If you like him, that's enough for me," she said with determination. "I've learned my lesson not to butt into anyone else's life." She drank some coffee. "Are you gonna see him again?"

So much for not butting in, he thought but kept his mouth shut. "I dunno. We haven't talked about it."

Her gaze grew soft. "Don't wait too long. If you feel somethin' for him, let him know. Before it's too late."

"Ma, he lives in Florida, and I'm here."

She shrugged. "So? Lotsa couples live together and barely see each other and still make it work. All I'm sayin' is, it don't have to be a problem if you don't make it one."

"All right. I gotta go. Pulled an afternoon shift. Talk to you later."

Nico mulled over her words as he got ready for work. It was sweaty as balls and he wished he could wear shorts, but he had to keep to the dress code and showed up in thin gray pants and a light-blue polo. This time he was traveling the uptown loop, which took them past Columbus Circle, up Central Park, to Harlem and the Apollo Theatre and 125th Street. Then down to the Met, Carnegie Hall, and up to Times Square. The hop on, hop off bus company Nico worked for was one of the few that provided live tour guides—most of them used audio in multiple languages, which he knew many people needed, but he loved being able to give the customers his personal backstory to places he'd been to in the city. And if people wanted audio in their language, it was provided with headsets.

The problem was, Nico foresaw that his job would be phased out in the coming years, which was why he hoped for a management position with the company.

At five he finished, turned in his trip sheets, and hustled to the train for the second part of his evening, working at La Dolce Vita. He walked in around six thirty to see his mother and Aunt Justine sitting at their usual corner table with salads. The restaurant was full, and Joey and Bobby were running from the kitchen to the dining room.

"Oh good, you're here. It's like a fuckin' zoo tonight. Everyone and their mother decided they needed to eat Italian. It's hot as fuck out there. What happened to sushi, for fuck's sake?" Joey complained, and Nico laughed.

"The two of us can handle it."

"My mom's been helpin' out, but I told your mother she ain't allowed." His lips twitched. "That didn't go over too good."

Nico cut his mother a look, and she smiled sweetly at him. "I'll tell her."

"You're okay with her, right? You talk it out about your father?"

Hearing those words still brought pain to his heart, but Nico ignored it. "Yeah. We're cool. I'm just gonna go say hi."

"Make it quick. We got a lotta orders." Joey pointed, and Nico waved him off.

"Yeah, yeah." He hurried over to his mother and aunt. "Hi, Aunt Justine." He kissed her cheek, then his mother's. "Ma. Why didn't you say you'd be here tonight?"

"Eh. I wasn't sure, but Justine and I decided it's not right to have you boys work so hard."

"If the two of us can help, we are. I'll make sure Joanne don't tire herself out. Don't you worry," Justine pronounced.

"Okay, okay." He raised his hands in the air. "I'm gonna go work."

Joey had been right, and he barely had time to go to the bathroom. It slowed down after eight thirty, and Nico finally had a chance to sit for a moment and eat some chicken *piccata* and spinach. He checked his phone and saw a text from Ford, about an hour earlier.

Was hoping you'd let me know how the talk went with your mother if you had one.

Damn, he'd forgotten Ford had asked to be kept in the loop. Nico pushed his plate away to answer.

Sorry. Been a busy day. We hashed it out, and we're good. What're you doing tonight?

Same thing I do every night. Sitting on my terrace, watching the boats.

Sounds good to me. I worked late, and now I'm at the restaurant.

Ford didn't answer right away, so Nico resumed his dinner and finished the chicken. His phone buzzed.

Next weekend is Labor Day. Would you want to come for a visit?

Nico was simultaneously thrilled and disappointed.

I wish I could, but it's one of our busiest days, since it's the end of the season. I've already got my hours.

I understand. It was a long shot.

Nico would've loved to ask Ford to come visit him, but how could he? With working every day on the bus and then at night in the restaurant, it wasn't fair.

Maybe in a few weeks, he replied.

I'd like that.

With regret, Nico saw his break was over and a few people had trickled in, waiting to be served.

I gotta go. We're busy as hell tonight.

He didn't wait for a response and shoved his phone into his pocket. He wished he could chuck all this and run to Florida, but if he wanted to prove to the company he was management material, he couldn't slack off and dump his responsibilities on one of the busiest holidays. But damn. What he wouldn't give to see Ford again.

He laughed to himself. *You're acting like a lovesick*

idiot. He's just another guy.

Oh, yeah? the voice inside his head asked. *If you believe that, I got a bridge I'd like to sell you.*

Chapter FOURTEEN

Ford flexed his fingers and rolled his shoulders. He'd had several Mohs surgeries, which took intense concentration and precision. As he finished his charts, a glance at the clock told him it was close to four. It was Friday afternoon, and they were closing early for the holiday weekend.

He sighed and rubbed his face. He really wished Nico could've found a way to visit, but he understood.

A quick knock on his door, and Marisol poked her head in. "Dr. St. Claire, why are you still here?"

He smiled. "I could ask you the same."

"Oh, my boyfriend has to work late." She made a face. "He's a manager at Publix, and since it's a holiday, they want everyone in. You couldn't pay me to go to a supermarket on a holiday weekend. But we're going to a barbecue at my neighbor's. Maybe the beach, and definitely a movie where it's cool."

"Well, I have no fun plans. Maybe I'll go through my closet and get rid of things I didn't wear this summer and donate them."

"Nooo, Dr. St. Claire. That's no way to spend your weekend." She hesitated. "Eva said you met someone in New York City." At his surprised expression, she ducked her head. "She overheard Dr. Nova tell Dr. Diamond. I'm sorry if I'm prying, but can't he come visit you?"

"You're not prying. We've known each other over five years. And yes, I asked him if he could come visit, but his work is in tourism, and Labor Day Weekend is very big in New York City."

Marisol cocked her head. "So why don't you go see him?"

Ford sighed. "I've already gone there twice this summer."

She rolled her eyes. "That was business. This is for pleasure."

He could feel his face grow warm. "Uh, well, when I asked him, he didn't suggest I come see him. If he wanted me to come, I figure he would've asked me."

Muttering to herself, Marisol raised her gaze to the ceiling. "*Madre de Dios*. Men. You're so dense. He probably doesn't want to ask you to come up again. I bet he'd love it if you surprised him. What do you have to lose?"

Ford thought about Marisol's words as he drove home, and while taking a shower. It was crazy…wasn't it? To pick up and go to New York on a whim, to see someone he didn't know all that well? But he put all that out of his mind, recalling Nico's passion. His searing kisses and delicious mouth on his dick. Even more importantly, he wanted to hear more about the conversation Nico had with his mother. Despite Nico saying all was good, having life-altering news like that dropped in your lap wasn't something a person talked about once and brushed aside. It stayed in your mind and heart. Ford wanted to be there for him if he needed to talk. Or simply wanted to be held.

"I'm an idiot, I know." Still, he booked a ten p.m. flight to New York and hastily tossed things into a carry-on. In the Uber on the way to the airport, he thought about telling Nico, but remembered Marisol's words: *I bet he'd love it if you surprised him.*

"Let's hope so."

Since he only had a carry-on and PreCheck, he didn't need to wait all that long. On the plane, he almost texted Nico, but instead, came up with a better idea.

"This is gonna be fun."

He again stayed at the Knickerbocker and woke up the following morning with anticipation thrumming through his body. He'd never done anything so reckless, and he couldn't stop grinning as he ate his yogurt and fruit. A check of his watch, and he motioned the server over.

"Can you charge it to my room?"

"Of course."

He signed the receipt, added a tip, and hurried out the door. The red-and-blue bus Nico worked for sat at the curb, and from afar, he spotted Nico's dark, wavy hair. Ford's heart pounded as he walked over and waited in line. Nico's eyes met his as he took the tickets from people farther up ahead, and his jaw dropped. At his turn, he handed Nico the ticket.

"Surprise."

Those blue-green eyes glowed. "Doc, nice to see you again. Here for business?"

"No." Ford's happy smile matched Nico's. "This time, I'm hoping it's purely pleasure."

"I think that could be arranged."

Ford took a seat in the front this time, to be able to watch Nico in action. He settled in and listened to Nico tell his funny stories about getting trapped in the elevator on the ninetieth floor of the Empire State Building, his favorite non-touristy place to get food in Chinatown, and where to find the best sales in Macy's Herald Square.

When the ride ended, he waited for the last person to get off.

Nico stood at the door. "I have four more trips on my shift today. I can't spend the day with you."

"That's where you're wrong." Ford held up four tickets. "I bought a ticket for each one."

Nico blinked. "That's…are you kidding? You didn't have to do that. I could've met you after." He cast his gaze downward for a moment. "I-I have to work tonight too."

Ford crossed his arms. "Funny enough, I'm really, *really* hungry for some eggplant *parmigiana*. Maybe you know where I can get some." He winked. "With some special Andretti sauce on the side."

"That's the extra-spicy kind. Sure you can handle it?" Nico was everything deliciously wicked and tempting.

"Challenge accepted."

Nico held out his hand. "Ticket please. The next tour is starting."

They stopped for lunch, and Nico seemed a bit disconcerted. "I, uh, I usually just pick up something quick, like a sandwich or something."

Ford took his arm and led him to the side. "Do you really think I care what we eat?"

Nico leaned in and kissed his cheek. "Tuna or turkey?"

Ford held him for a second. "Turkey. Mustard. Whole wheat."

They ate their sandwiches at one of the small tables set out in the open spaces. Nico kept darting glances at him. "I still can't believe you came."

Ford popped the last piece of his sandwich into his mouth. "It was either that or clean out my closet. You won."

"Ha-ha. I'm just sorry we can't do stuff while you're here."

"Hmm, and here I thought you'd be happy to be able to stay in the hotel so you wouldn't have to take the train all the way in every morning."

In the middle of wiping his hands, Nico stopped. "You want me to stay with you the whole weekend?"

"You sound surprised." Ford leaned forward. "I came to spend time with you. Here in the restaurant or anywhere. It's not the place that matters. It's who you share it with."

The tension built in the air between them, and if they weren't outdoors surrounded by thousands of people in the heart of Times Square, he would kiss Nico until neither of them could breathe.

Nico's tanned cheeks grew red. "That sounds good to me." He chewed on his lip. "Uh, my mother and Aunt Justine will probably be at the restaurant tonight."

"Is that a statement or a warning?" Ford joked. "I'm okay with meeting them if you want me to."

"Just giving you a heads-up. They'll probably have lots of questions."

"It'll be fine," Ford reassured him, with more confidence than he felt. His infrequent interactions with Lenny's parents had left him slightly sick to his stomach. It wasn't easy spending hours with people who didn't think you were fit to clean their toilets.

Nico crumpled up the wrappers and stuffed them into the takeout bags. "Time to boogie."

Ford liked the quick pace of New Yorkers, who always seemed to be in a rush to get where they were going. Nico explained certain things that made a person stand out as a tourist.

"First is slow-walking. Like, this ain't a stroll down memory lane. Keep it moving." He windmilled his hands. "Second is standing at the top of the subway steps to check your phone." Nico huffed. "Move the fuck outta the way. People need to get past you." Ford pressed his lips together to smother a smile. "Third is you all standing at the corner, waiting to cross when there's no car. Cross. You ain't gonna get killed if there's no car in sight. Fourth, when you're on line to order your coffee or whatever, make sure you know what you want when you get to the cashier. Don't stand there with your head in the clouds and take twenty minutes to figure out how you want your fucking coffee."

"*On* line?" Ford's brow wrinkled. "We stand *in* line."

Nico patted his cheek. "And that's number five."

Ford busted out laughing. "You have very strong opinions."

Nico shrugged. "I'm from New York. I like what I like and want what I want." Ocean-blue eyes captured his, and Ford's breaths grew short.

"I'm from Florida, and I feel the same."

Four hours later, Nico finished his shift. Ford pulled out his phone to call a car, but Nico frowned.

"Saturday evening in the city on a holiday weekend? No fucking way am I letting you waste over a hundred dollars on an Uber. We'll take the train."

They fast-walked to the station, which was packed. Nico said this was normal, and they didn't get a seat until the train passed Smith and 9th Street in Brooklyn. At first, having heard the stories of how dangerous riding the train could be, Ford was a little apprehensive, but being with Nico, sitting beside him with their thighs pressed together, all his misgivings melted away.

They reached 77th Street, and he followed Nico to the restaurant. It was filled to capacity, as Nico had told him to expect, and Joey growled at him.

"Where you been…ohhh, well…*hello*." The frown turned upside down when Ford stepped through the door. "What're you doin' here? Nico, you dog, you didn't say you were havin' company this weekend. How you doin'?"

Ford shook his hand. "I'm well. And Nico didn't know. I surprised him."

"Yeah?" Teresa bustled up to them, and Ford kissed her cheek. "I love a surprise. Ford, so nice to see ya. I wish I could chat, but I gotta go take Mrs. Carlucci's order." She hurried away.

Nico nudged Ford's shoulder. "I'm sorry to leave you, but I gotta go to work."

"Not just yet, lover boy." Joey put an arm around Nico and leaned in close to both of them. "You gotta introduce him to your mother and mine. They haven't stopped staring since you walked in the door."

"*Marone a mia*," Nico groaned. Ford pressed his lips together in a futile attempt not to laugh. "All right. C'mon, Ford. It's not gonna get any better if we wait."

It was quite a different experience meeting Nico's mother and aunt than it was Lenny's parents all those years ago. Lenny had brought them all to the Ritz Carlton for dinner, and later Ford wondered if it was to forestall a scene, as his mother would never create drama in public. The years after were no better. Ford could count on one hand the number of times they'd had a conversation in twenty years.

In contrast, Nico's mother was all smiles when he stood in front of her. Nico held his hand.

"Ma, this is Ford. He surprised me and came for a visit this weekend."

"That's such a thoughtful thing to do. Right, Justine? Nice to meet you, Ford. Call me Joanne. We're not formal here."

"It's my pleasure, Joanne." Nico's mother was beautiful, her skin smooth and unlined. She wore little makeup, and her silver hair lay in thick waves to her shoulders.

"And my aunt Justine, my mother's sister."

"Hiya, Ford." Justine was a slightly younger version of Joanne, but her hair was dark brown.

"Hi, you're Joey's mother? He's a great guy, and Teresa is so nice."

Her face brightened. "She's a doll. And Joey's a good kid."

"How long are you gonna stay?" Joanne asked.

"Only until Tuesday. Then it's back to the office for me."

"Siddown, Ford." She patted the empty chair beside her. "Let's talk awhile. Nico's gotta go help. We'll keep Ford company."

"That's what I'm afraid of," Nico muttered. "Don't bombard him with questions, please." He kissed his mother and aunt. "I'll bring you somethin' to eat. You want that eggplant parm? Or something lighter?"

Without giving him a chance to respond, Joanne spoke up. "Bring him a little something of everything to taste. We got ziti Siciliana with the eggplant inside. That's a special tonight. He needs to know what good food is. And some more garlic bread."

"I'm good with anything. I know it's all delicious. I haven't stopped thinking of the meal I had here. Nothing tasted good after that."

"That's 'cause it's made with love," Joanne stated, and Nico sighed like a martyr.

"It's okay," Ford reassured him. "I'll eat whatever you bring."

Nico hurried off, and Ford was left with the two women staring at him. He prepared himself for the barrage of questions he was certain was coming.

"So…you met Nico on his bus route?" Joanne began.

"Yes. I'd left my wallet on the seat, and luckily, he found it. He returned it, and later that night I saw him at a bar and we talked some more."

Her gaze sharpened. "You're older than him. Closer to my age, I'm thinkin'."

Ouch. Ford hadn't considered that perspective. "I'm forty-two." He held his breath, wondering if she'd tell him he was too old for her son.

"That's fourteen years older than Nico. Maybe that's a good thing." She eyed him speculatively. "Nico needs someone steady, not these guys who only like him because he's good-lookin'. He's got ambition, you know? My boy's got a head on his shoulders."

"I agree. He's smart and determined. I'm sure he'll do well no matter what he chooses to do."

"But you're livin' there, in Florida. How do you think that's gonna work with you two?"

Seemed like Joanne had him and Nico in a relationship, but the two of them hadn't discussed it yet. Ford wasn't sure how to answer, but the truth had always worked, so he said, "We haven't really talked about that. We're still getting to know each other."

Nico brought over plates of calamari with dipping sauce, garlic bread, stuffed mushrooms, and antipasto—cheese, peppers, salami, and prosciutto-wrapped melon.

"You two behaving?" He fixed the women with a stare, but they merely smiled.

"We're getting to know each other."

"*Oddio!*" Nico raised his eyes to the ceiling, and touched Ford's shoulder. "Have some of this. The mains are coming soon."

"I could survive on just this. It all looks amazing."

"This? *Pah*, this is nothin'. Some nibbles for the table." Joanne arched a brow. "Obviously, you didn't grow up in an Italian home. Food is love."

Ford's hand trembled as he chose a stuffed mushroom. "No, I didn't. Definitely not."

She patted his free hand. "Well, you're here now. That's all that matters."

The rest of the evening passed quickly, and Ford was again, as he was the time before, filled to the brim with delicious pasta—three different types—as well as chicken and fish. To Joanne and Justine's dismay, he turned down dessert, but Nico backed him up.

"Ma. It's enough. We're gonna go. Joey an' Tre are gonna cash out and walk you home."

"Go, go. I know you two wanna be alone."

Ford's face grew hot, and Justine laughed. "Aww, he's blushin'. So cute. But your mother is right. Go on. We'll take care of everything."

Ford rose to his feet. "It was wonderful meeting you both, and thank you for sharing your dinner table with me."

Joanne waved him off. "Wait until you come to the house. You'll see."

He didn't know how to respond, so he kissed her cheek, then Justine's. "I hope to see you again."

With Nico by his side, they left the restaurant, and he pulled out his phone to order a car. Nico put his hand over the screen.

"Do you still want me to stay the night?"

Ford's heartbeat raced. "I want you to stay the whole weekend. If you can."

Nico's grin lit up his face. "Yeah. I'd like that. So I'm gonna need to go to my place and pick up some things. Can we go there first?"

"Of course." He was eager to see where Nico lived. Fact was, he wanted to know everything about him.

They reached the house and walked inside. Ford had never known buildings like this, houses all in a row, attached on both sides. Some, like Nico's, had apartments on the ground level.

"This is so different from where I live," he remarked,

watching Nico put clothes and accessories in an overnight bag. "They don't have houses like this."

"Yeah? I'll bet. These were built about seventy-five years ago. My grandfather bought it for peanuts. My aunt Justine lives on the next block, Joey and Tre live around the corner, and my best friends, Anthony and Jack, are a coupla blocks away." Nico finished and stood in front of him. "I'm ready."

Ford leaned in and kissed Nico. "I am too."

Nico dropped the bag, cradled his face in his hands, and deepened their kiss. Ford moaned and held on to Nico's shoulders, fearing his legs might give way. Their tongues battled, teased, and tangled, and he ran his hands over Nico's broad, hard chest.

"I wanted to do this all night," Nico's husky voice rasped in his ear, and Ford's breath hitched. "I can't wait to show you more."

"I want that." Ford gasped when Nico's fingers danced up and down the length of his straining cock. "I want it all."

"And you're gonna get it." Nico took his hand and placed it over the thick bulge in his pants. "Let's go."

Chapter
FIFTEEN

The door to the hotel room shut behind him, and Nico set his bag on the floor. Ford removed his wallet and keys from his pocket and waited. Nico advanced on him, watching those fiery golden-brown eyes spark with lust.

"Nico…I can't believe you're here." Ford sighed when Nico's hand encircled his nape.

"I can't believe it either." He pressed small kisses on Ford's stubbled cheek, trailing along his jaw and neck, inhaling his scent, memorizing it to his blood. "And we have the whole weekend together." His fingers traced the edge of Ford's waistband. "All night, I wanted to drag you out of that restaurant and do this." He cupped his crotch and squeezed, hearing Ford's breath hitch, loving how Ford shivered in his arms.

"We're in sync, then, because that's all I was thinking

of as well."

Ford helped him by kicking off his shoes and yanking off his jeans and briefs. His cock swung free, and Nico grasped him. He was hard and heavy, his length hot in his grip, and Nico couldn't resist. He sank to his knees, took the glistening head between his lips, and lapped up the sticky precome. "*Mmm.*"

"Oh fuck, Nico," Ford cried out, and Nico released him and rose to kiss him once again.

"Taste yourself. Taste how much you want me."

Ford licked his tongue and sucked. "Trust me, I know how much I want you. Inside me. On me. I can't think about anything else except you fucking me until I can't move. I want you to stick your thick cock in me and make me scream."

"Fuck me," Nico breathed. Hearing the usually calm Ford get unexpectedly dirty was the biggest fucking turn-on, and he quickly stripped naked. Ford's hungry eyes ate him up, and Nico grinned, lazily stroking his dick and running a hand over his body.

"Like what you see?" he purred, and watched as Ford finished getting undressed. He was beautiful—lightly tanned skin, long, well-muscled legs, and the prettiest fucking cock Nico had ever laid eyes on. Ford's chest rose and fell rapidly, and Nico licked his lips, savoring every inch of Ford. "I know I'm loving the sights of New York right here. C'mon."

He put a hand on Ford's shoulder, felt him tremble, and steered him to the other room, where they fell together onto the bed in a knot of legs and arms, mouths reaching, lips warm and welcoming. Their kisses grew intense. Needy. Demanding and harsh. The prod of Ford's dick hit his stomach, leaving a sticky swipe of precome.

"I'm so damn lucky." Ford gazed up at him, the absolute trust slaying Nico to his core.

"I was thinkin' the same thing." Nico brushed their lips

together, moving downward to press his mouth against the rapid flutter of Ford's pulse at his neck. He nipped the tender skin and left it reddened. He did it again and again, liking the sight of his mark on Ford, wanting to leave him covered with them.

Mine. All mine, and no one else can touch.

That thought excited him, and he flicked at Ford's nipples, biting them lightly, then harder. Ford wriggled and moaned under him.

"Nico, my God, what're you doing to me?"

"You ain't seen nothin' yet, baby." Ford's dick jerked, leaving a small sticky puddle on his belly, and Nico grinned. "You like when I call you that?"

"I like every damn thing about you. Except the fact that you're not inside me."

"So anxious. That's what I like." Nico tongued a path over Ford's belly. He buried his face in the musky scent of Ford's groin. "So perfect." He sucked two fingers and slid one past the tiny pink opening of his hole.

"Oh fuck," Ford gasped. "Nico, please."

"Soon. Gotta make you ready for me."

"I'm so fucking ready, you have no idea," Ford growled, sending a thrill through Nico. He'd never heard a man so desperate for him. So eager.

Nico kissed Ford's hole, working his tongue in and out, and hearing Ford wail, moved quicker. Faster. He held Ford's legs apart, lapping and sucking. He could've spent hours eating Ford and listening to him loving it. But he had to get in this man before he exploded.

"Condoms," Nico ground out, his dick so painfully hard, it hurt to move.

Ford groaned. "Oh God, I left them in my suitcase. It's in the closet."

Nico had to wait and take a breath. "I'll get them." He left the bed and found the stuff he needed. Ford watched him with lust-filled eyes, and Nico had the condom on and slicked up in seconds flat. "I'll go slow."

Ford nodded, and Nico watched his face as he pushed into Ford's willing body, inch by inch. Ford took him in, his passage sucking him deep until he was fully seated. "Oh God, you're so fucking tight and hot and everything. Fuck, I need to move. I have to…" Nico thrust deep, and Ford's eyes grew wide.

"God, Nico. I'm so full of you." Ford clutched his shoulders, digging his fingers in while locking his legs around his waist, sending Nico farther into him. "Oh, oh…"

"Yeah, that's it." Nico rolled his hips, the walls of Ford's ass creating the most perfect friction. "Baby, you're fucking amazing." He buried his face in Ford's neck, biting and sucking, and Ford writhed under him, hand working his dick. "That's right," Nico urged. "Come for me. On me. Spread it all over us. I'll lick it off."

"*Nicooo.*" Ford arched and stiffened, then came, shooting over his hand and both their bellies. Nico was enthralled— Ford's eyes shot bright, golden fireworks, and his face flushed pink. He gasped and shuddered to completion.

Lost in the beauty of Ford's orgasm, Nico found his throbbing cock squeezed, and he had no time to breathe— his own climax slammed into him. Nico blew apart and collapsed on a shaking Ford.

Boneless and drifting, he lay on Ford, sated beyond belief, his mind fuzzy. When he finally regained the ability to put two brain cells together, Ford was holding him, kissing his hair, his face, his neck. Nico could easily stay like this forever.

"Am I awake or dreaming? Not that I care."

Ford's smile curved against his cheek. "I think we're awake."

Still half-erect, Nico shifted, and Ford's breath stilled. "Does that feel good or bad?"

"I don't think anything you could do to me would feel bad."

He slipped out of Ford, and after getting rid of the condom, slid next to him and slung an arm around his neck, rolling Ford so he lay on top. He kissed Ford. "That was fucking amazing. You"—he kissed Ford again—"are fucking amazing."

Ford's lashes lowered, hiding his beautiful eyes. "No one's ever said that to me. I never…sex was never like that."

"Yeah? Tell me what it felt like with me." Nico wasn't used to pillow talk, but it was warm and sweet lying beside Ford, and he wanted to prolong the afterglow.

"Like you owned me. Every piece of me. And I was happy to give it all to you."

Nico's dick twitched at Ford's words. "You like when I take over?"

Ford blushed. "It's more than that. It's not easy to explain."

Nico ran his nose down Ford's cheek. "I can wait."

Ford settled in closer. "With my ex, he was always in charge. He decided when we had sex, and I thought I had to do whatever he wanted to keep him. I guess in the back of my mind, I was always afraid he would leave me."

"Why?"

Ford's gaze shifted away, his body tense. "Because he knew where I came from. The poverty and ugliness. He'd tease me about how he rescued me—like a damn pound puppy. I never felt good enough."

Nico froze. "Did he hurt you?"

"No. Never. Not physically, at least. Mentally, he'd play games, asking me if I thought other guys were hot or if I'd ever want to fuck them. He'd tell me it was all a game, but I didn't think it was funny. I loved him."

"When you're with someone, you don't want nobody else. Even to think about. That's cheating," Nico said firmly.

"I agree. I know there are poly couples, and if that's what they want, that's great, but it's not for me."

He pulled Ford closer, as if by holding him tight he could squeeze out all the hurt from his body. "Me neither. More power to them, and live and let live, ya know? But I'm not about to share you with nobody."

Ford shivered. "That's what I've always wanted. Someone who's into me. Only me. I loved everything we did here tonight."

"Yeah?" Nico stroked Ford's cheek with his thumb and traced his slightly swollen lips. "I did too. And we got all night."

Ford smiled. "I know."

Nico opened his eyes. The clock by the bed read 3:42. An ugly hour. Ford, naked, lay sleeping beside him, and Nico's dick swelled. Damn, he wanted him again. They'd kissed and cuddled before falling asleep holding each other.

Trying hard not to disturb Ford, he slid out of bed and used the bathroom. On his return, he burrowed under the covers and closed his eyes.

"Everything okay?"

Nico rolled to his side. "Yeah." Ford's foot stroked up his leg, sending a ripple of desire through him. He shifted closer. "And getting better, I'm thinking."

Ford reached out. "I want you."

"You got me." Nico settled his mouth over Ford's, his tongue pushing past Ford's lips. Ford sucked it eagerly. Greedy for more, Nico reached and found Ford open for him. He stuck one finger inside, then another, and Ford gasped, moving his hips to the rhythm Nico set.

"Yeah, baby, that's it. You like this, don't you?"

"So good." Ford took their shafts in hand, and Nico fingered him deep, rubbing his tender spot.

"Jesus," Ford cried out, his hand moving rapid-fire on their cocks. Those long fingers stroked him hard and fast until they both exploded, their harsh cries splitting the night.

"*Mmm.*" Nico sighed. "Now I think I can get back to sleep."

"Happy to have helped," Ford replied and pressed a soft kiss to his cheek. "I like waking up and having you here."

"Me too," Nico whispered, wishing it would always be like this. Knowing it couldn't.

At seven thirty that morning they had breakfast in the room and showered together, Ford gave him a spectacular blowjob, and Nico hoped the people next door didn't hear his begging and pleading. Nico offered to return the favor, but Ford noticed the time and said Nico would be late.

"Make it up to me tonight."

Nico dressed quickly. "I will." He hesitated. "But I gotta work at the restaurant later. I'm sorry, I wish—"

"Hey"—Ford silenced him with a lingering kiss—"I know, and I already said it's fine. I came here spontaneously, so I'll take what I can get. And anyway, I like your family. Don't apologize for them. I appreciate how much they love you." His smile was sweet yet sad, and Nico disliked the sadness suddenly darkening Ford's bright eyes.

"Just warning you that it's gonna be more of the same as yesterday. Maybe worse."

"It's no big deal." Ford shrugged. "Better to have someone who cares about you than no one at all. Have you decided what you plan to do about your father?"

"No. I mean, my mother and I talked it out, but I can't imagine ringing his bell and saying, 'Surprise. Guess who?' " The idea made him sick to his stomach.

Ford frowned. "I don't think that would be wise, no,

but there are other ways to go about it."

"Yeah, well, I'm not ready to think about it yet." The whole situation sent him to a place he didn't want to visit. Not with Ford here for such a short time. He wanted to drown in physical pleasure and leave his painful reality behind.

"I understand, and I'm not trying to push you into anything."

"I know. It's okay." He gave Ford a quick uptick of his lips so he wouldn't think he was angry. It was the best he could manage.

He picked up his phone and checked for messages as he slipped on his shoes. One in particular had him snickering. There was still time before he had to check in for work.

"Hey, c'mere." He put an arm around Ford. "Just in case you were wondering how my family felt about you." Nico showed Ford his mother's message.

It was nice of Ford to spend his time with us. He's very polite and good-looking. I think he's a winner.

"A winner, huh?" Ford preened, eyes twinkling. "I guess that makes you my prize." He kissed Nico, who briefly considered saying to hell with the job and calling in sick. He groaned.

"I gotta go. I'll be back about five."

With regret, he brushed his lips to Ford's and left the suite. His phone buzzed, and it was Anthony. He talked as he walked past the crowds. "Yo, what's up? I'm working— gotta go pick up my stuff at the office."

"Yeah? Working, huh? Bet you were working it last night too." Anthony cackled. "I heard your Florida man was in town."

Nico sighed. "Joey's got a big mouth. Yeah. He's here. And?"

"And? What the fuck, and? You tell me. You two gettin' serious or what?"

"He lives in Florida. Remember?" Nico slowed as he

approached the building where the bus company office was located.

"Yeah, but things can change. Maybe you'll move down there."

"You're kiddin', right? My mom ain't leaving Brooklyn, and I can't leave her. And he's got a big practice, so don't say he's gonna be movin' up here for me." Even as he spoke, a pang hit his heart, which he immediately dismissed. "We're just havin' fun."

"Everyone liked him," Anthony said softly, but Nico heard him over the sounds of the crowds in Times Square.

And despite his words, Nico wanted to hear and tried to sound casual. "Oh, yeah?"

"Uh-huh. Joey said he's really into you. Tre, of course, is in love with him and thinks he's the one."

Nico snorted. "Okay, sure, whatever."

"Nah, seriously. Joey said his mom and yours were talkin' about it when he walked them home after they closed the restaurant. They thought he was a great guy, sweet, and your mom said he's the type she always wanted for you."

"Glad everyone's got an opinion about my love life," Nico groused.

"Maybe 'cause you finally got one to talk about," Anthony shot back. "Just don't get in your head about nothin'. He likes you and you like him. Go with it. You got a right to be happy, ya know?"

Nico knew what he was talking about but chose to ignore it. "You and Sergio still hot 'n heavy?"

"Yeah, 'course."

"And you like living with him?" It was hard to fathom a player like Anthony settling down with anyone. He'd always been about the score, and after a few weeks, would grow tired of the guy and moved on.

"Yeah. It's been great. There's somethin' about wakin' up with the person you're into that's special. You'll see."

Recalling how it had been with Ford that morning, Nico had an inkling of what Anthony meant and couldn't disagree. He'd stayed with guys overnight, but in the morning it was "See ya" and out the door. Fun but forgettable. Not with Ford. There was so much more about him he wanted to discover.

"I gotta go. Talk to you later."

"Me 'n Sergio are gonna come by the restaurant for dinner. Maybe we can all go out after. I'll see what Jack's up to. Or who he's into, more like it."

"Maybe," he hedged. With Ford and him having only a couple of days to spend together, Nico wanted as much alone time with the man as possible. And he didn't know how Ford would feel about it. But he did miss hanging out with his friends. "Catch you later."

Being the Sunday of Labor Day weekend, the tours were all full, and the time flew. By five o'clock, his wallet was bursting with tip money. He should've been exhausted, yet thinking of another night with Ford, anticipation ran hot and heavy through his veins. Upon his return to the hotel suite, he lay on the bed and tossed the bills into the air above him, laughing as they fluttered down. Ford grinned.

"A good day, I'm gathering?"

"Yeah. Over two hundred bucks. Buses were packed." He yawned. Ford sat next to him and massaged his shoulders. Nico groaned with pleasure.

"Oh God, that feels amazing."

Ford's mouth hovered by his. "I've been told I have very gifted hands."

"Don't do this when we can't get naked," Nico whined. "I gotta go to the restaurant."

A warm chuckle sounded in his ear, and Ford tickled the lobe with the tip of his tongue, then sucked it. "You have a lot to make up for." Ford continued to press light kisses on his ear and neck, and Nico gave himself a moment to sink into pleasure. "I spent the whole day thinking about you. And what happened last night."

"Yeah?" Hearing Ford's confession made him happy. "Me too. I'm sorry it can't be just the two of us tonight."

"I don't mind."

God, he'd found the most understanding man alive.

He changed into jeans and a T-shirt, and again they were off on the train to Brooklyn. This time there were no seats, and they held on to a pole, pressed up together by the crowd. Not a bad thing.

"My friend Anthony and his boyfriend are gonna be there too. Anthony wanted to go out after and hang out, but I didn't give him a yes or no without talkin' to you first."

The train screeched to a halt, discharged passengers, and took more on. Ford waited to respond until they started moving.

"I'll do whatever you want. Obviously, I want to be alone with you, but if you want to spend time with them, I'm fine with it. I'd like to meet your friends."

"You kinda already have." The train jerked, pushing him against Ford, who caught him and held on to him even after his balance had steadied. Nico didn't mind.

"I did?" Ford's brows drew together.

"Yeah. That first time at Stonewall. They were the couple sucking each other's faces off."

Ford turned red. "Oh, yeah. They were, uh, into each other."

"That came later on at home." Nico cackled, and Ford put a hand over his eyes.

"Oh, Jesus."

"Come on, Doc. You know that was a good one."

They reached their stop, and when they entered the restaurant, his entire family and group of friends were there.

"There they are," Joey called out, waving his hand. "Ford, siddown over here. There's a bowl of pasta with your name on it." Joey indicated a table in the back, where Nico's mother, Aunt Justine, along with Anthony and Sergio all sat. Jack was there as well, but alone.

Nico nudged Ford's shoulder. "Go ahead. I'll check in. Be strong."

He watched as everyone greeted Ford, who first said hello to his mother and aunt before his friends. Nico liked that he showed respect.

Joey found him in the kitchen. "Looking good, huh? Anthony said he wanted to go out after, but you weren't sure."

"I mean, he's only here a coupla days. You think I wanna hang out with you jokers or what?" Nico picked up an order. "How about you stop obsessing over my love life and we just fuckin' work?"

"Nah, this is much more fun."

Joey took several plates and followed him to a party of six. After serving their meals, Nico took more orders and returned to his family's table.

"You okay?" he leaned in to whisper to Ford and was caught up in his scent—a mixture of his light cologne and warm skin that drove Nico wild.

"I'm fine. We're discussing which sunscreens are best."

Nico glared at the group. "You people really makin' him work on his vacation? Come on, guys."

"He said he don't mind," Anthony called out from across the table. "I asked 'cause Sergio burns so easy."

"I'm fine with it," Ford reassured him. "And I told Anthony we'll go out with them after for a drink."

"Are you sure?" Nico frowned at the thought of Anthony pushing Ford to go out.

"Absolutely. I don't mind spending time with your friends, because I get to be with you. And when it comes down to it, being with you is all that matters."

Nico blinked. *Damn.* When Ford said things like that,

it made him believe what they were doing was more than fooling around until the lust fizzled out. Was it possible this could be something more?

Chapter SIXTEEN

"Welcome to Maxie's." Nico held open the door to the bar. "Not sure Frank can make you a martini the way you like it, but he'll try."

"I'm fine with beer." He didn't want Nico to think he couldn't fit in with everyone else. It was almost like when he first met Lenny and had to learn to mingle with the beautiful people. Only now, with Nico, there was no pretending. He liked these funny, loving people who didn't play games and laid it on the line. With Lenny's friends, he'd been forced to listen to which events they'd attended, malicious gossip about people only moments ago they'd introduced as friends, and golf scores, pretending he gave a damn. It was all about making Lenny happy. With Nico's friends and family, he didn't have to fake anything. He liked them and wanted them to like him.

Maxie's was a far cry from the silent spaces with tablecloths and candlelight, idle conversations, and power deals. It was a dark and sticky room with remnants of drinks spilled and lifelong friendships formed over a winning home run or an impossible catch.

It was a place Ford had never belonged to and now yearned to be part of more than anything, along with the group of warm, funny people who accepted you as one of them.

A scattering of patrons sat at the bar, a noisy group played pool, but two tables were open, so they pushed them together.

Ford nudged Nico. "I want to buy the first round."

"You don't gotta do that," he murmured, but a smile tugged up the corner of his lips and his face glowed with affection.

"I know."

Nico rubbed his back. "Hey, everyone. Ford's buying. What're you all having?"

"Thanks, Ford."

"Dude, thanks."

He and Nico took their orders and ambled up to the bar, where they were greeted by a silver-haired man with twinkling eyes. "Nico, whassup? Haven't seen you in a while."

"Been workin', Frank. Want you to meet my friend Ford. He's from Florida."

"Florida? I been to Naples years ago. Nice beaches."

"They are some of the prettiest. I live in Fort Lauderdale."

Nico gave him all the orders, and Frank talked while he poured. "I bet you all laugh at us in the winter when we're freezin' our asses off. Whatcha do for a livin', Ford?"

"I'm a doctor. A dermatologist."

Frank slid two bottles across the bar. "A derma—what?"

Nico snorted. "Skin, Frank. Ford is a skin doctor."

Frank's brows rose high. "No shit? Lemme ask you somethin'. I got this spot on my shoulder—"

Before Ford could answer, Nico cut him off. "Frank. Ford didn't come here to work or give free advice."

He put a hand on Nico's shoulder. "Hey. I don't mind. It's okay. Frank, has it been bothering you?"

Frank nodded. "It's gotten a little bigger, and I dunno, it kinda itches."

Ford tensed, and forgetting everything, else, leaned in closer. "Would you mind showing it to me?"

"Ford—" Nico began, but he held his hand up.

"No, Nico. I'm serious." Everything else fell to the wayside. "Frank? Show me?"

While Nico delivered the drinks to the table, Frank pulled down the edge of his T-shirt, revealing his shoulder and a large brown spot. To Ford's trained eye, it appeared slightly raised and with jagged edges. Not a good sign, but he didn't want to sound any alarms.

"I think you should see a doctor and have a biopsy."

Frank's eyes grew wide. "Biopsy? What're you talkin' about? It's just one of them moles."

"Maybe, but it could be melanoma, which is very dangerous if left untreated."

"Mela—what? This is nuts. It's probably nothin'. And I don't got a doctor. No health insurance, ya know? I gotta wait until I'm sixty-five for Medicare." He released his shirt. "It'll be fine. I'm sure it's nothin'."

"Frank, I really don't think you should wait." Ford tried not to be an alarmist, but dammit, he was worried.

A customer called to Frank, and he shrugged. "Gotta go."

Nico returned to his side while he struggled not to run after Frank and try to shake some sense into him.

"Ford? What's wrong? You look upset."

He rubbed his face. "I am. I'm not happy that Frank is brushing this off. It could be deadly. Melanoma isn't something to fool around with. If you don't treat it, you can die."

Nico paled. "Shit. But what can he do? He doesn't have that kinda money to pay for operations and stuff like that. Dammit." Nico peered over his shoulder at Frank. "He's family, you know? Anthony's uncle. Always been there for us."

Ford deliberated. "I might have something, but it'll have to wait until tomorrow. There's nothing we can do about it now."

"Okay. And thanks for treating everyone."

"Being with you is a treat for me. I'm happy to do it."

They rejoined the group, and Anthony raised his bottle. "To new friends. And new beginnings."

Ford smiled. "I'll drink to that."

Nico slid his hand up Ford's thigh, and his breath hitched. "What're you doing?" he whispered, lips against his beer bottle.

"What do you want me to do?" Nico's fingers teased along the inside of his leg, and Ford ached with restrained pleasure.

"Not here. Not in front of everyone. I won't be able to hide what you do to me."

Nico withdrew his hand. "*Mmm*. I can't wait to get you alone."

"What're you two whispering over there?" Joey called out.

"Nothin'," Nico countered.

"I call bullshit. Not with that shit-eating grin Nico's tryin' to hide."

Ford's cheeks burned. Thank God the bar was dark.

"Stop teasin'. You're embarrassing Ford." Teresa shoved Joey. "I'm so happy you're here again, Ford. When do you leave?"

"Tuesday."

"Not Monday?"

"No. I don't work on Tuesdays."

"So you get an extra night together."

He glanced at Nico. "That's my plan."

Nico's mouth drooped. "I gotta work." He perked up. "But we can have dinner in the city."

"I'd love that." Ford fell into the blue of Nico's eyes, forgetting they were surrounded by people.

Nico took a sip of his Scotch. "I don't wanna think about you leaving right now," he murmured.

"Me neither."

Joey got them a second round, and Ford excused himself to use the restroom. On his return, he paused to watch the pool game going on. The guys were decent but not great, and when one of them missed, Ford made a face that didn't go over well with the crew playing because of one of them sneered. "You got somethin' to say?"

"Not after that shot," Ford told him. "It said it all."

"Oh, damn, Jimmy. He called you out." A heavily tattooed guy dressed all in black snickered.

"You think you can do better than me, old man?" The lug called Jimmy went nose to nose with him, and from the corner of his eye he spotted Anthony, Joey, and Nico all rising to their feet, but he merely smiled.

"Yeah. I do."

Jimmy's friends jeered. "Man, this dude don't know who he's talkin' to. Jimmy's the best in Bay Ridge, probably all of Brooklyn."

Jimmy folded his arms. "You sure you don't wanna think about it? Wouldn't wanna make you look like an ass in front of all your friends."

"I'll take that chance." This was getting fun.

Nico stepped up. "Ford, maybe—"

"It's fine." He winked, and Nico, face filled with surprise, whispered to all the others who had circled them.

In high school, he'd had a job delivering cases of beer and soda to a pool hall. Was it illegal? Yeah, because he wasn't twenty-one, but people tended to look the other way in that business. The bar owner, whose family life wasn't much different from his own, took a liking to him and taught him all he learned when he was on the professional pool circuit.

"Rack 'em," Ford ordered. He found a cue he liked, chalked the tip, and leaned over the table. "Nine ball," he called out, and took the shot.

He stood back, and with satisfaction watched six balls roll into the pockets while hearing the chatter behind him.

"What the fuck?"

"Motherfucker played you, Jimmy."

"Son of a bitch, he's a ringer." Jimmy smacked his cue on the table. "You fucking played me."

Ford shrugged. "You asked if I could do better than you, and I did. Facts speak louder than words." He walked away, and his friends—as he now considered them—crowded around him.

"Ford, that was the bomb," Joey crowed.

"Where'd you learn to play like that?" Anthony demanded. "That's some pro-level shit."

It was Nico who shocked him the most, by kissing him in front of everyone. "You were awesome." He lowered his voice. "And your ass looked amazing when you bent over that table."

"And there he goes." Jack snickered. "Another one's bit the dust."

They returned to their seats, where Nico asked Jack, "What're you talking about?"

"You and Ford. All cutesy and coupled up. First Joey and Tre, Anthony and Sergio."

"Shut up," Nico snapped, to Ford's surprise. There was no joking behind his words.

"Why? You think I don't see it? Thought you learned your lesson with the last one."

"Jack, what the hell?" Seated next to Jack, Teresa pushed his shoulder. "Stop it."

"Why? 'Cause you like this one? Give it some time. I thought you'd never fall for a guy like this again, but looks like that ship has sailed."

"We're not—" Nico began but stopped. "What the fuck do I need to explain anything to you for?" He downed his Scotch.

"I ain't gonna listen to your bullshit when it's over." Jack finished his beer and tossed out a twenty. "Guess you do like the fancy clothes and nice restaurants." He rose to his feet. "Not to mention the big bank accounts."

Ford glanced at each of Nico's friends, but they all avoided his eyes. What just happened? Big bank accounts? What was Jack insinuating?

An uncomfortable silence descended on the table, and Ford met Teresa's eyes. She smiled. "That was a great shot, Ford. I never learned to play pool. Maybe you can teach me one day."

He appreciated her attempt to alleviate the tension. "Sure. I'd love to."

"We gotta go," Nico announced.

"We do?" Surprised at the sudden shift of events, Nico wore an expression he hadn't seen before. One etched in sharp, deep lines of anger and pain.

"Please?" Nico whispered, sounding so broken that Ford's heart hurt.

"Thanks, everyone. I hope to see you soon."

Everyone murmured farewells but didn't try and stop them.

Ford called for a car, and they left, but he made a mental note to make a phone call to Bruce Sandler about Frank.

Nico said nothing on the ride into the city. Once inside

his suite, Ford called room service and ordered them drinks and some crackers and cheese.

"That's gonna cost a fortune," Nico muttered, staring out the window.

"I don't care." He slipped his arms around Nico's waist. "What happened back there with Jack? Talk to me, please?"

Nico pulled away from him and paced the room. Ford let him, understanding that whatever it was, it had been eating away at his soul for a while. At the knock on the door, he answered, and room service wheeled in their drinks and a small charcuterie board. Ford picked up Nico's Scotch and handed it to him as he passed by.

"A double?" He took a sip.

"If you need the bottle, that can be arranged too." Ford plucked the drink out of his hand. "But I'd rather you tell me what's going on in your head." He cupped Nico's cheek. "Or is it your heart?"

Nico's gaze fell to the floor, those thick dark lashes hiding his beautiful eyes, and Ford led him to the sofa. They sat, and still holding Nico's hand, he waited.

"The year I turned twenty-one, I got a summer job as a cabana boy on the beach at one of the country clubs on Long Island. I'd heard the tips were great. And, man, they were right."

"You were the kid who'd bring out the chairs and towels for people?"

"Yeah. Plus drinks and food. They'd give me money for sunscreen if they ran out. Every club along the beach on the South Shore has them."

"Okay."

"That summer I met this guy, Payson, and he used to slip me his number whenever he gave me my tip. And it was a big tip—fifty or a hundred bucks each day."

Impressed, Ford nodded. "That could add up to a lot of money."

"It did. And he kept asking me to meet him in the city at his apartment. He'd bring me little gifts—cologne, small leather stuff, expensive bathing suits. After a few weeks, I figured why not? The country club didn't have any strict rules, and trust me, I saw lots of the ladies spend extracurricular time with cabana guys."

"So you had a summer fling. Can't say I blame him."

Nico's smile came and went. "It started in the summer, but it continued. Soon I was seeing him in his apartment in Tribeca—he had a huge penthouse. He took me to his house in the Hamptons during the winter, where we'd be snowed in, but I didn't care."

"You fell in love with him," Ford surmised.

Nico lifted a shoulder. "Yeah, well, everything was great until I started asking him why we never went out to dinner, or anywhere in the city. He was always at these events but never asked me to go with him."

Ford understood now why it had meant so much to Nico to come to The Pierre. It showed Nico he was valued, seen, and appreciated.

Nico continued. "He'd say he wanted to keep me to himself, or that I'd be bored."

"All true," Ford admitted. "Still not a reason to keep your lover sequestered." He ran his knuckles down Nico's cheek. "Just so you know, I was thrilled to have you with me."

Nico's face showed enormous strain. "Yeah." He shrugged. "One night, I made such a stink about ordering in dinner again that he took me out, I don't even remember where. On our way from the car to his building, he met a couple he knew from work."

"What was his job?"

"Hedge-fund manager."

Made sense. "Money to burn, huh?"

"You know it." Nico sighed. "Can I have some of that drink now?" Ford reached over and handed him the tumbler.

Nico took a sip. "Anyways, Payson tried to hurry me inside the building, but they waylaid him, and he introduced me as his personal assistant."

Ford winced. "And did you say anything to him?"

"Yeah. I asked him what the fuck was going on. Why wouldn't he tell them I was his boyfriend?" He stopped to take another drink. "He laughed at me and said, 'Boyfriend? I'm the manager of a multibillion-dollar hedge fund at the age of thirty-five. Do you think I'm going to date a twenty-one-year-old cabana boy? Come on. It was a summer thing that went on longer than I expected because let's face it"—Nico's voice broke—"you give great head and you're a great fuck, but that's it.' "

Seeing how Nico's hand trembled, Ford took his glass away and held him close. "Nico, Nico. I'm so sorry. What a bastard. What a total piece-of-shit human."

Nico's lips touched his neck. "I walked away and never saw him again."

"I'd hope not." Ford stroked his back. "He hurt you badly. Someone like that doesn't deserve a man like you." He rested his cheek to Nico's. "And I don't blame you for not trusting people. Jack was dead wrong to talk to you like that. He owes you an apology."

"He won't. Jack sees things in black and white. He didn't like Payson and said I was stupid to think a guy like Payson could want someone like me for anything else but sex. He was right."

That didn't sit right with Ford. "I'm sorry, but he was wrong. Those potshots at you, saying you're interested in me for my money and what comes with it—"

Wild-eyed, Nico grabbed his shoulders. "That's not true. I swear I don't—"

"Shh." Ford cut off Nico's rush of words with a kiss. "I know you're not like that. And I'm not like Payson either, who only wanted to hide you away. Know what I want?"

Nico's lips finally kicked up in a true smile. "I might have an idea."

"Besides that." Ford chuckled and kissed him. "I want to show you off and let people wonder how someone like me got so goddamn lucky to have a guy like you. I know I'm older than you and we hardly know each other, but I can't stop thinking about you—I haven't since we met."

"You don't have to say that to make me feel better." Nico's subdued expression made him sad.

"I wouldn't, and I'm not. I hate that you still don't understand how much you're worth, that this man mangled your self-esteem to the point where you don't think someone might actually care for you because of who you are."

"*I* don't even know who the hell I am," Nico blurted out. "I'm gonna be twenty-nine and don't have a career, just a job. I live in the basement of the house I grew up in. I thought I'd have more by now."

"Where's it written there's a time frame for success? And as I see it, you *are* a success. You have wonderful friends who will always be there for you. A mother who loves you and the potential to have a father. You're part of a thriving family business that has an impact on the community. You have drive and ambition to do more and be better. You're not complacent—you're hungry. And that's a good thing."

"Thanks, but if all that's true, why don't I feel better?"

Nico's frustration needed to be kicked to the curb.

"How about I make you feel better and tell you what I feel about you?" Ford pushed him down until he lay flat under him. "I came this weekend because I missed your smile and that funny accent, especially when you say *coffee*." Nico's mouth opened in outrage, and Ford had to kiss it closed.

"*Mmm*, I guess I can forgive you for that slur." Nico kissed him back, and Ford's head spun with the desire pounding through his blood.

"I feel appreciated when I'm with you. I feel like I belong, and I'm not that poor kid from the trailer park, pretending to fit in." He cupped Nico's face. "You don't pretend to be anyone but who you are, and I admire that." He kissed Nico's cheek. "If you haven't figured it out yet, I'm crazy about you, Nico Andretti, and I don't care about anything except how I feel when I'm with you. To me, that's all that matters."

Chapter SEVENTEEN

"You are?" Nico hadn't known Ford all that long or well, but one thing he knew was that the man chose his words carefully.

Ford kissed Nico slowly as he tugged his shirt up and over his head. "I am. And I want to keep seeing you after I leave. We'll figure it out, but right now I want to make love to you." Ford kissed his throat, his shoulders, and sucked at his nipples until Nico thought they'd burst into flames. "With you."

"Touch me," Nico begged, his hands at his waistband, but Ford pushed them away.

"I plan to." Ford popped the tab of his jeans and undid the zipper. With the pressure off his dick, Nico sighed with pleasure. "Let me show you how you deserve to be treated." He mouthed the outline of his cock through the thin material, and Nico pushed his jeans and briefs past his knees to give him access. But Ford stood, taking his time getting naked as well. As he bent over to remove his clothes, Nico drank in the sight of his tight, round ass, muscled abs, and thick cock.

"Suck me," Nico begged. "I've been thinkin' of you on my dick all day."

"Funny, I've been thinking the same thing." Ford pulled Nico's clothes off, and he lay naked, his dick thick and hard and aching. Those lion-like amber eyes narrowed like a predator's, and Nico ached with want. Ford lowered his head and licked the precome gathered at the slit. Late-night stubble rubbed along his throbbing length, and Nico groaned.

"Oh, yeah. Please. Do it." He watched Ford take him into his warm, wet mouth. The flat of his tongue passed over the head of his dick, and Ford tightened his lips around his shaft and sucked. Nico's toes curled and spots danced in front of his eyes. When his vision cleared, the sight of Ford's golden-brown head bobbing on his cock was the epitome of his nightly erotic fantasies. Ford's tongue fluttered and swirled, and then he went deep, taking him to the back of his throat.

Thunder boomed in his head, and Nico panted and gasped for air. His legs twitched and he shivered from head to toe.

"Uhhhh, fuck," Nico rasped and came, erupting down Ford's throat. Ford swallowed it all and sat up with a broad smile and glistening lips.

"I hate to tell you, but you taste better than anything I've eaten tonight."

"Yeah? Well, I think I'll keep that to myself. I don't think I'll be lettin' Joey know that." Nico grinned and held out his arm. Ford lay in the crook of his shoulder, and Nico traced the bulge of his cock. "What should I do about this, *hmm*? Seven inches of heaven."

"Anything you want," Ford whispered into his neck.

"You can have anything and everything you need from me."

"I need to touch you and prove you're real. That what's happening here is real." His fingers teased its solid length, and Ford panted, his fingers curling to a fist on Nico's chest. Over his pounding heart.

"How you make me feel—like I'm flying to the sun—is real. I can't get enough of you. The more I touch you, the more I want you. The time I'm here with you isn't long enough. I want to know everything about you. That's as real as it gets."

Those words burned bright in Nico's heart. No matter what happened between them, Nico would never think of himself as less than and undeserving of love.

He worked Ford's heavy length, and from Ford's whimpers and gasps, pinpointed the moment he'd hit his climax. Nico made sure to capture it in his memory—the pink flush over his face, full mouth open, the sheen of sweat gilding his body, and the harsh cries of his completion as he pulsed out streams of hot, sticky liquid through Nico's fingers.

With Ford gazing at him through hazy eyes, Nico licked his fingers clean. "You taste pretty damn good yourself, in case you didn't know."

"Let me see." Ford reached up and kissed him, plunging his tongue into Nico's mouth. Their tongues played a leisurely game of tease tag, and he massaged the sweet curve of Ford's ass. To him, there was nothing sexier than a man's butt, and he fondled it, his desire rising.

Ford smiled against his lips. "Oh, to be young and able to get it up again quickly."

Nico held out his hand. "Let's shower. I'm not ready for what I have in mind."

Ford raised a brow but followed him to the bathroom, where they washed and dried, then naked, slid under the covers. Nico liked that Ford cuddled up to him, throwing a leg over his and holding him close.

"You're so warm."

"That's because you make me hot," Ford rumbled in his ear.

"Corny too."

"*Mmm*. Call me anything you want, I'm good right here." He wiggled his ass.

"Yeah, you are. Let's rest up. My first tour tomorrow is at ten, so we have a little extra time in the morning."

Ford kissed his shoulder. "I already know what I want for breakfast. Spicy Italian sausage."

Nico burst out laughing. "That was so bad."

Nico awoke and stretched. He looked over at a still-sleeping Ford, and slowly reached out and touched his hair. He'd never meant it to go this far, but it hit him like a pickpocket, swift and silent, leaving him unaware he'd become a victim until it was too late. Only it wasn't his wallet that had been stolen.

It was his heart.

What was it Anthony had said to him?

"Once I met him, I didn't need no one else, 'cause he makes me feel good about myself."

With Ford, he forgot he didn't have a fat bank account and couldn't afford to buy his own apartment. He didn't wish for dinners in expensive restaurants when sharing a simple plate of pasta made even a glass of water taste delicious.

"What's wrong?" Face grave and gaze intense, Ford sat up.

And because he didn't trust his voice, Nico leaned in and kissed him, freeing all the love he'd kept locked away for years. It poured out of him, like the sweetest honey, and Ford sucked his tongue, a bee to the nectar he offered.

"I want you." Nico rolled on top of Ford. "Wanna make sure you know how much." The scent of Ford's desire rose from him, and Nico watched as his body flushed pink and his dick grew full. "Wanna eat you out and hear you scream." A stream of liquid flowed from the head of Ford's dick, and Nico grinned. "You like that, baby? Want my tongue in you?"

He leaned down and lapped up the sticky precome, sliding his tongue up and over Ford's rigid shaft. Ford opened his legs and begged.

"Please, Nico. Want you so bad."

That pretty pink hole beckoned him, and Nico dived in, starving for a taste of Ford. He buried his face between Ford's legs and stuck his tongue in, sucking.

"Ahh, oh fuck." Ford nearly leaped off the bed, but Nico held him fast and continued to pump his tongue in and out. "Nico, *Nico*." Ford's head thrashed on the pillow and his hands scrabbled at the sheets. Loving how Ford was losing himself to his lust, Nico grabbed the lube and condom, sheathed his dick, and teased Ford's rim.

"Ready for me?" he purred, and Ford groaned as he sank the wide head of his dick in. "So fucking tight and hot. So perfect." He pushed in farther, and Ford gasped and reached out, grabbing his arm.

"Harder. All the way in me."

"Baby, I'm gonna go so far into you, I'm never gonna be able to leave without taking a piece of you with me." Nico thrust, and Ford hissed.

"Oh, fuck. Take it. Take everything."

Nico dragged his cock out of Ford's body, then hammered in again. Ford caught his rhythm, and soon they were moving together. The bed squeaked, the mattress shifted, and his blood roared in his ears. Ford's mouth hung open as he gasped for air, and Nico drove in farther, the absolute raw need to give this man pleasure paramount.

"You're mine, Ford. Even if you're not here, you're mine." He bit Ford's shoulder and sucked at the mark, then covered Ford's neck with kisses, drowning in his scent. Christ, it wasn't enough to make love to him. He wanted to be part of him. Wear him like a second skin.

"Yes," Ford keened. "Only you." His hand worked his shaft, and Nico watched as he came, hot ribbons of come spraying over his belly and chest.

Hearing Ford's words, his emotions in a tangle, Nico soared and gave in to the force of nature possessing his body. As Ford lay beneath him, trembling from his own orgasm, Nico's climax rushed over him like a tornado, tearing him apart. He must've blacked out, and he came to awareness, collapsed on top of Ford, still buried deep inside him.

He moved slightly, and Ford put his arms around him. "Don't go. Not just yet. It's so perfect."

"I won't," he promised.

"I want to be able to remember our time together after I'm back home."

Nico's heart shriveled a bit. "I don't wanna think about that."

Ford kissed his hair. "I hate the thought of leaving you too."

Nico sighed because there was nothing he could do to change things. This time when he moved, Ford didn't stop him. Nico got rid of the condom, his insides doing a funny twist seeing Ford lying in bed, looking at him with a soft smile.

"I'd better take a shower and get ready."

Ford, propped up on his elbows, cocked his head. "Is everything okay? You're not still upset about last night, are you?"

He shrugged. "I can't change what happened. I'm still pissed at Jack, but he's always sayin' stupid shit."

"He should apologize. He doesn't know what the hell he's talking about." Ford left the bed. "I meant what I said." He leaned in and kissed Nico. "I'm crazy about you. And for you. Everything will be all right."

Would it, though?

Nico shrugged. "Yeah. I know."

Accepting his answer, Ford checked the room-service menu. "I'll order breakfast while you shower."

"Okay. Get me anything. I'm fine with eggs, bacon, fruit…whatever you want."

He entered the bathroom and turned on the taps. Was it foolish to wish he didn't have to wash away Ford's smell from his body? He laughed. "Idiot. Don't go actin' like some lovesick jerk." Ford had changed from the man he'd first met. He'd become more self-assured, and that was a fucking turn-on. Nico liked him a little bossy and tough. But if it made Ford more attractive to him, other guys would see it too and make a move. Older guys who didn't have to work seventy hours a week. Men who didn't live paycheck to paycheck.

Would Ford grow tired of their differences and slowly slip away?

"Fuck it. Just enjoy what you got goin' on. You knew the score when you started this."

After giving himself a pep talk, he stood under the spray, and after he finished and came out of the bathroom, Ford was in one of the hotel robes, looking at his phone. Their eyes met, and his face lit up.

"I'd better go shower too. You're all clean and gorgeous, and I'm still a mess."

Nico caught his arm as he passed by. "You look fucking perfect to me." And he was, even with a face rubbed red from beard burn, bedhead, and his neck and chest littered with marks. His marks. Nico's dick swelled at the thought of Ford belonging to him. And him being Ford's man.

Ford's eyes smoldered. "Don't start, or room service is going to walk in on us and get an eyeful."

Nico kissed him slowly, his bones melting at the push of Ford's hot, slick tongue. "I wouldn't care. They'd be jealous of me getting to have you."

"You do have me. All of me. You know that, right?" Ford captured his face between both hands. "I'm not leaving you just because I'm going home." Another kiss. "You've become very special to me."

Joy burst through him, but he could only hold on to Ford and wish he never had to let him go.

With one last kiss, Ford retreated to the bathroom, and Nico heard the shower turn on. After getting dressed, he checked his phone and saw several messages from his friends.

First Anthony: *Jack's a dick. Don't pay attention to him.*

Then Joey: *Fuck what Jack says. Ford isn't Prickface. He's into you, and it's not fake. Tre says the same thing, and you know she's always right. She loves Ford.*

Nico bit his lip. "She's not the only one," he muttered to himself, safe in the knowledge that Ford was in the shower and couldn't hear him. *Love.* He rolled the word around on his tongue. Foreign yet so right when connected to Ford.

He scrolled to the next message.

Finally, at four thirty in the morning, a text from Jack: *Sorry.*

Nico blinked. "*Sorry?* What the fuck kind of shit is that?" he fumed.

At the knock on the door, he answered it, and a young guy in a white shirt and black pants with the name tag *Eduardo* pushed in the cart.

"All good, sir?"

"Yeah, thanks." He reached for his wallet.

"No need. Mr. St. Claire took care of it already." Eduardo smiled. "Would you like me to clear out the cheese platter and glasses?"

Nico winced at the waste of food, but there was no eating it after it had been out all night. "Yeah, please."

"You here visiting the city for the holiday weekend?"

"No, I live here."

Was he mistaken, or did Eduardo give him a funny look? Nico caught Eduardo glancing at his bare feet.

Ford, fresh from the shower and only wearing his robe, walked into the living room. "Oh good, the food is here. I'm starving."

There was no mistaking Eduardo's wide eyes or his gaze darting from Nico to Ford. "Have a good day," he said, hustling out with the leftovers from the night before.

"Guy probably thinks I'm a hookup," Nico grumbled as he poured himself a cup of coffee, then one for Ford. "Did you see the way he stared?"

Ford took his coffee. "No, and even so, why would you care what a stranger you'll never see again thinks? We know the truth."

Without answering, Nico sat and began to eat his eggs. What the hell did he know about the truth? He'd been lied to by his mother and grandparents, and now he was lying to himself. Who was he to be head over heels for someone like Ford? He'd done it again—fallen for an unattainable man.

With a face full of questions, Ford set his coffee on the table. "Nico, what's wrong now? You're back in that weird mood from last night. Is what Jack said still bothering you?"

"I dunno." He crunched on his toast. "Will it always be like this, people thinking I'm a boy toy or that you're paying my way? I hate that shit."

"I know you do, but the reality is, who cares? Again, if this is about the waiter, you'll never see him again. The people in your life who love you, your family and friends, they know who you are, and I think—at least, I hope—they like me and know I'm not the type of person who only cares about someone's looks."

"I guess I'd feel better if I was makin' more money."

"You applied for that job, right?"

"Yeah."

Ford ate some eggs. "Let's think about this. What's stopping you from applying to other companies for management positions? Why only the one you're working for?" His smile was kind, yet he seemed intent on making a point. "Sometimes we get set in our routine and don't look outside our own four corners. See what other companies have to offer, and apply there too. You're a great asset, and any company should be proud to have you."

Nico thought about that as he ate. "Maybe you're right. I don't owe them nothin'."

"Tonight after dinner, we could go through the job listings, and I can help you apply."

Nico finished his breakfast and made a face. "That's how you wanna spend our last night together?"

Ford's eyes danced. "We have to come up for air sometimes."

Nico snickered. "True that. I'd better get a move on. What're you gonna do today?"

Ford grew somber. "I know it's a holiday, but I plan to call Bruce Sandler—the dermatologist from the party at The Pierre."

"What for?"

"I want to talk to him about Frank. He can't let that spot go unchecked."

Nico frowned. "He doesn't have that kinda money. Not for what he considers a fancy doctor." He picked up his wallet and phone from the nightstand and slipped them into his pockets.

"Don't worry about it. I'll cover it for him."

Shocked, Nico stood still, his mouth open. "What?"

Ford put his arms around Nico and kissed him. "I have

more money than I know what to do with. Frank shouldn't have to worry about medical expenses. Whatever he needs, I'll pay for. I can tell Frank means a lot to you. And you mean a lot to me."

"Frank's not gonna accept charity."

Ford kissed him again. "Don't you worry. I'll make sure it's handled properly."

"That's…I dunno. You're…" Nico was at a loss for words, so he kissed Ford.

"Nico," Ford breathed, his eyes blazing fire, and settled his lips over Nico's, plunging his tongue in his mouth. They kissed as if starved for touch, even though they'd held each other all night. "If you don't leave now, you're going to be in trouble." He patted Nico's ass. "I'll keep it for later. After dinner."

Nico walked out, his head spinning.

Going to be in trouble? I already am.

Chapter EIGHTEEN

After checking his messages, Ford decided to venture out and buy Marisol and Adriana presents from the city. He headed onto Broadway, and the first thing he spotted was a tour bus. He couldn't be sure it was Nico's tour, as the company had routes going uptown and downtown, but simply knowing he was there put a smile on his face.

After a little time at M&M's New York, where he bought them cute but overpriced gifts, he wandered the streets uptown, stopping to take pictures of Rockefeller Center and Radio City Music Hall. Farther uptown, he passed by Carnegie Hall, and spotting Central Park, walked the perimeter, gazing at all the famous hotels—the Waldorf, the Plaza—and taking tons of pictures, knowing Marisol and Adriana would love to see everything.

His phone buzzed with a text, and seeing it was Nico,

his heart gave a little swoop. Ford laughed at himself for acting like a schoolkid with a crush, but that was how Nico made him feel—he was a teenager again, dreamy-eyed and unable to control his emotions.

What're you doing?

Ford took a selfie.

Guess.

You went to the park? Be careful of pickpockets.

Ford snorted.

Yes, Dad. I'm just going to have lunch.

Don't eat those dirty water dogs.

What's that?

Nico sent a rolling-eyes emoji. *Hot dog carts. If you have one, you might be in the bathroom all night. And that'll fuck up my plans for you.*

Ford tingled all over in anticipation.

I promise. What do you feel like eating tonight? I want to take you someplace special.

Your ass is pretty special. I plan to eat that. I know you like it.

Ford's breath hitched, and he darted a glance around, as if anyone could see the deliciously filthy words from Nico. He never thought he'd get turned-on by dirty talk, but after the incredible sex they'd had, Nico was opening his eyes to the kind of passion he'd been missing.

Another text popped up.

Did I shock you?

Ford hesitated for a second.

Yes, but I like it.

Yeah? You like the dirty talk? You like when I fuck you and make you scream? Shove my cock in your hole? Fill you up and split you in two?

Ford had to press his lips together to keep from panting.

Yes. Do it. All of it. Tonight.

Nico sent a devil's-horns emoji, and Ford blew out a

breath of pure frustration that he was sitting in the middle of New York City with a raging hard-on and couldn't move.

He'd worried at first that he wouldn't be sexually experienced enough for a man like Nico. He'd always thought his sex life with Lenny had been satisfying—Lenny would come to his room, kiss him, give him a blowjob and push inside him. Then Lenny would fall asleep, and after he woke up, Ford would give him a blowjob before he'd leave.

They'd started sleeping separately because Lenny had claimed he was too light a sleeper and Ford's tossing and turning woke him up. Later on, Ford figured it had all been a ruse so Lenny could come and go as he pleased without Ford noticing.

Twice-a-week sex with Nico would never be enough. Even now, after Nico had wrung out the most intense pleasure from him, Ford craved more. But, as he'd told Nico, it wasn't only the sex. He missed being with Nico, soaking in his bright spirit and joyful presence.

Finally able to leave the bench, he walked around until he found a cute place, Sarabeth's, where he ordered a salad and a club soda. While he was there, he made a reservation at Gallaghers, hoping that Nico would want a nice steak dinner. Ford had eaten at the one in Boca Raton, and it had been delicious. He wanted to make this last night with Nico special.

He ordered a cappuccino and stared into space as he sipped. Could he, somehow, make it work with Nico? He didn't mind flying up every other weekend or so, but he wanted more than stolen weekends in hotel rooms.

No use trying to figure it out on my own.

He called for the check. He needed to return to his suite and make a phone call.

By the time he entered the Knickerbocker, he was sweaty, so he showered and changed clothes. From his wallet, he took out the card Dr. Sandler had given him at the conference and placed the call.

The service picked up, and he told them it wasn't an emergency and to please connect him with the voice mail so he could leave a message. He could've used his personal cell number but didn't feel comfortable disturbing the man on a holiday weekend.

"Dr. Sandler, this is Dr. Ford St. Claire. We met at the conference in New York last month. I have something I'd like to discuss with you. Please call me at your earliest convenience."

With that done, he decided to lie down and take a nap. "I have a feeling it's going to be a very late night."

They waited at the hostess station of Gallaghers Steakhouse to be seated. Nico craned his head.

"I've heard about this restaurant. It's supposed to be one of the best steakhouses. Never thought I'd be eating here."

Ford's hand rested on Nico's nape. "You deserve the best."

Nico's eyes blazed turquoise heat. "Yeah? I got that. You."

Ford leaned in close. "You are so going to get lucky when I get you back to the hotel."

"I already am."

"Uh, gentlemen?" The sound of a throat clearing snapped him out of his lust-filled fog. The hostess waited with a knowing expression. "I have your table ready."

Holding hands, they followed her through the dining hall to a table for two in the corner. "Here you go. Enjoy your dinners."

They sat opposite each other, and Ford feasted on Nico's

gorgeous face. He would never get tired of looking at him.

"You need to stop staring at me like that," Nico murmured with a slight smile tipping up the corner of his delicious mouth.

"Like what?"

A busboy stopped by to fill their water glasses and set a basket of bread and butter between them. Nico waited for him to leave before continuing.

"Like you want to eat my face."

"Not your face." The words tumbled from Ford's lips, shocking him, and from his raised eyebrows, Nico as well.

"Yeah? You're gonna play that game with me here?"

"I'm not playing." He took a sip of water. "And what I feel is no game."

Nico flushed and lowered his gaze. Those thick, dark lashes fanned out over his cheeks.

The server appeared. "What can I get you gentlemen to drink?"

"I'll have an extra-dry martini. Nico?"

"Uh, Macallan, neat."

"Very good. Have you had a chance to look at the menu?"

"I've eaten at Gallaghers in Boca. The chilled seafood appetizer for two was delicious." He checked with Nico. "Would you like to try that?"

Nico swallowed. "Are you sure?"

"Absolutely." He nodded to the server. "Let's go with that. Is there still prime rib available? I know you run out."

"I'll check with the kitchen and put your order in now for this."

"Thanks."

Nico fidgeted until the man was out of earshot, then whispered loudly, "That appetizer is almost a hundred dollars on its own."

"I know."

Nico huffed. "I don't belong here."

"Stop that," Ford said, his voice sharp. "You belong any damn place you want to go. Understand?"

"Yeah, but—"

"No buts. We're going to eat our appetizer, and if they have the prime rib, we're going to get that with sides, and if you want dessert, we're going to get that too."

A wicked smile curved Nico's lips. "I like it when you get bossy. Turns me on."

Ford tipped his head. "I'll remember that."

Their drinks were served, and he was informed that they did have the prime rib.

"Two orders, please. Medium rare?" he asked Nico, who nodded. "With french fries and creamed spinach."

They drank and talked, Nico agreeing that it made sense to look beyond his company for opportunities.

"I did some lookin' when I was on break, and there are other jobs. What I'd really like is to go back to business school, but I can't afford it right now."

It was painful to sit and listen, knowing he had more than enough to pay for Nico's school, but that Nico would never take his money.

"I think you'd be great in marketing or advertising. You have a feel for people and understand what they like and want."

Nico thought as he ate his shrimp. "Yeah. That was gonna be what I studied, but things got knocked off course—I had to drop my plans when my mother got sick. Someday, though, I'll get that degree. My mom was so proud of me graduating from college, she'd go nuts if I got a master's."

"I know you can do it."

Their meals came, and Nico dug in with such gusto, it made Ford's heart swell. He would love to take him to Florida and walk with him on the beach, or Las Olas, window-shopping.

"What's the matter?" Nico's brows knitted. They'd

demolished almost all the food, leaving only scraps behind. "You look like you thought of somethin' you forgot to do."

"No. Just something I wish I could do but can't."

Nico leaned forward. "I know you're not thinkin' of me. 'Cause you can do me any way you want."

Ford choked on his water. "Dessert?" he managed to ask.

That dangerous smile of Nico's returned, and Ford felt a corresponding tug in his belly. He called over the server.

"Check, please."

Without even glancing at the bill, he gave over the credit card and scribbled a hefty tip. Nico had his phone out.

"Car will be here in a minute."

Nerves buzzing, he took Nico's hand, and they left the restaurant. The return ride was quick, and when they entered the dimly lit suite, Nico was all over him, his lips and hands everywhere.

"What do you want me to do?"

Ford wanted to hold him tight and whisper, *Love me*, but instead he swiftly undressed and helped Nico off with his clothes. "Lie on the bed, facedown."

Nico did, and Ford followed, aching and ready to burst out of his skin. He hovered over Nico and parted his legs. His mouth watered, and he ran his hands over the sweet curve of Nico's ass. Sighing, Nico spread himself open wider, and Ford's dick swelled as he took in the shadowed cleft. He ran his nose down it and spread him apart. With the point of his tongue, he licked across the hole, and hearing Nico grunt only spurred him on. He licked and lapped, circling the tiny opening, then sucked it again.

"Holy fuck," Nico groaned, his hips rutting into the bed. "Fuck, come on. I need it."

"Shh. Let me." Ford stuck his tongue inside Nico as far as he could. Hearing him sob, feeling his full-body tremors, Ford plunged in and out, his tongue flickering. Nico cried out and tore at the bedcovers.

"Fuck. Oh, God. Oh, Christ." His hips worked frantically.

But Ford didn't want Nico to come. He wanted Nico's cock, so he pulled out.

"No, what the hell? Ford!" Nico rolled over, and wild-eyed, pulled him close. "Why'd you stop? I was fucking close."

"Do it in me. Fill me up with your come," Ford groaned, and a feral smile broke across Nico's face. Ford lay trembling, loving how Nico's wet fingers speared him, stretching him wide.

"You hold me like a second skin. Like I'm part of you."

"You are," Ford breathed. "The best part."

Nico moved his fingers, rubbing his prostate, sending him into a frenzy. When Nico reached for the condom, he got on all fours. Nico returned and rubbed his rough cheek against his ass.

"You want it like this, baby? Want me all up in that gorgeous ass?" Nico blew a cool stream of air over the cleft, and Ford trembled.

"Yes," he choked. "Please."

Nico circled his dick on the rim, the wide head catching the nerve-rich opening, and Ford gasped and raised his hips higher.

"You like that?" Nico growled, continuing to tease him, now delving his fingers in again and again, spreading him open, hitting that spot so Ford saw stars. "Want it?"

"Fucking hell, yes," Ford cried out, uncaring how he pushed his ass into Nico's hand, greedy to be filled. "I need you, Nico. Please." He burned for this man.

Nico thrust deep, fingers digging into his hips. "Fuck, it's even better this way." Holding him by his waist, Nico hammered into him, withdrawing almost completely, then driving in, over and over. "You're fucking amazing."

Ford sighed and bit the edge of the pillow as Nico continued to pump him hard and fast.

"Oh, God. You're fucking huge. I love it." Sweat poured from his face, and he felt wild and primitive. Like they were two creatures rutting against each other. He let go and came, his unsteady legs no longer able to hold him up. He fell flat, drained yet whole. "I'm so in love with you."

Nico lay over Ford, and he thrust into his willing, boneless body and came. The pulse of Nico's dick inside his passage as it filled the condom with heat sent tremors through him. Nico kissed his neck, his cheek, his hair, and Ford turned his head to catch his mouth.

"Did you mean it?" Nico breathed, continuing to press his lips to Ford's. "What you said just before? Tell me."

"I know it's fast, but I've spent every day since we've met thinking of you. And I didn't want to leave—I couldn't—without telling you."

Nico pulled out, got rid of the condom, and faced him with an uncertain expression. "You meant it? You don't gotta say it to make me feel good."

It was painful to see the doubt in those beautiful eyes and hear the waver in his voice. Nico didn't only doubt Ford's feelings, he doubted himself, and that broke Ford's heart.

"Tell me why you don't believe me."

Nico picked at a stray thread on the bedcover and cast his eyes downward. "I dunno, Doc. Let's see. It's way too fast. You're successful, a doctor, have tons of money, and…" His expression darkened. "You wanna make me say all this?"

Ford scooted over to his side. "I'm still not seeing a reason. Nothing you've said is about who you are as a person. Because the Nico I've come to know is the most kind and giving person I've ever met. Someone who takes care of his family and friends and watches out for them. A man who works hard without complaining. A fantastic lover."

Nico's eyes softened. "I know the sex is incredible, but—"

Ford smoothly cut him off. "Yeah, it is. The best I've

ever had, and I don't lie." Nico's eyes glowed, and Ford took his hands, lacing their fingers together. "Sex and lust, no matter how exciting or intense, aren't love. Eventually the fire will burn itself out, and all you're left with are the memories of what used to be."

"Like you with your ex?"

Ford's heart lurched, but the searing pain he'd learned to live with after Lenny left him had faded, leaving him scarred and bruised but not broken.

"Yeah. He hurt me. Badly. And at the time I thought I'd never want to show my face again."

Looking confused, Nico asked, "Why? What happened? I mean, you said he cheated, which sucks, but why would you wanna hide? You didn't do nothin' wrong."

It had been so long since he'd relived the events that brought his life crashing down. But he wanted no secrets between him and Nico.

"When I met Lenny in our first year of med school, I was twenty-two and a virgin. He was charming and persuasive, and I fell for him. For lack of a better phrase, he swept me off my feet. What Lenny Nova wanted, he got."

"Like you."

Ford nodded. "I won't deny I allowed myself to be blinded by all that money, and it wasn't too hard, believe me. The fancy restaurants, the beautiful clothes, the parties I was able to attend. Because I was only too eager to forget where I came from, I shed my trailer-park life and embraced his life of luxury—the best of everything."

"Sounds like you were livin' the dream."

Ford fixed his eyes on the carpeting. "Until it turned into a nightmare." He chewed the inside of his cheek. "I'd sit with him at events and at country clubs, never speaking and feeling hugely out of place. If they discovered where I came from, I knew they'd slam the door in my face. His parents never accepted me, and I figured he probably kept me around to give them the middle finger."

"I get it. You were the wrong-side-of-the-tracks guy. Like me. We're always better, you know. The bad boys are always more fun." Nico winked at him, and a surge of love rushed over him in warm waves.

"Except I wasn't the bad boy. I molded myself into the man Lenny wanted me to be."

Nico trailed a finger down his cheek. "You don't gotta change who you are. You look pretty damn perfect to me."

Ford's smile was wry. "I've learned no one's perfect. All that glitter hid a lot of ugliness. And it's not like I wasn't satisfied with our sex life—I mean, what did I know? Sometimes Lenny wanted to do things I was uncomfortable with, but if I said no, he stopped. Turns out, he didn't drop it, just found someone else to scratch his itch." He swallowed. "Lots of somebodies. The big scandal hit when he was caught with the senator's son in the senator's town car, having sex. The kid was only nineteen."

Nico winced. "Damn."

Ford forced his numb lips to stop trembling. "Of course it made the news—prominent local doctor caught in compromising position with a senator's teenaged son? Nice and juicy, and the local news couldn't get enough of it. And because a senator's son was involved, it made national news. That's when all these people came out of the woodwork to say they too had sex with Lenny, and they were only too happy to give the blow-by-blow of their stories. So to speak."

"Jesus. Sounds like your ex was a walking erection."

"Basically. And I was portrayed as the foolish, suffering, duped fiancé."

Nico's brows flew high. "You were engaged?"

Ford sought to reassure Nico. "We talked about getting married, but I never pushed, and neither did Lenny. But being together for so long, and running our practice together, people assumed."

"Yeah, I don't get that either. Why are you still in business with him? Someone fucks me over like that, I'm out and I don't ever wanna see them again."

Ford sighed. "It's complicated. We own the practice together and have a joint business account. It's only been a year since we broke up, and I haven't had the time or energy to start dissolution proceedings."

"You should," Nico declared with a stubborn set to his jaw.

"Why? I don't love Lenny anymore. We're merely business partners. As I told you, we don't even see each other at the practice; we set our schedules for different days, worked it out, all very efficient."

"He's a sex fiend. Trust me, he still wants you. Why would he give up someone like you?"

"He had no trouble sticking it in anyone who breathed his way. I don't care anymore." Ford kissed him. "He doesn't want me, and I sure as hell don't want him. He can screw half of Florida for all I care, and he probably has." He slid his fingers through Nico's dark waves. "I have everything I want right here. With you."

"Yeah," he said softly. "And you gotta know"—he ducked his head, so adorably cute, Ford wanted to hug him and never let go—"I…I love you too. You're so different from anyone I've ever met, I still don't think it's real."

"How come?" Ford asked.

"Because." Nico shrugged. "Guys like you don't fall for guys like me."

"You know what I'm thinking?" Ford tipped up his chin to meet those beautiful eyes. He needed to chase away any doubts Nico had about his heart. "What do *I* have that would keep someone like you interested in me? You're young and beautiful, with tons of friends and a family who loves you. I'm older. Alone. And all I have is my work."

"Not true. You got me and the entire crew you've already met—who think you're the best, by the way." Ford grinned, and Nico bit his lip. "Not gonna lie, though. It'll take me some time to get used to this."

Ford pulled him close and buried his lips in Nico's hair. "We have all the time in the world."

Chapter NINETEEN

It was rough seeing Ford get into that car and leave. A piece of his heart went along with him, but they'd agreed to FaceTime and work out a schedule of visits.

The last thing Ford said to him was, "We'll work it out."

Nico tracked the cab, watching as it melted into the thousand other vehicles and disappeared from view. He shoved his hands into his pockets and headed toward the subway. After a weekend of running from tours to being with Ford to working at the restaurant, he needed to decompress. Sit in his apartment and think.

He reached home and fell onto the bed, staring at the ceiling. Now that Ford had left, their time together seemed dreamlike. Ford might say nothing was perfect, but Nico disagreed. He ran his tongue over his lips, tasting the last of Ford's kisses, and touched the sore spots all over his body from their hours of making love.

Making love. That was a new one to him. He wasn't a stranger to sex—he and Tommy DeLucca had traded blowjobs after baseball practice in high school. He'd lost his virginity to Tommy at sixteen and had been having sex ever since.

But making love? That hadn't happened. Except with Ford. No one had treated his body like it was precious. He and his hookups would prefer to get to the main event as quickly as possible. Any kisses had been more like a battle of mouths and tongues.

With Ford, he'd learned that a kiss was a sensual extension of touch. The merest hint of Ford's lips on his was enough to awaken and enhance his pleasure. One kiss wasn't enough. He needed Ford's mouth on his, his tongue.

"Fuck," he groaned. "Get a grip." Was this what being lovesick was like? He'd better find a cure because he couldn't walk around aching for Ford until they saw each other again. For a split second he wondered if his mother would ever consider moving, but immediately dismissed it. Her family was here, the restaurant, and most importantly, her doctors. No way could he even think of suggesting it.

His bell rang, and when he peered out the window, his mother waved at him.

"Hiya. You're finally home. Have a nice weekend?" She came inside, holding a pot. "I made meatballs. I thought you might be hungry."

For the first time, his stomach cramped at the thought of eating. He and Ford had attempted lunch, but he was too depressed to take more than a few bites of his burger, and Ford wasn't much better.

"I'm okay, but I'll save them for later, before I leave for work."

"Ford get off okay?"

Nico checked his phone and saw a text.

Taking off. I'll call you when I get home.

He wasn't used to this. Was that how a boyfriend acted? He could check with Anthony, but then he'd have to get into everything with him, and Nico wasn't ready to share his feelings. Not yet.

"Yeah. His plane took off about ten minutes ago." He sat on the couch, and after putting the pot on the stove, his mother took the chair opposite him. Sharp-eyed as ever, she peered at him.

"You miss him."

He shrugged. "Yeah. We had a great weekend."

"Don't gimme that. This is me you're talkin' to. You're crazy about him." He opened his mouth, and she glared. "Don't lie to me, Nico."

He sighed. "Okay, so I'm crazy about him. What am I supposed to do about it?" His voice rose. "He lives there, and I'm here. *Dammit.*" Frustrated that he'd so easily lost control, he rubbed his face. "I'm sorry, Ma. I didn't mean to go off on you."

Her eyes soft, she got up and sat next to him. "It's okay. I'm happy to see you finally connect with someone." Her face grew fierce. "You don't fall for just nobody. He better feel the same."

Nico allowed a grin. "Yeah. He does. We're together, although I don't know how it's gonna work. I almost didn't believe it 'cause...you know."

"No, I don't know. He's the lucky one, as far as I'm concerned. Yeah, he's a doctor and rich, but you?" She rested her hand on his cheek. "You're special. My son. *Gioia mia.*"

"*Te voglio bene*, Mamma." He kissed her.

"When you gonna see him next?"

"Dunno. We'll FaceTime."

She pursed her lips as if she'd bitten into a lemon. "Nah, that ain't gonna work. You need to go there and see him."

"Ma. I don't got the money for airfare. It's stupid

expensive, and I gotta work." He needed to fill out more applications for management jobs. And maybe he should look into marketing jobs. He didn't mind starting at the bottom. But losing his tip money would be a blow. That brought him in nice cash off-the-books. Plus, he wasn't sure he could swing it with working at the restaurant. It depended on the hours they wanted, which he'd heard could be long.

His head hurt.

"Eh, you can figure it out." She folded her hands in her lap. "Have you decided what you're gonna do about seeing your father?"

"Oh God, please." He raised his face to the ceiling. "No, Ma. I haven't. It's too much right now."

"I'm sorry. I shouldn'ta brought it up. You'll do what you feel is right when it's right."

"Yeah. Are you comin' to the restaurant tonight?"

"Yeah. Me 'n Justine'll be there."

He thought for a moment and decided what the hell. "All right, I'll see you there. I got some stuff to do this afternoon."

She kissed him good-bye, and he texted Anthony.

Bring Frank to the restaurant for dinner. Let's get him together with my mom. Since Maxie's was closed that night, it was the perfect opportunity.

When Anthony didn't respond right away, Nico got on his laptop and began to search for entry-level marketing jobs. Somehow, someway, he was going to make it all work. Job-wise, at least. His father was a different matter. Thinking about the situation made him sick to his stomach and he couldn't deal with how to see him. As far as Nico was concerned, both of them were victims, but he wasn't sure his father would see it that way.

His stomach growled, and he decided to heat up the meatballs and ate while he filled out a few applications. His good grades and degree from college should still mean something.

His phone buzzed.

Nice. I like it, Anthony replied. *How's you and the boyfriend?*

Nico rolled his eyes.

If you mean Ford, he left.

You'll need some cheering up.

Nico didn't respond, instead eating his lunch. A text came through from Ford, and his pulse spiked.

Landed about 15 mins ago. In the garage and heading home. I miss you already.

Nico's fingers hovered over the phone screen, as if he could touch Ford. "I'm such a dork." But he couldn't stop smiling.

Miss you too. Call me soon.

At seven that night, Anthony walked in with Sergio and Frank.

"Frank, how's it shakin'?"

"Haven't been here in a while, but Anthony insisted on takin' me out, so here I am."

Nico gave Anthony a hug and whispered, "Make sure he sits next to my mom."

"Leave it to me 'n Sergio. We're pros." Anthony strolled to the back, Sergio and Frank flanking him. He pulled out the chair by Justine. "Sergio, sit here. Frank, you sit by Joanne. I need to sit at the end."

"Yeah, you need room for all those muscles, huh?" Frank snickered, and they all laughed.

Nico watched with approval, then went to the kitchen to pick up several orders. When he reappeared, Frank and his mom were chatting. Nico dropped off his orders, and

Anthony excused himself from the table to join him at the front, where Nico was setting up the bread baskets and water glasses for the busboy to take to the tables.

"Mission accomplished. Frank is turnin' on the charm, and your mom's eatin' it up." Anthony reached over and grabbed a piece of bread.

"Dude, don't go stickin' your fingers in the bread. Who knows where they been?" Nico snickered. "Or should I say, I *know* where they been."

"Yeah, you do, and speakin' of stickin' fingers into things, how was the rest of the weekend with Ford?" Anthony smirked.

Nico grew warm but remained casual. "Good. We had dinner at Gallaghers, that steakhouse, you know? It was awesome. Best meal I ever had, aside from here."

"Damn, that had to run some big bills." Anthony snickered. "Snagged yourself a sugar daddy. Good for you."

Nico's hands balled into fists. "Don't you *ever* fuckin' call him that. You hear me?"

"Whoa, take it down a notch. I just meant he's got bucks and you lucked out."

But Nico didn't want to take it down. "Fuck that shit. It ain't like that between us. I'd be with him even if he had nothin'. Yeah, I'm lucky 'cause he's the nicest fuckin' man I've ever met. Got it?"

A slow grin spread across Anthony's face. "Oh, yeah. I got it. And so do you. Bad."

Nico avoided his eyes. "Whatever. Just don't go calling Ford names like that."

"I'll assume present company excepted," Anthony joked and leaned in close. "Happy for you, bro. I could tell you two had somethin' special that night at Maxie's when he showed us what a pool shark he was. You ain't never kissed nobody in front of us before."

Nico shrugged. "Yeah, well…"

"Don't be shy. It's awesome to find the right person." Anthony's gaze shifted to Sergio, who was deep in conversation with Justine. "Why should we have to hide who we love?"

"It's not that. I don't give a fuck who looks at me funny 'cause I'm with a guy."

"Then what?" Anthony's brows drew together.

"Look how you reacted. Like I'm with Ford 'cause he's got money. I don't want nobody thinkin' I'm only with him for that."

"I'm sorry. You're right. That was shitty of me. But there's nothing you can do to change perception. As long as Ford knows how you feel—and he does, right?"

Thinking about the things they said to each other, he confessed to Anthony. He had nothing to hide. "Yeah. We're in this together."

True happiness shone from Anthony's face. "Dude. That's fucking awesome. Happy for you."

"Thanks, now we just gotta figure out how to make it work."

"You mean the long-distance thing? Listen. You can be with a person in the city, and they're so damn busy, you never see 'em. If you want to, you make the time."

"But flights ain't cheap."

"Go on those travel websites and make your days flexible. You can find some cheapo prices."

Nico pondered Anthony's words for the rest of the night. When the restaurant closed, he watched with satisfaction as Frank offered to walk his mother home, while Anthony quickly told Justine he and Sergio would take her. Bobby, who'd asked to train as a waiter, wished him good night.

"See you tomorrow, Nico. How'd I do tonight?" Bobby waited anxiously.

"Great. Feel like doin' it tomorrow as well? Wednesday is a little busier, just lettin' you know."

"Yeah, definitely, thanks."

"Good. Be here before five. Joey's on tomorrow for the early shift."

Bobby nodded and ran out.

After making sure everything was in order, Nico left too, and got home around 11:15. He'd finished brushing his teeth when his phone rang, and seeing it was Ford, he jumped on the couch.

"Hi."

"Hi, yourself. Are you home? I didn't want to bother you at the restaurant." Ford's voice warmed him like a bowl of hot soup on a cold winter day.

"Yeah, I was just getting ready for bed."

"Wish I could be there with you, instead of here by myself."

"Me too." The ache of loneliness he'd been too busy to pay attention to while working flared, and he sighed. "But I'm really glad you called."

"Me too. I just wanted to hear your voice before I went to sleep."

"You're too sweet. Talk tomorrow?"

"Yes. Call me when you can." Ford hesitated. "Miss you."

"I miss you too. Night."

Yeah, he had the dopiest look on his face, but he didn't give one damn. And instead of going to sleep, he opened his laptop and began to check prices to fly to Florida.

He'd never done anything this outlandish, but when he stepped out of the Fort Lauderdale-Hollywood airport and saw the palm trees reaching up to the blue, blue sky, he couldn't contain his excitement. It had taken close to a month to work out the time off because the bus company had to find people to cover all his shifts, but they'd finally given him three days off. He'd asked for five but didn't argue. His mother was almost as excited as him, and he had to insist he couldn't bring an entire lasagna in his carry-on.

He did have a tin of homemade biscotti, though. Chocolate and almond.

Joey and Tre had already promised to work extra shifts and help Bobby with his.

"Anything for true love." Joey cackled.

Nico didn't care. He was going to see Ford and spend the weekend with him. He hoped Ford didn't mind the surprise, but since he couldn't be sure if he'd work it all out, he'd kept quiet.

They'd fallen into a routine. After he'd get home from the restaurant, they'd FaceTime well into the night, talking about their days—funny stories from Nico's tours, or serious stuff, like all the jobs Nico had applied to. Ford had helped him punch up his résumé and often found job openings Nico had missed. Ford had sent packages to his mother, Justine, and Teresa filled with top-of-the-line skin-care items, and Nico couldn't tell who was crazier about his boyfriend, he or his family.

They also confessed they missed each other, and Nico would whisper all the filthy, dirty, sexy things he wanted to do to Ford the next time they saw each other.

The Uber pulled up to a strip mall, and when he saw the pale stucco building with the Fresh Faces Dermatology Practice sign, his heart pounded.

It was lunchtime, and Nico knew Ford worked afternoons on Fridays. He hefted his bag—a new lululemon overnight bag gifted to him by Sergio—and pushed opened the glass doors.

Several patients sat in the waiting area, and the

receptionist greeted him. "May I help you?"

"Is Dr. St. Claire in?"

Her pretty brown eyes assessed him. "He's due in at one fifteen. Do you have an appointment?"

"No. But I can wait."

"I'm sorry, sir, but Dr. St. Claire has a full schedule today. Would you like to make an appointment?"

Nico smiled at her. "It's okay. I'm a friend. I'll just wait."

He took a seat next to an elderly man, who moved his cane. "I don't blame you for waiting for Dr. St. Claire. He's a good man."

Hearing someone speak well of Ford made Nico proud, and he laughed to himself. He was acting like a doting boyfriend.

"I think so."

The man eyed him up and down and smiled. "I see."

Good thing the old man did, because Nico had no idea what he was talking about. He pulled out his phone and saw he had about twenty minutes before Ford was due to come. Several patients were called in, and Nico admired the beautiful office, done in pale greens, peach, and blue. Definitely a Florida vibe. A man in a white lab jacket appeared—tall, with a short-cropped beard and black glasses. He spoke with the receptionist, and they shared a laugh. He scanned the room, and when their eyes met, he strolled over. The name tag on his jacket read, *Dr. Jose Diamond.*

"Hello. Adriana said you were waiting for Dr. St. Claire. Maybe I can help you?" His brown eyes twinkled. "Although I can't understand what someone with such beautiful skin would need to have done."

The old man next to Nico huffed and shifted in his seat.

"I'm a friend of his, not a patient."

"Oh?"

"Yeah. I'm here for a visit."

The doctor's gaze turned shrewd. "Ahh. And from the

accent, you're from New York. Now I see why he made all those trips up north."

Nico remained silent.

Another man walked out from the back, and Nico recognized Ford's ex, Lenny, from when he'd googled the clinic.

"Jose, babe, are you ready?"

Now Nico had both doctors standing in front of him, and the old man by his side, muttering.

Jose said, "I was just talking to…what did you say your name was?"

"I didn't." Nico crossed his arms.

Lenny chuckled. "He's sharp. Can we leave now?" Lenny took off his white lab jacket and pulled out his phone.

"He's here to see Ford. A friend from *Noo Yawk*." Jose smirked.

Lenny's brows rose high. "New York?"

"Last time I checked," Nico drawled.

Lenny's assessing gaze traveled up and down Nico. "I heard he had a good time at the conference dinner with his date. Was that you?"

"None of your business," a smooth voice interrupted. Nico's attention shifted to the doorway, where Ford stood in all his gorgeous glory. "Nico? What're you doing here?"

"Surprise."

Ford's gorgeous face was all he needed to see, and he left his seat to give him a kiss on the mouth. Ford's tongue met his for a brief moment, before he put his hands on Nico's shoulders and stepped away. Red spots burned on his cheeks, and his eyes gleamed golden.

"I can't believe you're here."

"I was able to get three days off. I'm here till Sunday night."

Remembering they had an audience, Nico slipped his arm around Ford's waist. Lenny and Jose stood wide-eyed, mouths hanging open, while the elderly man smiled with satisfaction. "To answer your question, yeah, I was his date."

"You're enjoying this, aren't you?" Ford murmured.

"Damn straight. Aren't you?"

Ford's eyes crinkled with laughter. "More than I thought possible."

Chapter TWENTY

Nico had come to Florida.

He was actually here.

To be with him.

Seeing Nico in his waiting area when he walked into the office was like a shot of adrenaline to his heart.

"I can't believe you surprised me like this."

Eyes sparkling, Nico squeezed him. "Two can play that game, Doc. I know you gotta work, and I'm fine sittin' here."

"I can't make you wait here for four hours. That's ridiculous." Suddenly aware that his staff, Lenny, and Jose, as well as Mr. Rosenstein and his aide were all avidly listening, Ford pointed to the chair. "Have a seat for a little while, until I figure it out."

He bypassed Lenny and Jose and addressed Mr. Rosenstein. "I'll be with you in a few minutes. Sorry about the delay."

The man waved a hand at him. "Don't mind me. Who am I to stand in the way of true love? Take all the time you need."

Ford laughed him off. "It'll only be a few minutes." He greeted the staff and entered his office. Footsteps sounded, and he grinned to himself, figuring Nico had followed him, wanting a more private hello.

Instead, it was an angry Lenny. "What the hell were you thinking?"

Ford checked his watch. "That I'm running behind and need to see Mr. Rosenstein, so if you'll excuse me?" He crossed his arms. "And you're supposed to have left the office already per our agreement."

Lenny advanced on him. "You have a fucking lot of nerve bringing your hookup here. We're a professional office."

Ford's jaw clenched, and he drew in a deep breath to calm his annoyance. "You are the last one to talk to anyone about being professional when you've screwed half of Florida and who knows where else." He pointed a finger in Lenny's face. "And do *not* call Nico a hookup."

"What else is he? An extra for a new *Godfather* movie?"

"Shut up and get out of here. I have patients to see."

"You're fucking him, aren't you?"

"What I do is not your concern. Now get out." He trembled with the effort to keep quiet.

"How much is he for the weekend? A piece of ass that hot must be a fortune." Lenny waggled his brows.

Ford shoved him against the wall. "Don't you fucking dare speak about him like that. Nico is a better man at his age than you'll ever be."

"Don't tell me you're in love with him?" Lenny laughed. "Of course you would be. Don't you know you're only supposed to screw them? You're not supposed to fall in love with them."

Disgusted, Ford let him go. "Is that what happened with me?"

"You were so eager to please. Like a puppy. Plus, you were pretty to look at, so I didn't mind." Lenny straightened his tie and adjusted his monogrammed shirt sleeves. "But after a few years, it got boring."

"You're right. It was boring. You were boring." Maybe it was petty and childish, but Ford was angry enough to stoop to Lenny's level. "Now that I've been with Nico, I know how unsatisfying sex with you was because you've never made me feel like Nico does."

Unfortunately, that didn't have the desired effect.

"For enough money, he'll tell you you're fucking king of the world," Lenny sneered.

"Get out. You're a pig."

Shaking, he turned his back and sank into his chair with his face in his hands. *Dammit.* Why couldn't he ever get the best of an argument with Lenny? He rubbed his eyes. By the time Marisol knocked on the door, he'd regained his self-control.

"Are you ready for Mr. Rosenstein? He's in Room 1."

"Yes, thanks. And sorry about all that."

She came into the office and shut the door behind her. "It's okay. We've been talking to Nico. He's so funny and sweet. He's been telling us all these New York stories." Her eyes danced. "And he's really hot. You leveled up, Dr. St. Claire."

He shouldn't laugh, but he couldn't help it. "Glad you approve. He's a very nice person." Feeling better, he rose to his feet. "All right. Let me see my favorite patient." He walked into the exam room. "Mr. Rosenstein. I feel like I've just seen you."

The old man's eyes twinkled. "And yet look at all the news." Ford helped him off with his shirt and began his exam while Mr. Rosenstein chattered away. "A very nice young man. He helped me when I dropped my cane. And a looker. I'm glad you took my advice."

With no change from the last time, Ford didn't like how Mr. Rosenstein looked thinner. "Are you losing weight?" He was afraid the man didn't have enough money to buy food.

"Maybe a little. Sometimes I'm just not hungry. Jim makes sure I eat."

Ford helped him off the table and with his shirt. When he reached the reception area, he walked Mr. Rosenstein to the chairs and beckoned to Jim. "Can I talk to you a moment?" He turned to Mr. Rosenstein. "Just a question I need to ask him."

Nico met his eyes, and he tipped his head to Mr. Rosenstein. Nico immediately began to talk with the man about everything going on in the city, while Jim walked with Ford to the office.

"Is Norman okay? He looks thinner than the last time I saw him."

Jim's face drooped. "His prostate cancer has spread, and the doctors say there's nothing more they can do for him. He knows he's dying, but he didn't want to tell you."

Grief put a hand around Ford's heart and squeezed. "Damn. I thought he'd beaten it after the surgery last year."

Jim wiped his eyes. "Me too. He's such a sweet man, you know? Never complains about anything."

"Did they say…do they know how long?" Just saying it made him sick.

"Not long. I'm sure that's why he came now instead of waiting. He really cares about you."

"I care about him too. Please let me know how he's doing, or I'll call to check up. Can I get you a ride home?"

"No, but thank you," Jim replied as they returned to the reception area. "Mr. Rosenstein has a meeting with a lawyer now. I think it's about a medical power of attorney."

They approached Nico and Mr. Rosenstein. Nico was still talking to the elderly man, who was all smiles. "Do you know this young man lives in the neighborhood where I grew up? Lillian and I moved to the city so we could be closer to all the museums and Broadway, but before that we lived in Bay Ridge too." He sighed. "I miss home—not the weather, but everything else. Just listening to Nico talk brings back memories."

"Norman, next time I come for a visit, I'll bring you some of my mother's cooking. You'd love it." Nico rummaged in his overnight bag and pulled out a tin. "Here. She made some biscotti for Ford, but I know she won't mind if I give some to you." He put five in a plastic bag and handed it to Jim.

"Ahh, now this is better than any of that junk from the grocery store. Thank you." He tried to stand but couldn't on his own, and Nico and Jim helped him. "Getting old stinks," he grumbled, and with Jim at his elbow, they left.

Ford watched them leave and sighed. "Thanks for talking to him."

"I was taught to respect older people. He's a sweet man."

Ford leaned in close. "You're sweet."

"And you get to taste me later." He winked, and Ford cursed himself that he had another three hours to work.

The afternoon sped by, and he was closing down his computer when Marisol stuck her head in his office. "Dr. St. Claire, can I talk to you a sec?"

"Of course, please sit."

"I know you're anxious to leave, but I didn't want to let it sit all weekend."

A sense of foreboding fell over him. "It's fine. Please. What's upsetting you?"

She closed the door behind her, then took the chair in front of him. "I know I'm just an assistant—"

"Don't say that. You're much more than that."

She flashed him a smile. "Thank you. I was talking

about it with my boyfriend, and he said I definitely have to tell you."

"Are you okay? Is something wrong?"

"I'm fine. But…Dr. Diamond asked me to help him sometimes when he comes in to do the Botox and fillers, and I figured why not. It was a way to make extra money."

"I see. I wish you'd mentioned it to me, but it's fine."

"I'm sorry. I figured it was on my days off, so it wasn't a big deal. Anyway." She twirled her fingers in her curls. "I worked for him a couple of times, and it went okay. But something felt off."

"Off?" Ford's brows pulled together.

"Yeah. Like, something's weird about him. I mean, he wasn't unprofessional to me, but just…I don't know. Just off."

Confused, Ford wasn't sure where this conversation was heading, but Marisol was smart and had good common sense. "Go on. I'm listening."

"One patient asked him where he went to medical school, and he dropped the syringe, then made a big production about needing to replace it, and he never answered the question. And the patient didn't ask again. Last week when I was assisting him, another patient asked what medical school he went to, and he said in Arizona."

"Okay." Clearly, he was missing something.

Marisol met his eyes. "Two days ago, he told a patient he went to school in Texas. So when I went home, I told my boyfriend, and we looked him up."

Feeling slightly sick, Ford nodded. "He wasn't listed anywhere, was he?"

She shook her head. "We found an aesthetician license for him in California. He's not a doctor."

"Which means he can't be doing these procedures. He's putting the practice at risk for a huge malpractice suit. Marisol, thank you for telling me."

"I'm sorry, Dr. St. Claire, but I didn't want you to get in trouble, in case anything bad happens."

He grimaced. "It already has. I appreciate it."

She gave him a face filled with sorrow and left.

He paced the office. What the hell was Lenny doing bringing in someone like that?

He picked up the phone and called Lenny. It went to voice mail. "You stupid son of a bitch. I know about Jose—your fake doctor friend. He'd better not show up here next week, or I'll have him arrested for impersonating a doctor and practicing without a license."

Feeling a bit better, he shut off the light in his office, locked the door, and went into the waiting area. His anger melted away the moment he spied Nico. They had a whole weekend together, and he didn't intend to bring his bad mood home with him. He'd deal with Lenny and the fake Dr. Diamond on Monday.

"Ready to go?" He put on a smile.

"Am I ever. And I'm starvin'." Nico picked up his overnight bag and crossed the room to the front desk. "Ladies, have a good weekend. Been great chattin' with you."

"Bye, Nico. Thanks for all the recipes." Adriana waved her phone. "I have them all saved here. And I'll send you some of mine."

"Dr. St. Claire, have a great weekend," Marisol said. "Make sure you show Nico a good time." She giggled.

"Or vice versa," Nico answered for him, and Ford's face burned while Marisol and Adriana laughed.

"All right, everyone. See you Monday." He and Nico left, and kept shooting looks at each other on their way to his car. "I still can't believe you're here."

"In the flesh, baby."

They reached his car, a new Mercedes coupe, and Nico whistled. "Damn, nice wheels."

"One of my weaknesses." They got inside, and he began to drive.

"One? I dunno, Doc. I can think of a few. That place behind your ear. That soft spot behind your knees." Nico ran a hand up his thigh, and thank God he was stopped at a red light, because he might've rear-ended the car in front of him. "Me sucking your dick."

"You're gonna be the death of me, aren't you?"

"What a way to go, *hmm*?"

Ford turned into his garage, and they exited the car and took the elevator up. The sun was setting, and he brought Nico out to the terrace. Twenty stories high gave him a bird's-eye view of the city and the Intracoastal. The evening sky glowed pink and violet.

"Every night since I left you, I'd sit out here and wish I were in New York. With you."

Nico stood at the railing. "This place is awesome. I could stare at the water all day. Watch the boats glide by. Look at all those yachts." He whistled.

Lenny had been dying to buy a boat—a symbol in Florida that you made it—and when he did, they'd spent every weekend on it for six months, entertaining. He'd even hired a captain, who Ford had later discovered was one of Lenny's regular lovers. Along with the house in the Las Olas Isles, Ford was only too happy for Lenny to keep the yacht.

"What's wrong? You look like you've seen a ghost."

In a way he had. The ghost of a life he'd lived as a lie. But he couldn't say that.

"I'm just so damn happy you're here. Not that I'm complaining, but what made you decide to come?" He ran his hands over Nico's arms, his broad shoulders, as if afraid it was all a dream and he'd vanish before his eyes.

"I hated being without you," he said with that shy smile that devastated Ford's heart. Nico nudged his cheek with his nose. "I still can't believe I did it. But everyone told me to surprise you, so I hope you don't mind. I didn't even ask if you have plans this weekend."

Laughter bubbled from his chest. "Plans? You're looking at my weekend plans. Wondering what you were doing while I watch the boats."

Nico's gaze was drawn to the water. "Those babies must cost a fortune."

"Some of them do." Ford nuzzled his hair, drawing comfort from his familiar scent. "But having you here with me is priceless." He cupped Nico's cheeks, mapping out those fabulous cheekbones and tracing his lips. "I missed you. So damn much."

That shy smile reappeared, sending Ford's heart into free fall.

"I missed you too."

Unable to hold off any longer, he settled his mouth over Nico's, who made sounds that were warm, inviting. Deep in his throat, reverberating through his chest like a big cat. It let Ford know exactly how much Nico wanted him.

Fire exploded between them, his pulse accelerated, and he gathered Nico closer as he trailed kisses on his cheek and neck. "Let's go inside."

"You gotta feed me first if you want me to last the night."

Laughing, he held out a hand. "Come on. We'll walk a few blocks and pick a place on Las Olas."

Nico's eyes lit up. "Lemme change. I've been wearing this all day, and I wanna put on somethin' clean."

It was a sultry night, and Ford put on shorts and a T-shirt, as did Nico. They had a delicious Mexican dinner, and hand in hand, took a stroll on the Riverwalk. Afterward, they got ice cream at Kilwins and traded licks on their walk home. Back in the apartment, they again gravitated to the terrace.

"I could stand out here forever." Nico leaned on the railing, still licking his cone. "It's already getting chilly at night at home."

Ford nuzzled his neck. "I'm beginning to get very jealous of that ice cream."

Nico grinned and pushed him onto the chaise. Ford's heart stuttered as he watched Nico sink to his knees. He crunched the last of the cone, then pulled down Ford's shorts and briefs to reveal his hard dick.

"We-we're outside," Ford stammered, but he was aching for Nico's touch.

"*Mmm*, I know." Nico wrapped a hand around his cock and licked the head. "Twenty stories in the sky."

Ford gasped as Nico slid his cool lips down the length of his erection. All reason flew out of his brain as Nico's tongue flicked and swirled over his shaft, and Ford struggled to contain his moans. Nico's fingers danced along his rigid length before sliding past his taint to tease his rim, and Ford knew he couldn't hold out any longer.

"Nico, God," Ford whispered. "Please. Let's go inside. I need you in me."

Nico released him, and they almost ran into the bedroom, where they shed their clothes and eagerly rolled onto the bed. Ford reached into his nightstand drawer and handed Nico the lube and condom.

"Prepared?" Nico sheathed and slicked his cock.

"I've gone through three bottles of lube since I came home, thinking of you. Every morning in the shower and at night after we talk."

Nico's eyes lit up. "Yeah? You jerk off to me? *Mmm*, that's hot. I do too. I dream of that pretty cock of yours in my mouth." His breathless words set Ford squirming. "Now you got the real thing." Cool fingers entered him, spreading him open, and Ford sighed at the familiar touch he'd longed for.

"I dreamed of this. Of you."

Nico replaced his fingers with the head of his dick. "Me too. My bed is lonely without you." He gave several shallow thrusts, not going deep like Ford wanted.

"My heart is," Ford confessed.

"Mine too. It's empty." Nico lowered to kiss the points of his nipples, and Ford arched his back, giving himself over fully to Nico's wet mouth. "You fill it up."

Ford's heart soared at Nico's words. He was ready to make sure that when Nico left on Sunday, he'd know exactly how Ford felt about him.

"And now I'm gonna fill you."

He inched in slowly, halfway, then withdrew, and Ford rocked with him, urging him on. But Nico continued to move at a deliberate pace, sending Ford into a frenzy.

"I can't hold it. I need you so bad." He grabbed Nico's shoulders and rolled him over so he was on top. He took Nico fully, the thick shaft piercing him to the core. "Oh God, oh God," he sobbed, stuffed full. "So good."

Nico held him by the waist and thrust up, a feral grin curving his lips, those startling eyes locked on his. He grasped Ford's dick, and Ford trembled, moving quicker. Nico's dick was splitting him in two, while his fingers moved rapid-fire up and down his cock.

"Fuck me, you love it, don't you? You love taking my cock."

Ford couldn't answer, all sensation concentrated at the point where he and Nico were joined, and he writhed on top of Nico, straining to take more of him, all of him. Everything. He never wanted this to end, hot skin meeting hot skin, Nico's hands all over him. The burning, throbbing ache as his climax hit, and he cried out.

"Nico," he moaned. "Nico."

A moment later Nico came, and Ford clasped his pulsing dick as it emptied into the condom.

"I love you," Ford whispered.

Pale moonlight spilling in past the half-drawn curtains lit Nico's smiling face.

"You know…no one's ever said that to me except you. I still don't believe it's real. That you're real."

"Then I'd better keep saying it." Ford leaned over and kissed his soft lips. "I love you. I don't want to have met you and learned what it all means, only to have it snatched away because of a few miles between us."

Nico licked his lips. "More than a few."

Ford turned on the light next to the bed. "You are like every wish I never dared to dream, every miracle I didn't trust was real. I love you, Nico."

Nico kissed his hair. "I love you, too."

He got rid of the condom, and they lay in bed, wrapped around each other. Ford could tell Nico wasn't asleep.

"Is something bothering you?"

"Your ex—what did he say when he went after you in the office?"

"Exactly what I expected."

"Which tells me nothin'." Nico sat up. "He said some shit, didn't he? About me."

Ford so didn't want to have this conversation. "All Lenny does is talk shit. And I don't care what he says."

"Tell me." The stubborn set of Nico's jaw made it clear he wasn't about to drop the conversation, and since Ford would never tell Nico Lenny thought he was a paid escort, he put a different spin on it.

"He couldn't understand what a gorgeous, hot guy was doing with someone like me. He laughed at me, said I was a fool." He kissed Nico. "Now can we drop it? We have the weekend to ourselves, and I don't want to waste our time talking about my ex."

"He's the fool," Nico grumbled and pulled him close, clinging to him. "Who would let you go? I'm the lucky guy."

"We both are."

The next day, Ford took Nico for a drive along A1A, and after a seafood lunch, they walked hand in hand along the shoreline. Ford told Nico that Dr. Sandler had agreed to see Frank and he was taking care of the bills.

"Is Frank gonna be okay? He and my mom have been sorta seeing each other."

Ford squeezed Nico's hand. "I can't tell you about his medical condition, but Sandler is one of the top doctors in New York. Frank's in great hands."

Nico told him how Joey had finally bought Teresa a ring but was waiting for the holidays to propose. Anthony and Sergio were going strong, but Jack had sort of stepped away from their friends group, something they were sad about but didn't know how to fix.

"Why not just ask him what's going on?" Ford suggested. "Maybe he feels left out since you're all coupled up."

"Maybe. But whenever we talk to him about dating, he tells us to shut up and that he's not interested."

"Then let him be. He'll work through his problems. I'm more interested in yours."

"Me? I don't have any."

"No? What about seeing your father?"

Nico dropped his hand and wandered farther into the water, up to his calves. Obviously, he'd touched a raw nerve. Ford followed him, waiting for Nico to speak.

"I don't know what to do. So I try not to think about it."

"I'm sorry. When the time is right, you'll know."

A heartbreaking, quick smile was all he received in return. There was so much more Ford wanted to say to him, but Nico had retreated, and for the rest of the afternoon remained quiet. Ford chose to leave him alone to think and hopefully work through that anger and pain.

At dusk, they were on the terrace having a drink, when Ford received a call from Lenny. He wanted to ignore it, but after what Marisol had told him, he needed to hear Lenny's explanation.

"What is it?"

"Who the hell are you to talk to me that way?" Lenny spit out. "What the fuck is wrong with you?"

"That's not a response to my voice mail. You brought in someone who isn't a doctor to perform medical procedures. We could lose our practice. What the fuck is wrong with *you*, Lenny? Are you screwing him? Is that what this is all about? Did you promise him a job in the heat of the moment, and you're so blinded by your dick that nothing else matters?"

"You're the one blinded by that hot piece of Italian ass. Better make sure you have enough cash in the bank. That one looks like he's expensive."

Ford's stomach dropped as Nico abruptly got up from his chair and went into the house.

"You bastard," he swore. "Go to hell. I'm talking to my lawyer on Monday." He ended the call and ran into the apartment. He found Nico sitting in the bedroom, staring at the wall.

"I knew it. He thinks I'm with you for your money. That's what he said to you, isn't it?"

He wasn't going to lie to Nico. "Yes. But that's because money is all Lenny thinks about." He held Nico's face in his hands. "He couldn't possibly understand that what we have has nothing to do with money. Because looks will fade, and the money might dry up, but you're part of my heart and my soul."

"I don't know pretty words like that. I'm just an ordinary guy."

How could he explain to Nico that what was in his heart transcended everything that had come before him?

That being with him chased away the inadequacies of that lost, lonely kid from the trailer park who was never clean enough, never fed enough…simply never enough of anything to feel worthy.

"You're anything but ordinary. You fill me with hope and magic—the extraordinary. Seeing you makes me happy. Touching you brings me to life. I could lose it all tomorrow and be happy with you in one room because there's no price tag on how you make me feel. We are the lucky ones because we'll always have love. And in the end, that's what matters."

Chapter
TWENTY-ONE

Was it always going to be this way? Knowing he failed to meet the standard of the man Ford should be with? For years he'd put on the face of a happy, good-time guy who didn't care whom he was with because he'd been told the truth—he was the reflection in the mirror and nothing more. Nico listened to Ford, but though the words were pretty and he knew Ford meant them, that damn self-doubt was an evil thief, stealing his joy.

Since Payson, he'd talked himself into believing love was a lie. That it was for suckers, for fools. No reason to tie yourself down when there were so many willing guys to meet. Sex in a relationship would become boring. Routine. Why would he want to see the same face next to his on the pillow every morning?

Ford changed that. Changed him. One touch from him

wasn't enough. A single kiss had him craving more. Each morning found him lonely for strong arms holding him tight and a wake-up kiss that brightened his life more than the midday summer sun. He had no clue that falling in love was willingly handing your heart to someone else for safekeeping.

Unlike with Payson, Ford wasn't ashamed to be seen with him. But at what personal cost?

"I don't wanna hurt your business," he said quietly, all the while tasting the bitterness of his thoughts.

"Explain, please." Ford's narrowed eyes revealed nothing but confusion. "How would you be doing that?"

Nico shrugged and hung his head. "If Lenny thinks I'm a gold digger, then other people will too."

"And?" Ford quirked a brow, and Nico grew irritated that he didn't understand.

"*And?* You don't need people thinkin' I'm a money-honey. That I'm just a hot piece of ass, like he told you on the phone. I heard him. "

"You are gorgeous. And sexy."

Nico's heart twisted with each word. "You're proving my point, and I don't like it."

"Don't be silly," Ford responded, maddeningly calm. "I'm stating the obvious. Anyone with eyes and a brain can look at you and see that. And let's turn it around to me. People will think, *What's Ford trying to prove by having a hot, young lover? Is he trying to hold on to his youth? That guy can do much better.*"

"They'd better not," Nico growled, instinctively possessive. "And I know what you're tryin' to do. But people are always gonna think I'm with you for your money."

"So what? Fuck them," Ford snapped, and Nico realized how rarely he'd heard him curse. "I'm serious, Nico. When Lenny's scandal broke, I discovered that people I thought were my friends, all of them knew he was a serial cheater, yet they never came to me. That's when I learned that the only one I can rely on to create my happiness is me, and I don't have to behave as others think I should. I know who you are; I know you don't care about the money. That is the person I love." His mouth drooped. "Meanwhile, I have a huge problem, which might have lasting complications."

Hearing Ford's concern, Nico put aside his personal misgivings. Ford needed him, and he was ready to help however he could, even if it was only by listening. "What's wrong? Can I help?"

When Ford told him about Marisol's discovery of Jose Diamond's fraud, Nico couldn't believe it.

"So lemme get this straight. Your ex brings in someone who lies about bein' a doctor? What the fuck is wrong with him? Do you think he knew this guy is a fake? I mean they're obviously together."

"Yes but no matter what, I wouldn't trust him to tell me the truth about anything. Whether he did or didn't might not matter if there's liability. Or even if there isn't. I was foolish enough to go along with it, and failed to do my own due diligence. I stupidly trusted Lenny."

Nico wasn't certain he grasped the situation, but from Ford's dour expression, he knew it wasn't good.

"You mean, you could be blamed if this guy hurts someone?" That didn't sound fair to him, but that was what the lawyers would figure out.

A host of expressions played on Ford's face—fear, pain, anger—all of which made Nico see red and want to hold Ford and keep him safe. "Yes. All of us will be in trouble. I'll have to speak to my lawyer on Monday, but as far as I'm concerned, I have to leave the practice." Darkness shrouded his bright eyes.

Channeling his protective instincts, Nico wrapped an arm around Ford. He'd never allow anyone to hurt this man and would do whatever he could to prevent it from happening. "How does that work?" Ford leaned into him, and Nico kissed the top of his head, hoping he could offer the comfort and support Ford needed.

"Dissolution, and we split the assets and close it." A shudder ran through Ford. "It can get ugly—and it will. Lenny's capital was used to set up the practice, so I'm sure he'll try to weasel the greater share of the practice's assets, even though we set it up fifty-fifty. Besides that, he has a regular weekly spot on a morning news station, and I write a column for the newspaper. The goodwill built up is in both our names."

"Sounds complicated, but I bet since you both want out, it might not be as bad as you think," he said, trying to put a positive spin on the situation.

Ford's smile was wry. "All I know is with Lenny, I foresee it getting very ugly." He kissed Nico's cheek. "But this isn't why you came to see me. I don't plan on spending the rest of your vacation talking about my business failure."

"Why not? Isn't that what people should do? Talk about their shit? I know that Anthony and Sergio talk about their jobs and future. And Tre and Joey have a plan for after they get married and she starts havin' kids. You helped me see that I shouldn't pigeonhole myself by only applying to my company. I've got my résumé out to a buncha places."

Ford nodded with satisfaction. "I'm glad. And anyone who hires you will be lucky to get someone with your drive and ambition."

But Nico wasn't in the mood to be placated. "Don't brush me off. I wanna help you, like you helped me. Maybe I don't have a fancy graduate degree—*yet*—but I have street sense about people." He nudged Ford. "After all, I knew enough to lock you in when I met you."

"Thank you." Shiny-eyed, Ford leaned on his shoulder. "I've never had anyone on my side. I've always been alone, hiding where I came from, putting up walls so I couldn't be seen. Loving you allows me to break down those walls because I know you'll always be there to pick me up."

"Hold you up, I think is what you mean. 'Cause I promise, I'll never let you fall."

They kissed to seal their bargain, and as Ford snuggled into Nico's arms, Nico yawned. "Don't fall asleep," Ford warned and turned on the bedside lamp.

"Yeah?" Nico rolled over and flung his leg over Ford's hip. "Why's that?"

"Because…I have a patient who just happens to own one of the big clubs in South Beach, and I may have texted him when you were in the shower earlier to ask if he could put us on the VIP list for tonight."

Nico cocked a brow. "VIP, huh? That's what you are to me. Very Important Penis." Ford's face burned. "You're so fucking adorable, I could eat you up."

Ford tugged him close, lips barely touching. "That's later tonight."

As promised, they didn't have to wait, and after they were seated at a prime table, Nico made sure to take pictures and send them to Anthony and Joey. Immediately, his phone blew up with texts. He laughed and showed them to Ford.

Joey: *No way. Me and Tre waited two fucking hours and never got in. You bum.*

Anthony: *Damn. Looks sick. Have fun. Sergio says hi and to make sure you dance.*

With Ford's hand around his nape, fingers playing in his hair, he snuggled in close and held up his phone.

"Let's take a selfie, and I'll send it to the guys."

Ford indulged him, and when Nico held the camera

up, kissed him. Nico sent it and set his phone on the table, ready to pay attention to his man.

"I'm having the best time. Thank you." Nico angled Ford's mouth to his and sucked hungrily on his tongue. They were surrounded by hundreds of people, yet no one existed outside the two of them at their table. Ford filled every black corner of his mind with the sunlight of his smile. Pleasure crackled like Fourth of July fireworks exploding in the sky, and he shifted closer to deepen their kiss.

"How did I get so lucky?" Ford nibbled on his ear, and under the table, hidden from sight by the darkness and strobe lights, Nico teased along Ford's thigh. "What're you doing?" he hissed, and Nico's grin grew wicked.

"Something wild and fucking hot." With a napkin in one hand, Nico unzipped Ford's jeans and slipped his hand into Ford's briefs. Heat radiated from him. "You're ready to explode, aren't you, baby?" he murmured and squeezed Ford's thick, hot dick.

"*Mmph.*" Ford couldn't respond, a strangled moan the best he could manage. His eyes fell half-shut, and his breathing turned labored. Nico was enthralled and turned-on by his passion.

"Fuck me, baby, you should see yourself. So hot for it. You like getting off in public? Like how your big cock feels in my hand?"

Nico leaned forward to touch their mouths, and Ford shivered, his gaze traveling down to where Nico slowly pulled him out of the confines of his briefs.

"Jesus. Wh-what if someone sees?" But Nico watched him, riveted to the sight of the cockhead sliding through his fist. "Fuck," Ford whispered. "Oh God, feels so good. So fucking good."

The lights played off Ford's wild, lost face, and his hips rolled as he found his rhythm. Nico shifted closer to keep their privacy intact, though Ford had put up no resistance to Nico bringing him off in public. Ford thrust up again and again, his head flung back, eyes squeezed shut. Nico knew he'd passed the point of no return, and he closed the space between them to catch the harsh cry of Ford's orgasm in his mouth. The sticky release spread over his hand and the napkin he had ready.

God, he was beautiful in this untamed state of pleasure, and Nico reveled in knowing he'd been the first to give Ford this experience. There'd never been a sweeter man, yet his eyes glowed with a feral light. Nico's heart banged.

"Goddamn, you're so hot, I wanna flip you over and fuck you right now."

Ford buried his face in Nico's neck, but his soft cock, still in Nico's hand, jerked.

"You'd like that, *hmm*?" Nico chuckled low and licked his lips. "Look at you, coming all over my hand. I'm gonna suck your come off my fingers like fucking maple syrup, but I know you'll taste sweeter."

Nico released him, and as promised, licked his fingers clean. Ford zipped up, then gulped a glass of water.

"I can't believe…I mean, I've never…" He ducked his head, and Nico grew afraid he regretted what they'd done and was upset, until he saw the edge of a shy yet blissful smile. "It was so sexy, *forbidden*," he murmured. He rubbed his cheek to Nico's. "I loved every single second." His gaze dropped to Nico's crotch. "But you—"

"I'm fine. I get off on making you happy."

And it was true, he realized. Giving Ford pleasure, seeing him in the throes of his climax, was so fucking beautiful, it left him warm and sated, as if he'd come himself.

"Let's dance," Ford said abruptly and stood, holding out his hand. Surprised, Nico assessed the dance floor, full of writhing bodies.

"It's packed. There's hardly any room."

A devilish grin curved his lips. "That's what I'm

counting on."

The pounding beat rattled through his body. Nico had been to a few clubs in the city, but this scene was wild. Half-naked women and men rubbed up against each other, hands and lips roaming over any and all exposed body parts.

"Damn. Gives new meaning to the term *dirty dancing*," Nico muttered.

Ford pulled Nico closer. "Hold me."

They moved in synchronicity, chest to chest, their groins aligned, and Ford wrapped an arm around his waist and captured his mouth for a hot, wet kiss. Tongues teasing and playful, Nico sighed and looped his arms around Ford's neck. The music thumped in a sensual beat, and the dance floor swelled with the surging crowd. Ford cupped his ass, and Nico ground against him, his cock still full and aching for release. It didn't matter that they were on the dance floor with a thousand people surrounding them. He was desperate for that friction, and Ford's smile was nothing but pure wickedness as he bit Nico's neck.

"Do it. Come for me. Right here." He stuck his tongue in Nico's ear. "Give it to me."

Oh God, he hadn't come in his pants since he was a horny teenager, but when Ford's hands groped his ass, then moved lower, between his legs, Nico hissed. "Fuck me, oh God, fuck *me*."

Still on fire from watching Ford, Nico groaned. Warmth flooded his briefs, and he swayed. Ford held him tighter as his climax rushed over him, and he rode Ford's leg like a dog in heat. He sighed and rested his head on Ford's shoulder.

"I love you," Ford whispered, holding him by the waist as they left the dance floor. "Let's go home."

"I wish it were my home," he replied, his voice lost in the music.

The valet brought the car around, and he slid into the passenger seat. Ford drove away into the night, and they were on 95 North, traveling for about ten minutes, when Ford asked, "Did you mean it?"

Half-asleep, Nico opened an eye. "What?" He was woozy from the sex and drinks—they had to order bottle service, and being the driver, Ford had barely touched his. Never one to waste anything, especially the stupidly expensive liquor, Nico had drunk over half the vodka himself.

"About how you wish my apartment was your home."

That chased away all desire to sleep. He hadn't meant for Ford to hear, but the drowsy haze of the liquor and sex had short-circuited the connection between what should remain in his brain and not spill from his lips.

"Well, uh, yeah, sure, but that's impossible. Between the restaurant and my mom, I can't leave New York."

"They have good doctors down here too, you know. And stellar dermatologists."

Ignoring Ford's attempt to lighten this life-changing discussion, Nico sat up straight. "I know, but I can't ask her to leave her life because I wanna move in with you. That would be as crazy as me asking you to leave Florida and come to New York to be with me."

There. He'd said it. The challenge lay in the air between them and remained unanswered as they drove through the night. When they arrived at Ford's apartment, he immediately shed his sticky pants and underwear and got into the shower. Part of him hoped Ford would join him, but he was left solo, and when he'd dried off, found Ford waiting for him, sitting on the bed.

Ford remained silent but held out his arms, and Nico slid into them as if they were all he needed. They clung to each other, chests rising and falling, each breath counting off the seconds until they'd be apart again.

"I'm sorry," Ford whispered. "That was unfair of me, asking you to give up your whole life for me."

Nico latched on to his neck, lips nipping and sucking

at Ford's collarbone. It left a mark, a tingle of red against a sea of light skin. A mark he'd think about a thousand miles away in his lonely bed.

"If it were only me, I'd chuck it all to be with you. I hope you understand why I can't."

"I do." Ford kissed him. "And that dedication to your family and your selflessness are both reasons why I fell in love with you. It'll work out, don't worry."

Nico kissed him, desperate and hungry, and as they made love, he held on to Ford as if by letting him go, he'd lose a piece of himself in the process.

Chapter
TWENTY-TWO

Physically, he was in his office on Monday morning at 10:05, but mentally, Ford was a thousand miles away. Specifically, in a little corner of Brooklyn with a dark-haired, blue-eyed man who'd stolen his heart. Their weekend together had been perfect, but saying good-bye to Nico at the airport the night before had been bittersweet, and he'd lingered in his car, trying to recapture the unique taste of Nico's kisses.

As he'd made Nico promise him, he'd texted Ford when he landed and was home.

You know, only my mother makes me do this.

Smiling, Ford answered: *Because both of us love you. I miss you already.*

Miss you too. Tell me what happens after you talk to the lawyer.

His patients came and went in a steady stream, and by lunchtime, he was grateful for the break. His lawyer, Art Heron, called as he finished his lunch. Ford had placed a call early that morning and left a message.

"Thanks for getting back to me so quickly."

Art had handled the split with Lenny and the division of their property, and was well aware of the person they were dealing with.

"I have to tell you, Ford, this was not on my bingo card of shit your ex was going to pull. Do you think he knew this guy isn't a doctor?"

As much as he and Lenny were strangers now, Ford wanted to believe there was some good in him. Simply for the fact that he'd spent almost half his life believing himself to be in love with the man.

"I want to say no. For all that Lenny is a piece of shit in his personal life, he is a good doctor and does value the practice. But aside from that, what do you suggest I do?"

"Get while the getting is good. Seriously, this could blow up in your face at any moment. If you want, I can contact Lenny's attorney and start dissolution proceedings."

"Can we do that, even though it's a partnership?"

"Hold on a sec." Art hummed under his breath. "Yes, there's a clause here that allows one partner to dissolve the practice if it's found that the other partner engages in any practice or behavior that has or may bring the goodwill of the business in disrepute." A humorless laugh escaped him. "I think this is about as disreputable as one can get. And he can claim he didn't know, but Lenny was the one who brought him in, and as such will have to fall on the sword."

He hated what was happening, yet tears pricked his eyes at the thought of their hard work gone, as if it had never existed. He heard loud voices outside his door, and sensing a confrontation was about to occur, he ended the conversation.

"Thanks, Art. I guess, start the paper work and get back

to me?"

"We'll need to hire a forensic accountant. I don't trust Lenny—he'll try and pay you off with a million dollars and think that'll suffice."

Ford blinked. "Uh, okay. I have no idea what the practice is actually worth."

"Trust me, Ford. When we get through, you're going to be a wealthy man."

As soon as the conversation ended, his door slammed open, and Lenny, eyes spitting fire, stormed inside. Marisol and Adriana hovered behind him in the hallway, wide-eyed and scared.

"Lemme tell you, if you even think of calling the police on Jose, I'll—"

"You'll what? You're sleeping with him, aren't you?" His eyes narrowed. "You are *unbelievable*. You have the goddamn nerve to talk to me about Nico when you're busy screwing this guy who pretends to be a doctor."

"I didn't know," Lenny whined. "I met him at a convention in California, and we hooked up for the weekend. He said he wanted to move to the East Coast and join a practice. I didn't think—"

"Yeah, you did, except it was with your dick and not your brain. You idiot. Do you realize the trouble we're in because you can't keep it in your pants?"

"It'll be okay."

"Why? You think your family can smooth this over with their money?" Ford barked out a laugh. "He'll be lucky if he's not arrested for pretending to be a doctor. And you for facilitation." Proud for not revealing his nerves, Ford crossed his arms. "*Hmm.* I think that's a felony. He'll probably do jail time." Of course, Ford had no idea what he was talking about, but he wanted to hurt Lenny for all the pain he caused.

"Jail time? Are you fucking kidding me?" If it wasn't for his life imploding, it would've been comical to see Lenny's eyes bug out of his head. The man rarely lost his cool—even during the scandal, he was able to make jokes. "I'll take over his patients, and he'll assist me. No one has to know."

The sheer audacity of Lenny's nonchalance took Ford's breath away. It made his choice that much easier.

"He must be great in bed for you to risk your license. But I don't give a damn what happens to you anymore, Lenny. You made your bed when you shared it with every guy who waved his dick at you. I've contacted my attorney, and I plan on taking steps to dissolve our partnership."

"Wha-what?" Lenny's voice cracked before he reasserted himself. "You're not serious."

"Watch me," he said, the confidence in his decision growing with each passing minute. "I don't know why I continued to work with you as it is. My attorney thought I was foolish, and Nico couldn't understand it."

"Nico?" Lenny sneered. "Your fuckboy?"

Ford rose, his hands balled into fists, and advanced on Lenny. He itched to smash them in Lenny's face, but he refrained. "I don't owe you any explanation."

Nasty Lenny returned with that smirk Ford despised. "Your little Wise Guy plow you good this weekend? Is that why you're feeling so cocky?" He snickered. "So to speak. He'll grow tired of your boring vanilla ass as soon as he finds a richer sugar daddy. And he will because you're not going to bleed me dry from this." Lenny's handsome face twisted into a mask of ugliness. "I'll see you in court." Breathing heavily, he opened the door.

"I'll see you in hell first," Ford answered and slammed it shut behind him. Shaking with anger, Ford slumped in his chair. How did it come to this? He'd given Lenny so much—his virginity, twenty years of his life, and most of all, his love and trust. While he'd never regret the choices he'd made, Ford did resent the wasted years of loving Lenny without Lenny loving him in return.

Everything happened for a reason, though, and if he'd never met Lenny, he wouldn't have been in this practice where he was asked to be an expert witness. He wouldn't have needed to be in New York City to meet with the lawyers. And most importantly, he never would've met Nico.

Nico.

A smile curved his lips. God, he missed him already. The red haze of anger melted away the longer his thoughts lingered on their weekend. He could almost hear that husky growl in his ear giving his opinion on what to do about Lenny.

Nico had that blunt, no-nonsense way of looking at life. He was a black-and-white kind of man—he loved with his whole heart, and if you hurt him or anyone he cared about, you no longer existed in his world.

His intercom buzzed. "Dr. St. Claire, your next patient is here. Mrs. Morrison is in Room 2."

He pinched the bridge of his nose and drew in a deep breath. He had to be grateful for the distraction of a busy schedule. Since he couldn't be with Nico, work was the next best thing to keep him occupied and forget about the shit storm about to rain down on him.

"I'll be right in."

Friday found him at dinner with Art, who was being very patient and understanding as he walked him through the contract. The week had been long and arduous, with Lenny calling him throughout, making veiled threats, but Ford ignored him. As far as he was concerned, Lenny's actions showed his desperation. Art agreed, and a wry grin tipped his lips, softening his normally stern features.

"Maybe next time you'll listen to me and not stay in business with your ex. I know you thought you could handle Lenny, but now you can see he's a loose cannon."

"You're right. I'd hoped the different schedules would work and we could coexist. It's just that we worked so hard to get the practice to flourish, and now it's all in the toilet." That suffocating feeling of failure, something he'd thought he'd beaten after going to college and medical school, sent its ugly tendrils up to choke him. Success was an illusion. "Everything we accomplished, wiped out." Morose, he finished his martini, and for the first time, seriously considered getting drunk.

"Don't think of it that way. It's a chance for a fresh start—new beginnings. You have opportunities. You're young."

"Maybe." Earlier in the day he'd received word that Mr. Rosenstein had entered hospice, so Art's words had little effect on his bleak mood.

"Definitely. From my review of the business records, you'll end up with around two million dollars, which should enable you to either buy into an existing practice or start from scratch. I've spoken with Lenny's attorney, and he's working on the details of the dissolution."

"Like getting him to agree?" It was his turn to fake a smile. "If I know anything, it's that Lenny will be fighting it every step of the way. He hates to lose."

"If he knows what's good for him, he'll sign off," Art said darkly. He closed his iPad case and slipped it into his briefcase. "I doubt he'll want an investigation into his business practices. I predict it'll be done within the month."

Ford hoped so because the last thing he wanted was a protracted court fight. The holidays were on the horizon, and he'd been invited to spend them with Nico and his family. He'd hoped to have it all settled.

At home and ready for bed, he placed his nightly call

to Nico, who listened carefully to everything Ford relayed about his meeting with Art.

"So by the end of the year, you and Lenny should be kaput, right? You can tell him to fuck off."

Despite his sour mood, Ford's lips twitched. He loved Nico's no-bullshit way of laying it out there. Ford missed him so much, he wished it were possible to reach out and touch him. *Damn technology.* Why hadn't they made that possible yet?

"Yes. The practice will close. I'll have to start planning what to do next—where to relocate and informing my patients. I feel saddest about losing the staff, especially my assistant, Marisol. She's been with me for years."

Uncharacteristically quiet and serious, Nico leaned closer to the screen. "Why not make a really big move? Come to New York."

"New York? You mean, move there?"

"Yeah," Nico answered softly. "Move here and live with me."

Ford blinked. "I hadn't considered that," he answered cautiously.

Nico's face fell. "I guess it makes sense. All your patients are there. If you came here, it'd be like starting over. I get it." He forced a smile. "Listen, I gotta go. Early morning tours, and the trains are all fucked up as usual. I'm sure you'll figure out where to go and how to do it. You're smart."

"Wait. Are you angry with me because I didn't say yes?"

"Nah. I get it. Don't worry about it, Doc." Nico blew him a kiss. "Talk to you soon."

Before he could answer, Nico had ended their call. Automatically, Ford went to reconnect, but held off to think. They hadn't ended the conversation with an "I love you." Ford blew out a heavy sigh and headed out to his place of peace—the terrace—and sat on the chaise, his mind not on the glittering lights over the water, but on the conversation he'd had.

"It's not as simple as Nico thinks. All my patients are here—my connections. My medical license. My entire professional life."

Why did it sound like he was making excuses not to be with Nico? A good boyfriend would jump at the opportunity to live together—after all, he'd already asked Nico on his last visit to leave his life in New York and be with him. They'd discussed why Nico couldn't move, and Ford had understood. Now Nico had lobbed the ball back in his court, and Ford had resisted without half as good a reason.

"He can't expect me to just walk away from my livelihood." That argument didn't sound nearly as valid when reasoned out loud. "And yet I had no qualms about asking him to leave his job and family behind, along with the restaurant, to be with me." Ford hated to think that the reason he hesitated was he believed his work mattered more than Nico's. Had he become elitist? He winced at the thought.

"He had every right to feel upset. I'm the one who said no."

With the weekend looming, Ford knew he should start looking at listings of practices for sale, or medical office space to buy. Starting fresh at the age of forty-two was a scary thought—as a kid he didn't have enough life experience to be scared when Lenny suggested they open their own office straight out of med school, only a driving need to put as much distance between himself and his rundown past. He went along with whatever Lenny said to make him happy.

Having grown up with a mother who abused him and cared little about his welfare, Ford had learned to put his needs second because to speak up or to ask for what he wanted made him a target. It had left him mute in the face of Lenny's subtle digs at his lack of upbringing and trailer-park background, giving Lenny a free pass for his indiscretions.

The enormity of what he'd have to face in the days and

weeks ahead weighed heavily on his shoulders. First thing Monday morning, he'd speak with Marisol. She deserved to know the future of the practice. As much as he wanted to keep her, he couldn't expect her to stay while he was searching for a new place and getting settled. He would give her a very generous severance and hope she'd be okay.

Ford spent a few more minutes scrolling, but his heart wasn't in it, and he set his phone down, wondering instead what Nico was doing and thinking. He picked up his phone again. There was still time to remedy his mistake.

Chapter
TWENTY-THREE

It had been a shit morning, and it wasn't even ten o'clock. After his conversation with Ford, he'd spent a sleepless night, wrestling with himself. He had every right to feel hurt that Ford had immediately dismissed his suggestion without taking a second to think about it, but maybe he was being too sensitive and not seeing it from Ford's point of view.

He fell asleep at about four, and of course, slept through his alarm. Then his coffeemaker leaked all over the counter and the train was delayed, forcing him to stand the entire trip to the city for his morning tour shift. He had no time to buy a coffee and winced as a throbbing headache began to pound behind his temples.

"You look rough, man," Dave said around a bite of muffin. Nico told his morning story of woe, Dave rummaged in the paper bag at his side and handed him a cup. "Here. I bought two because I didn't have a chance to have any before I left. You're welcome to it."

"Thanks. You're a lifesaver." He took a hefty gulp and sighed as the hot liquid flowed through him. "Damn, that's good. I can't wait to finish up today and go home and get into bed."

"Me neither." At the familiar voice, he turned and saw Ford's smiling face. Nico almost dropped the cup.

"Wha-what're you doing here?" All his hurt melted away, and he wanted nothing more than to hug him and kiss those hesitantly smiling lips.

Golden eyes twinkling, Ford held up his ticket. "I'm here to take a tour."

Nico took it from him. "Sit up front," he murmured in Ford's ear as he mounted the steps of the bus. "That way I can look at you all throughout the tour."

"Your wish is my command." Ford grinned and did as told, taking the seat directly behind the bus stairs.

"How long are you here for?" Nico asked as the people entered the bus. "Why didn't you tell me you were coming?"

"I didn't know until after we spoke last night." Ford's smile vanished, and he hung his head. "I hated how our conversation ended, and I couldn't stand thinking you were hurt and angry with me. I wanted to make sure you were okay and talk with you about my next steps. I realized I wasn't being fair to you. I barely slept last night."

Nico's heart tumbled. "Me neither," he admitted.

Ford's expression turned hopeful. "I took the earliest flight in this morning, and I'm booked on the latest one out I could find tomorrow night. Can we talk later?"

Warmth unfurled in his chest. He knew Ford loved him, but Nico wouldn't have asked him to drop everything and come to New York to see him. Hearing that Ford went to such lengths to make sure he was okay left Nico no doubt that they'd work out their differences.

"Yeah, of course, but I gotta work at the restaurant."

"Funny, but suddenly I'm dying for lasagna."

Ford insisted on a car to Brooklyn, and Nico didn't say no. Ford held his hand, his thumb tracing along the skin, causing goose bumps up and down his arms. For once he cursed the fact that there was little traffic and they were moving quickly over the Brooklyn Bridge. The car turned a corner, and he slid into Ford.

"Hi, there." Ford darted a glance at the driver, whose gaze remained intent on the road. It had begun to drizzle, and the air had turned foggy. He wrapped an arm around Nico, pulling him close.

"Hi, yourself." Nico's words hung on a smile, and he pressed a kiss to the sweet curve of Ford's cheek. Ford turned so his lips rested on the edge of Nico's mouth, and Nico sighed with contentment.

"Touching you has been the best part of my day. Do you know how hard it was to sit so close to you all day and keep my hands off you?" Ford nuzzled his ear. "It's been less than a week, but it feels like a year."

"Yeah. It sucked."

Ford caught his eye, and winked. This intimacy, so new and fresh, flowed so easily between them, it scared Nico. Could this really be his life? Was he finally the lucky one to have won a prize like Ford? He kept waiting to be disappointed, but Ford continued to smash his negativity and replace it with pure joy. And yet tomorrow he'd have to watch Ford leave, taking another piece of happiness with him.

Ducking the raindrops, they walked into La Dolce Vita, and Nico watched as Joey and Teresa rushed to hug him.

"Dude, we didn't know you were comin'. Someone didn't bother to tell us." Joey glared at Nico, who grinned.

"Don't blame him," Ford hastened to correct Joey. "He didn't know either. I have some things I need to talk to him about, and I didn't want to do it over the phone or text."

Teresa kissed him. "Find yourself a man who hops on a plane just to talk. Nico, you dog, your man is the best."

"Don't I know it." He took Ford's hand. "Let's go say hi to my mom and Justine."

With Ford at his side, he approached their table. "Ma, look who surprised me today."

"Joanne, it's great to see you. And Justine as well. Both looking gorgeous as always." Ford kissed her first, then Justine, and Nico didn't know whose smile beamed brighter, his aunt's or his mother's.

Her brown eyes filled with light, she held out her arms. "Now that's a good boyfriend, am I right, Justine? I was just tellin' her an' Frank, I haveta ask Nico when Ford is comin' to visit again, and here you are. How long are you stayin'?"

"Only until tomorrow night, I'm afraid. And thank you again for the biscotti. They were delicious."

"You could have this all the time if you lived here, ya know."

"Mom," Nico warned. "Please."

Ford took it in stride with his natural warmth. "I'd probably gain a hundred pounds. And I'm glad to hear Frank is doing well. How is he feeling?"

"He's good. Thanks you every day for your help in making sure he got diagnosed and payin' for his treatment. It's a gift from God, I swear." She wiped her eyes. "You and that doctor both are lifesavers. Praise Jesus, we're lucky it hadn't spread to his lymph nodes, but he's gotta be checked for the rest of his life."

"I'm very glad we were able to help him. Dr. Sandler

is an excellent doctor. Tell Frank I said hi next time you see him."

"I'm gonna go bring him his dinner in a little while, so I will. He's dying to get back to Maxie's, but the doctor said not to for a few more weeks, since he's still recuperating from the surgery. It took a lot outta him."

The rain started up in earnest, and several customers came in, soaking wet even with umbrellas. Teresa got them seated, and Bobby brought them bread and water.

"I gotta get to work," Nico said, not without some regret. "Have a seat, and we'll bring you out somethin' to eat."

"Thanks." Ford's smile held a promise of what was to come.

Nico left him and went straight into the kitchen to wash up and see what was going on. Joey was there, joking with the cooks. "Yo, Nico, you really didn't know Ford was comin'?"

Nico swiped a breadstick. "Not a clue." He debated whether to tell Joey and decided an abbreviated version would probably be best, leaving out the issue of Jose and his fake medical degree. "See, he and his ex are closing their practice, so he needs a new space. I told him he should move up here. We sorta had a disagreement."

"A fight, you mean? Was that your first? And he got worried and flew up here to make sure you weren't mad at him, huh?"

"Whoa. You got all that from me saying we had a disagreement?" Nico laughed, but Joey was no fool.

"It's the truth, isn't it? I bet he's afraid you'll break it off if he doesn't."

Nico thought about Joey's words. "I dunno. I mean, he asked me to move down there, and I said I couldn't because of my mother and my jobs. He knows the score."

Joey's sharp eyes met his. "Listen. Maybe he's afraid you're at—whaddya call it—a standoff, and it's a choice he's gotta make: move here, or you break up with him. 'Cause you've said you won't go to him."

"Can't," Nico pointed out. "There's a difference."

"Whateva." Joey waved him off. "Just make sure he knows you ain't going nowhere."

"He knows." At least Nico hoped he did.

"Haven't you been sayin' he's a little, you know, antsy about your age difference? Make sure he knows you'll work it out, 'cause I'm tellin' you, he's the one. I know it, Tre knows it, and most importantly, you know it. Now go take table four's dinners to them."

"Who are you, my boss?" Nico joked and flipped him off but took the plates. "Make yourself useful. Go bring Ford somethin' to eat."

Maybe Joey was right and he needed to reassure Ford that nothing, not even distance, would keep them apart.

In Ford's hotel room later that evening, Nico, already naked, lay on the bed, watching Ford undress. The rain hadn't let up, and even in the quick dash from the car to the hotel, they'd gotten pretty drenched. "Do you think the hotel wonders why you're back here every few weeks?"

Ford hung his wet jeans over the chair and faced him wearing only a pair of tight black briefs. "Not anymore. When I checked in, they said it was nice to see me again, and I said I was here to visit my boyfriend." He crawled onto the bed, and Nico curled his hand around his neck. "My very sexy, delicious, hotter-than-hell boyfriend."

"Yeah? I like hearing that." He was an achy mess of conflicts and emotions, eager to hold Ford yet wanting to clear the air between them first.

Ford leaned over and licked his nipples into stiff points. "I like you. I love you."

As much as Nico wanted to make love, he knew they needed to talk, so he rolled up to a sitting position. "Before we get into it, I wanna say something."

Turning serious, Ford dipped his head. "Okay. I'm listening."

"I don't wanna break up. Even if we have to live in separate states for now, I'm not going to give up the best guy I've ever met. That would be pretty damn stupid of me. But I hated how our last phone call ended." He leaned in close and kissed Ford. "I'm sorry I acted like a dick and brushed you off."

Ford's smile was sad. "I didn't know what to think, and the worst part was, with all the shit going on in the office, I couldn't give you my full attention. I'm sorry I made it sound like I don't want to be with you full-time. I want to be with you forever. You walked into my heart and made it your home."

So this was love. The stripped-to-the-bare-bones feeling where you couldn't hide, no matter how badly you'd been hurt in the past, because none of it mattered anymore. Only this man and his words that calmed all the hurt and drove out the demons of his loneliness.

"I want you forever too. We might not have the easiest road, but you're who I want walking by my side, every step of the way."

"Then we'll keep on doing what we have been. Together."

Ford dived in for a kiss, and Nico pushed his tongue past his lips and met Ford's. They playfully teased and danced as Ford's hands roamed over him, tweaking his nipples to red points, stroking his stiff cock until it throbbed, cupping his aching balls.

"I need you in me," Ford whispered.

"I need that too."

Ford stopped kissing him and gazed at him so intently, so seriously, that Nico's heart drummed double time. "What's wrong?"

"Nothing." Ford brushed their lips together. "It's never been more right than in this moment." His beautiful eyes glowed with passion. "Can we…would you want to make love without a condom?"

Nico shivered at the thought. "Go bare?" he asked hoarsely, imagining being fully skin-to-skin with Ford. Nothing between them. "I—yeah. I want that." His fingers clutched Ford's shoulders. "I've never done it without a condom."

Ford's eyes grew soft. "It'd be my first time as well. I didn't with Lenny, and after him, I didn't think I'd ever trust another person. Until you."

Lust curled deep in his belly, and he slanted his mouth over Ford's for a harsh, demanding kiss. He swallowed Ford's breath to his lungs, felt his pounding heart as if it beat in his own chest.

"Nico, please."

Hearing Ford's whispered cry, Nico's passion rose hot and bright, and he spread Ford wide, his avid, hungry gaze sweeping over his fit body. He loved the curls of hair on his chest leading down to the thick brown patch where his perfect cock lay swollen and heavy. Nico's mouth watered, and he took the entire length to the back of his throat.

"*Mmm*," he hummed, smiling around the rigid shaft at the strangled moan of desire escaping Ford. His hips thrust, and Nico swirled and licked the girth while picking up the saliva escaping to wet Ford's rim. He teased the opening while Ford squirmed under him, mouth open and gasping, eyes blazing hot.

"Fuck, oh God." Ford's ass lifted off the bed, and Nico pressed in farther with his fingers, curling them as he probed. "Nicooo, please." Ford thrashed on the bed, his hands reaching and grabbing Nico. "Fuck me already, goddammit."

He released Ford's dick with a juicy *plop*, and slicked himself up, lined the head of his cock with Ford's hole, and sank slowly. "Oh, Jesus. Oh, God." Ford's velvety, hot passage clasped him tight as he pushed. "So hot, so fucking perfect." Nico's head spun, and he struggled not to blow apart immediately.

"Move," Ford demanded, pulling at his arm, but Nico kept a slow slide until he was fully buried inside Ford's body.

"Ford," he breathed. "I didn't know."

Their eyes locked, and Nico swore he felt his heart shift, making room for half of Ford's.

"Me neither. It was never…I never…" Ford's long fingers ghosted along his cheek. "Nothing's ever come close to this. To us."

He eased out of Ford only to drive back in, the friction on his unsheathed dick a miracle he'd never believed possible. Ford's hand flashed on his erection, and the rising cries of his need spurred Nico on. The bed squeaked in protest as he thrust hard, and he crushed his mouth over Ford's, sucking his tongue. Slick with sweat, their bodies slammed into each other, each demanding power, neither ceding control.

"*Ti senti così bene sul mio cazzo, amore mio,*" he crooned, switching to Italian, and Ford clawed him and rose to sink his teeth into his shoulder, but Nico barely felt the sting. He lost himself in the friction on his dick and the beautiful sight of Ford writhing beneath him, caught up in his orgasm.

Ford's ass clamped on to Nico's dick, pulsing in rhythm as his release spread between them, and Nico continued to pump into him, riding out wave after wave of pleasure. Lashes fluttering, Ford squeezed his ass, and his fingers trailed down the crease.

It was more than he could handle, and his teeth bared

in a snarl. He emptied into Ford, his cock aching from the squeeze holding him tight. "*Ti amo*." He kissed Ford's neck. "*Amore mio*."

"I cherish you. My love."

He rested on Ford's chest, listening to the rapid pounding of his heart, the slide of Ford's fingers through his hair calming his still-shaky nerves. Rain lashed the windows, and he jumped slightly at a *boom* of thunder. "What the hell was that?"

Ford yawned and stretched, then held on to him. "Who cares?"

"*Mmm*, you're right." Nico lifted off of Ford. "That was incredible. Do you know how wild it feels to be inside you with nothing between us? It's like a silk glove clamped on my dick, making me part of you."

"You're always a part of me, wherever I am."

Nico kissed him. "Let's take a shower."

A buzzing sounded in his ear, and he cracked one eye open. Eight a.m. The noise continued, and when his brain cells finally fired, he slapped the bed for his phone and hit the screen.

"Yeah?" he grunted.

"Nico, tours are canceled today."

He yawned and rubbed his face with his free hand. "Huh? Why?"

"You're kiddin', right? Have you looked outside?"

"No, I literally woke up because you called." He swung his legs off the bed, careful not to wake a still-sleeping Ford, and padded over to the window. "Damn. It's really raining out there."

Sheets of rain poured from a sky mottled as gray as a pigeon's wing. An ugly sky of unending clouds and low visibility. Few vehicles were out on the street and even less people. Nico watched as one poor soul had his umbrella whipped out of his hand by the howling wind. It sailed down Broadway, and he raised his hands to the sky in defeat. He'd been that guy and felt sorry for the soaked commuter.

"*Rain* ain't the word. Try monsoon. So it's all canceled. Ain't no one gonna be looking for a tour." Carlos chuckled.

It had been over a month since he'd applied for the management job, and he hadn't heard anything. "Hey, you wouldn't happen to know if they started hiring for those management jobs, would ya?"

"Nah, bro. You gotta talk to the office."

What he'd expected. "Okay, thanks."

He ended the call and smiled as Ford slipped his arms around him from behind and kissed under his ear.

"Good morning."

That smooth, deep voice played havoc with his insides, and he turned into Ford's embrace.

"Sure as hell is."

"Did I hear that you're not working today?"

"You did." He settled his mouth over Ford's, enjoying the pleasure of a leisurely kiss. "What time is your flight?"

"Late."

Nico cupped his ass. "What should we do to pass the time?"

Ford dragged him over to the bed and pushed him onto the mattress. "I think we'll figure something out. Let's have breakfast. I think we'll both need our strength."

Nico understood these were moments they'd draw upon. They'd drench themselves in the honey of their love, creating a time capsule of every touch, kiss, and heated glance to be opened when the nights grew long and lonely.

He watched as Ford placed their order for eggs and bacon

and waffles, and he pulled on his jeans while Ford put on sweat pants. Nico scrolled through his phone, checking his messages, while Ford checked his.

"Dammit," Ford said, looking at his phone.

"What's wrong?"

"My flight's been canceled because of the weather. I'd better rebook, and then I'll have to log into the office calendar and contact my patients to reschedule. Hopefully I can get a flight out in the morning."

Nico sat and watched him, wishing he wasn't so happy over Ford's misfortune. It gave them one more night before he had to leave, which was one more night they'd spend together.

Nico would take what he could get.

Chapter
TWENTY-FOUR

It had been a frustrating morning, one he'd spent mostly on hold with the airlines. The rain that kept pouring from the sky only served to heighten his already foul mood. The problem wasn't Florida—it was impossible to get a flight out of New York.

"Please, I'm a doctor and need to get back to my office." He cringed hearing himself say it, but he did have skin-cancer surgeries scheduled.

"I'm sorry, Doctor, but the only flight I can get you on is the 10:28 p.m. tomorrow night to Miami."

"I'll take it," he answered in a hurry, afraid if he hesitated, the seat would disappear.

"Okay, I have you all booked in a confirmed seat. I'd get to the airport earlier than usual because all the delays will make it super crowded."

"Thanks." He ended the call and found Nico sitting on the bed, staring at him with an odd look. "What?"

"Nothing. I know it's a pain in the ass for you, but not gonna lie, I like having you for an extra day."

Ford sat next to him and tipped up his chin to softly kiss his mouth. "I know. And I do love being here with you. It's just that with everything up in the air at the office, being absent even one day may be too long. I'm afraid of Lenny coming in and pulling some shit."

A range of emotions played over Nico's face. "I know. I hate that you're going through this."

"At least I'm here with you, and not stuck in some hotel room alone."

"Yeah, about that." Nico made a face. "At some point I'm gonna have to go home. I can't wear the same clothes three days in a row."

Ford quirked a smile. "I like you in nothing at all, but I get it." He peered at the window. "Do you think we can get a car?"

Nico snorted. "Surge pricing will cost you a fortune. No way am I gonna let you waste your money."

"You're sweet. I guess we'll make a run for the train, then. And if we get wet, I'll have to borrow your clothes, if that's okay."

"You think I'm gonna be mad about your sexy ass in my clothes? I may never wash them again." Nico winked, and Ford's heart filled with so much joy, he couldn't stop smiling. "That was the first thing I noticed about you when you took that tour." Nico reached around and patted his butt. "A work of art."

Ford's cheeks burned. "Silly. You're the one. The perfect combination of sexy and sensual and sweet. You're beautiful."

With breakfast finished and umbrellas in hand, they made a run for the subway station. Ford was surprised to find the train half-empty, and mentioned it to Nico, who shrugged.

"It's Sunday, and the weather sucks, so people are staying home."

"Makes sense. It's good you have the trains. In Florida we get these kinds of torrential downpours all summer long, but we have to drive."

"Yeah, that would suck. A lotta people in the city don't even bother with getting their driver's license, since they're never gonna own a car."

It was such a different world, and yet Ford found himself enjoying all of it. The crowded streets filled with people dressed in wildly contrasting styles. The quiet of the Brooklyn streets at night, compared to the frenetic hustle of the city. The small mom-and-pop stores and restaurants in Nico's neighborhood, where people looked out for each other.

They reached Nico's apartment and kicked off their wet sneakers and socks. Ford sat on the couch and watched as Nico turned on the lights. "You know what? I think I finally understand."

"What?"

"Why you love it here in the city. If I lived here, I'm not sure I'd want to move either."

Nico stretched out on the couch and put his head in Ford's lap. He couldn't resist running his fingers through those dark, silky waves. "It's not perfect. We got a shitload of problems to deal with, our taxes are ridiculous, there's too much crime, and the rent is too damn high." He quirked a smile. "But I still love it. Everyone who means anything to me is here." He glanced up. "Except you."

"I'm here now." Ford leaned down and met his kiss halfway. Nico's lips were gentle and sweet in contrast to the furious rain and wind pummeling the windows. Ford forgot about the shit storm waiting for him at the office and contemplated a lazy day spent snuggled in bed with Nico.

Nico's phone rang, and he groaned. "It's my mother."

Ford laughed. "Great timing."

"Hey, Ma. What is it?"

Ford could hear her voice through the phone.

"Are you downstairs? I thought I heard noises."

Nico rolled his eyes.

"Ma, you got Superman hearing or what? How can you hear anything with all this rain out there?"

"Never mind that. Did Ford get off okay? The weather's really bad."

Nico met his eyes, and Ford clamped a hand over his mouth to keep the hysterical laughter inside.

I got off okay, all right. Twice last night and once this morning.

"Actually, he's right here with me. His flight got canceled, so he's stayin' until tomorrow."

"Ain't that nice. Tell you what. I got a nice soup on the stove. Why don'tcha come upstairs and have some?"

"Ma. We're—"

"Joanne, we'd love to," he called out, and Nico's eyes widened in surprise.

"Hi, honey. Don't you listen to my son. You need some good home cookin'. The soup'll be ready in about half an hour. You two come up here then."

Before Nico could answer her, she ended the call, and Nico rolled up to sitting and shot him a dark look. "Why'd you agree? We'll be stuck up there all afternoon."

Ford reached for Nico's jeans. "Half an hour is plenty of time for what I want to do to you."

The rest of his day and evening were spent in the circle of Nico's family, and Ford gathered all their warmth to carry with him when he left. As a child, he'd seen the other kids at school getting picked up by their mothers or fathers and given hugs. Parents would show up for school plays, science fairs, and spelling bees, but never his mother, who informed him through the ever-present cigarette smoke that she didn't have time to waste on crap like that. As her next of kin, he'd received notification of her death while he and Lenny were on vacation in the Virgin Islands. He had her cremated and her ashes spread over the ocean, as he remembered she'd once said she loved the beach.

"You okay, honey?" Joanne patted his hand. "You look sad." A knowing expression lit her eyes. "Aw, I get it. You gotta leave tomorrow. Don't worry, you'll be back in no time for the holidays."

Let her believe what she wanted. He had no wish to expose long-buried grief, and he breathed a sigh of relief that she didn't dig deeper. "I know. I can't wait."

Nico gazed at him with thoughtful eyes but said nothing. Later that night, they returned to his hotel after Nico worked a very slow shift at the restaurant. Knowing he was leaving and wouldn't return for a month made him desperate for Nico, and the moment they entered the room, he kissed him. But for the first time, Nico put him off.

"Hold up."

Ford blinked. "What's wrong?"

Nico crossed his arms. "You tell me. At dinner you were in your head. Even my mother noticed."

"It was nothing." He reached for Nico to kiss him. There wasn't a chance in hell he was wasting their last night talking about his mommy issues.

But Nico was willing to take that chance because he refused Ford yet again.

"Bullshit. Talk to me. What's wrong?"

Pain washed over him. "Your mother mentioned the holidays and family…I should've cared more when my mother died, but it meant nothing to me. When I was little, my mother would dump me with the lady in the trailer next to us—who was a better mother to me than she was—and go do her thing at the strip club."

Nico paled. "Ford, what're you talking about?"

Perhaps he'd always remained that same scared kid who'd tucked away his true feelings for fear of getting hurt. But Nico wasn't Lenny, with that smile that danced on the edge of cruelty. Nico understood him. Loved him. He shouldn't fear telling him.

"When I was ten, she'd leave me alone, cursing that she shouldn't have to pay to have someone watch me, and I learned to do things on my own, including the holidays. I'd put up tinsel and whatever stuff I could find at the dollar store. I even bought a little fake tree with the money I earned from helping people around the trailer park with their errands."

Nico took his hand and held it tight.

"She didn't like that I'd told people I'd done it all myself, and smacked me, saying it made her look bad, like she wasn't being a good mother." Nico's face reflected his horror at Ford's story, but now that he'd begun to speak, he couldn't stop the bleeding. Old scars never fully healed.

"When I told her she wasn't, she ripped apart whatever I'd done and dumped the tree in the garbage." He fixed his gaze on the geometric pattern of the carpeting under his feet. "That year I spent Christmas in the emergency room. She said I fell down the stairs."

"Oh my God," Nico breathed and hugged him. "I'm so damn sorry."

"I'm okay now. But I've never told anyone."

"Not even your ex?"

Nico's surprise stopped him. "Especially not him. I

wanted to push all the ugliness of my childhood out of my mind. Lenny knew I was poor but nothing else." He grimaced. Reliving those days had him cringing, but it allowed him to see the equal and loving relationship he had with Nico.

"I can't imagine you anything but strong and confident." Nico played with his fingers.

"In my work, yes." His lips twitched. "My personal life is another story. I was in love, or so I thought, and did whatever he wanted, too afraid to upend a seemingly perfect life. I let him control everything in our relationship—our practice, our social life…our sex life." His cheeks warmed. "Give Lenny a smooth path, and he's a great guy. But any obstacle, no matter how small, sets him off." He shuddered, remembering the rants when he'd perceive some injustice against him.

"He's a piece of shit," Nico pronounced, and Ford kissed the strong set of his jaw.

"Sitting there with your family and all your friends, I wished I had a mother because I never did, really. And I'm so damn sad about it."

"Baby…" Nico kissed his wet eyelashes and face and held him as the tears flowed freely for the first time. "I love you. My family is yours. *Tutte bene.* It'll be fine. You're with us now. *Ti amore. Sei il mio cuore, sei l'amina mia.*"

"Have I mentioned how sexy you are when you speak Italian? I don't even know what you're saying, but it makes me hard. I definitely leveled up in boyfriends."

"It means I love you. You're my heart and my love."

Ford rested his cheek to Nico's. Those love words finally smoothed the broken edges of his soul. Nico's kisses, soft lips, and seeking tongue gave him peace. "I love you, Nico. So damn much." He cupped Nico's face. "And while we're baring our souls tonight, I know you might not want to hear this, but I think you should try to see your father."

Nico's eyes grew as stormy as the sky outside. "I don't want to talk about that. Not on our last night together."

"Nico. I'm not on death row. I'll be back in a month. But life is too fucking short, and he should know what an amazing son he has."

Nico sank to the bed. "What if he doesn't want to know me? He can say go fuck yourself, I don't give a damn about you."

"Then you have your answer. And I can help you with that—I'm an expert on knowing what it feels like to have a parent treating their child like shit." He ran his nose down Nico's cheek, inhaling his scent along with the smell of fear. "It'll be okay. Because no matter what, you'll still have me. Us. That's never going to change."

Nico met his eyes, so anxious, lost, and vulnerable. "I'm scared."

Ford hugged him. "I know. But that's when it's worth fighting for. I know you can do it."

Nico buried his face in his neck. "I-I will. I'll do it this week."

"Good."

They held each other, their love more powerful than the raging storm outside.

The following morning dawned bright, with the sky a freshly washed shade of blue. Ford decided it would be nice to thank Sandler in person for taking care of Frank, and so he pulled the business card from his wallet and placed the call.

"Ford, how are you? How's sunny Florida?"

Ford smiled. "The same. I'm in town and wondered if you had time for me to stop for a visit."

"How about lunch? I can order us some sandwiches."

"Sounds good. What time?"

"Is one good? That's my usual time."

Ford could hear Nico waking up in the bedroom and was anxious to join him. "I'll be there."

"See you then."

He pounced on Nico and kissed him. "I'm going to see Frank's doctor at one."

"What time is it now?" Nico asked, his voice still rough with sleep. Between his messy dark waves spread over the bright-white pillowcase and the morning stubble shading his face, Nico was a wet dream come to life, and Ford grasped his shaft. He was still open from earlier and sank down on him, hungry to be filled.

"It's get-inside-me o'clock."

Nico groaned and rolled him underneath to thrust hard and fast. "Mission accomplished."

Ford rose to meet Nico, wishing they could stay like this forever. He came with a harsh cry, and Nico followed a second later, filling him with warm come. Nico latched on to his neck, sucking. "That's for when you're not with me, so you remember who you belong with."

"I couldn't forget. And the best thing is, I know I'll never have to."

At one in the afternoon, he walked into Sandler's office and stopped at the doorway in admiration. From the outside it looked like an older apartment building, nice enough, with a doorman, but nothing special. Indoors however, it was understated elegance. Soft, muted tones of lemon and sage green for the furniture, and gray carpeting. Quiet classical music played in the background.

The receptionist greeted him. "Dr. St. Claire? Dr. Sandler's expecting you. Follow me, please."

She led him to a small room with a long table. Sandler stood at the window, and a smile broke out over his face when he saw Ford. They shook hands, and Sandler held on to his arm.

"Ford, how are you? I can't tell you how it made my day to get your call. Sit, please."

They'd had a few calls after he'd referred Frank, so he was aware Frank was responding to treatment and was well on his way to recovery.

"It's good to see you again too."

"I have curried chicken salad, turkey, and tuna. I'm banned from roast beef."

Ford's lips twitched. "Not a problem. I'm fine with any of these."

They ate for a while. Ford set his half of the sandwich aside. "Your space is beautiful. Very different from mine in Florida."

"Thanks. I'll tell my wife, as she's the decorator of the family." Sandler fiddled with his cup. "How's the office doing? Things still okay with your partner?"

A bit of an odd question, but Ford could answer it without giving away too much. He liked and respected Sandler but would never reveal Lenny's stupidity.

"Actually, we're dissolving the practice. It should be finished by the end of the year. Things weren't going as well as I'd hoped, so we're calling it quits."

Sandler's gray brows flew up. "That's so interesting."

"Not really. It should be pretty simple. We each have our own patient lists. We'll split everything according to our partnership, then go on our separate ways." The pain in his stomach tightened like a knot, and his appetite vanished. Awaiting his return was an angry Lenny and all the problems he'd created. Ford couldn't stick his head in the sand and ignore his world imploding around him, but for one more day he'd pretend to be Scarlett O'Hara and think about it tomorrow.

"From where I sit, it's not so simple, son. I'm sorry you had to get mixed up with him. Have you found a new place?"

"Not yet," Ford admitted.

"And yet you're up here. Visiting that young man I saw you with at the dinner?" Sandler's lips curved in a grin. "Still seeing each other?"

Ford lifted his chin. "Yes. Yes we are."

"Good for you. And him. I wish you luck. You're a good man, Ford. What you did for Frank, I'm not sure anyone else I know would've bothered." He drummed his fingers on the table. "Let me ask you this. Have you thought about maybe relocating here? If the two of you are serious, maybe you want to think about it."

Ford sighed. "First of all, I'd have to get licensed. It would mean a competitive market I don't know much about, with no patients initially. I'd be starting over from scratch, and at my age, that's not easy."

Sandler laughed. "Your age looks pretty good from where I'm sitting." He peered at him over his glasses. "Let me tell you what I have in mind."

Chapter
TWENTY-FIVE

"You're shitting me."

Nico sat on the couch, staring at Ford, uncertain he'd heard him correctly. Ford had checked out of his hotel, and Nico had given him the keys to his apartment so he could hang out there instead of sitting in the airport for hours. He'd just walked in the door when Ford sprang the news on him.

Excitement sparkled in Ford's eyes. "No. I'm not. But it's something we need to discuss. I know you want to say yes immediately, and I do too, but it might mean a ton of changes for us both."

"Tell me you're kidding. You get an offer to buy into a practice that in five years will be yours. Here. In the city. Meaning you're gonna move and live up here, and we can be together, and you think I'm gonna have a problem with it? Are you high?"

"Let's sit and talk for a moment. I know you have to get to the restaurant, so I'll lay out all the facts as I see them." Ford pointed to the couch, and they settled next to each other. "It's going to take a significant chunk of my assets, so we might not be able to do all the things we have been. For a while, at least. Would you have a problem living in the city? I know you want to stay close to your family, but the train ride would be outrageously long for me every day to the practice."

"I don't care about goin' to fancy places, you know that. Movin' to the city…I never thought about it 'cause I knew I'd never be able to afford it. I always figured I'd stay here."

Leaving the neighborhood was a wrinkle he hadn't contemplated. Family stayed together.

"Like I said, you don't have to decide right now. Dr. Sandler's not on a timetable, and he wants me to think about it. There's a lot to consider."

"Like what?" To him, it seemed simple. If Ford's practice was closing, there was nothing to keep him in Florida. Now that he'd had an offer to join a practice, Nico couldn't find a single obstacle.

"I still have to get my license here and either sell my apartment or sublet it. Plus, I need to figure out how much I'll actually end up with after the partnership is dissolved, and buy a place up here. To me, it doesn't make sense to rent, not at these prices. That'll also eat into my savings."

"Pfft. You'll ace your test." Nico brushed it off. "Damn, I love that apartment."

"I do too. But the good thing is that fees are higher here. Sandler has a very exclusive client list, as his wife was an interior designer to a lot of the rich and famous in the city. I'll be grossing much more than I was in Fort Lauderdale, so if I can sell it, we can buy something else."

We?

"Uh, there might be a problem."

Ford's brows rose. "Such as?"

"I can't afford to pay for an apartment in the city, and I certainly can't afford one here and one in Florida."

"I understand. I don't expect you to."

Was he deliberately being dense? "I won't live with you if you pay for everything."

Ford leaned over and kissed him. "So you'll pay what you can. But being in a relationship means give and take at different levels at different times. Sometimes you give more and sometimes you take. We'll make sure you contribute what you feel comfortable with, but understand this." Ford held him by the shoulder. "I have more money than you. That's a given. Please don't put a wall between us based on that. If I lost all my money tomorrow, would you leave me?"

"No, but—"

"No buts. I mean it. We have to get this out of the way for good. I'm never going to make you feel less than if you have less than me. But don't make me feel bad about having more. If I want to spoil you or your mother, please let me. It gives me pleasure to do it, since I had so little growing up."

It made sense to Nico. "I'll try. It's something I'll have to work on, but I won't let it break us up."

Ford's happiness met his own. "Nothing will," he reassured Nico. "Realistically, it could all be settled by year's end."

That brightened Nico's spirits even more. "This all sounds almost too good to be true. But I'm not tellin' nobody." His mother always warned not to say anything to anyone before something was a done deal because you might jinx it. He'd always been a little bit superstitious.

"Right now, there isn't anything to say. Nothing has been finalized yet."

Looking at the clock on the stove, Nico saw it was time for him to leave for the restaurant. "I gotta go. Call me when you get home, and I'll speak to you tomorrow."

Ford handed him the keys. "Here. Don't want you to forget these."

"Keep them. I got an extra set, and so does my mom. No need to spend money on hotel rooms no more. When you come for the holidays, you'll stay here with me."

Ford's expression grew serious, and Nico became afraid. "What? Did I do somethin' wrong?" He swiped a hand over his cheeks. "Is something on my face?"

"Nothing's wrong. It's so damn right. I'm scared maybe it's happened so fast that you're going to wake up and wonder what you're doing with me."

"Time for you to take your own medicine, Doc. Enough with that ridiculous talk." Nico pounced on him, capturing his mouth in a kiss that would have to last through the long weeks of separation. "I know exactly what I'm doin' with you." He continued to kiss and touch Ford, mapping out the perfect cut of his cheekbones and the full pout of his lips. "And it's only gonna get better."

"Nico." Ford sighed, kissing him on his neck, his shoulder, while holding him close. Heat poured off him, and Nico knew he had to leave, or they'd end up naked. One final kiss, and he extricated himself from Ford's clinging arms.

"I gotta go. Sorry."

Hazy-eyed, Ford rubbed his face. "I'll lock up and talk to you later." He brushed the messy hair off his brow and frowned. "Don't forget what we talked about earlier. Your father."

At those two words, all the energy and good vibes were sucked out of the room. "Yeah, I guess."

"What's wrong? Are you having second thoughts?" He swung his feet over the couch and sat up straight.

Nico had barely given it any thought at all. Every time the suggestion came up, from his mother or Ford, his stomach turned. "You do know he cheated on my mom when they were engaged. He's not a good person."

"Nico…I know we're different people, but if I had the chance to know who my father was, I would take it."

He cocked his head. "You sure there wasn't anything your mother said or that you found after she died that could give you a clue?"

Pale-faced, Ford wiped his eyes. "No," he whispered. "Like I said, all I know is that he drove a Ford." His attempt at a smile faltered. "Not exactly evidence to go on. I want to feel sorry for her and what she went through, but ten-year-old me still remembers the broken wrist and a concussion from Christmas morning. In my case, I think I would've been better off if I'd never known her at all."

"C'mere." There was little he could say to soften the horror of Ford's childhood, so he offered his heart and his arms to hold him tight. Ford clung to him, and Nico felt the warm tears on his neck.

It took only a second before Ford pulled away and put on a brave face. "Sorry. I don't know why I'm so emotional about it lately. Maybe because you and I are so close, and your family accepted me like one of their own, which brings into stark relief everything I missed."

"I told you," Nico murmured, ready to fight and slay whatever dragons Ford had to conquer. "You're my family. You're my home."

Ford's kiss lingered, and then he pushed him away. "You have to get to the restaurant."

"Yeah, yeah." His anxiety gone now, Nico planted a kiss on Ford's cheek. "I'll talk to you later."

He walked around the corner with a spring in his step, and before he entered the restaurant, he checked his emails. His heart pounded at the one from the bus company. He started reading it, and his spirits sank.

"We're sorry…"

That was all Nico needed to see. He didn't get selected. "Fuck." He kicked the wall. "Screw them. I gotta get outta there. Fuckin' dead-end place." He scrolled farther down, past all the crap, and saw an email from one of the other places he'd applied to—the marketing department of one of the largest credit card travel companies.

"Thank you for applying for a position as an entry-level social media marketing specialist. We'd like to schedule an interview…" A *whoop* escaped him, and he didn't bother to read the rest of the email. He had an interview, and suddenly the world seemed brighter. This was it. He was going to make sure he'd get this job and work his ass off. He wanted Ford to be proud to introduce him to all the fancy-ass people he'd no doubt be meeting, and marketing specialist sounded a fuckton better than tour-bus guide. He slipped the phone into his back pocket and entered the restaurant. His mother beckoned him over.

"Ford left yet?"

"Later tonight. I left him in my apartment, and I gave him his own set of keys."

"Good." She nodded with approval. "He shouldn't waste his money on hotels no more."

He wasn't planning on telling her about the offer Ford had gotten until things were more settled. But he did want to feel her out about him possibly moving out of the neighborhood and see her reaction. The restaurant was slow, so he sat across from her as she ate her salad.

"Lemme ask you somethin'—and it's all hypothetical—but…would you be upset if I ever moved away?" At her raised brows, he hurried to finish. "Not to Florida or another state. But like to the city or a different area of Brooklyn closer to the city."

"You scared me for a sec. I thought Ford talked you into movin' in with him." She took a sip of water. "I don't wanna be like my father, who made it his way or no way. But I can't lie, I'll miss havin' you downstairs."

It was exactly his fear. "I'm not going anywhere—"

"But you're thinkin' about it." He didn't answer, and she smiled. "Don't feel bad 'cause you want to follow your heart. You know how lucky I am to have a son like you? All these years together, you stuck by me to help. No questions asked. You did more than I could've ever hoped for. You were always my blessing from God. But now it's time for you to find your own way."

"I love you, Ma. And if I do move, I'll still see you at the restaurant and come by on the weekends. So it's not gonna be that different."

She held out her hand, and he took it. "And if it is, it is. All I want is for you to be happy. Don't make the same mistakes I did, trying to live your life to please other people. You gotta please yourself."

"You're talking about Nonno and my father." Again, his anxiety kicked into high gear. "Ford wants me to contact him. To have closure either way."

Hopeful eyes met his. "Are you gonna do it?"

He lifted a shoulder. "Yeah, probably. I'm just not sure how."

She squeezed his hand. "You'll figure it out. You always do."

The next morning he woke at seven, and with the information from his mother, found his father's dental office. Madison and 57th Street. "Not too shabby. You coulda given my mother a good life."

He'd debated whether to contact him at home or at his office, and decided the former would look weird and stalkerish. Leaving open the tab with his father's office info, Nico clicked over to the job interview. That, more than anything, was of prime importance.

"How fucking awesome would it be to tell Ford I got this job? Don't get ahead of yourself. You don't have it yet." He cleared his throat and put the call through. It was over in five minutes, and he had an interview in two days.

"Fuck, yeah." He couldn't keep the smile from his face. Now for the hard part. He downed two double espressos.

"Dr. Gargano's office. How may I help you?"

"I, uh, need an appointment."

Smooth, real smooth.

"Okay, sir, are you a patient?"

"No, I've never seen him before."

But he's my father.

"Is there something specific, or is it a general checkup?"

You should only know.

"Uh, I think it would qualify as an emergency. Is there any way he could see me today?"

"Let me check his schedule. Tuesdays aren't usually too bad." He could hear her clicking. "I could fit you in at the end of the day, say around 4:45? Does that work?"

"Yeah, it's fine."

"Wonderful. May I have your name, please?"

"Nico Andretti."

"Very good, Mr. Andretti. Any dental insurance?"

"No, no insurance."

"Very well. There's a one-hundred-dollar fee for the consult, which includes an exam. Any X-rays are an additional one hundred and twenty-five dollars, and a cleaning will be another one twenty-five. We do have a new patient special—the exam, cleaning, and X-ray for three hundred dollars total. We take credit cards and cash."

His head spun. *Damn.* Dr. Fischetti on Fourth Avenue and 89th Street only charged him $75 a visit unless he had a cavity. "Okay, sure, no problem."

"All right, then. I have you scheduled for 4:45 this afternoon. Thank you."

"Yeah, thanks."

He ended the call, and sick with nerves and the two double espressos, made it to the bathroom in the nick of time before he threw up.

The office was bright white with pictures of people showing perfect teeth. Nico had flossed and brushed carefully, not because he expected an exam, but because he wanted to show he took care of himself and wasn't a bum. He'd made sure to iron a fresh shirt and wear slacks.

The receptionist gave him a clipboard to fill out, and he realized when he wrote the address down, that if his father saw it, he'd know right away. Whatever. He handed it back and waited in the reception area. All day he'd waited for this. From the time he'd called that morning, he hadn't been able to take a true deep breath.

"Mr. Andretti?" A woman in blue scrubs waited by the door to the inner office. "Follow me, please."

He was taken not to an examination room, but to an office, where he came face-to-face with pictures chronicling his father's life: a wedding picture with a blond woman, pictures of two children—both girls—at their college graduations.

Sisters. I have two sisters.

The door opened, and Nico swallowed. Hard. His heart pounded in a wild rhythm. He drew in air, hopeful he wouldn't pass out.

His father sat in front of him and studied him. "Are you here to see me for a dental appointment?"

His face was all strong lines and stern frowns, his dark hair cut short to prevent the waves Nico struggled to tame and lost the battle with most days. Eyes like blue-green chips of ice stared at him unwaveringly. No warmth or gentleness residing there. But Nico knew he smiled, that was evident in the pictures covering the credenza behind his desk. Especially with his daughters.

My sisters.

Did he not see it? To Nico, it was as if he looked into a mirror—thirty years in the future.

Swallowing his nerves, Nico clasped his shaking hands. "Not exactly."

"I didn't think so. You're related to Joanne Andretti?"

That hostile gaze pinned him, but Nico grew angry as the seconds ticked away. Why should he be on the defensive? All he did was be born. He wasn't the one who'd cheated and run away.

"Yeah." He lifted his chin. "I'm her son. And yours."

"What did you say?" Gargano—because Nico couldn't think of this angry man as his father—growled even as he paled.

"You heard me. I'm your son. You ran away, and she was pregnant. She raised me with only her parents to help her." Nico's words held no warmth. "While you were having your fun with your side chick, my mother was dealing with all the shit you left her."

A high flush spread over Gargano's cheeks. "I didn't know."

"And if you did?" Nico glared. "Would you have given a shit? No. Because you'd already replaced my mother and had a nice new life. You made a brand-new family."

A muscle ticked in Gargano's jaw. His eyes twitched. But he stayed silent.

Nico focused on the pictures behind Gargano. "I see I have sisters."

"My daughters are off-limits to you."

Hurt by the obvious slight, Nico concentrated on

everything good in his life—Ford, his mother and aunt, Joey and Tre, Anthony and Sergio. Even Jack. All these people loved and cared about him.

"Yeah? Why's that? I'm not good enough? Or is it 'cause I remind you of what a lousy thing you did?"

"You have no idea what it was like being under the thumb of that man. He made us miserable. And I couldn't live like that. I told Joanne, but she refused to make a choice."

"No shit. You wanted her to pick between her father and her husband-to-be? You think that's fair?"

"You don't understand."

"You're damn right I don't," Nico lashed out.

"What do you want from me?"

"What does that mean?" Nico asked, confused. His brows pulled together. "I came to talk to you. You're my father."

"And yet you waited all these years to confront me. There must be a reason." Gargano's assessing gaze swept over him. "What do you do for a living? Did you go to college? I know the old man didn't put much stock in education."

Ignoring the slight to his grandfather, Nico folded his arms. "Yeah. I have a college degree in business. I'm, uh, between jobs at the moment." He'd be damned if he'd tell him he worked as a tour-bus guide.

"Now I see," Gargano said, and Nico almost flinched at the contempt radiating from him. "You came to hit me up for money. You think I'm too afraid to tell my family about you."

"Are you fucking crazy?" Nico spat out. "I just found out recently that you didn't know. My mother didn't tell you, but she also didn't tell me. My grandparents didn't want you to have anything to do with me because of the way you humiliated my mother." He bared his teeth in a snarl. "All this time I was told you knew she was pregnant and didn't care."

"I didn't," Gargano stated, his face shiny with sweat. "I had no idea she was pregnant."

"Yeah, I know. Bet you would've tried to force her not to have me." Gargano flushed red, and Nico, heartsick, knew he was right. "Yeah, I thought so. And you know what? Up until now, I was so angry with them for lying to me, but I'm glad to see they were right to keep you out of my life. You *are* that son of a bitch they claimed."

"I have a family," Gargano hissed. "I can't just bring you home and introduce you as the illegitimate son I never knew existed."

"Can't or won't?" Nico challenged, though his head and heart already foreshadowed the answer.

Gargano huffed in frustration. "I never told Eileen I was engaged before I met her. We met about a year after that. She wasn't the woman I was with when I called off the wedding. That relationship didn't last."

"Relationship? You mean the woman you were cheating on my mother with."

Gargano shifted in his chair. "Look, I loved Joanne, but that old man was impossible. I wasn't going to let him tell me how to live my life."

"And now you have what you wanted, and everything was perfect until I popped up. I don't fit in."

Gargano's eyes darted to a frame on his desk, and Nico snatched it up. It was a family portrait. Gargano's wife—small, blond, slim—looking up at him like he roped the moon for her. But it was the girls, his sisters, Nico focused his attention on.

"They're very pretty," Nico said softly. Dark hair fell in waves to their shoulders, and their father's bright blue-green eyes—and Nico's too—stared back at him.

"Tessa and Lucy. Tessa is an anesthesiology resident, and Lucy's clerking for a state supreme court judge." Gargano's pride was evident, and Nico's throat thickened with grief at possibilities made impossible by lies and heartbreak. He squared his shoulders.

"I didn't come here to ask you for money. I didn't even want to come, but my boyfriend said if I didn't, I'd always wonder what if."

"Boyfriend?" Gargano blinked. "You're gay? I-I never would've guessed."

Nico's smile was bright. "Why, what'd you expect, rainbows or a pink tutu? Bet you're really happy to have met me now." Gargano refused to meet his eyes. "Yeah, you'll go to the grave with your secret gay son. I know you don't think I'm good enough to meet your daughters. My sisters. That's your loss and theirs. Because I'm a damn good person, and you'll never get the opportunity to have me as your son. You know what? You can have all the money in the world, and you still wouldn't deserve me."

Without another word, he strode out of the office, ignoring the receptionist calling after him, and pushed the button for the elevator. He began to shake and walked up to the park and found a bench. Tears streaked down his face, and he knew Ford was busy, but he needed to talk to him. He took a chance and made the call.

"What's wrong?" Ford's worried voice wrapped around him like a hug.

"How do you know something's wrong?"

"Because you should be on the way to the restaurant, and you're calling me earlier, and you sound stuffed up. Nico, are you crying?" A FaceTime request from Ford popped up, and he had no choice but to answer it. "You *are* crying. What's the matter, love?"

"I went to meet Ray Gargano."

It took Ford a second to register the significance of what he'd said. "Oh, fuck. It didn't go well? I'm so sorry."

Hearing Ford curse like that had him laughing through

the dampness of his tears. "Yeah. Not well. You could put it that way." He related their confrontation—he hardly thought of it as a conversation—and when he was done, waited for Ford's reaction.

"Bastard," Ford swore. "He's not only a liar and a cheater, he's a homophobe. I'm sorry you had to go through it, especially by yourself, but now you know you tried. From his reaction, you're better off without him. He's not good enough for you."

"You're sweet. But I wish…I wish I could meet my sisters. They're beautiful and so smart—one's gonna be a doctor and the other's a lawyer." He chewed his lip. "Guess they got the brains and the beauty."

"You had better not be thinking what I think you are," Ford scolded, his mouth tight with anger. "You're smart as hell and fucking gorgeous. Having a postgraduate degree doesn't prove anything."

"Maybe," he hedged, remembering their discussion and unwilling to argue. Exhausted, frustrated, and sad didn't begin to describe his state of mind.

"You could contact them on your own. They're adults. You don't need their father's permission."

"I couldn't do that. It wouldn't be right."

Ford's expression grew soft. "I'm sorry. I wish I could be there to hold you and tell you everything will be all right."

"Talking to you helps." It wasn't a lie. As always, Ford's serenity settled his frazzled nerves, and Nico could now take the train home and talk to his mother. He intended to tell her everything. "I gotta get going. Thank you for being there for me."

"Always and forever. Love you."

"Love you, too."

It wasn't until he was on the train that he realized he'd forgotten to ask Ford how his conversation with Lenny had gone.

Chapter
TWENTY-SIX

It bothered Lenny that he'd come in on a Tuesday—not his regular day—but as far as Ford was concerned, their contract had been voided and he could do whatever the hell he wanted. There was a certain kind of peace that came with knowing that in less than two months, there would never be a need to talk to or see Lenny again.

Lenny had huffed and puffed, strutting around the office, proclaiming how this past year had been their best yet and there was much to look forward to. Ford ignored him and tried to concentrate on his charts, but his thoughts centered on Nico and the meeting with his father.

If he hadn't already decided to move to New York, the conversation with Nico would have tipped the scales. It hurt to see Nico, alone and in so much pain, be a thousand miles away, and him unable to do anything but offer words of advice. His lover needed him there, face-to-face, to encourage and help him through the emotional minefield of seeing his father, and the devastating wreckage left behind after that conversation.

He warred with wanting to be at Nico's side and caring for his patients, who depended on him in a different way.

"Only a few short months, but God, so much to do in the interim." He scrolled through his phone and the pictures of the two of them, along with Nico's friends and family.

His phone buzzed with a text from Nico.

Told my mother about meeting Ray. She's sorry but said it's his loss not to have had me as a son.

Nico wasn't alone. He wasn't Ford, living life and getting by solely on grit, determination, and the drive to fit in. Nico had his place. It was alongside his mother, aunt, cousin, and best friends. He'd been loved and accepted since birth. Looking at the two of them, people would automatically assume Nico was after Ford's life, when all along, it was Ford who envied what Nico had: love, family, and a home.

She's right. And we're the lucky ones to have you.

I'm lucky to have you.

With that weight off his chest, Ford signed and dated his last chart of the day, then hit the buzzer for the front desk. "Marisol, can you come here, please? Thanks."

Time to have his own difficult conversation. Something had been bothering her all day, and he hoped Lenny hadn't tried to poison her mind with his lies about the future.

"Yes, Doctor."

A minute later a quiet knock sounded on his office door. "Come in."

Marisol appeared and couldn't meet his eyes.

"Sit, please."

Head bent, keeping her gaze firmly on the floor, Marisol perched on the edge of her seat.

"Marisol, what's wrong? Have you heard rumors or

people talking?" At her slight nod, he smiled. "Look at me." She raised her head and met his eyes. "I'm sure you're afraid of losing your job. Trust me, I've been heartsick about it."

"So it is true?"

"Tell me what you've heard."

She continued to fidget with her hands. "Dr. St. Claire. I-I feel so bad. Dr. Nova, he said you were leaving, and though he begged you to stay and keep the practice open, you refused."

Typical Lenny, with his lies, half-truths, and innuendos. "It's not that simple. The fact that Dr. Nova brought in Jose Diamond, who'd been impersonating a doctor, put us all at risk. I can no longer trust him to act in the best interests of this practice, and we're dissolving the partnership."

Her long lashes swept down. "I'm so sorry. I know I'm the one who caused all these problems—"

"No," he interrupted her. "You saved us from a potential malpractice suit. Hopefully, there won't still be one in the future. But don't think for a second it's your fault." He sighed. "I'm just really sorry to lose you. If you want, I can give you references for some of the practices around here."

"Thanks, Dr. St. Claire, but when I told my boyfriend what was happening, he said now's the time to make a move."

"Oh. What does that mean?"

"Remember I told you once, he has family in New York City? His cousin and uncle run a livery cab service, and they've offered him a piece of the business. Tomas said there are tons of medical-assistant jobs I can get, and they pay more than they do here."

"So you're leaving?"

She gave him a quick nod. "I'm sorry. This has been the best job I've ever had, and I don't want to leave it or you. I wish we could wait until you find another practice here, but we can't afford to be out of work." Her smile was sweet.

"We wanna get married and start a family. Tomas's aunt has a hookup with the city and can get us a rent-controlled apartment." She blotted her eyes with a tissue. "I should be excited, you know, but I still hate leaving."

"I completely understand." Truly happy for her, Ford couldn't wait to let her in on his news. "But honestly, it sounds like a great plan. For both of us."

"Huh?" Her face screwed up. "I don't understand."

"I went to New York this weekend—that's why I didn't come in yesterday. There was a terrible rainstorm the night before, and all the flights were canceled."

"Oh." Realization dawned in her expressive face. "Dr. Nova said…" Red spots appeared on her cheeks. "Forget it."

Anger filtered through his joy at the news he was about to impart. "I'm sure whatever he said wasn't flattering. But trust me because I'm telling you the truth. Yesterday I talked with a doctor I met when I went to the conference during the summer. He has a beautiful office and a high-quality practice. Marisol, he offered me a partnership, and I plan to tell him yes."

Her mouth made an O, and her eyes grew comically wide. "You're moving to New York too?"

"Yes." He laughed. "And now that I hear you'll be in the city, I want you to come work for me. Teamwork makes the dream work."

"I can't believe it," she said in amazement. "This went from the worst to the best day. I'll have everything I've ever wanted—my family together, Tomas, and working for you. Thank you, Dr. St. Claire. I'm so happy I could cry."

"Don't do that," he joked. "I'll fill you in on all the details so you'll be ready. But my plan is to have this wrapped up by the end of the year, and move in the new year. Does that work for you?"

Her eyes shone. "Yes, yes it does. I can't wait to go home and tell Tomas. Thank you."

She hugged him, and he watched her almost run out of the office. Ford sat in his chair and laughed at himself. "Guess you're really doing this." Anticipation swirled inside him, and he made some notes concerning his apartment, his car lease, and licensing requirements for New York. Not that there would be any problem, but he needed to talk to Sandler, who said he knew many people on the licensing board and could smooth the way for his application.

"Well, well, look at you." Lenny slouched in the doorway.

His guard up, Ford shut down his computer and tried to affect a bored, uninterested face. "What do you want? I'm getting ready to leave."

"Had a nice weekend with your boy toy?" Lenny sneered.

"I'm not about to discuss my personal life with you." He gathered his personal items from the drawer, hoping Lenny would get the hint and leave.

"You're not serious about dissolving the practice, are you? Why would you shoot yourself in the foot? Our billings are way up, and we were just voted South Florida's top dermatology practice. In five years we can retire."

"I don't want to spend five more minutes with you, never mind five years." Time to lay it on the line. "I refuse to be tied to you any longer. I don't need you anymore. I have a new life, and I'm ready to move on. Your stupidity could've cost me everything, including my license. There's no need to keep up this farce of a partnership. Just let it go, Lenny. It's time."

He brushed past Lenny, who dogged his footsteps to the front. Only Adriana remained behind the desk.

"You think your bought-and-paid-for hottie is going to want to see you all the time? He's got bigger fish in his pond—hedge-fund billionaires and Wall Street bigshots with fatter bank accounts and dicks than yours."

Ford's stomach turned in disgust, especially knowing

Adriana heard Lenny's crude language.

"Leave me alone, Lenny. Go find someone else to bring into the practice, and stop harassing me. It's over." Maybe he should tell Lenny the truth. "I'm leaving Florida and moving to New York. We won't ever have to see each other again."

"Moving? To be with him?"

"I can't believe I was stupid enough to have once loved you." He took out his car fob. "I feel sorry for you."

"I cared," Lenny called out after him. "In the beginning I loved you."

Before walking through the door, Ford spun around. Lenny stood pale-faced, but Ford refused to allow one ounce of sympathy. "But you took what I gave you and abused it."

He left, and in the safety of his car, gripped the steering wheel to keep from shaking. It wasn't how he'd wanted it to end. Lenny had left him no choice. He started the engine, but his phone rang, and seeing it was Jim, Mr. Rosenstein's aide, his stomach did a free fall.

"Hello?"

"Dr. St. Claire? It's Jim. I'm sorry to have to tell you, but Mr. Rosenstein passed away this morning."

Tears filled his eyes and spilled down his cheeks. "I'm so sorry. He was such a nice man. I meant to come to see him, but I was in New York this weekend."

"He was in no shape for people to visit and had orders to allow no visitors except myself. But he went in his sleep, so there was no pain."

"I'm glad for that at least. I appreciate you telling me. Thank you." About to end the call, Jim stopped him.

"Wait, Dr. St. Claire. There's something else. Mr. Rosenstein left me as the executor of his estate, and you are his beneficiary—well, you and me."

A smile came to his lips. "That was very sweet of him, to leave me a token of thanks for taking care of him."

Jim chuckled. "It's more than a token. You weren't

aware, but Mr. Rosenstein was a very wealthy man. He lived very modestly because he didn't believe in showing off. A result of his time spent in the camps, during the war."

Ford had known about Mr. Rosenstein's painful past, but he was surprised to hear the rest. In all the years he'd seen the elderly man, there had never been a hint of it.

Jim continued. "He would talk about his family after they came over from the war. How they lost everything and built up their business. Mr. Rosenstein's family owned one of the largest spice companies in the United States." He named the company, one that even Ford recognized, and he sat in the parking lot with his mouth hanging open like a fish.

"Are you serious?"

Jim laughed. "That was my response when I found out as well. And yes. Very. You know how Norman loved to tell stories. I just sat and listened because it was all fascinating to me. Like a history book. He didn't like to talk about what happened over there. He spoke more about meeting his wife and their life together. She was a model for some very famous designers in the 1960s and '70s."

"I recall him showing me her picture. She was very beautiful," Ford remarked, still shocked by what he was hearing.

"Mr. Rosenstein owns several commercial buildings here in Florida that house animal shelters he and his wife adopted their dogs from, and he left them the buildings, plus a substantial trust. He also owns an apartment in New York City."

"Yes, I think he mentioned that to me recently."

"There are stocks and bonds, as well. A lawyer from Erskine and Friedbaum will be calling you in the next few days. Obviously, I don't know what's in the will, but Mr. Rosenstein was insistent that it be handled as quickly as possible. He knew you were very busy and didn't want to cause you to have to take time away from your work."

"He was special, wasn't he?"

"One of a kind. I'll speak to you soon, Dr. St. Claire."

"Thank you. Good night, Jim."

Twilight had morphed into a night sky sprinkled with a thousand stars, and Ford sat staring out into the darkness. "What a sweet man. I'll make sure to donate some of what he's given me." He started the car and drove home.

"I'm sorry, can you repeat that?"

Two weeks after Mr. Rosenstein's death, Ford sat in the office of Toby Friedbaum, stunned by what the lawyer had read to him.

Friedbaum's blue eyes crinkled as he laughed. "Yes, seven million dollars is a hard number to wrap your brain around, isn't it? And that is exclusive of the apartment."

A buzzing sounded in his ears. "I don't know what to say…or think. Are you sure it all goes to me?"

"This isn't all of it, Dr. St. Claire. Several charities have already received their portion, but it's actually Norman's aide, Jim, who received the bulk of the estate."

"He deserves it. Jim was very good to Mr. Rosenstein."

"As I hear you were. I won't lie, we were a little concerned when Norman told us how he wanted his estate handled. We've known Jim for over twenty years, but for Norman to make such a large bequest to his doctor…" Ford met Friedbaum's eyes and could see he knew about Lenny's scandal.

"I never expected anything from him. He wanted to see me every three months, and I told him it wasn't necessary, but I figured he was lonely. I didn't send a bill because I knew his insurance wouldn't cover such frequent visits."

"Nice to see there are still good people in the world." Friedbaum printed out some papers and slipped them in a folder, then handed it to Ford. "This is a list of everything Mr. Rosenstein left you, along with legal documents transferring ownership. Sign them, have them notarized by your attorney, and we can begin the process of getting the assets to you."

Still reeling, Ford shook his hand, and clutching the folder, made his way to the car. He slipped the list out of the folder and read it.

"A one-bedroom apartment at 360 Central Park West. I'm guessing that's a great location because it's Central Park." Ford scanned the rest, which was a confusing combination of money market accounts, trusts, bonds, and stocks. He checked his watch and figured he'd take a chance and see if Nico was at lunch.

"Hi, are you busy?"

"Nah. I'm on a lunch break."

"You have your second interview tomorrow?"

"Yeah. I've been practicing from these questions I found on the Internet that they've asked potential hires in the past. It would be great to get my foot in the door of a huge company like that. The benefits would be amazing."

His faster-than-usual speech signaled how nervous Nico was. He'd confessed it'd been like a kick in the stomach to be passed over for the management training at his bus company, but personally, Ford thought the job he was interviewing for was a much better fit for his goals.

"You'll kill it. And I have some news."

"Oh, yeah? Is it about that meeting with the lawyers? Sad about that man. I'll say a prayer for him."

Ford smiled to himself. Nico was such a mix of sensuality and sweetness. "It is. He left me…a lot."

"What's that mean?" Nico's voice dropped. "Like a hundred grand or somethin'?" Ford bit his lip and hit the screen for a FaceTime. He needed to see Nico's expression.

He was in a coffee shop, wearing a blue-and-black scarf wrapped around his neck. His hair fell over his brow, and he pushed it away to peer at Ford. "Whoa, you're sitting in your car." His eyes narrowed. "What's going on? How much did he leave you?"

Ford grinned. "Seven million dollars, plus an apartment on Central Park West, which I'm assuming is a great area."

Nico's jaw dropped. "Get the fuck outta here. You lie."

"Nuh-uh."

"That's dollars? Like US money?"

"It's not Monopoly money, baby. I'm still shaking. We aren't ever going to have to worry about money again."

"I-I can't believe this. Now you won't haveta take out a loan to buy your practice."

"I know. And something else, equally important." Completely serious, he fixed Nico with an intent stare. "I want you to go back to school and get that master's degree."

As he spoke, Nico started shaking his head. "No. I'm not gonna take your money. No way."

"You're still worried what people will think, aren't you?" Ford's heart ached for Nico. "You're afraid people will assume you're with me for the money. Who cares, Nico? We know the truth."

" 'Cause I'm not gonna be what people like Ray Gargano think I am. He assumed I was gonna hit him up for cash. Funny, isn't it, that money was the first thing in his head but the last thing in mine."

That bastard. The damage he caused Nico from that one meeting would be a scar on his heart for a long time. Ford vowed to make sure to love Nico harder than his father could ever hurt him.

"We'll talk about it."

"Where's that apartment? I can look it up."

Ford repeated the address.

"*Marone a mia,*" Nico breathed, and Ford grinned. He

loved hearing Nico speak Italian. "It's right on the park. Fucking hell. Even a one-bedroom is worth a ton." He continued to shake his head. "I don't fucking believe it."

"Well, you'd better. It's going to be ours."

Nico blinked and gaped at him. "Ours? You mean… you wanna live there?"

"Uh, hello. Earth to Nico. I'm moving to the city, as you call it, in a few weeks. Now we have a place to live."

"But a place like this? All these rich people live there."

"We're rich, Nico," he said gently. "Even without this money, we have it all because we have love. And that's what matters."

Epilogue

Six months later

"Ohh, this is gorgeous." Eyes wide, his mother walked through the apartment. She'd been after them to see the final renovation since he'd moved, but Nico had wanted it to be completed, down to the bathmats and towels. And with Ford settling into the new practice, he'd left it to Nico to decorate.

"Ford's partner's wife was a decorator—*interior designer* is the fancy term for it—and she took me 'n Tre to all the places you gotta know people to get into." He ran his hand over the gleaming-white quartz waterfall island. "Pretty, huh?"

"Beautiful." She took Frank's hand, and the bright light spilling in from the windows overlooking the park hit her engagement ring, sending rainbows against the pale-blond wooden floors. "You did a great job, honey."

They'd had so much to celebrate over the holidays: Ford moving in, Nico's new job, Joey and Teresa's engagement, and the biggest shocker—Frank surprising everyone by asking Nico's permission to marry his mother. He'd moved in with her, and Nico couldn't have been happier that she now had a man who adored her and treated her like a queen.

"No reason to wait. Gotta grab every moment of life," Frank had told him, and Nico couldn't agree more.

"Ain't it stunnin'?" Tre hooked her arm through his. "I said to Nico and Ford, it belongs in one of those magazines with all the expensive apartments. Leslie was so nice to help me too with my house. Free of charge. She's got some really famous clients."

"Teresa, that ring is stunning." Ford handed Nico's mother a glass of sparkling water and Frank a beer. "Did you and Joey set the date yet?"

Teresa spread out her hand to admire the two-carat ring. "Yeah. The weekend after Memorial Day. It's gonna be at our house. I don't need nothin' that's gonna cost us a bundle. Especially now that we've got a mortgage." She rested her hand on her stomach. "And a little surprise on the way."

"You're pregnant?" Nico couldn't stop smiling and hugged her. Gently.

Her face shone with happiness. "Yeah. It's early, though. I didn't wanna walk down the aisle with a big belly, so I should be okay in a month or so."

They all crowded around and congratulated her and Joey, who, puffed up with pride, bragged, "I already got him a Mets cap and a onesie."

Ford laughed. "What if it's a girl?"

"She can wear it too. It don't matta. Lulu's got a Mets collar. We're a loyal family."

Nico hugged Ford's waist. "We are."

"So how does it feel to be workin' in an office?" Anthony asked Nico. "Bet it's a lot different from them bus rides."

"Yeah, it sure is. I love it. And my supervisor liked some of my suggestions."

"Make sure he don't take credit if it's your idea," Jack warned.

"Negative Nelly, I know that. He's gonna bring me to the meeting so I can tell everyone." Nico frowned. "He's not gonna stab me in the back."

"Just looking out for you."

"That's what friends are for," Ford jumped in. The relationship between them and Jack was still somewhat strained, but Jack had started to show up more regularly whenever they hung out. Which, Nico had to admit, hadn't been as often.

"You're right," Nico relented. "And I gotta tell you, the work you did on Joey and Tre's house was real nice. Great tile job in the kitchen."

"I know, right?" Tre piped up with a big smile. "I was scared of a fixer-upper, but Jack made it look easy."

Joey had surprised them by buying a house near Bensonhurst, and Aunt Justine moved with them to the downstairs apartment they set up for her.

"And my apartment is be-yootiful," Justine crowed. "Now I get to watch my grandbaby grow up and take care of him or her when Teresa goes to work."

"I'm thinkin' of maybe rentin' out your apartment, Nico. Now that we're sellin' the restaurant to Bobby and his family, it'll be steady income for me and Frank, since he's not gonna be working full-time at Maxie's."

"Yeah, good idea," Nico reassured her. "I still can't believe you and Aunt Justine are selling the place."

"I don't wanna be tied down no more. Justine's gonna be with Joey and Teresa, and Frank and me wanna travel—he wants to go all over Italy. It was my father's dream to own the restaurant, not mine." Her eyes grew soft as she gazed at Nico. "All I ever wanted was a family. And I got the best—having you, Nico. But the restaurant…" She shrugged. "So one more month, and it'll be done with."

"No more lasagna." Ford pretended to pout.

"For you, sweetheart, anything." She kissed his cheek, and Nico's heart swelled with more love than he thought it could contain. His mom and Ford had bonded as deeply as if they were related by blood, and Nico knew how Ford had longed for that kind of relationship. "I have my two boys together now. I couldn't be happier."

"Me too, Ma." Nico raised his glass to Ford, who winked at him.

Nothing could've prepared him for the complete happiness of coming home and spending every evening with Ford. How could he have ever thought that seeing the same face on the pillow every morning would get boring? Waking up to Ford curled around him was like celebrating Christmas and his birthday every single day.

And he'd never had a lover leave him so blissful and wrecked. Even that morning, knowing their friends and family were coming for a visit, Ford had kept him in the bed, kissing him from head to toes, leaving no inch of skin unloved by his tongue. Ford had edged him for an hour before taking Nico's aching, throbbing cock between those fabulous lips and sucking him all the way down.

Nico's cheeks grew warm, thinking of his scream of pleasure as his climax rocketed through him. His body tingled with anticipation of their night to come. He'd promised revenge on Ford and couldn't wait to be inside him.

"Are we all ready for dinner?"

They were off to La Dolce Vita for a family celebration. They'd closed the restaurant for the evening, so it was friends and family only—Ford had invited Bruce and Leslie Sandler, as well as Marisol and her husband, Tomas, and they were meeting them at the restaurant. Nico and Ford surprised everyone by getting a car and driver for each of them.

"Thanks, bro." Joey hugged him while Tre kissed his cheek.

"Wow, thank you." Anthony and Sergio each hugged Ford, and Jack squeezed his shoulder. "Cool, thanks."

"Justine, Mom, and Frank will come with us," Ford said, and Nico stopped talking to Joey to stare at him. A beautiful yet nervous smile overtook Ford's face. "Joanne said if I felt comfortable enough, she'd love it if I called her that. You don't mind, do you?" He searched Nico's face anxiously.

His eyes burned with the tears he held back. God, how did he get to be such a sap? But Nico knew he'd do anything to be able to keep that absolute joy on Ford's face.

"I think it's fantastic."

An hour later, they met at the restaurant, where Ford introduced Marisol and Tomas to everyone. She and Tre hit it off, and soon the two of them were exchanging numbers and making plans. Tomas, a little quiet at first, came alive when Joey started talking sports, and Joey invited him to their Sunday games.

"Only requirement is you gotta bring something tailgate-ish. Wings, nachos, chili, hot dogs…"

"Did someone mention the holy grail of food groups?" Bruce and Leslie stood at the door, and Nico and Ford greeted them. Bruce was still the funny, wisecracking man Nico remembered, and Leslie pretended exasperation but played along. Ford spoke of him almost as a father figure.

"Come meet my mom, her fiancé, and my aunt."

They sat at a table in the center of the room, and all were soon chatting like old friends. Nico, Joey, and Bobby brought out platters of antipasto, both hot and cold, as well as salads, and set them along with plates, cutlery, and napkins.

"Everybody," Nico called out. "We got the antipasto here and more food comin'. There's red and white wine on the counter, and water and club soda too. We're not fancy here, so help yourself and dig in."

The door opened, and Tre ran over to tell whomever it was that it was a private event and that the restaurant was closed tonight. She didn't seem to be getting through because she continued to shake her head. Nico decided to help her get rid of them, and Tre glanced over her shoulder, looking relieved.

"Oh, good. I tried tellin' them we're not open, but they don't care. They were askin' to speak to you." She stepped aside, her face a mask of curiosity.

"Me?" He put a pleasant smile on and opened the door wider. And almost passed out.

Facing him were the two women in the picture on their father's desk—a little older, of course, but still as pretty. Blue-green eyes widened as they met his.

"Nico?" one of them asked—he didn't know if she was Tessa or Lucy.

"H-how do you know my name?"

"It's kind of rainy, can we come inside?" the other asked, cheeks pink and teeth chattering, despite her being bundled up in a wool jacket and a cashmere scarf.

He could be a piece of shit and tell them to leave, that he had nothing to say, but he opened the door and let them in. Tre gave him the raised eyebrows. "It's okay. I'll tell you later," he murmured.

"You betta," she hissed. "They look exactly like you."

She returned to Joey, who was talking to Ford. She whispered in Ford's ear, and he immediately left them to join him. His hand rested at Nico's waist, supporting him. Nico led them to a corner of the room. A room which had suddenly gone too quiet for this crowd.

Tessa and Lucy stared at him, and he at them, until Nico couldn't stand it any longer. "Why are you here?" He ran a shaky hand through his hair. "Which of you is Tessa and which is Lucy?"

They side-eyed each other. The one with the scarf spoke

first. "I'm Tessa. Last weekend, we went to see our parents, and they were having an argument. Seems my father told my mother he'd been visited by someone claiming to be his son, and he didn't want her to find out from anyone else, in case this person decided to go to her."

"I wouldn'ta done that," he muttered. "It's not her fault."

"It's not our father's either," Lucy piped up. "He said he had no idea your mother was pregnant. You can't blame him."

Nico folded his arms. "I don't blame him for that. I blame him for cheating on my mother while they were engaged and dumping her right before the wedding. And I don't care what you say, that's an extremely shitty thing to do. It says a lot about a person."

Tessa and Lucy shared a quick, stunned glance, cluing in Nico that their father had conveniently forgotten to mention that not-so-minor detail. "Uh, he…he didn't say that. Only that he didn't know she was pregnant, and you just popped up in his office, demanding to be part of our family."

"That's not what happened. I didn't demand anything."

Ford held him tighter, and Tessa's brow furrowed. Her gaze shifted from him to Ford, then back again. "Is he your boyfriend?"

"*He* is Ford, and yeah, he is."

"Oh, that's nice." Her smile was nervous. "I have a fiancé, and Lucy's serious with her boyfriend too."

He didn't know what to say, so he repeated her words. "That's nice."

Tessa blew out a breath. "Look, I'm sorry, Nico. This is awkward as hell for us too. But we came because…because we wanted to meet our brother. When we found out that Dad wasn't even going to tell us about you, we got really angry with him."

"Wait, what? You wanted to meet me?"

For the first time, Tessa and Lucy, his *sisters*, laughed

and Tessa nodded. "Well, yeah. I mean, you're our brother. We have nothing against you. Our father didn't cheat on our mom, and what happened between them isn't your fault either." She put a hand on his arm, and he trembled. "I'm so sorry about the way this turned out for you, Nico, and we don't expect to have a big family reunion." She peered over his shoulder. "But it looks like you have a wonderful, close family of your own."

"Yeah, I do."

Lucy tucked a strand of hair behind her ear. "Do you… do you think maybe Tess and I could see you sometimes, get to know you? And Ford too." Her anxious but hopeful eyes shifted to Ford.

"I'd like that. It's nice to meet you both."

Tessa hesitated, and Nico sensed she was the more serious one. "My dad and I were always close, so this hit me hard. I wasn't sure I wanted to even see you. But I kept thinking about you and wondering how I would feel in your place, knowing I had siblings but couldn't talk to them. And it was keeping me up at night because I was so damn sad. Finally, I told Lucy, this is stupid. It happened almost thirty years ago, and the three of us aren't to blame. I had tonight off work, and I grabbed Lucy, and we came here."

"How did you know where to find me?"

"We asked our father, and he told us about the restaurant your mother's family owned and suggested to start here."

"He did?" he asked, shocked that Ray had helped them.

His face must've reflected his tumbling emotions because a wry smile quirked Tessa's lips. "I'm not saying he's happy about it. But we're both adults, and we make our own decisions. My father's not thrilled with my fiancé, Luke. He turned down working for a lucrative pulmonary practice and chose to open a clinic in the Bronx."

"He sounds like a wonderful person," Ford said. "And maybe you can put him in touch with me. I'm a dermatologist, and I'd be happy to help out sometimes if he has people with skin issues."

Tessa's pretty eyes grew wide. "Oh, wow, yes, I'm sure that would be very helpful. If you give me your card, I'll have him reach out."

Nico felt it was up to him to say something at that point. "I'm glad you came by. Since I saw your pictures, I couldn't stop wishing I could meet you, but I gave up hope because of how I left it with your father."

Lucy's brow puckered. "He's your father too."

Nico frowned. "No, sorry. I'll never be able to think of him like that. But if I end up with you as sisters, that's better than I could've hoped for." He lifted his chin. "He thinks I came to see him to get money from him. But that's not true. All I wanted was to know who my father was." He swallowed, his throat tight. "And for him to know me."

Tessa brushed her eyes, her lashes spiky with tears. "I'm sorry, Nico. Maybe one day…"

But Nico knew better. In his heart he knew there would be no father-son reconciliation.

Her phone buzzed. "We'd better go. We have dinner plans, and the guys are waiting." She hesitated. "Is it okay if I give you a hug?"

He nodded, and she wrapped her arms around him. She smelled like sunshine and flowers. Lucy held him tightly too.

"Can we have your number? Would you mind if we texted you sometimes? Maybe we can all get together."

A little dumbstruck, Nico said, "Uh, yeah, sure." He recited his number, watched them enter it in their phones, and felt the buzz of his seconds later. They waved and then left. He stood watching them, unaware for how long, until Ford held him in his arms.

"You okay?"

Nico turned and studied his face. Those sparks of sunlight in his warm amber eyes. The high cut of his cheekbones and the full, soft lips Nico couldn't not kiss when they were this close. It was brief but gave him the energy he needed.

"I've got you, Ford. I'm great."

"Yeah, you are."

Hand in hand, they approached their friends and family, who were trying and failing to pretend disinterest. All conversation died, and Nico knew he owed them an explanation.

"Those were my half sisters. Tessa and Lucy."

His mother gasped. "I knew it. I said to Frank, they look exactly like Ray. And you."

"Yeah, they're really pretty. And smart. Tessa is an anesthesiology resident, and Lucy clerks for a judge." He huffed. "Ray told them about me and about the restaurant. That's how they knew where to find me."

"Are they nice? They seemed happy to talk to you. I saw them smilin'."

Nico rushed to soothe his mom's anxiety. "Yeah, yeah. It's all good. We'll keep in touch. They want to, and I think it would be nice."

He gazed around the table, at his mom and Frank, at Aunt Justine with Teresa and Joey, who were about to take a huge step. Anthony and Sergio, still going strong a year later. Nico had no doubt they'd be the next to get married. Jack had revealed a bad breakup with a guy he'd been seeing, and he'd apologized for taking it out on them. Nico suspected he'd fallen hard, and understood his pain. If Jack felt like talking about it, they'd be there for him.

New friends like Tomas and Marisol, Bruce and Leslie, who fit in with the crew as seamlessly as if they'd always been there.

Most of all Ford, who gave him all the love and support he could ask for, and more.

Bobby brought out the mains—mussels, chicken *parmigiana*, baked ziti. Chicken marsala and veal *piccata*.

Eggplant rollatini. Two different kinds of fish. Fettucine with shrimp. Calamari. Spinach with garlic and broccoli rabe.

The table was filled with the trays of food and bottles of wine. He caught his mother's eye, and from her beaming face, knew she'd never been happier. He stood and raised his glass.

"To my family, *mia famiglia*. You are all that matters to me."

He leaned over and kissed Ford, soaking in the lifetime of love on his lips.

Thank you for reading Nico and Ford's story. I hope you'll consider leaving a review, which helps indie authors more than you can imagine. Reviews are like M&Ms-there are never enough! If you're curious about Alexi and Cam, the custard vendors on the Coney Island Boardwalk, you can find their story in *Under the Boardwalk* and the sequel, *Down by the Sea*. They might be my sweetest couple ever!

FELICE STEVENS writes romance because what is better than people falling in love? Her favorite part of a romance novel is that first kiss…sigh. She loves creating stories of hopes and dreams and happily ever afters. Her stories are character-driven, rich with the sights, sounds and flavors of New York City and filled with men who are sometimes deeply flawed but always real.

Felice writes gay romance because she believes that everyone deserves a happily ever after. Having traveled all over the world, she can safely say that the universal language that unites people is love. Felice has written in a variety of sub-genres, including contemporary, paranormal, and she has a mystery series as well. You can find all her book listed on her website.

Felice is a two-time Lambda Literary Award nominee and the Lambda award-winner in Gay Romance for her book, *The Ghost and Charlie Muir*.

BOOKBUB
https://www.bookbub.com/profile/felice-stevens

NEWSLETTER
https://tinyurl.com/y85e69ab

READER GROUP
https://www.facebook.com/groups/FelicesBreakfastClub/

FACEBOOK AUTHOR PAGE
https://www.facebook.com/felicestevensauthor/

INSTAGRAM
https://www.instagram.com/felicestevens

GOODREADS
https://www.goodreads.com/author/show/8432880.Felice_
Stevens

WEBSITE
felicestevens.com

PAYHIP STORE
https://payhip.com/FeliceStevensAuthor